KT-569-338

Michel Bussi has won fifteen literary awards, making him one of France's most prestigious crime authors. When not writing fiction, he is a Professor of Geography at the University of Rouen and a political commentator. *After the Crash*, his first book to be published in the UK, was a No. 1 bestseller, and has been translated into 26 languages around the world. *Black Water Lilies* is his second novel to be translated into English.

Also by Michel Bussi

After the Crash
Don't Let Go

Praise for *Black Water Lilies*

'This **elegant crime mystery** shimmers as delicately as the paintings of Claude Monet that lie at its heart . . . A bestseller in France, it is **a dazzling, unexpected and haunting masterpiece**'
Geoffrey Wansell, *Daily Mail*

'**A work of genius** befitting the masterpiece by Monet at its heart. The award-winning author weaves **an enchanting tale that kept me absolutely hooked**, as Bussi cleverly breaks all the perceived rules of plotting in a story containing riddles within riddles. It works on multiple levels and left me completely baffled, yearning to work out how the different strands connect. But every loose thread is meshed neatly together in the final stages until the jaw-dropping big reveal at the end. The result is simply stunning' Jon Coates, *Daily Express*

'Murder always seems especially appalling against a beautiful back-drop, which is why Michel Bussi's novel begins so strikingly: a corpse is found stabbed and battered in a stream that runs through the famous gardens of Giverny . . . A good deal of eccentric **Gallic charm**' Jake Kerridge, *Daily Express S Magazine*

'Bussi's portrait of the difficulties of investigating a closed community is **fascinating**, and the novel ends with **one of the most reverberating shocks in modern crime fiction**'
Joan Smith, *Sunday Times*

'The plot is set in Giverny, where Monet planted and painted water lilies. It's where the characters live, the murders are committed, the clues are scattered, and the police investigate . . . [An] **intelligent and absorbing** book' Marcel Berlins, *The Times*

'To say that Michel Bussi's *After the Crash* made a considerable mark is to understate the case. The **highly original** premise had critics seeking out new adjectives to lavish praise on this narrative of the tragic aftermath of a plane crash . . . *Black Water Lilies* (translated by Shaun Whiteside) is quite as accomplished a piece of work as its predecessor, with the details of the slowly unfolding mystery exerting a **mesmerising** effect' Barry Forshaw, *Crime Scene*

Praise for *After the Crash*

'A novel so **extraordinary** that it reminded me of reading Stieg Larsson for the very first time. Bussi's novel brings with it the same thrill of discovering a truly original voice . . . It is one of the most remarkable books I've read in a long time; **Bussi breaks every rule in the book**, but I doubt I'll read a more **brilliant** crime novel this year'
Joan Smith, *Sunday Times*

'There's a **great premise** to this thriller, which is already a huge bestseller in the author's native France . . . You find yourself quite frantic to know the truth, before this cleverly constructed, smart mystery concludes by delivering **a delicious sting in the tail**'
Deirdre O'Brien, *Sunday Mirror*

'A **richly satisfying** story about the sole survivor of an airline crash . . . an old-fashioned puzzle in the manner of a mystery from the Golden Age of crime . . . **hugely enjoyable**'
Eilis O'Hanlon, *Irish Independent*

'**Thriller of the Month** . . . A suspense novel that's been on the bestseller list for two years in France'
Joanne Finney, *Good Housekeeping*

'*After the Crash* will keep you solidly gripped for its total duration. [The] provocative premise – and its aftermath in the present – sets in motion a truly **compelling tale** by the talented Michel Bussi, a writer who well knows exactly how to keep the reader turning page after page even when it's past time to turn out that bedside lamp'
Barry Forshaw, *Good Book Guide*

'An **original** voice . . . [Bussi] borrows elements from old-fashioned clue-puzzle mysteries to provide a **breathtakingly suspenseful thriller** . . . extraordinary' Meadhbh McGrath, *tn2 Magazine*

'Splendidly engineered . . . a **compulsive** page-turner'
Maxim Jakubowski, *Lovereading*

Black Water Lilies

MICHEL BUSSI

Translated from the French by Shaun Whiteside

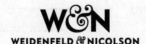

WEIDENFELD & NICOLSON

First published in Great Britain in 2016
by Weidenfeld & Nicolson,
This paperback edition published in 2017
by Weidenfeld & Nicolson
An imprint of the Orion Publishing Group Ltd
Carmelite House, 50 Victoria Embankment
London EC4Y 0DZ

An Hachette UK Company

1 3 5 7 9 10 8 6 4 2

First published in France in 2011 as *Nymphéas Noirs* by Presses de la Cité

Copyright © Presses de la Cité, a department of Place des Éditeurs 2011
English translation copyright © Shaun Whiteside 2016

The rights of Michel Bussi and Shaun Whiteside to be identified as
the author and translator of this work, respectively, have been asserted
in accordance with the Copyright, Designs and Patents Act 1988.

All rights reserved. No part of this publication may be
reproduced, stored in a retrieval system, or transmitted,
in any form or by any means, electronic, mechanical,
photocopying, recording or otherwise, without the prior
permission of both the copyright owner and the above publisher.

All the characters in this book are fictitious, and any resemblance
to actual persons living or dead is purely coincidental.

978 1 474 60176 4 (Mass Market Paperback)
978 1 474 60177 1 (eBook)
978 1 409 16323 7 (Audio)

A CIP catalogue record for this book is
available from the British Library.

Typeset by Input Data Services Ltd, Bridgwater, Somerset

Printed and bound by Clays Ltd, St Ives plc

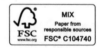

www.orionbooks.co.uk

In memory of Jacky Lucas

*'With Monet, we don't see the real world,
but we grasp its appearances.'*

F. Robert-Kempf, *L'Aurore*, 1908

*'No! No! No black for Monet!
Black is not a colour!'*

Georges Clemenceau,
at the foot of Claude Monet's coffin
(Michel de Decker, *Claude Monet*, 2009)

In the following pages, the descriptions of Giverny are as exact as possible. The places exist, whether it's the Hôtel Baudy, the Ru and the Epte, the Chennevières mill, the school in Giverny, the church of Sainte-Radegonde and its cemetery, the rue Claude Monet, the Chemin du Roy, Nettles Island or, of course, Monet's house and the water-lily pond. The same can be said of locations in the neighbouring area, such as the museum in Vernon, the art museum in Rouen, the hamlet of Cocherel.

The information about Claude Monet's life, his works, and his heirs is authentic. That is also the case for the other Impressionist painters mentioned, notably Theodore Robinson and Eugène Murer – however, the Robinson Foundation and the International Young Painters Challenge are my own invention.

The cited thefts of artworks come from real news stories.

All the rest, I have imagined.

Three women lived in a village.

The first was mean, the second a liar, and the third an egotist.

Their village bore the pretty name of a garden. Giverny.

The first lived in a big mill on the banks of a stream, on the Chemin du Roy; the second occupied an attic flat above the school, Rue Blanche Hoschedé-Monet; the third lived with her mother, in a little house with the paint flaking off the walls on Rue du Château d'Eau.

They weren't the same age. Not at all. The first was over eighty, and a widow. Almost. The second was thirty-six and had never deceived her husband. Yet. The third was nearly eleven and all the boys in her school wanted her to be their girlfriend. The first dressed always in black, the second put on make-up for her lover, the third plaited her hair so that her tresses flew out behind her in the wind.

All three were quite different. But they had something in common, a secret. All three dreamed of leaving. Yes, of leaving Giverny, the famous village that compels swarms of people to travel across the entire world just to stroll in its gardens for a few hours. Because of the Impressionists.

The first woman, the oldest, owned a pretty painting; the second was interested in artists; the third, the youngest, was good at painting. Very good, in fact.

Many would find it strange, wanting to leave Giverny. But these three women viewed the village as a prison – a big, beautiful

1

garden, but surrounded by a fence. Like the grounds of an asylum. A trompe-l'oeil. A painting from which you could not escape. The third woman, the youngest, was looking for a father. The second was looking for love. The first, the oldest one, knew certain things about the other two.

But once, for thirteen days, thirteen days only, the gates of the park were opened. The dates were very precise: from 13 May to 25 May 2010. But the rules were cruel – only one of them could escape. The other two would have to die. That was how it was.

Those thirteen days passed like a parenthesis in their lives. Too short. Cruel, too. The parenthesis opened with a murder, on the first day, and finished with another, on the last day. Strangely, the police were only interested in the second woman, the most beautiful; the third, the most innocent, had to carry out her own investigation. The first, the most discreet, was left in peace to keep an eye on everyone. And to kill.

It lasted thirteen days. Long enough for an escape.

Three women lived in a village.

The third was the most intelligent, the second the most cunning, the first the most determined.

In your opinion, which one managed to escape?

The third, the youngest, was called Fanette Morelle; the second was called Stéphanie Dupain; the first, the oldest, that was me.

PICTURE ONE

Impressions

DAY ONE
13 May 2010
(Giverny)

Assembly

1

The clear water of the stream is tinted pink, in small threads, like the fleeting pastel shades of water in which a paint brush is being rinsed.

'Neptune, no!'

Further down the stream the colour is diluted and clings to the green of the weeds that hang from the banks, the ochre of the roots of the poplars, the willows. A subtle, faded shade . . .

I quite like it.

Except that the red does not come from the palette a painter has been cleaning in the river, but from the battered head of Jérôme Morval. The blood is escaping from a deep gash at the top of his skull, neat and clearly defined, washed clean by the Ru, a branch of the river Epte, in which his head is now immersed.

My Alsatian approaches, sniffs. I call him again, more firmly this time:

'Neptune, no! Come back!'

I suspect it won't be long before the corpse is found. Even though it's only six in the morning, someone out for a walk will pass by, or a painter, or a jogger, someone out collecting snails . . . they will discover the body.

I'm careful not to go any closer. I lean on my stick. The ground in front of me is muddy, there's been a lot of rain the past few days, and the banks of the stream are soft. At eighty-four, I'm not really the right age to pretend I'm a water-nymph, even in such a piffling stream less than a metre wide, half of which used to be diverted to feed the pond in Monet's gardens. (Apparently this is no longer the case – there is an underground pipe which feeds the lily pond these days.)

'Come on, Neptune. Let's keep going.'

I lift my cane in his direction, as if to keep him from poking his snout into the gaping hole in Jérôme Morval's grey jacket. The second wound. Right in the heart.

'Go on, move! We're not going to hang about here.'

I look one last time at the wash house just opposite where I am standing, then continue along the path. It is impeccably maintained. The most invasive trees have been sawn off at the base and the banks have been cleared of weeds. You have to remember, several thousand tourists walk along this path every day. You might pass someone with a pram, or in a wheelchair, an old woman with a cane. Like me.

'Come on, Neptune.'

I make a turn a little further on, at the spot where the brook divides into two branches, cut off by a dam and a waterfall. On the other side you can see Monet's gardens, the water lilies, the Japanese bridge, the greenhouses . . . It's strange, I was born here in 1926, the year of Claude Monet's death. For a long time after Monet's passing, almost fifty years, those gardens were closed, forgotten, abandoned. Today, the wheel has turned again and every year tens of thousands of Japanese, Americans, Russians, and Australians travel round the world just to linger here. Monet's gardens have become a sacred temple, a Mecca, a cathedral . . . In fact, it won't be long before those thousands of pilgrims descend upon us.

I look at my watch. 6.02. Another few hours of respite.

I walk on.

Between the poplars and the huge butterburs, the statue of Claude Monet stares at me with the malicious expression of an angry neighbour, his chin devoured by his beard and his skull concealed by a piece of headgear that vaguely resembles a straw hat. The ivory plinth indicates that the bust was unveiled in 2007. The wooden sign hammered into the ground beside it explains that the master is watching 'the meadow'. His meadow. The fields, from the Ru to the Epte, from the Epte to the Seine, the rows of poplars, the wooded slopes that undulate like soft waves. The magical places he painted. Inviolable . . . Varnished and on show for all eternity.

And it's true – at six in the morning, the place can still be deceptive. I look in front of me at a pure horizon consisting of fields of wheat, of maize, of poppies. But I won't lie to you. For most of the day, Monet's meadow is, in fact, a giant car park. Four car parks, to be precise, clustered around a bitumen stem like a water lily made of tarmac. I think I can afford to say this kind of thing, at my age. I have seen the landscape transform itself, year after year. Today Monet's countryside is just a commercial backdrop.

Neptune follows me for a few metres, and then sets off, running straight ahead. He crosses the car park, pees against a wooden barrier, then lopes on into the field, towards the confluence of the Epte and the Seine. For some reason this little wedge of land between the two rivers is known as Nettles Island.

I sigh and continue on my way. At my age, I'm not going to go running after him. I watch as he scampers away, then circles back, as if he's taunting me. I don't want to call him back yet, it's still early. He disappears once more into the wheat. That's how Neptune spends his time these days – always running a hundred metres ahead of me. Everyone who lives in Giverny knows this dog, but I don't think many people know he's mine.

I walk along the car park and towards the Moulin des Chennevières. That's where I live. I like to get back home before the crowds arrive. The Moulin des Chennevières is by far the most beautiful building in the vicinity of Monet's gardens, and the only one built beside the brook, but ever since they transformed the meadow into fields of metal and tyres, I feel like a species on the

7

brink of extinction, a rare animal that has been put in a cage so that inquisitive people can come and have a look. There are only four bridges over the brook to get from the car park to the village, one of which crosses the steam just in front of my house. I feel that I'm besieged until six in the evening. At that hour, the village closes down again, the meadow is given back to the willows and Claude Monet can reopen his bronze eyes, without coughing into his beard at the smell of hydrocarbons.

In front of me, the wind stirs a forest of sea-green wheat, studded with the red pearls of scattered poppies. If someone viewed the scene from the other side, along the Epte, it would inevitably remind them of an Impressionist painting. The harmony of orange tones at sunrise, with just a hint of mourning, the tiniest black speck in the background.

A widow dressed in dark clothes. Me.

A subtle note of melancholy.

I call again: 'Neptune!'

I stand there for a while, savouring the momentary calm, until a jogger arrives. He passes in front of me, headphones jammed in his ears. T-shirt. Trainers. He bursts into the meadow like an anachronism. He is the first of the day to spoil the picture; others will follow. I give him a little nod, he returns it and disappears, the noise from his headphones like the buzzing of an electronic cicada. I see him turn towards the bust of Monet, the little waterfall, the dam. I imagine him running along the brook, he too taking care to avoid the mud at the edge of the path.

I sit down on a bench and wait for what will happen next.

There are still no coaches in the car park when the police van screeches to a halt on the Chemin du Roy, between the wash house and my mill, around twenty paces from the drowned body of Jérôme Morval.

I stand up.

I wonder about calling Neptune one last time but he knows the way home, after all. The Moulin des Chennevières is nearby. I cast one last glance at the police getting out of their vehicle and then I leave. I go back to my house. From the fourth floor of my mill you get a much better view of everything that is happening.

And much more discreet.

2

Inspector Laurenç Sérénac begins by marking out a perimeter of several metres around the corpse, attaching a wide orange plastic tape to the branches of the trees above the stream.

The crime scene suggests that this will be a complicated investigation. Sérénac is reassuring himself that his reaction when the call came in to the police headquarters in Vernon was sound; he had set off immediately with three colleagues. Right now, Officer Louvel's chief task is to keep away the rubberneckers who are starting to crowd along the brook. It is incredible, in fact – the village seemed deserted when the police van drove through it, but a few minutes later it was as if the entire population had converged on the murder scene. Because it certainly is a murder. You don't need three years at the police training academy in Toulouse to be sure of that, Sérénac thinks, observing the wound to the heart, the gash in the skull and the head immersed in water. Officer Maury, supposedly the best forensic specialist at Vernon headquarters, is carefully picking out footprints in the ground, just in front of the corpse, and taking a mould of the prints with quick-setting plaster. It was Sérénac who gave him the order to immortalise the muddy ground before they even began to examine the corpse. The man is dead, he can't be saved. Trampling all over the crime scene before everything is bagged and photographed is out of the question.

Inspector Sylvio Bénavides appears on the bridge. He stops to get his breath back. Sérénac had asked him to run along to the village with a picture of the victim, to see if he could get some initial information – especially the identity, if possible, of the murdered man. Inspector Sérénac hasn't been working in Vernon for long, but it didn't take him much time to work out that Sylvio Bénavides was very good at following orders, organising, filing meticulously.

9

The ideal deputy, to a certain extent. He suffers, perhaps, from a slight lack of initiative, but Sérénac senses this may stem more from an excess of timidity than a lack of competence. And the man is devoted – yes, devoted – to his job as a policeman. Because, in fact, Bénavides must view his superior, Inspector Laurenç Sérénac, fresh from police academy in Toulouse, as some kind of unidentified police object . . . Sérénac was dropped in as boss of the Vernon station only four months ago, without even having reached the rank of detective chief inspector, so were they really expected to take seriously – here, north of the Seine – a cop who wasn't yet thirty, who talked to both criminals and colleagues with his southern, Occitan accent, and who already approached each crime scene with an air of disillusioned cynicism?

Sérénac isn't sure. People are so stressed up here. Not just in the police. It's even worse in Vernon, a large Parisian suburb that has spilled into Normandy. The border with the Île-de-France passes through Giverny, a few hundred metres away, on the other side of the main river. But people here think of themselves as Norman, not Parisian. And they're proud of it. It's a kind of snobbery. Someone once told him, in all seriousness, that more people had been killed at the Epte, that ridiculous little stream that had once defined the border between France and the Anglo-Norman kingdom, than had died at the Meuse or the Rhine.

'Inspector . . .'

'Call me Laurenç, for Christ's sake . . . I've told you that before.'

Sylvio Bénavides hesitates. It hardly seems the fitting moment to discuss it, given that Inspector Sérénac is talking to him in front of officers Louvel and Maury, about fifteen rubberneckers and a blood-drenched corpse.

'Erm. Yes . . . fine, chief. I think we'll be walking on eggshells . . . I had no trouble identifying the victim. Everyone here knows him. He's a local bigwig, apparently. Jérôme Morval. A well-known ophthalmologist, with a surgery on Avenue Prudhon in Paris, in the 16th arrondissement. He lives in one of the nicest houses in the village, 71 Rue Claude Monet.'

'He lived . . . ' Sérénac corrects him.

Sylvio takes it on the chin. He looks like someone who's just been called up to the Russian front. A civil servant who's been seconded to the sticks – or a cop transferred to Normandy. The image makes Sérénac smile. He's the one who ought to be sulking, not his deputy.

'OK, Sylvio,' Sérénac says. 'Good job. Not worth stressing about it for the time being. We'll examine his CV later on.'

Sérénac unhooks the orange tape.

'Ludo, have you finished with the prints? Can we come on over now?'

Ludovic Maury nods, then moves away, carrying various plaster moulds. As he approaches, Inspector Sérénac's feet sink into the mud. He clings with one hand to the branch of the nearest ash tree, and with the other, points at the inert body.

'Come here, Sylvio. Take a look. Don't you think it's strange, the way this crime's been committed?'

Bénavides steps forward. Louvel and Maury turn round as well, as if this were their superior's entrance exam. They are keen to see him in action.

'Look at the wound, there. Whatever it was went straight through the jacket right to the heart, so clearly Morval was killed with a sharp weapon. A knife or something of the kind. Even without consulting forensics, we may hypothesise that this was the cause of death. Except that if we examine the tracks in the mud, we will notice that the body was dragged several metres to the edge of the water. Why take all that trouble? Why move a corpse? Then, the murderer picked up a rock, or another heavy object, and bashed in the top of his skull and his temple. Again, why would anyone do that?'

Louvel almost raises a timid hand.

'Perhaps Morval wasn't dead?'

'Perhaps,' says Sérénac. 'But given the size of the wound to the heart, I don't think so . . . And if Morval were still alive, why not simply stab him again where he lay? Why move him and then stave his skull in?'

Sylvio Bénavides says nothing. Ludovic Maury studies the site. There is a rock at the edge of the brook the size of a large football, covered with blood. He has taken every possible sample from its surface. He attempts a reply.

'Because there was a rock nearby? He grabbed the weapon closest to hand . . .'

Sérénac's eyes shine.

'I don't agree with you there, Ludo. Take a good look at the scene. There's something even stranger. Look at the stream, twenty metres along. What do you see?'

Inspector Bénavides and the two officers look along the banks. They haven't the faintest idea what Sérénac is getting at.

'There *are* no other rocks!' Sérénac says triumphantly. 'There isn't a single other rock along the whole length of the river. And if you study this one more closely, there is no doubt that it too has been moved here. There is no dry earth stuck to the rock, the crushed grass underneath it is fresh . . . What is it doing here, this providential rock? The murderer must have brought it here; it's blindingly obvious.'

Officer Louvel tries to drive the locals back towards the right bank of the brook, towards the village side, although having an audience doesn't seem to bother Sérénac in the slightest.

'If I may sum up what we know so far,' the inspector continues, 'we can assume the following: Jérôme Morval is stabbed somewhere on the path, a blow that is probably fatal. Then his murderer drags him to the river. Six metres away. Then, as our man is a perfection- ist, he digs up a rock from somewhere nearby, something that must weigh not far off twenty kilos, and comes back to crush Morval's skull . . . But it isn't over yet. Observe the position of the body: the head is almost entirely submerged in the stream. Does that position look natural to you?'

'You just said, Chief,' Maury replies, almost appalled. 'The mur- derer struck Morval with the rock, beside the river. Then the victim slid into the stream—'

'As if by chance,' Inspector Sérénac says ironically. 'No, guys, I'm prepared to take a bet on this. Imagine picking up that rock and smashing Morval's brain in, there, on the bank. And the corpse's head would be found, beautifully submerged in the water at a depth

12

of ten centimetres? The chances are less than one in a thousand. Gentlemen, I think the situation is much simpler. We're dealing with the triple murder of a single individual. One, I stab you. Two, I smash your head in. Three, I drown you in the stream . . .'

A rictus grin appears on his lips.

'We're dealing with someone highly motivated. Someone stubborn. And someone very, very angry with Jérôme Morval.'

Laurenç Sérénac turns towards Sylvio Bénavides.

'Wanting to kill him three times wasn't pleasant for our ophthalmologist, but in the end it's better than killing three different people once each, isn't it?'

Sérénac winks at an increasingly embarrassed Inspector Bénavides.

'I don't want to spread panic in the village,' he goes on, 'but nothing about this crime scene seems to have been left to chance. I don't know why, but it almost looks like a composition, staged. As if every detail has been chosen. This precise location, in Giverny. The sequence of events. The knife, the rock, the drowning . . .'

'An act of vengeance?' Bénavides suggests. 'A kind of ritual? Is that what you think?'

'I don't know,' Sérénac replies. 'We'll see . . . So far it doesn't seem to make any sense, but I'm fairly certain that it makes sense to the murderer.'

Louvel continues in his feeble attempt to herd the onlookers back towards the bridge. Sylvio Bénavides remains silent, concentrating, as if trying to sort Sérénac's flood of words.

Suddenly, a brown shadow emerges from the clump of poplars in the meadow, passes under the orange tape and paddles through the mud.

An Alsatian! Officer Maury tries unsuccessfully to hold it back.

The dog merrily rubs itself against Sérénac's jeans.

'Hey,' the inspector says, 'our first witness.'

He turns back towards the locals on the bridge.

'Does anyone know this dog?' he calls.

'Yes,' an elderly man dressed as a painter, with velvet trousers and a tweed jacket, replies immediately. 'It's Neptune, the village dog. Everyone meets him sooner or later. He runs around after the kids in the village, the tourists. He's part of the landscape, you might say.'

'Come here, big fellow,' Sérénac says, crouching down to Neptune's level. 'So you're our first witness? Tell me, did you see the murderer? Do you know him? Come and see me later, give me a statement. We still have a bit of work to do here.'

The inspector breaks off a willow branch and throws it a few metres away. Neptune responds to the game. Runs off, comes back. Sylvio Bénavides watches his superior's behaviour with astonishment.

At last Sérénac straightens up again. He takes a while to itemise his surroundings: the cob and brick wash house overlooking the brook; the bridge over the stream and, just behind that, a strange, crooked, half-timbered building, dominated by a kind of four-storey tower. Engraved on the wall is its name: *MOULIN DES CHENNEVIÈRES*. Nothing must be neglected, he notes in a corner of his mind; we'll have to question all potential witnesses, even if the murder was probably committed at around six o'clock in the morning.

'Michel, make the public stand back. Ludo, pass me a pair of plastic gloves; we'll go through the doctor's pockets. We're going to have to get our feet wet if we don't want to move the body.'

Sérénac throws aside his trainers, his socks, rolls his jeans halfway up his calves, slips on the gloves that Officer Maury holds out to him, then walks into the stream barefoot. His left hand holds Morval's body steady while the other searches his jacket. He removes a leather wallet, which he holds out to Bénavides. His deputy opens it and checks through the papers.

No doubt about it, the victim is Jérôme Morval.

Sérénac continues to explore the corpse's pockets. Handkerchiefs. Car keys. Everything passes from gloved hand to gloved hand and ends up in a transparent bag.

'Hang on. What the—'

Sérénac's fingers extract a piece of crumpled card from the outside pocket of the corpse's jacket. The inspector lowers his eyes. It is a simple postcard. The illustration depicts Monet's *Water Lilies*, a study in blue: a reproduction of the kind sold by the million throughout the world. Sérénac turns the card over.

The text is short, the letters typed: ELEVEN YEARS OLD. HAPPY BIRTHDAY.

Just below those five words is a thin strip of paper that has been cut out and glued to the card. Nine words, this time: *The crime of dreaming, I agree to its creation.*

The freezing water of the stream suddenly feels like two steel fetters around the inspector's ankles. Sérénac shouts at the onlookers who are crowding around the Norman wash house as if they were waiting for the bus:

'Did Morval have any kids? An eleven-year-old, for example?'

Once again the painter is the quickest to reply:

'No, Inspector. Certainly not!'

Bugger . . .

The birthday card passes into Inspector Bénavides' hand. Sérénac raises his head, looks around. The wash house. The bridge. The mill. The village of Giverny waking up. Monet's gardens, a little further off. The meadow and the poplars.

The clouds clinging to the wooded riverbanks.

The crime of dreaming, I agree to its creation.

He is suddenly convinced that something is out of place in this postcard landscape.

3

High up in the tower of the Moulin des Chennevières, I watch the police. The one wearing a pair of jeans, the boss, still has his feet in the water, the other three are standing on the bank, surrounded by that stupid crowd, nearly thirty people now, who don't want to miss a thing, as if this were a scene in the theatre. Street theatre. Stream theatre, in fact.

I smile to myself. It's stupid, don't you think, making puns to yourself? And am I any less stupid than those rubberneckers just because I'm up here on the balcony? It's the best seat, believe me. I can see without being seen.

I hesitate. I laugh nervously.

What should I do?

The police are taking a large plastic bag from the white van – something to stuff the corpse into, no doubt. The question keeps scurrying around in my head. What should I do? Should I go to the police? Go to the station at Vernon and tell them everything I know?

Are they capable of believing the delirium of a mad, old woman? Is the solution not to simply shut up and wait? Just for a few days. To observe, play the quiet little mouse, and see how things develop? I'll also have to talk to Jérôme Morval's widow, Patricia. Yes, of course, that's what I must do.

But talking to the police, on the other hand . . .

Down by the stream, the three policemen are dragging Jérôme Morval's corpse, like a large piece of thawed meat dripping with blood and water, over towards the bag. They're struggling, poor things. They look like amateur fishermen who have harpooned a fish that's too big for them. The fourth policeman, still in the water, is watching them. From where I'm standing, you might even say that he's enjoying himself. Yes, as far as I can tell, he's smiling.

I may be torturing myself for nothing. If I talk to Patricia Morval, there's a risk that everyone might find out, that much is certain. Especially the police. That widow, she's a chatty one . . . although I'm not a widow yet, not completely.

I close my eyes for a minute.

I've made up my mind.

No, I'm not going to talk to the police! I'm going to turn myself into a little black mouse, be invisible. For a few days at least. After all, if the police want to find me they can; at my age I can't run very fast. All they need to do is follow Neptune . . . I open my eyes and look at my dog. He is lying a few dozen metres away from the police, in the bracken. He doesn't miss a thing.

Yes, I'll wait a while, at least until I'm a widow. That's the norm, isn't it? The minimum standard of decency. After that, there will always be time to improvise, to act, when the right moment comes. A long time ago, I read a fairly incredible detective story. It was set in

16

an English stately home or something of the kind. The whole plot was explained through the eyes of a cat. Yes, you heard me correctly, a cat! The cat saw everything but no one paid it any attention. It was the cat who, in a sense, led the investigation. It listened, observed, nosed about. The novel was even clever enough to make you think that, in the end, the cat itself was the murderer. I won't spoil it for you, I won't reveal the ending, you might want to read the book if you get the opportunity . . . Anyway, that is exactly what I plan to do: to be a witness to this business, as beyond suspicion as the cat in my stately home.

I turn my head towards the river again.

Morval's corpse has almost disappeared, swallowed up by the plastic bag; it looks like a sated anaconda. Only a glimpse of the head peeps out between the two serrated jaws of a zip that hasn't quite been pulled shut. The three policemen on the bank seem to be taking a break. From up here it looks as if they're just waiting to have a smoke.

DAY TWO

14 May 2010
(Moulin des Chennevières)

Familiarity

4

They're getting on my nerves, the people at the hospital, with all these papers. On the table I stack up the sheets of different-coloured paper as best I can. Prescriptions, medical insurance certificates, marriage certificates, residence certificates, examination certificates. I slip them all into brown envelopes. Some for the hospital. But not all. I'll weigh them and send them from the post office in Vernon. I put the pointless papers in a white folder. I haven't filled in everything, I haven't understood everything, I'll ask the nurses. They know me now. I spent yesterday afternoon and a good part of the evening there.

In Room 126, playing the widow-to-be, worried about her husband who's about to leave this world; listening to the soothing words of the doctors and nurses. Their lies.

He's done for, my husband is! I'm well aware of it. If they knew how little I cared.

Let's just get it over with. That's all I want.

Before leaving the house, I walk over to the flaking gilded mirror to the left of the front door. I look at my creased, wrinkled, cold face. Dead. I wrap a big black scarf around my braided hair. It almost looks like a chador. In this place, the old women are condemned to the veil, no one wants to see them. That's how it is. Even in Giverny. Especially in Giverny, the village of light and colours. Old women are condemned to the shadows, to darkness, to the night. They pass, forgotten.

Well, that suits me.

I turn around one last time before going down the stairs of my keep. That's what people usually call the tower of the Moulin des Chennevières. The keep. I automatically check that there's nothing lying about, and at the same moment curse myself for being stupid. No one comes here anymore. No one will ever come, ever, and yet seeing the slightest object out of place makes me chew my nails. It's a kind of obsessive compulsive disorder, a tic, which doesn't bother anyone else but me.

In the darkest corner one detail alarms me. I have a sense that the painting has slipped slightly in relation to the rafter. I slowly cross the room. I press down on the right-hand bottom corner of the frame, to straighten it slightly.

My *Water Lilies*.

Black water lilies.

I hung the painting at the precise point where it could not be seen from any of the windows – as if anyone could see through the fourth-floor windows of a Norman tower built in the middle of a mill.

My lair . . .

The painting hangs in the corner that is least well lit; in a blind spot, you might say. The gloom makes the dark patches floating on grey water look even more sinister.

Flowers in mourning.

The saddest ever painted.

I struggle down the stairs. I go outside. Neptune is waiting in the courtyard. I push him out of the way with my cane before he can jump up on my dress: the dog hasn't worked out that I am finding it increasingly difficult to keep my balance. I spend several long minutes locking the three heavy locks, slipping my key-ring into my bag, then checking once again that each lock is properly secure.

In the courtyard of the mill, the big cherry tree is losing its last blossoms. It's a hundred years old, apparently. They say it might have known Monet! They're lovely, in Giverny, the cherry trees. A whole series of them has been planted in the car park of the Museum of American Art, which became the Museum of Impressionisms a year ago. They're Japanese cherry trees, from what I've heard, and they're smaller, like dwarf trees. I find them a bit strange, these exotic new trees, as if there weren't already enough trees in the village. But what do you expect, that's just how it is. Apparently the tourists love the pink of the cherry trees in spring. If anyone asked my advice, I would say that with the ground of the car park and the cars all covered in pink petals, it all looks a bit too Barbie. But no one does ask my advice.

I clutch the envelopes against my chest so that Neptune can't damage them and I hobble up the Rue du Colombier. I take my time, I catch my breath in the porch of an ivy-covered guest house. The coach for Vernon won't be here for two hours. I have time, all the time in the world to play being a little black mouse.

On the Rue Claude Monet hollyhocks and orange irises pierce the tarmac like grass along the stone façades. That's the charm of Giverny. I continue at my octogenarian pace. As usual, Neptune is already far ahead. Eventually I reach the Hôtel Baudy. The windows of the most famous restaurant in Giverny are hidden behind posters advertising exhibitions, galleries or festivals. The glass panes are exactly the same size as the posters. It's odd, if you think about it; I've always wondered if it was a coincidence, if the dimensions of all those posters were specifically designed to fit the windows or, on the contrary, if the architect of the Hôtel Baudy was a visionary who, when he designed those windows in the nineteenth century, had somehow managed to predict the standard size of future advertisements.

Several dozen visitors are sitting around tables outside the Hôtel Baudy, on green cast-iron chairs, under orange parasols, seeking to recapture the same emotion the colony of American painters felt when they landed here more than a century ago. That's strange too, when you think about it. Those American painters came here, to this tiny village in Normandy, all those years ago, in search of peace and concentration. The very opposite of what Giverny is today. I don't think I understand very much of what Giverny is today.

I sit down at a free table and order a black coffee. A new waitress brings it to me, a seasonal worker. She's wearing a short skirt and a little Impressionist-style waistcoat, with mauve water lilies on the back. To me, that seems bizarre too.

Having seen all changes that have taken place in the village over the years, I sometimes have the feeling that Giverny has become a giant theme park. And I sit here sighing and grumbling to myself like a mean old woman, no longer understanding anything about anything. I study the crowd around me. A pair of lovers reading the same Green Guide in duet. Three children, less than five years old, squabbling in the gravel; their parents must be thinking that they'd be better off by a pool than by a pond full of toads. A faded American woman tries to order her café liégeois in Hollywood French.

They're here.

The two of them are sitting three tables away from me. Fifteen metres. I recognise them, of course I do. I've seen them from my window at the mill, from behind my curtains. The inspector who paddled in the brook by the corpse of Jérôme Morval and his shy deputy.

Of course they're looking in the other direction, at the little waitress. Not in the direction of an old black mouse.

5

Inspector Sérénac's sunglasses lend the façade of the Hôtel Baudy an almost sepia tint, in the style of the Belle Époque, and the legs of the pretty waitress crossing the street turn the colour of a golden croissant.

'OK, Sylvio. I want you to supervise new searches along the brook for me. Of course everything has already been sent to the lab, the footprints, the rock, Morval's body . . . But we might have overlooked something . . . the wash house, the trees, the bridge, I don't know. You'll see when you get there. Take a walk around and see if you can find any witnesses. As for me, I must pay a visit to the widow, Patricia Morval. Can you brief me about this fellow Jérôme?'

'Yes, Laur . . . er, chief.'

Sylvio Bénavides takes out a file from under the table. Sérénac watches the waitress.

'Would you like something? A pastis? A white wine?'

'Ah, no, no. Nothing for me.'

'Not even a coffee?'

Bénavides prevaricates.

'Go on, have some tea.'

Laurenç Sérénac raises an authoritarian hand.

'*Mademoiselle*? A tea and a glass of white wine. A Gaillac, if you have such a thing?'

He turns back towards his deputy.

'Is it so hard to call me by my Christian name? Sylvio, I'm what – seven years, ten years older than you? We're the same rank. You don't have to be formal with me just because I've been in charge of the station for the past four months. In the South, even the new recruits call inspectors by their first name.'

'In the North, you have to know how to wait . . . It'll come, chief. You'll see . . .'

'I'm sure you're right. They say I have to give it time, to acclimatise . . .'

Sylvio fidgets with his hands, as if hesitating to contradict his superior.

'If you'll forgive me, I'm not sure it is a question of differences between the North and the South. For example, my father is retired now, but he spent his whole life building houses in Portugal and

France for clients younger than himself, who all called him by his first name, while he had to use their surname. I think it has more to do with, I don't know . . . ties versus blue overalls, manicured hands versus hands covered with grease – do you see what I'm getting at?'

Laurenç Sérénac spreads his arms, parting his leather jacket and revealing his grey T-shirt.

'Sylvio, do you see a tie anywhere? We're both inspectors, for God's sake.'

He laughs.

'Well, as you say, it will just take time. I like your humble, second-generation Portuguese thing . . . Anyway: this guy Morval?'

Sylvio lowers his head and studiously reads his notes.

'Jérôme Morval is a child of the village who managed to make a good life for himself. He was born in Giverny, but his family moved to Paris when he was still a boy. Papa Morval was a doctor too, a GP, but he didn't make a huge amount of money. Jérôme Morval married quite young, one Patricia Chéron. He was less than twenty-five. The rest is a success story. Little Jérôme pursues his medical studies, specialising in ophthalmology, first opening a surgery in Asnières with five other colleagues and then, when Papa Morval dies, he invests his inheritance in his own ophthalmological surgery in the 16th Arrondissement. Things seem to have gone rather well. From what I understand, he is a well-known specialist in cataracts, which means he has quite an elderly clientele. Ten years ago, he bought one of the finest houses in Giverny, between the Hôtel Baudy and the church . . .'

'No children?'

The waitress sets down their order and walks away. Sérénac interrupts his deputy just before he can answer.

'Pretty girl, no? She has cute legs under that skirt, don't you think?'

Inspector Bénavides hesitates between a weary sigh and an embarrassed smile.

'Yes . . . I mean no . . . Well, as I was saying, the Morvals. They've never had any children.'

'Right . . . And enemies?'

'Morval led quite a limited life as a local dignitary. No politics. No responsibilities in local associations or anything like that . . . No real network of friends. On the other hand, he had—'

Sérénac turns round abruptly.

'Hang on! Hello you . . .'

Bénavides feels the hairy shape sliding under the table. This time he sighs openly. Sérénac holds out his hand and Neptune comes to rub himself against it.

'My only witness, for the time being,' whispers Laurenç Sérénac. 'Hello there, Neptune!'

The dog recognises his name. He presses against the inspector's leg and enviously eyes the sugar sitting on the saucer of Sylvio's cup of tea. Sérénac lifts a finger towards the dog.

'Behave yourself, now. We're listening to Inspector Bénavides. So, Sylvio, you were saying?'

Sylvio continues in a monotone. 'Jérôme Morval had two passions. All-consuming ones, as they say. To which he devoted most of his time.'

'Now we're getting somewhere,' said Sérénac, still stroking the dog.

'So, two passions . . . art and women. As far as art is concerned, apparently we're dealing with a serious collector, a gifted auto-didact, with a strong preference for Impressionist paintings, of course. And he had an obsession, from what I've been told. Jérôme Morval dreamed of owning a Monet! And if possible, not just any old Monet. He wanted to discover a *Water Lilies*. That was what your ophthalmologist had in mind.'

Sérénac whispers in the dog's ear:

'A Monet no less! Even if he managed to give every fine bourgeois lady in the 16th back her sight, a *Water Lilies* would still seem to be beyond the means of our good doctor. These passions, you were saying . . . Heads, art. And tails, women?'

'There are rumours. Apparently Morval was less than discreet. His neighbours and colleagues were particularly keen to mention the situation of his wife, Patricia. Married young. Financially dependent on her husband. Divorce out of the question. Condemned to turn a blind eye.'

Laurenç Sérénac drains his glass of white.

'If that's a Gaillac . . .' he says, pulling a face. 'I see what you're getting at, Sylvio, and I'm finally beginning to like this doctor. Have you been able to get hold of the names of any of his mistresses, jealous husbands . . . ?'

Sylvio sets down his tea. Neptune looks at him with moist eyes.

'Not yet. But apparently, as far as mistresses are concerned, Jérôme Morval also had an obsession.'

'Really? An impregnable citadel?'

'You could put it like that . . . it's the village schoolteacher. She's the most beautiful girl in the area, apparently, and he'd got it into his head to add her as another trophy in his collection.'

'So?'

'So, that's all I know. That's all I got from a conversation with his colleagues, his secretary and the three principal art dealers he worked with.'

'Is she married, this teacher?'

'Yes. To a particularly jealous husband, or so they say.'

Sérénac looks down at Neptune.

'Now we're getting somewhere, my old friend. Sylvio's good, isn't he? He might look a bit awkward, but he has the brains of a computer.'

He gets to his feet. Neptune runs off down the street.

'Enjoy your paddle in the Ru, Sylvio. I hope you haven't forgotten your boots and your fishing line! I'm off to present my condolences to the widow Morval . . . 71, Rue Claude Monet, that's right, isn't it?'

'Yes. You can't go wrong. Giverny is a tiny village built on the side of a hill. It consists of two long parallel streets, the Rue Claude Monet, which runs through the whole village, and the Chemin du Roy, the main road at the bottom of the valley which runs alongside the brook. There's a series of small alleyways that climb quite steeply between the two main streets, but that's it.'

The waitress's tanned legs cross the Rue Claude Monet and head towards the counter of the bar. The hollyhocks lick at the terracotta brick walls of the Hôtel Baudy like pastel-coloured flames. And Sérénac thinks the scene is very picturesque.

6

Sylvio wasn't wrong. Number 71 Rue Claude Monet is without contest the most beautiful house on the street. Yellow shutters, a Virginia creeper devouring half of the façade, a deft mixture of freestone and half-timbering, geraniums dripping from the windows and spilling from huge clay pots: an Impressionist façade *par excellence*. Patricia Morval must have green fingers, or at least she must know how to field a small army of competent gardeners. There can't be a shortage of those in Giverny. A brass bell hangs on a chain by a wooden gate. Sérénac tugs on it. A few seconds later, Patricia Morval appears at the oak door. She has clearly been waiting for him. The policeman pushes the gate open and she steps aside to let him in.

Inspector Sérénac always enjoys this moment in an investigation. *The first impression.* Those few instants of pure understanding, of instinctive psychology, captured live. Who is he going to be dealing with? A woman desperately in love, or a crisp and indifferent matron? A lover struck down by fate or a merry widow? Rich, now. Free, at last? Avenged, after her husband's indiscretions. Feigning grief and pain, or not? At that moment it's hard to say, as Patricia Morval's reddened eyes are hidden behind large, thick glasses.

Sérénac steps into the hall. In fact it is a vast vestibule, narrow and deep. He suddenly stops, dumbfounded. Covering the entirety of the two walls, which are over five metres long, are two enormous paintings of water lilies reproduced in a rather rare variant: in tones of red and gold, with no sky or willow branches. If Sérénac is right this is probably the reproduction of a painting Monet produced during the last years of his life, the final series, after 1920. It isn't hard to work it out. In his later years, Monet followed a simple creative logic: narrowing his gaze, eliminating scenery, focusing on a single point in the pond, a few square metres across. The hall is doubtless intended to recall the walls of the Orangerie, even if it is far from the hundred linear metres of *Water Lilies* displayed in the Paris museum.

Sérénac goes into a room. The interior decoration is classical, with a few too many knick-knacks of different kinds. The visitor's attention is particularly drawn to the paintings on display. About ten of them. Originals. As far as Sérénac can tell, there are some names that suggest real value, both artistic and financial. A Grebonval, a Van Muylder, a Gabar . . . Apparently Morval had taste and a good nose for an investment. The inspector reflects that if his widow can keep at bay the vultures who will sniff out the scent of paint, then she will be sheltered from poverty for a long time to come.

He sits down. Patricia won't stand still. She nervously moves the perfectly arranged ornaments around. Her purple suit contrasts with her rather dull, milky skin. Sérénac puts her at about forty, perhaps younger. She isn't really pretty, but a kind of stiffness in her bearing gives her a certain charm. More classical than classy, the policeman would say. The appeal is minimal, but well looked after.

'Inspector, are you absolutely sure that it was murder?' she says in a sharp, slightly disagreeable tone. She adds: 'I've been told about the scene. Isn't an accident a possibility? Jérôme might have tripped and fallen onto a rock, or a flint, and then drowned . . .'

'Anything is possible, madam – we have to wait for the forensic report. But as the investigation stands, I must admit that murder seems the most likely option. By a long way.'

Between her fingers, Patricia Morval is torturing a small statue of Diana the Huntress that is resting on a side table. A bronze. Sérénac resumes charge of the discussion. He asks questions, Patricia Morval replies, seldom using more than three words, and often the same ones, barely varying the same high, sharp tone.

'He had no enemies?

'No, no, no,'

'You didn't notice anything in particular over the past few days?'

'No, no.'

'Your house looks enormous; did your husband live here?'

'Yes . . . Yes. Yes and no.'

This time Sérénac doesn't give her the choice. He needs to understand the nuance.

'You'll have to tell me more, Madame Morval.'

Patricia Morval slowly utters the syllables, as if counting them.

'Jérôme was rarely here during the week. He had a flat beside his surgery, in the 16th. Boulevard Suchet.'

The inspector notes the address, remembering that it is a stone's throw from the Musée Marmottan. Surely not a coincidence.

'Did your husband often sleep elsewhere?'

A silence.

'Yes.'

Patricia Morval's nervous fingers rearrange a freshly picked bouquet of flowers in a long vase covered with Japanese motifs. A striking image comes to Laurenç Sérénac's mind: those flowers will rot on their stems. Death will congeal this sitting room. The dust of time will settle on this harmony of colours.

'You had no children?'

'No.'

A pause.

'And your husband didn't either? On his own, I mean?'

Patricia Morval compensates for her hesitation with a tone of voice that has dropped an octave.

'No.'

Sérénac takes his time. He extracts a photocopy of the *Water Lilies* postcard found in Jérôme Morval's pocket, turns it over and holds it out to the widow. Patricia Morval is obliged to read the five typed words: ELEVEN YEARS OLD. HAPPY BIRTHDAY.

'This card was found in your husband's pocket,' the inspector explains. 'Perhaps you have a cousin? A friend's child? Can you think of any child your husband might have intended to give this birthday card to?'

'No, I don't think so. Honestly.'

Nevertheless, Sérénac gives Patricia Morval time to think before he starts again:

'And this quotation?'

Their eyes slide over the card and read the strange words that follow: *The crime of dreaming, I agree to its creation.*

'I've no idea. Sorry, Inspector. '

She seems genuinely indifferent. Sérénac puts the card down on the table.

'It's a photocopy, you can keep it. We have the original. If anything occurs to you . . .'

Patricia Morval's agitated movements have slowed, like a fly trapped in a jam jar that has worked out it can't escape. Sérénac goes on.

'Did your husband have any enemies from a professional point of view? I mean an operation that went wrong, or an unhappy client? Someone who made a complaint?'

The fly suddenly becomes aggressive again.

'No! Never. What are you insinuating?'

'Nothing, I assure you.'

He looks at the paintings on the walls.

'Your husband had a good eye for a painting. Do you think he might have been implicated in, how can I put it, some kind of smuggling operation, receiving stolen goods, perhaps without even knowing it?'

'What do you mean?'

The widow's voice rises to the heights again, even more unpleasant than before. This is classic, the inspector thinks. Patricia Morval is shutting herself away by denying it was murder. To admit that her husband was murdered would be to admit that someone could hate him enough to kill him . . . And that would mean admitting the guilt of her husband, to a certain extent. Sérénac has learned all this – how to shed light on the dark side of the victim without pointing his gun directly at the widow.

'I don't mean anything by it, nothing specific. I can assure you, Madame Morval, I'm just trying to find a lead. I was told about his . . . let's call it his quest . . . to own a painting by Monet.'

'You are quite right, Inspector. It was a dream. Jérôme was known as one of the best experts on Claude Monet. And so yes, he had a dream to own one for himself. He worked hard for it. He was a highly gifted surgeon and he would have deserved it. He was a passionate man. And it wasn't just any painting, Inspector. He wanted to own a *Water Lilies*. I don't know if you can understand, but that was what he was searching for. A canvas painted here, in Giverny. His village.'

Taking advantage of the widow's monologue, Sérénac's brain stirs into action. *The first impression!* After talking to Patricia Morval for several minutes, he is starting to have an idea of the nature of her mourning. And contrary to all expectation, the impression is tending more towards the idea of inflamed passion, of thunderstruck love, rather than the faded, dull indifference of the abandoned wife.

'I'm sorry to bore you like this, Madame Morval, but we both want the same thing – to find the person who murdered your husband. I will have to ask you some more . . . personal questions.'

Patricia seems to freeze in the pose of the nude painted by Gabar on the opposite wall.

'Your husband hasn't always been, let's say . . . faithful. Do you think that . . . ?'

Sérénac spots Patricia's flash of emotion. As if all the tears stored up inside her were trying to douse the fire in her belly.

'My husband and I met when we were very young. He courted me – and others – for a long time, a very long time. It was many years before I yielded to it. When he was young he wasn't the kind of boy to set the girls dreaming. I don't know if you see what I mean. He was probably a bit too serious, too awkward. He . . . he lacked confidence with the opposite sex. And girls sense this kind of thing. Then, over time, he became more sure of himself, much more charming too, and more interesting. I think, Inspector, that I had a lot to do with that. He grew richer, too. As an adult, it was as if Jérôme had to exact his revenge on women . . .

On women, Inspector. Not on me. I don't know if you can understand.'

I hope so, thinks Sérénac, telling himself that he will need names, facts, dates.

Later . . .

'I expect you to be tactful, Inspector. Giverny is a small village with only a few hundred inhabitants. Don't kill Jérôme a second time. Don't sully his memory. He doesn't deserve that.'

Laurenç Sérénac nods reassuringly.

First impressions . . . His conviction is now forged. Yes, Patricia Morval loved her Jérôme. And no, she would not have killed him for his money.

But for love, who knows . . .

One last detail strikes him. It's the flowers in the Japanese vase that persuade him of it: time has stopped in this house. The clock broke down the day before. In this drawing room, every square centimetre is still infused with the passions of Jérôme Morval. Of him alone. And everything will stay like that, for all eternity. The paintings will never be taken down from the walls. The books on the shelves in the library will never be opened. Everything will remain inert, like a deserted museum devoted to a man who has already been forgotten. An art lover who will leave nothing behind. A lover of women who will probably be mourned by none of them. Except by his own wife, the one he abandoned.

A life spent accumulating reproductions. A life without issue.

As he leaves the house, the intense light on the Rue Claude Monet explodes on the inspector's face. Silvio appears at the end of the street less than three minutes later, no boots on his feet but the bottom of his trousers covered with mud. This amuses Sérénac. Sylvio Bénavides is an elegant man. Probably much cleverer than his meticulous side makes him look. From behind his sunglasses, Laurenç Sérénac examines the fine profile of his deputy, whose shadow stretches along the walls of the houses. Sylvio isn't exactly thin. Narrow would be a more precise description, because paradoxically the beginnings of a little pot-belly can be seen under his checked shirt, which is buttoned up to the neck and tucked neatly into his beige cotton trousers. Sylvio is probably wider in profile than face-on, Laurenç thinks with amusement. He's like a cylinder. It doesn't make him ugly, quite the contrary. It lends him a kind of fragility, a waist like a young tree trunk, lithe and supple, as if it could bend without ever breaking.

Sylvio approaches, a smile on his lips. Quite definitely, what Laurenç likes least about his deputy, physically at least, is his habit of slicking his short, straight hair back or to the side, with a seminarian's parting. A simple brush cut would be enough to transform him. Sylvio Bénavides stops in front of him and puts both hands on his hips.

'So, chief, what about the widow?'

'Very much a widow! Very much. And you?'

'Nothing new . . . I talked to a few neighbours. They were asleep on the morning of the murder and don't know anything. As to the other evidence, we'll just have to see. Everything has been bagged up or put in a sample jar. Are we going back to base?'

Sérénac consults his watch. It's 4.30 p.m.

'Yes. Or rather, you are. I have an urgent appointment.'

He explains to his astonished deputy.

'I don't want to miss the end of the school day.'

Sylvio Bénavides thinks he's understood.

'You are looking for a child who is about to celebrate their eleventh birthday?'

Sérénac gives Sylvio a complicit wink.

'You could say that . . . And I'd also like to see this jewel of Impressionism for myself: the schoolteacher Jérôme Morval coveted as much as a painting by Monet.'

7

I wait for the coach below the lime trees in the little square that contains the town hall and the school. It is the shadiest corner of the village, just a few metres away from the Rue Claude Monet.

I'm almost alone. Really, this village has become the oddest place: it only takes a few metres, a simple bit of street, to pass from all the hubbub and queues of the besieged museums and galleries to the deserted alleyways of a simple country village.

The bus stop is in front of the school, or almost. The children are playing in the playground, behind the wire fence. Neptune is standing a little further off, beneath a lime tree, waiting impatiently for the release of the caged children. He loves that, Neptune does, running after the little ones.

Just opposite the village school is the studio of the Art Gallery Academy. Their motto is painted in huge letters on the wall: OBSERVATION WITH IMAGINATION. There's a whole programme. Throughout the day, a regiment of limping pensioners, wearing boaters or panamas, leaves the gallery and scatters around the village in search of divine inspiration. They are impossible to miss, with their red badges and their old-lady shopping trolleys used to transport their easels.

Don't you think that's ridiculous? One day someone will have to explain to me why the hay, the birds in the trees or the water in the river hereabouts aren't the same colour as anywhere else in the world. It's beyond me. I must be too stupid to understand, I must have lived here for too long. Like when you live beside a very handsome man for too long and stop noticing.

Anyway, these particular invaders don't leave like the other tourists at six o'clock. They hang around until nightfall, sleep in the village, go out at dawn. Most of them are American. I may only be an old woman observing the whole circus through a cataract, but that doesn't stop me thinking that all these old painters parading in front of the school will end up influencing the children of the village, putting ideas in their heads. Don't you agree?

The inspector has spotted Neptune standing under the lime tree. They really stick together, those two. He cavorts with the dog, their play a mixture of joyful struggle and caresses. I stay in the background, on my bench, like an ebony statue. It may seem strange to you that an old woman like me should stroll around the whole of Giverny and that no one, or nearly no one, should notice. Even less so the police. I suggest you just try it. Go and stand on a street corner, any corner, a Parisian boulevard, in the square by a village church, wherever you like. Stop for, I don't know, ten minutes, and count the people passing. You will be surprised by the number of old people. There will always be more old people than anyone else. First of all, because that's just how it is, there are more and more old people in the world. Secondly, because that's all old people have to do, hang about in the street. And then, no one notices them. That's just how it is. You turn to gaze at a girl's bare navel, you push your way past the senior executive in a hurry, or the gang of young people filling the pavement, you glance at the buggy, the baby in it and the mother behind it. But an old man or woman . . . They are invisible. Precisely because they pass so slowly that they are almost part of the decor, like a tree or a streetlight. If you don't believe me, just try it. You'll see.

To come back to the issue at hand, and since I have the privilege of seeing without being seen, I can assure you that he is insanely charming, this young policeman, with his short leather jacket, his tight jeans, his stubble, his crazy hair, blond as a wheat field after a storm. You can understand why he might be more interested in melancholic schoolteachers than the mad old women of the village.

8

After giving Neptune one last pat, Laurenç Sérénac leaves the dog and walks towards the school. As he approaches, about twenty children run out in front of him squealing, a mixture of all ages. As if he were scaring them away.

The wild beasts have been unleashed.

A little girl of about ten runs at the head of the group, her bunches flying in the wind. Neptune follows her, as if attached to a spring. Indeed they all follow, spilling into the Rue Blanche Hoschedé-Monet and scattering along the Rue Claude Monet. As suddenly as it came alive, the Place de la Mairie falls silent again. The inspector walks forward another few metres.

For a long time afterwards, Laurenç Sérénac will think about that miracle. All his life. He will weigh each sound, the shouts of the children fading away, the wind rustling the leaves of the lime trees; every smell, every flash of light, the whiteness of the stonework on the town hall, the convolvulus climbing along the railing of the seven front steps.

He didn't expect it. He didn't expect anything.

Much later, he will understand that it was the contrast that left him thunderstruck, a tiny contrast lasting barely a few seconds. Stéphanie Dupain was standing by the door of the school and hadn't seen him. Laurenç caught the look in her eyes as she watched the children run away laughing. A faint melancholy, like a fragile butterfly. As if their satchels contained their teacher's dreams.

Then, a moment later, Stéphanie notices the visitor. Immediately, the smile appears, the mauve eyes sparkle.

'Can I help you?'

Stéphanie offers the stranger her freshness. A great gust of freshness, cast out to the four winds, to the beloved landscapes of the artists, to the tourists, to the laughter of the children on the banks of the Epte. Keeping nothing for herself. A gift.

Yes, it's that contrast that so troubles Laurenç Sérénac. That vague sense of suppressed melancholy. As if he had glimpsed, just for an instant, a cave filled with treasure, and his sole obsession, from now on, would be to find its entrance again.

He stammers, also smiling: 'Inspector Laurenç Sérénac, from Vernon police station.'

She holds out a delicate hand.

'Stéphanie Dupain. The only teacher of the only class in the village.'

Her eyes are laughing.

She is pretty. More than pretty, even. Her pastel-coloured eyes, with their hints of water lily, marry different tones of blue and mauve according to the sunlight. Her lips are a delicate shade of pale pink. Her little, light dress reveals bare shoulders that are almost white. Porcelain skin. A slightly crazed chignon imprisons her long, light brown hair.

Jérôme Morval plainly had good taste, and not just in paintings.

'Come in. Please.'

The gentle air of the school contrasts with the crushing heat of the street. When Laurenç enters the little classroom and observes the twenty or so chairs behind the tables, he feels a kind of pleasant discord at this sudden intimacy. His eye slides over vast maps displayed on the wall. France, Europe, the world. Pretty maps, deliciously old. The inspector's gaze suddenly stops on a poster, near the office.

INTERNATIONAL YOUNG PAINTERS CHALLENGE

Robinson Foundation
Brooklyn Art School and Pennsylvania Academy
of the Fine Arts in Philadelphia

It seems like the ideal place to start.

'Are any of your children putting themselves forward?'

Stéphanie's eyes shine.

'Yes. They do every year. It's almost a tradition here. Theodore Robinson was one of the first American painters to come and paint in Giverny alongside Claude Monet. He was the Hôtel Baudy's most loyal guest! Then he became a renowned art teacher in the United States. The least the children of Giverny can do today is to take part in his foundation's competition, don't you think?'

Sérénac nods.

'And what do the laureates win?'

'A few thousand dollars. And more importantly a training course lasting several weeks at a prestigious art school . . . New York, Tokyo, St Petersburg. The venue changes every year.'

'Impressive. Has a child from Giverny ever won?'

Stéphanie Dupain laughs and gives Laurenç Sérénac a tap on the shoulder. He shivers.

'If only . . . Thousands of schools from all over the world take part in the competition. But you have to give it a go, don't you? Did you know that Claude Monet's own sons, Michel and Jean, once sat at the desks of this school?'

'Theodore Robinson never came back to Normandy, did he?'

Stéphanie Dupain stares in astonishment at the inspector. He thinks he spots a hint of admiration in her wide eyes.

'Do they give art history classes at the police academy?'

'No, but you can be a policeman and like art too, can't you?'

She blushes.

'Touché, Inspector . . .'

Her porcelain cheeks, marbled with freckles, assume the pink of wild flowers. Her lilac eyes flood the room.

'You are quite right, Inspector. Theodore Robinson died of an asthma attack in New York at the age of forty-three, just two months after he had written to his friend Claude Monet about returning to Giverny. He never saw France again. His heirs set up a foundation, and the international competition, a few years after he died in 1896. But I'm boring you, Inspector. I don't imagine you've come here for me to give you a lesson.'

'Actually, I'd love that.'

Sérénac says that just to make her blush again. It works.

'And what about you, Stéphanie Dupain. Do you paint?

Once again, the young woman's fingers float in the air nearly touching the inspector's chest. The policeman forces himself to see this gesture as merely the reflex of a teacher who is used to leaning in close to her children, looking into their eyes as she speaks to them, touching them.

An incendiary innocence?

Sérénac hopes he isn't blushing as much as she is.

'No, no. I don't paint. I don't . . . I have no talent.'

Very briefly, a cloud passes over her bright irises.

'So what about you? You don't have a Vernon accent! And

your first name, Laurenç, that's not very common in these parts.'

'Well spotted. Laurenç is the equivalent of Laurent, in Occitan. My personal dialect would be local to Albi, to be precise. I've just been transferred.'

'Well, in that case, welcome! Albi? So your taste in painting must derive from Toulouse-Lautrec?'

They smile.

'Partly . . . I suppose Lautrec is to the people of Albi what Monet is to the Normans.'

'Do you know what Lautrec said about Monet?'

'I'm going to disappoint you, but I have to confess that I wasn't even aware that they knew each other.'

'They did. But Lautrec said the Impressionists were a bunch of brutes. He even said that Monet was an idiot because he wasted his huge talent painting landscapes rather than human beings.'

'It's a good thing Lautrec died before he saw Monet going off to live like a hermit and paint nothing but water lilies for thirty years.'

Stéphanie laughs out loud.

'That's one way of looking at things. Or you might consider that Lautrec and Monet chose opposing fates. For Toulouse-Lautrec, an ephemeral life of debauchery spent chasing the desires of the flesh; for Monet, a long contemplative life devoted to nature.'

'Complementary rather than opposing, wouldn't you say? Does a person really need to choose? Can't you have both?'

Stéphanie's smile drives him mad.

'I'm incorrigible, Inspector. I don't imagine you've come here to talk about painting. You're investigating the murder of Jérôme Morval, I assume?'

She nimbly lifts herself on to the desk and crosses her legs. The movement is quite natural but the cotton fabric of her dress slips halfway up her thigh. Laurenç Sérénac can hardly breathe.

'And what does that have to do with me?' the teacher whispers innocently.

9

The coach is parked just in front of the Place de la Mairie. There is a woman driver behind the wheel. She doesn't look like someone who wanted to be a boy, or a truck driver; no, she's just an ordinary little woman who could just as well be a nurse or a secretary. I don't know if you've noticed, but it's increasingly common to see women driving these enormous great hulks, especially in the countryside. You never used to see that in the old days, female bus drivers. I'm sure it's because it's only old people and children who take public transport in the villages. That's why it isn't considered a man's job anymore.

I painfully lift my foot on to the running board of the bus. I pay the girl, who gives me my change and then I sit down at the front. The bus is half full, but I know from experience that a number of tourists will board on the way out of Giverny and most will get off at Vernon railway station. There's no stop directly outside Vernon Hospital, but in general the drivers take pity on my poor legs and set me down before the stop. Now you can understand why women drive buses – they accept this kind of thing.

I think about Neptune. Yesterday I took a taxi back from Vernon. It cost me exactly thirty-four euros. An incredible amount, don't you think, for less than ten kilometres? Night rate, he told me, the man behind the wheel of the Renault Espace. They definitely take advantage – they know very well that there's no bus to Giverny after nine in the evening. And, by the way, you will notice that it's always men behind the wheels of taxis, never women. They must circle around the hospital all night like vultures, just waiting for an old woman to come out, an old woman who never learned to drive. At times like that you suspect they already know you aren't about to haggle! Well . . . I say all that but it's possible I will be very happy to find one not long from now. Because from what the doctors have told me, this evening may be the last one. So there's a risk it could stretch on into a good portion of the night.

It really bothers me, having to leave Neptune hanging about outside.

10

In the classroom, Inspector Laurenç Sérénac is trying to keep his eyes away from the bare skin of the teacher's legs. He clumsily fumbles in his pocket while Stéphanie Dupain studies him candidly, as if the pose that she has adopted, sitting on the desk with her thighs crossed, were the most natural in the world. Normally, Laurenç Sérénac muses, none of the children in her class would see any mischief in this . . . normally . . .

'So,' the teacher asks again. 'How does this relate to me?'

The inspector finally extracts from his pocket a photocopy of the *Water Lilies* postcard.

ELEVEN YEARS OLD. HAPPY BIRTHDAY.

He holds out the card.

'They found this in Jérôme Morval's pocket.'

Stéphanie Dupain decodes the phrase attentively. As the teacher leans over and turns away slightly, the ray of sunlight shining through the window reflects off the white paper and illuminates her face, a reading woman bathed in a halo of light that is suggestive of the work of Fragonard. Degas. Vermeer. For just a moment, Sérénac is touched by a strange idea, an impression: not one of the young woman's gestures is spontaneous; the grace of each movement is too perfect, calculated, studied. *She is posing, for him.* Stéphanie Dupain straightens up, elegantly, her pale lips open gently and release an invisible breath that turns the inspector's ludicrous suspicions into dust.

'The Morvals had no children. So you thought of the school.'

'Yes. That's the mystery. Are there any eleven-year-olds in your class?'

'Several. I look after more or less all the children, from the ages of six to eleven. But to my knowledge none of them is going to celebrate a birthday in the coming days, or weeks.'

'Could you draw up a precise list for us? With parents' addresses, dates of birth, anything that might be useful.'

'Might the card have anything to do with the murder?'

'It might . . . or it mightn't . . . We're just feeling our way around at the moment. Following different lines of enquiry. By the way, does this phrase mean anything to you?'

Sérénac points towards the bottom of the postcard. She frowns slightly in concentration. He loves all of her mannerisms.

She continues to consider the words. The fluttering of her eyelids, the trembling of her mouth, the curve of her neck. A woman who knows how to read the inspector's fantasy. How could she toy with him like this? How could she know?

The crime of dreaming . . .

'So . . . does it mean anything to you?' Sérénac stammers.

Stéphanie Dupain gets abruptly to her feet. She walks towards the bookshelves, bends down and then comes back, all smiles. She hands him a white book. Laurenç has a sense that the teacher's heart is beating fast under her cotton dress, like a quivering sparrow that doesn't dare to pass through the open door of its cage.

'Louis Aragon,' Stéphanie's clear voice rings out. 'I'm sorry, Inspector, I'm going to have to give you another lesson.'

Laurenç pushes an exercise book aside and sits down on a pupil's desk.

'As I said before, I'd love that.'

She laughs again.

'You're not as well up on your poetry as you are on your painting, Inspector. The phrase on the postcard comes from a poem by Louis Aragon.'

'You're incredible . . . '

'No, no, I don't deserve any credit. First of all Louis Aragon was a regular visitor to Giverny, one of the few artists to remain in the village after Claude Monet's death in 1926. Also it's taken from a famous poem by Aragon, the first one of his to be censored, in 1942, by the Vichy government. I'm still worried about lecturing you, Inspector, but when I tell you the title of the poem, you will understand why it's a tradition in the village to teach it to the children of the school every year.'

'"Impressions"?' Sérénac hazards a guess.

'Wrong. Although you're nearly there. Aragon called his poem "Nymphée" – Nymphaeum, which is of course reminiscent of nymphéa, our word for water lilies.'

Laurenç tries to sift through this information in his mind.

'So, if I'm following you correctly, Jérôme Morval would, logically, be familiar with these lines as well . . .' he paused, thinking again. 'Thank you. It could have taken us days to work that out. Although I'm not sure, for the moment, where this will take us.'

The inspector jumps up and turns towards the teacher. She is now standing in front of him, their faces nearly level, only about thirty centimetres apart.

'Stéphanie . . . Can I call you Stéphanie? Did you know Jérôme Morval?'

Her mauve eyes settle on him. He barely hesitates before diving into them.

'Giverny is tiny,' says Stéphanie. 'There are just a few hundred people . . . '

'That's not an answer, Stéphanie!'

A silence. Only twenty centimetres separate them.

'Yes . . . I knew him.'

The mauve surface of her iris is flooded with light. The inspector floats on it. He has to keep going. Or sink. None of his cheap cynicism is of any use to him.

'There . . . there are rumours.'

'Don't be embarrassed, Inspector. I'm aware of them, of course I am. Jérôme Morval was a ladies' man, isn't that what they say? So I'm not going to claim that he didn't try to get close to me. But . . .'

The surfaces of her water-lily eyes ripple. A light breeze.

'I'm married, Inspector Sérénac. I am the village's teacher. Morval is its doctor, in a sense. It would be ludicrous for you to go off down the wrong track. Nothing ever happened between Jérôme Morval and me. In villages such as ours, there is always someone ready to spy on you, to spread lies, invent secrets.'

'My fault. I'm sorry if I seemed rude.'

She smiles at him, there, just in front of his mouth, then suddenly disappears again towards the bookshelves.

'Here, Inspector. Since you have the heart of an artist . . .'

Laurenç sees that Stéphanie is holding out another book to him.

'For your own edification. *Aurélien*, Louis Aragon's finest novel. The most important scenes are set in Giverny. From chapter sixty to chapter sixty-four. I'm sure you'll love it.'

'Th . . . thank you.'

The inspector can't find anything else to say, and rages inwardly at his silence. Stéphanie has caught him off guard. What does Aragon have to do with all this? He feels he's missing something, like he's skidded and lost control. He takes hold of the book with fake self-assurance, presses it against his thigh, arm dangling, then holds out a hand to Stéphanie. The teacher grips it.

A little too hard.

For a little too long.

For a second or two. Just long enough for his imagination to start working. This hand in his seems to be clinging to it, seems to be shouting, 'Don't let me go. Don't abandon me. You are my only hope, Laurenç. Don't let me fall into the depths.'

Stéphanie smiles at him. Her eyes are glittering.

He must have been dreaming, of course. He's going mad. He has been getting his wires crossed since his first investigation in Normandy.

This woman isn't hiding anything.

She's simply beautiful. She belongs to someone else.

He gabbles as he retreats. 'Stéphanie, will you . . . I mean, could you think about drawing up a list of children, for me? I'll send an officer to pick it up tomorrow.'

They both know he won't send an officer, that he will come back himself, and that she hopes he will too.

11

The Vernon coach turns into Rue Claude Monet and makes its way towards the church, in the part of the village where the flood of tourists is less dense. If you can say that . . . I love going through the village in a coach like this, sitting at the front watching the panorama pass by. We pass the Demarez and Kandy art galleries, the Immo-Prestige estate agency, the Clos-Fleuri guest house, the Hôtel Baudy. The coach catches up with a group of children who are walking along the street, satchels on their backs. The children push their way to the side when the driver sounds the horn, heedlessly crushing hollyhocks and irises. Two other children scamper into the field opposite the Hôtel Baudy. I recognise them, they're always together, those two. Paul and Fanette. I see Neptune as well, he's beside them, running through the hay. The dog won't leave the kids alone, particularly Fanette, the girl with the plaits.

I think I'm getting indulgent, you know. I worry myself sick over my old dog, when he can get along very well without me. The kids from the village always look out for him.

At the very end of the street I see the next stop. I can't suppress a sigh. It's the exodus! More than twenty passengers are waiting, with their suitcases on wheels, and paintings wrapped in brown paper.

12

Fanette holds Paul's hand. They are hidden behind the haystack in the large field that separates the Chemin du Roy from the Rue Claude Monet, level with the Hôtel Baudy.

'Shoo, Neptune! Clear off! You'll give us away.'

The dog looks at the two eleven-year-old children and doesn't understand. His coat is covered in straw.

'Go on! Idiot!'

Paul bursts out laughing. His long shirt is open. He throws his schoolbag down beside him.

I like Paul's laugh, Fanette thinks.

'There they are!' the little girl suddenly exclaims. 'At the end of the street! Come on . . .'

They dart off, Paul barely having the time to pick up his bag. Their footsteps echo down Rue Claude Monet.

'Paul, hurry up!' Fanette cries again, catching the boy's hand.

Her plaits fly in the wind.

'There!'

She turns abruptly when they reach the church of Sainte-Radegonde and sprints along the gravel path without slowing her pace, then crouches down behind the thick green hedge. This time Neptune hasn't followed them, he sniffs at the ditch on the other side of the road then urinates on the low houses. Because of the slope of the bank it almost looks as if they are buried. Paul stifles a giggle.

'Shh, Paul. They'll be here in a minute. You're going to give us away.'

Paul retreats a little way and sits down on the white grave behind him. One buttock on the plaque dedicated to Claude Monet, another on the one dedicated to his second wife, Alice.

'Careful, Paul! Don't sit on Monet's grave.'

'Sorry.'

'Doesn't matter!'

I really love Paul, when I tell him off and he apologises and goes all shy.

Fanette bursts out laughing as Paul shuffles forward, unable to stop himself from leaning on the other plaques attached to the grave, the ones dedicated to other members of the Monet family.

Fanette peers through the branches. She hears footsteps.

It's them!

Camille, Vincent and Mary.

Vincent is the first to arrive. He studies his surroundings with the concentration of an Indian scout. He looks suspiciously at Neptune, then shouts:

'Faaanette! Where are yooooou?'

Paul giggles again. Fanette puts her hand over his mouth.

45

Camille reaches the church too. He is smaller than Vincent. His chubby arms and his belly spill out of his open shirt. He is out of breath. The inevitable little fat boy of the gang.

'Did you see them?'

'No! They must have gone further off . . .'

The two boys continue on their way. Vincent shouts, even more loudly:

'Faaanette! Where are yoooou?'

They hear Mary's strident cry coming from a little further away.

'You could at least wait for me!'

Camille and Vincent have already gone by the time Mary reaches the church. The little girl is rather tall for her ten years. Her eyes are weeping behind her glasses.

'Boys, wait for me! We don't care about Fanette! Wait for me!'

She turns her head towards the graves, and Fanette instinctively lies down on top of Paul. Mary hasn't seen anything, she ends up going straight on, down Rue Claude Monet, angrily dragging her sandals along the tarmac.

Phew . . .

Fanette gets up, all smiles. Paul flicks the gravel from his trousers.

'Why do you not want them to see us?' he asks.

'They annoy me! Don't they annoy you?'

'Well, maybe a bit . . .'

'You see. Wait. Camille, he never stops going on about his science marks, "blah blah, blah blah, I'm the first in the class, listen to me" . . . Vincent's even worse, I hate the way he clings to me all the time. Boring, boring, boring! He won't let me breathe. As for Mary, I don't need to tell you, with all her complaining, being teacher's pet and saying bad things about me . . .'

'She's just jealous,' Paul says gently. 'What about me? I don't cling to you too much, do I?'

Fanette tickles his cheek with a leaf.

It's not the same with you, Paul. I don't know why, but it's not the same.

'Idiot. You know you're the one I like. For ever . . .'

Paul shuts his eyelids and tastes the pleasure. Fanette adds:

'Usually, at least. But not today!'

She gets up and checks to see if the coast is clear. Paul rolls his eyes.

'What? Are you leaving me behind too?'

'Yep. I have an appointment. Top secret!'

'Who with?'

'Top secret, I said! Don't follow me. Only Neptune's allowed to do that.'

Paul twists his fingers round each other, his hands, his arms, as if trying to hide an intense fear.

It's because of that murder. Nobody in the village has been talking about anything else since this morning! The police are strolling about the streets as if it was dangerous for us too . . .

Fanette insists. 'Promise?'

Paul doesn't want to, but he swears:

'Promise!'

DAY THREE

15 May 2010

(Vernon Hospital)

Rationality

13

The luminous alarm clock above the bed says 1.32. I can't sleep. The last nurse I saw went past over an hour ago now. She must think I'm asleep. Asleep. You must be joking! How could anyone sleep in such uncomfortable armchairs?

I watch the liquid dripping slowly from the bag. How long can they keep him going like this?

Days? Months? Years?

He isn't sleeping either. He lost the power of speech yesterday, at least that's what the doctors said. He can't move his muscles anymore, but his eyes are open. According to the nurses he understands everything. They've told me a hundred times that if I talk to him, if I read to him, he will hear me: 'It's important for your husband's morale.'

There's a pile of magazines on the bedside table. When the nurses are there, I pretend I've been reading out loud to him. But as soon as they go I shut the pages again.

Because, obviously, he understands everything, he will understand.

I look at the drip again. What are they for, these drips? The nurses told me that they are keeping him alive, but I've forgotten the details.

Minutes pass. I'm worried about Neptune, too. My poor dog, all alone in Giverny. I'm not going to stay here all night, all the same.

The nurses weren't hopeful. He hasn't blinked for the last ten minutes. He just goes on staring at me. It's driving me mad.

2.12.

A nurse came by. She told me to try to sleep. I pretended to listen to her.

I've made my decision.

I wait for a while, I listen, and check that there are no sounds from the corridor. I stand up. I wait a little longer, my fingers quivering, and then I unplug the drips. One by one. There are three.

He looks at me with crazed eyes. He has understood. Definitely, he's understood this.

What did he expect?

I wait.

How long? Fifteen minutes? Thirty minutes? I've picked up a magazine – *Normandy Magazine*. They're writing about the huge operation to gather all the paintings for the 'Impressionist Normandy' exhibition that is taking place this summer. It's the only thing everyone will be talking about around here from June onwards. I read on in silence. As if I don't care that he's dying right here beside me. Besides, it's true.

From time to time I look at him over the top of the magazine. He stares at me with rolling eyes. I watch him for a few minutes, then plunge back into my reading. His face is a little more distorted each time. It's quite grotesque, believe me.

At about three in the morning I have a sense that he is truly dead. My husband's eyes are still open, but they are frozen.

I get up and start plugging the drips back in as if nothing has happened. And then no, thinking about it, I unplug them again. I press the alarm button.

The nurse comes running. Professional.

I look panicky. Not too much, though. I explain that I went to sleep, that I found him like this when I woke up. The nurse examines the unplugged tubes. She looks annoyed, as if it's her fault.

I hope I won't create any problems for her. I'm certainly not going to cause a fuss.

She runs off to find a doctor.

I feel a strange emotion. Somewhere between anger, stillness, and freedom.

And this doubt.

What do I do now?

Reveal everything to the police, or continue to play the role of the little black mouse in the alleyways of Giverny?

14

The five photographs are spread out on the station desk. Laurenç Sérénac is holding a brown envelope.

'Good God,' says Sylvio Bénavides, 'who could have sent that?'

'We don't know. We found the envelope in this morning's post. It was sent from a post box in Vernon, yesterday evening.'

'Just photographs. No letter, no message, nothing?'

'No explanation, no. But it's as clear as can be. We're dealing with a kind of collage of Jérôme Morval's mistresses. A "best of". Sylvio, could you cast your eye over them? I've already had time to admire . . .'

Sylvio Bénavides shrugs and leans over the five pictures; Jérôme Morval is present in each one, but each time he is accompanied by a different woman, none of them his wife. Jérôme Morval behind a desk, leaning on the knees of a girl he is kissing full on the mouth, and who might be the secretary at his surgery. Jérôme Morval on the sofa in a nightclub, with his hand on the breast of a girl in a sequined dress. Jérôme Morval bare-chested, lying beside a white-skinned girl, on a sandy beach that looks as if it might be somewhere in Ireland. Jérôme Morval standing in a sitting room decorated with paintings that look like his own, while a girl in a skirt is kneeling with her back to the photographer, but not to the ophthalmologist.

Jérôme Morval walking along a country lane, above Giverny – you can recognise the bell-tower of Sainte-Radegonde's church – hand in hand with Stéphanie Dupain.

Sylvio Bénavides whistles.

'This is the work of a professional!'

Sérénac smiles.

'I thought so too. He was incredibly confident, our ophthalmologist, and yet he didn't have the physique of a movie star . . .'

Bénavides, disconcerted, looks at his boss for a moment.

'I wasn't talking about Morval, I was talking about the man who took the pictures!'

Sérénac glances at him.

'You're incredible, Sylvio. Anyway, go on, sorry.'

Bénavides blushes and continues.

'I meant, chief, that these pictures must be the work of a professional private detective. *A priori*, I would say that the photographs, at least the ones of the office and in the drawing room, were taken through a window, with a zoom lens that even a standard paparazzo would have trouble affording.'

Sérénac examines the pictures again. He gives a cheeky grimace.

'I wouldn't say they're great. The interior photographs are a bit blurred, aren't they? But who am I to criticise? Clearly Morval liked beautiful women. That's what I should have done, really, be a private detective rather than a cop. It's a cool job.'

Sylvio doesn't respond to that. 'In your opinion,' he asks, 'who, apart from his wife, could have commissioned these photographs?'

'I don't know. We'll question Patricia Morval, but when I met her she wasn't particularly forthcoming about her husband's infidelities. And I also have the impression that in this case we're going to have to treat the evidence with caution.'

'What do you mean?'

'Well, for example, Sylvio, I think you will have noticed that the nature of these five photographs is very different. In some, like the one taken in the nightclub, the one in the drawing room, and the one in the office, this blasted Morval is, without a doubt, sleeping with the girl in question . . .'

Bénavides frowns.

'Fine, OK,' says Sérénac, 'perhaps I'm being a little too hasty. Let's just say that Morval is intimate enough with them to stroke their breasts or be offered a little treat. But if you look at the photograph on the beach, or particularly the one taken near Giverny, there's nothing to confirm that these girls were definitely Morval's mistresses.'

'The last one,' Bénavides suggests, 'is also the only girl we can actually identify. It's Stéphanie Dupain, the village teacher, if I'm not mistaken?'

Sérénac nods.

'On the other hand, chief, I don't see what you're getting at with your comments about Morval's little hit parade. Surely playing away is playing away, isn't it?'

'I'll tell you what I'm getting at. I don't like – I *really* don't like – getting anonymous presents. I'm even less keen on basing a criminal investigation on something sent by a poison-pen. You understand, I'm a big boy now, I don't like somebody prompting me where to look.'

'So what does that mean?'

'It means, for example, that just because Stéphanie Dupain is included in this series of photographs, she isn't necessarily one of Morval's mistresses. But perhaps someone wants us to put two and two together . . .'

Sylvio Bénavides scratches his head, thinking about this hypothesis.

'OK, I follow you so far. But still, you can't simply discount these photographs.'

'Why not? Particularly since we haven't got to the bottom of the mystery. Come here, Sylvio, and take a look at what it says on the other side.'

One by one, Sérénac turns over the five pictures on the desk. On the back of each photograph there are some numbers.

23-02 on the picture of the office. *15-03* for the one in the night-club. *21-02* for the beach. *17-03* for the one in the drawing room. *03-01* on the back of the one showing the country lane near Giverny.

'Bloody hell,' whistles Bénavides. 'What does that mean?'

'No idea.'

'They look like dates. Could they be the days when the photographs were taken?'

'Yes, but would they all really have been taken between January and March? That would mean our king of the cataract was in excellent health, don't you think? And I would bet my right arm that the photograph on the Irish beach wasn't taken in winter.'

'So?'

'So, we'll find out, Sylvio! We have no choice. We'll go rooting about. Do you want to play a game?'

Bénavides smiles suspiciously. 'Not really, no . . .'

'Well, let's say you don't have any choice.'

Sérénac gathers the five photographs together, shuffles them and then spreads them out in a fan, like cards. He holds them out to Sylvio.

'We each take a turn, Sylvio. Each of us draws a girl. And then we both have to find out their name, their CV and their alibi on the day of Morval's murder. We'll meet up in two days and see who's winning.'

'You're weird sometimes, chief.'

'No, Sylvio. It's just my way of presenting things. And what would you rather do than find out the identity of these girls? Surely you don't want to let Maury and Louvel take our place in the hunt for these heavenly creatures?' Sérénac laughs. 'Fine, I'll start if you can't make your mind up.'

Sérénac draws the photograph of Morval kneeling over the girl in the office.

'The secretary playing doctors and nurses with her boss,' he observes. 'We'll see. Your turn . . .'

Sylvio sighs then picks a card. He turns the photograph over. It's the one in the nightclub.

'You lucky thing!' exclaims Sérénac. 'The girl with the sequins.'

Sylvio blushes. Laurenç Sérénac takes another turn. He picks the photograph of the girl on her knees in the sitting room.

'Chef's special. The girl with her back to us. Your go.'

Sérénac holds out the last two cards to Bénavides. He draws. Fate deals him the photograph on the beach.

'The stranger at the Irish seaside,' Sérénac observes. 'You're doing well, my little piglet.'

Sylvio Bénavides taps the photographs on the desk, then measures up his superior with an ironic smile.

'You don't fool me, chief. I don't know how you managed it, but I was sure from the outset that you would keep the photograph of Stéphanie Dupain for yourself.'

Sérénac returns his smile.

'No flies on you, are there? I'm not going to reveal my trick, but you're right, boss's privilege, I get to keep the beautiful teacher. And don't pay too much attention to those codes on the back, Sylvio, 15-03, 21-02 . . . I'm sure that when we've put names to those four other girls the numbers will speak for themselves.'

He puts the photographs in his desk drawer.

'So, shall we get started?'

'Ok, let's go. Wait a moment, Chief. Before we start, I've brought you a little present. To show that even if you do spend most of your time pulling my leg, I don't bear a grudge.'

Bénavides gets to his feet before Sérénac has a chance to defend himself. He leaves the office and comes back a few moments later holding a white paper bag.

'Here, fresh out of the oven, so to speak.'

Sylvio Bénavides pushes the bag across the table and turns it upside down. About twenty brownies spill out of it.

'I made them for my wife,' Sylvio explains. 'Usually she loves them, but for the last fortnight she hasn't been able to swallow a single thing. Even accompanied by my home-made custard.'

Sérénac slumps down in his chair.

'You're like a mother to me, Sylvio. I admit it. In fact I asked to be transferred to this godforsaken hole just so I could have you as my deputy!'

'Don't go too far . . .'

'And when's the baby due?'

'Any day now. She's scheduled to give birth in exactly five days. But afterwards, you know . . .'

Sérénac munches his first brownie.

'Christ! They're divine. Your wife is missing out.'

Sylvio Bénavides bends down to retrieve the file resting against his chair. When he straightens up his superior is on his feet again.

'And with a cup of coffee,' Sérénac adds, 'they'll be out of this world. I'm just popping down for one. You want one too?'

The printout that Sylvio is holding unspools all the way to the floor.

'No thanks.'

'Really, nothing?'

'OK, then. A tea. No sugar.'

Many minutes later Inspector Sérénac comes back with two paper cups. The brownie crumbs have been cleaned from the table. Sérénac sighs, as if to tell his deputy that he's allowed to take a break. No sooner has he sat down than Bénavides starts his summing-up.

'So, chief, I'll cut to the chase. The autopsy report confirms that Morval was stabbed first. He died in the minute that followed. It was only then that someone crushed his skull with a rock, then put his head in the stream. The crime happened in that order, forensics are sure of it.'

'Given the doctor's track record, perhaps three jealous husbands were in it together. A conspiracy of cuckolds. That would explain the ritual aspect, like *Murder on the Orient Express*.'

Bénavides stares at him in consternation.

'I'm joking, Sylvio, only joking . . . OK, I'm going to be serious for two seconds. I admit, there's something strange about this case. A connection between all the elements that isn't quite coming together.'

A flash appears in Sylvio's eyes.

'I absolutely agree with you, chief . . .' He hesitates. 'By the way, I have something to show you. Something that's going to surprise you.'

15

Fanette has been running, as she does every day at the end of school. She has left the other children in the class behind, and since then she has been playing hide and seek through the lanes of Giverny to avoid bumping into Vincent, Camille or Mary again. It's too easy! She knows all the lanes by heart. Once again, Paul wanted to go with her, just him, not the others. He told her he didn't want to leave her alone because of the criminal who might be stalking the streets, but she stuck to her principles and said nothing.

It's my secret!

There it is, she's nearly there. She passes the bridge, the wash house, that wonky old mill with the tower that scares her.

I swear to you, Paul, tomorrow, I'll tell you who it is, the secret meeting I've been having every day for a week. I'll tell you tomorrow.

Or the day after.

Fanette continues on her way, along the path towards the meadow. James is there.

He is standing a little further off, in the wheat field, in the middle of four easels. Fanette silently steps forward.

'It's me!'

A big smile distorts James's white beard. He holds Fanette tightly in his arms. Just for a moment.

'Hurry up then, little imp. To work!' There aren't many hours of daylight left. Her school day ends far too late.

Fanette goes and stands at one of the easels, the one that James lends her – the smallest one, suited to her height. She leans towards the big varnished wooden paint box and helps herself to tubes and brushes.

Fanette doesn't know much about the old painter she met a week ago, except that he's American, that his name is James, and that he paints here almost every day. He told her that she is the most gifted little girl he's ever met, and he has met a great many, from all over the world. He used to be an art teacher in the United States, he tells her. He never stops saying that she talks all the time, and even though she's very gifted, she needs to concentrate more. Like Monet did. She needs to be able to observe and imagine. That's James's refrain. Observe and imagine. And paint quickly, too, that's why he brings four easels, to be able to paint as soon as the light settles on a corner of the landscape, as soon as the shadows move, the colours change. He told her that Monet brought six easels with him when he walked in the fields. He paid children her age to carry everything, early in the morning and late in the evening.

The nerve of it! James was just trying to trick her into carrying his things, Fanette thought. She guessed what he was up to, but pretended to believe him.

James is nice, but he tends to get himself muddled up with old Monet a bit too much.

And to treat me as if I'm an idiot!

'Stop day-dreaming, Fanette. Paint!'

The little girl tries to reproduce the Norman wash house, the bridge over the stream, the mill beside it. She has already been painting for quite a while.

'Do you know who Theodore Robinson is? Our teacher talked about him.'

'Why?'

'She's entered the class for a competition. An international competition, Mr James. Yes, INTERNATIONAL . . . The Robinson prize! If I win I'll get to travel to Japan, or Russia, or Australia . . . I'll see. I haven't decided yet.'

'Well, well!'

'Not to mention the money . . .'

James gently sets down his palette on his paint box. Sooner or later, he is going to dunk his beard into the paint. As he does every day.

Green, today.

I'm a bit mean, I never tell him when his beard is covered in paint. It makes me laugh too much.

James comes over.

'You know, Fanette, if you work hard, if you believe it, then you really do have a real chance of winning that competition.'

He's scaring me a bit.

James must notice that Fanette is peering at his beard. He runs his finger over it, spreading the green paint a little more.

'Don't tease me.'

'I'm not teasing you, Fanette. I've told you before. You have a gift. There's nothing you can do about it, that's just how it is. You were born with it. And you know it, too. You have a talent for painting. More than that, even. A little touch of genius, in a way. But none of that matters if . . .'

'If I don't work, is that it?'

'Yes, you must work. It's indispensable. Otherwise, talent . . . well . . . Anyway, that's not what I wanted to say to you . . .'

James moves slowly. He tries to step over the ears of wheat to avoid crushing them. He shifts the position of one of the easels as if the sun up there had suddenly put on a sprint.

'What I was trying to say, Fanette, is that genius is useless if you're not capable of . . . how can I put it? Capable of being selfish.'

'What?'

Sometimes James comes out with complete nonsense.

'Selfishness! My little Fanette, genius annoys every person who doesn't have it, which is to say almost everyone. Genius takes you away from the people you love, and makes others jealous. Do you understand?'

He rubs his beard, smearing the paint all over the place. He doesn't even notice. He's old, James is. Old old old.

'No, I don't understand at all!'

'Let me put it another way. If I take myself as an example, it was my absolute dream to come and paint in Giverny, to discover Monet's landscapes for myself. You can't imagine, in my village in Connecticut, the hours I spent looking at reproductions of those paintings, how many times I dreamed of them. The poplars, the Epte, the water lilies, Nettles Island . . . Do you think it was worth it, leaving my wife, my children, my grandchildren, at the age of sixty-five? What was more important? My dream of painting here, or spending Halloween and Thanksgiving with my family?'

'Well . . .'

'You see, you are hesitating. Well, I didn't hesitate! And believe me, Fanette, I don't regret a single thing. But I live here almost like a tramp. And I don't have a quarter of your talent. So do you see what I mean when I say you need to be selfish? Do you think those first American painters who stayed at the Hôtel Baudy in Monet's time didn't take risks too? That they didn't have to leave everything behind?'

I don't like it when James starts talking like this. It's as if he's thinking exactly the opposite of what he says. As if he really does regret it, he is bored to death, as if he is thinking about his family in America all the time.

Fanette picks up a brush.

'Well, Monsieur James, I must get back to work. Sorry to be selfish, but I have a competition to win.'

James bursts out laughing.

'You're right, Fanette. I'm just a grumpy old fool.'

'And a mad one. You haven't even told me who Robinson is yet!'

James steps over and looks at Fanette's work. Narrows his eyes.

'Theodore Robinson was an American artist. He was the most famous Impressionist where I come from, the United States. He was the only American artist ever to become close personal friends with Monet. Claude Monet usually avoided other people like the plague. Robinson stayed in Giverny for eight years. He even painted the wedding of Monet's favourite stepdaughter, Suzanne, to the young American painter Theodore Butler. And it's strange, Fanette, another of his most famous paintings depicts precisely the same scene that you are painting at the moment . . .'

Fanette nearly drops her brush.

'What?'

'It's an old painting from 1891, a famous painting that shows the brook stemming from Epte, the bridge over it, the Moulin des Chennevières. In the background you can see a woman in a dress, her hair knotted in a scarf . . . and in the middle of the stream is a man watering his horse. That's the title of the painting, by the way. *Père Trognon and His Daughter at the Bridge*. That was his name, the horseman, he was from Giverny . . .'

This time Fanette has to struggle not to laugh.

Sometimes, James really takes me for a complete fool.

Père Trognon – he says the first thing that comes into his head!

James is still studying the little girl's painting. The old painter's beard is practically poking her in the eye. His fat finger passes barely an inch from the still damp paint.

'It's good, Fanette. I like the shadows around your mill. It's very good. It's a symbol of your fate, Fanette. You are painting the same scene as Theodore Robinson did, and I have to say I think your version is better. Trust me, you are going to win this competition! A life, you know, Fanette, is just two or three opportunities that you mustn't allow to slip by. That's what's at stake, my pretty one, a life! Nothing less.'

James sets off to move the easels again. You would think he spends more time moving his canvases than he does painting on them. You would think that the sun is too quick for him.

He doesn't care.

Almost an hour has passed when Neptune comes and joins them. The Alsatian sniffs suspiciously at the paint box, then lies down at Fanette's feet.

'Is that your dog?' James asks.

'No, not really. I think he belongs to pretty much everyone in the village, but I've adopted him. He likes me best!'

James smiles. He is sitting on a stool by one of the easels, but every time Fanette looks at him, he looks as if he's dropping off on to his canvas. His beard is going to end up looking like a rainbow.

No. No, I've got to concentrate.

Fanette continues with her study of the Moulin des Chennevières. She twists the shapes of the little half-timbered tower, reinforces the contrasts, the ochre, the tiles, the stone. James calls the tower 'the witch's mill'. Because of the old woman who lives there.

A witch . . .

Sometimes James really treats me like I'm a baby.

Except that Fanette is a little bit scared. James has explained to her why he doesn't like that house very much. He says that because of the mill, Monet's water lilies nearly didn't exist. The mill and Monet's garden are built on the same stream. Monet wanted to build a dam, introduce locks, divert the water to create his pond. No one in the village wanted him to do it, because of illness, marshes, all that kind of thing. In particular his neighbours. In particular the people who lived in the mill. There were lots of problems. Monet got angry with everyone, he put lots of money into his campaign too, he wrote to the prefect, another man she's never heard of, a friend of Monet's, Clemenceau was his name. And in the end Monet got it, he did, his lily pond.

It would have been such a shame . . .

But it's still stupid on James's part not to like the mill because of that. That stupid fight between Monet and his neighbours was ages ago.

Sometimes James can be silly.

She shivers. But what if the person who lives in the mill really is a witch!

Fanette goes on working a while longer. The light fades, making the mill look even more sinister. She loves it. James has been asleep for a long time.

Suddenly Neptune leaps to his feet. The dog growls nastily. Fanette turns round with a start towards the little clump of poplars just behind her, and catches the silhouette of a boy of her age.

Vincent! A blank look.

'What are you doing here?'

James wakes up with a start. Fanette is shouting:

'Vincent! I hate it when you turn up like that, as if you're spying on me. How long have you been there?'

Vincent doesn't say anything. He studies Fanette's painting, the mill, the bridge. He looks hypnotised.

'I've already got a dog, Vincent. I've already got Neptune. He's enough for me. And stop looking at me like that, you're scaring me . . .'

James coughs into his beard.

'Erm . . . umm. All right, children, it's good that there are two of you. Given the light, I think it's time to pack away all our materials.

You can help me. Monet said that wisdom was getting up and going to bed with the sun.'

Fanette hasn't taken her eyes off Vincent.

Vincent scares me when he appears like that out of nowhere. Behind me. As if he were spying on me. Sometimes I think he's insane.

16

Inspector Laurenç Sérénac's cup is frozen in his hand. His deputy is like a student who has written an extra piece of homework and is paralysed, caught between the desire to show it to his teacher and the fear of doing so. Bénavides' right hand has disappeared into a thick file. He takes out a sheet of A4 paper.

'Look, chief. To get a clear view of things, I've started doing this . . .'

Sérénac takes another brownie, sets down his cup of coffee and leans forward, surprised.

'It's just a way of organising my ideas. I'm obsessed with this kind of thing, writing notes, pulling summaries together, drawing sketches. I've divided the sheet into three columns. In my view, there are three possible scenarios: the first, that it's a crime of passion, somehow connected to one of Morval's mistresses. In which case his wife would be a suspect, of course, or a jealous husband, or another mistress . . . We have no shortage of leads in that direction.'

Sérénac glances at him. 'Thanks to our anonymous letter . . . Go on, Sylvio . . .'

'The second column focuses on art, his collection of pictures, the paintings he was looking for, the Monets, the *Water Lilies*. Couldn't the murder be connected to stolen goods? A black-market sale? Something to do with art and money . . .'

Bénavides looks up at the ten or so pictures on the wall of the office that his boss hung up as soon as he arrived. Toulouse-Lautrec, Pissarro. Gauguin. Renoir . . .

'Which is a stroke of luck, if I may say so,' Sylvio adds. 'Painting seems to be your area, Inspector.'

'Pure coincidence, Sylvio . . . If I had suspected, when I was transferred to Vernon, that my first corpse would be found dunked in the stream at Giverny . . . I was already interested in art before I started at the police academy, which is why I spent most of my training in Paris with the art unit. You're not into art, Sylvio?'

'Just cookery . . .'

Laurenç laughs, his mouth still full of brownie.

'Well I can certainly attest to that . . . I've alerted my former colleagues in the art unit to the case. They're going to look into thefts, stolen goods, dodgy collections . . . parallel markets . . . I was able to dip my toes into that world, back then, and you wouldn't believe the business – there are millions and millions at stake. Anyway, I'm waiting to hear from them. So, your third column?'

Sylvio Bénavides peers over his page.

'As far as I'm concerned, the third area of investigation – and don't laugh at me, Chief – is the children. Eleven-year-olds, in particular. There's no shortage of clues, either: that postcard and the quote from Aragon. Morval might have had a child with one of his mistresses, and not told his wife . . . Also, according to the experts who have analysed the physical properties of the card found in Morval's pocket, it is quite old. About fifteen years old, perhaps more. The typed text, HAPPY BIRTHDAY, ELEVEN YEARS OLD, is thought to date back to the same period, but the addition, the quote from Aragon, is more recent . . . Now that's weird, isn't it?'

Inspector Sérénac whistles with admiration.

'I stand by what I said, Sylvio. You're the ideal deputy.' He gets abruptly to his feet and heads for the door. 'Even if you are a little . . . pernickety. Come on, then, Sylvio, shall we go to the lab?'

Bénavides follows him without a word. They walk along the corridors and down a badly lit staircase.

'One of the things that needs to be done as a matter of urgency is to look for witnesses. You can write that down on your page, Sylvio. It's hard to believe that in a village where everyone paints from morning till night not one person claims to have seen anything on the day of Morval's murder, and that the only witnesses who have come forward are an anonymous paparazzo, sending us dirty photographs, and a dog that just wants to be stroked. Have you found out anything about the house beside the wash house? That crooked old mill?'

Sérénac takes a key from his pocket and opens a red fire door bearing the slogan: *LAB ARCHIVES DOCUMENTATION*.

'Not yet,' Bénavides replies. 'I'll go there as soon as I have a second.'

'In the meantime, I've been thinking about another mission to keep the whole station busy. I'll need a team of several men to do it . . . Now, chef's surprise!'

He walks into the dark room. There's a cardboard box on the first table. Sérénac opens it and takes out a plaster cast.

'Size forty-three,' he announces proudly. 'It's the sole of a boot. There can't be two the same anywhere in the world! According to Maury, this mould is more precise than a fingerprint, freshly imprinted in the mud on the banks of the brook a few minutes after Morval's murder. To cut a long story short, the owner of this boot is, at the very least, a direct witness to the crime . . . if not a candidate for the title of murderer.'

Sylvio opens his eyes wide.

'And what are we going to do with it?'

Sérénac laughs.

'I hereby officially launch Operation Cinderella!'

'I swear, Chief, I'm trying, but sometimes I really do have trouble with your sense of humour . . .'

'You'll get used to it, Sylvio. Don't worry.'

'I'm not worrying. To be honest I don't really care. So what's this Operation Cinderella?'

'Well, this version is a little more rural, and a bit muddier . . . The mission will be to recover all the boots belonging to the three hundred inhabitants of Giverny.'

'Is that all?' Sylvio runs his hand through his hair.

'So, that will probably come to . . . how many?' Sérénac goes on. 'A hundred and fifty boots? Two hundred at most . . .'

'Christ. Inspector . . . it's a surreal idea.'

'Exactly! I think that's why I like it.'

'But in the end, Chief, I don't understand. Surely the killer will have thrown his boots away? In any case, unless he's a total cretin, he's not going to hand them over to a policeman who comes and asks for them?'

'Exactly, my fine fellow. It will be a process of elimination. So the good inhabitants of Giverny who say that they don't have any boots, or who say that they've lost them, or who offer us very new boots that by chance were bought only yesterday, will be very high on our list of suspects . . .'

Bénavides looks at the plaster boot-sole. A big smile spreads across his face.

'If I may say so, Chief, you do have some totally ridiculous ideas . . . But worse than that, they might actually work! And Morval's funeral should be in two days. Imagine if the whole place is flooded . . . Every person in Giverny is going to curse you!'

'Because you go to funerals in your boots, in Normandy?'

'Well, if it's completely pouring down, then yes.'

Bénavides bursts out laughing.

'Sylvio, I think I have trouble with your sense of humour too.'

His deputy doesn't respond.

'Five hundred boots,' he murmurs. 'Which column will I put that in?'

They say nothing for a few minutes. Sérénac looks around the room, at the thick shelves of archives covering three out of the four walls, the corner with a tiny makeshift laboratory, the fourth wall reserved for documentation. Bénavides picks up an empty box, a red one, and writes 'Morval' on the side. Suddenly he turns towards his superior.

'Inspector, did you pick up the list of eleven-year-olds? That would give me something else for my third column . . . It's the one with the least information, and yet . . .'

Sérénac interrupts him. 'Not yet. Stéphanie Dupain is supposed to be putting it together for me. Given the nature of the photographs we've received, I'd say she's no longer the top suspect in terms of the line-up of Morval's mistresses . . .'

'Except that I've done some investigation into her husband,' Bénavides says. 'Jacques Dupain. And he has pretty much the ideal profile.'

Sérénac frowns.

'Tell me more. What do you mean by the ideal profile?'

Bénavides consults his notes. 'Ah, well sometimes it can be useful to have a deputy who's a bit pernickety.'

Sérénac seems enormously amused by the remark.

'So, Jacques Dupain. Forty years old. Estate agent in Vernon, and quite a mediocre one at that. An occasional huntsman with some other Givernois, and pathologically jealous as far as his wife is concerned. What do you say to that?'

'I want you to keep him under close surveillance.'

'Seriously?'

'Let's just say it's a kind of intuition. No, more than that, a premonition.'

'What do you mean?'

Sérénac runs his finger along the boxes on a shelf. *E, F, G, H* . . .'

'You're not going to like it, Sylvio . . .'

'All the more reason for you to tell me.'

'I have a feeling that another drama might be brewing . . . '

I, J, K, L . . .

'You'll have to give me more than that, boss. As a general rule, I'm not keen on police intuition. I'm more of a fan of collecting evidence. As much as possible. But you've intrigued me.'

M, N, O, P . . . Sérénac suddenly says:

'Stéphanie Dupain . . . She's the one in danger.'

Sylvio Bénavides frowns. 'What makes you think that?'

'I told you, intuition . . .'

Laurenç Sérénac takes three photographs from his pocket and throws the one of Stéphanie Dupain on the table. It lands just beside the plaster sole. Bénavide looks at him quizzically.

'I don't know. When she takes your hand, her grip is too tight, and there's a look in her eyes that's slightly too intense. I sensed a cry for help. There, I've said it!'

Bénavides approaches the table. He is smaller than Sérénac.

'A cry for help? With all due respect, Chief, and since you like straight-talking, I think what you're saying is absolute rubbish. You're getting all mixed up.'

Sylvio picks up the photograph from the table and studies the graceful outline of Stéphanie Dupain walking hand in hand with Jérôme Morval.

'At a pinch, Chief, I can understand where you're coming from. Just don't ask me to agree with you.'

DAY FIVE

17 May 2010
(Giverny Cemetery)

Burial

17

It's raining, as it always does at funerals in Giverny.

A fine, cold rain.

I'm alone by the grave. The freshly turned earth all around makes the place look like an abandoned building site. Tiny trickles of muddy water sully the marble plaque. *To my husband. 1926–2010.*

The grey concrete wall nearby gives me a bit of shelter. Right at the top. Giverny Cemetery is built on a slope behind the church, in terraces. It has been progressively extended, stage by stage, the dead gnawing away at the hill little by little. The celebrities, the wealthy ones, the glorious ones, are still buried down below, near the church, near the village, near Monet.

There's no mixing: they're all together, keeping each other company, the patrons, the collectors, the more or less famous painters who have paid a fortune for the privilege of resting there for all eternity. Idiots. As if they could hold a ghostly little gallery opening when there was a full moon . . .

I turn round. Right at the bottom, at the other end of the

cemetery, they've nearly finished burying Jérôme Morval. A lovely grave in the finest of spots, among the Van der Kemps, the
Hoschedé-Monets and the Baudys. The whole village is there, or
nearly. A hundred or so people, all in black, bare-headed or under
umbrellas.

A hundred people, plus me, all on my own. No one cares about
an old man or an old woman dying. All in all, if you want to be
mourned, you're better off dying young, in your full glory. Even
if you're the biggest bastard of the lot, if you want to be grieved
for, you should make sure you go out first. For my husband, the
priest got the whole ceremony over with in less than half an hour.
He's a young fellow, from Gasny. I've never seen him before.
Morval, on the other hand, got the Bishop of Évreux! A relative
on his wife's side, apparently . . . That one's taking about two
hours.

I know it may seem strange to you, two funerals happening in
the same cemetery, and not that far apart. Does the coincidence
seem disturbing to you? A bit too much? Be sure of one thing,
then, and one alone: nothing is a coincidence in this scenario.
Nothing is left to chance – quite the contrary. Each element is in
its proper place, at exactly the right moment. Each piece in this
criminal chain of events has been cleverly arranged, and believe
me, I swear on my husband's grave, nothing's going to put a stop
to it.

I raise my head and I can tell you, from up here it's a tableau
worth looking at.

Patricia Morval is kneeling by her husband's grave. Inconsolable. Stéphanie Dupain stands a little way behind her, a serious
expression on her face, her eyes red too. Her husband is supporting her, his arm around her waist, his face closed, water dripping
from his large eyebrows, his moustache. Around them is a crowd
of nameless people, relatives, friends, women. Inspector Sérénac
is also there; he stands a little apart from the others, near the
church, not far from Monet's grave. The bishop is finishing his
eulogy.

Three wicker baskets are positioned in the grass. Everyone

is supposed to take a flower and throw it on to the coffin in the hole: hollyhocks, irises, pansies, lilacs, tulips, cornflowers . . . Only Patricia Morval could have devised such a morbid idea. *Impression, dying sun* . . . Even Monet wouldn't have dared come up with that.

They've gone as far as to sculpt a grey water lily on a vast granite plaque. Talk about bad taste . . .

At least the light's given out. The famous light of Giverny, one last time before the darkness of the hole. You can't buy everything. It may even be a sign that God exists.

The fresh earth of the grave at my feet is starting to slide in ochre runnels along the path between the graves . . . Of course, down below, not a single inhabitant of Giverny has a pair of boots. Inspector Sérénac must be chuckling to himself. We take our amusement where we can . . .

I shake the black scarf that I have been using to cover my hair. It's drenched too. The children are a little further off. Some of them are standing with their parents, others aren't. I recognise some of them. Fanette is crying. Vincent is behind her, but he clearly doesn't dare comfort her. They are serious, like the incongruity of death when you're eleven years old.

The rain is easing off a little.

As I observe this scene, a strange story comes back to me, one of those riddles that we used to ask each other when I was a child, at sleepovers. A man goes to the funeral of a member of his family. A few days later that same man, for no apparent reason, kills another cousin. All the interest in the riddle lies in finding the motive for the murder by asking questions. It could last for hours . . . No, the man didn't know the cousin . . . No, it wasn't about revenge. No, it had nothing to do with money. No, it wasn't about a family secret either. We could go on like that for a whole night, asking questions in the dark, under the blankets.

The rain has stopped.

The three baskets of flowers are empty.

The drops slide gently down the marble plaque marking my husband's grave. Down below, the crowd finally disperses. Jacques Dupain is still gripping his wife's waist. Water drips from her long hair, soaking the dark swell of her breasts. They pass in front of Laurenç Sérénac. The inspector hasn't taken his eyes off Stéphanie Dupain for a moment.

It's that devouring look, I think, that reminded me of the riddle from my childhood. I found the answer in the small, battle-weary hours of the morning . . . At the funeral the man had fallen madly in love with a stranger. The woman had disappeared before he could speak to her. He had only one possible hope of seeing her again: killing another member of the family and hoping that the beautiful stranger would come to the next committal . . . Most people who had tried to find the solution to the riddle thought it was some kind of trick, that it wasn't fair. Not me. The implacable logic of the story, of the crime, fascinated me. It's strange how memories come back to you. I hadn't given it a thought for years. Until my husband's funeral.

The last silhouettes move away.

I can admit it now, because I know.

It's the ideal setting.

DEATH IS GOING TO STRIKE ONCE MORE IN GIVERNY.

A witch's promise.

I look at the loose soil around my husband's grave. I'm more or less certain that I will never come here again. Not alive, at least. I no longer have anything to do, there isn't another funeral to keep me company. Minutes pass, maybe hours.

At last, I leave.

Neptune is waiting patiently outside the cemetery. I walk along the Rue Claude Monet as the day gently fades. The flowers spill down the walls, beneath the streetlights. A gifted painter could doubtless make something of the gloom of this village.

The lights are starting to go on in the windows of the cottages. I pass in front of the school. In the nearest house, the round skylight on the upper storey glows. The bedroom of Stéphanie and Jacques Dupain. What could they be doing, saying, as they dry their sodden clothes?

You too, I should imagine, wish you could slip beneath the mansard roof and spy on them. But this time I'm sorry. However seriously I take my role as a black mouse, I can't climb up drainpipes.

I just slow down for a few seconds, then go on my way.

18

Laurenç Sérénac walks carefully in the darkness, trusting simply to the crunch of his footsteps on the gravel. He had no trouble finding his deputy's house – he simply followed Sylvio Bénavides' directions to the letter: go along the Eure Valley to Cocherel, then left up the hill after the bridge towards the church, the only landmark in the hamlet that was illuminated after 10 p.m. Sérénac had parked his motorbike, a Tiger Triumph T100, between two monumental pots of flowers, after spotting his deputy's name on the letterbox in the beam of the headlights. It was only then that things got complicated: no doorbell, no light, just a gravel path and the shadow of the building fifty metres ahead. He steps forward again, trusting to fate . . .

'Bugger!'

Sérénac's knee has just bashed into a brick wall. Less than a metre tall, and just in front of him. His hand gropes its way along some cold stones, an iron grille, dust. Just as he works out that he's bumped into a barbecue, a light flickers in the distance and then, a moment later, a huge veranda lights up. At least his shout has roused the neighbourhood. The outline of Sylvio Bénavides appears at the glass door.

'Straight on, Chief, follow the gravel path, just watch out for the barbecues.'

'OK, OK,' grumbles Sérénac, thinking that his advice has come a little too late.

He walks along the dark gravel, again trusting his ears, his feet and his deputy's directions. Less than three metres further on, his leg crashes into yet another wall. The inspector, bent double, pitches forward and his elbows crash into a kind of iron cube. Sérénac cries out with pain again.

'Are you all right, Chief?' asks Sylvio's confused voice. 'I told you to watch out for the barbecues . . .'

'Bugger,' Sérénac growls as he gets back up. 'I didn't realise there was more than one of them. How many barbecues have you got? Do you collect them?'

'Seventeen!' Sylvio replies proudly. 'You're right, I do collect them. Me and my father.'

The darkness hides Sérénac's stunned reaction. As he approaches the veranda, he is still swearing.

'Are you taking the piss, Sylvio?'

'What?'

'You really want me to believe that you collect barbecues?'

'I don't see what the problem is. You'd see them, in the daylight. There must be several thousand fugicarnophiles in the world . . .'

Laurenç Sérénac bends down and rubs his knee.

'Fugi-whatsit means "collector of barbecues", I suppose?'

'Well, I'm not absolutely sure it's in the dictionary. I'm just an amateur, but there's a man in Argentina who has almost three hundred barbecues from a hundred and forty-three different countries, the oldest of which dates back to twelve hundred years BC.'

Sérénac is rubbing his painful elbows.

'Are you pulling my leg?'

'You're getting to know me, Chief; do you think I'd make up something like that? You know, everywhere in the world, since fire was discovered, men have eaten cooked meat. There is no practice more universal, or that provides a greater link to our ancestors, than the barbecue.'

'And sure enough, you've got seventeen of them in your

garden . . . Perfectly normal. I suppose they're better than garden gnomes.'

'Original, cultural, decorative . . . also, at the end of the day, they're good when it comes to inviting the neighbours over.'

Sérénac runs his hand through his hair. 'I've been transferred to a land of lunatics . . .'

Sylvio smiles.

'Not really. Another time I can tell you about Occitan traditions and the difference between Cathar and Cévenol barbecues . . .'

He climbs the three steps up to the veranda.

'Come in, Chief . . . Did you find the place all right?'

'Apart from those last twenty metres, yes! Apart from your barbecues, it's quite smart round here. The mills, the cottages . . .'

'Yes, I like it, especially the view from up here. You can't see much at this time of night, of course, but during the day the view is superb. And Cocherel is quite a strange place.'

'Stranger than a club of fugicophiles?'

'Fugicarnophiles. Well, there have been a great many deaths here. A huge battle in the Hundred Years War was fought on the slopes opposite, with thousands killed, and then it happened again during the Second World War. And do you know who's buried in the churchyard just behind?'

'Joan of Arc?'

Bénavides smiles. 'Aristide Briand.'

'Oh, really?'

'I bet you haven't the faintest idea who he is?'

'A singer?'

'No, that was Aristide Bruant. People always get them mixed up. Aristide Briand was a politician. A pacifist. The only French person ever to win a Nobel Peace Prize.'

'It's very kind of you, Sylvio, to educate me about Normandy like this . . .'

He looks at the timbered cottage.

'For a simple police inspector on a wretched salary, your official residence is pretty grand.'

Touched by the compliment, Sylvio's chest swells. He

raises his eyes towards the roof of the veranda and its framework of natural beams. Some wires have been stretched between the timbers so that the vine planted there can twirl its tendrils around them.

'You know, chief, when I bought this place more than five years ago, it was a ruin. Since then I've done a bit of DIY . . .'

'What did you do?'

'Just about everything.'

'No!'

'Yes . . . It's in the genes, Chief, you know, a Portuguese thing. The great North-South divide . . .'

Sérénac bursts out laughing. He takes off his leather jacket.

'You're drenched, Chief.'

'Yep, bloody Norman funeral.'

On the veranda, Laurenç Sérénac puts his jacket over the back of a plastic chair that nearly topples backwards under its weight. He sits down on the one next to it. Bénavides apologises.

'It's true that plastic garden chairs aren't very comfortable. I got them from a cousin and they're fine for the time being. Maybe in a few years' time, I'll have a look at the antique shops of the Eure Valley, when I've made detective chief inspector . . .'

He smiles and sits down as well. 'So, this funeral?'

'Nothing special. A lot of rain. A crowd of people. The whole of Giverny was there, from the oldest to the youngest. I asked Maury to take some pictures, we'll see what we can get out of them. You should have come, Sylvio; there was a granite water lily, flowers in baskets, even the Bishop of Évreux. And I can assure you, not a single Givernois was wearing boots! It was a classy affair.'

'Talking about boots, Chief, I saw at the station that Louvel was coordinating that line of enquiry. We should get some idea by tomorrow.'

'Let's hope that it reduces the list of suspects,' Sérénac says, rubbing his hands as if to warm himself up. 'At least, one advantage of that interminable funeral was that it has given me the opportunity to do some overtime at the home of my favourite deputy.'

'Well, that's lucky, given that you only have the one! I'm sorry, Chief, for asking you to come here, but I'm not too fond of leaving Béatrice alone here in the evenings.'

'Don't worry, I understand. Anyway, I hadn't finished telling you about the funeral. Patricia, the widow, was in tears from start to finish. Honestly, if she's putting it on then she deserves an Oscar. As far as the mistresses go, however, there wasn't a single one crying by Morval's graveside.'

'Apart from the schoolmistress, Stéphanie Dupain.'

'Are you trying to be funny?'

'Not on purpose, I swear.' He lowered his eyes and gave a discreet smile. 'I know very well that's it's a touchy subject.'

'My God, but he really loosens up, my favourite deputy, when he's playing at home! To reply to your comment, Sylvio, yes, Stéphanie Dupain was at the funeral and I would even go as far as to say that she was more beautiful than ever, she even made the rain seem more pleasant, but she did not leave the arms of her jealous husband for a single second.'

'All the same, boss, just watch out.'

'Thank you for your advice, but I am a grown up, you know.'

Slightly annoyed, Laurenç Sérénac looks around at the veranda. The salmon-coloured brickwork is impeccable, the roofbeams have been sanded down, and the sandstone edging has been polished and bleached.

'Did you really do all this yourself?'

'I spend all my weekends and my holidays doing DIY with my father. We do it together. It's great!'

'You stagger me, Sylvio, really you do. The only reason I can tolerate your shitty climate is because it puts eight hundred kilometres between me and my family.'

They both laugh. Sylvio looks a little worried, no doubt because of the noise they are making.

'Right, shall we get down to it?'

Laurenç spreads out the three photographs he has of Jérôme Morval's mistresses on the plastic table. Sylvio does the same with his two.

'Personally I don't understand why anyone would cheat on their wife. I just don't get it.'

'How long have you known your Béatrice?'

'Seven years.'

'And you've never been unfaithful?'

'No.'

'She sleeps up there, just above us, doesn't she?'

'Yes, but that doesn't change a thing.'

'Why have you never cheated on her? Your wife is the most beautiful woman in the world, is that it? You have no reason to desire any other?'

Sylvio's hands fiddle with the photographs. He is already regretting having brought his superior here.

'Stop it, boss, I didn't invite you here to—'

'What's she like, this Béatrice of yours?' Sérénac cuts in. 'She isn't pretty, is that what you're trying to tell me?'

Sylvio suddenly puts both hands flat on the table.

'Pretty or not pretty, that isn't the question! That's not how it works. It's silly to expect your wife to be the most beautiful woman in the world. What would that mean? It's not a competition. There will always be women more beautiful than the one you live with somewhere. And even if you manage to pull Miss World, even Miss World, at the end of the day, is going to grow old. You'd have to get a new Miss World into your bed every year.'

In response to his deputy's tirade, a strange smile spreads across Laurenç's face, which Sylvio finds odd, particularly since he seems to be looking over Sylvio's shoulder.

'So you're saying I'm not the most beautiful woman in the world?'

Sylvio's head snaps round as if the spring that attaches it to his neck has come loose and it might go on spinning. His face is scarlet.

Béatrice, behind him, seems to glide across the tiles of the veranda. Laurenç thinks she's ravishing, even if that's not exactly the right word. Stunning, perhaps. Tall and dark, with her long black hair and dark eyelashes forming a curtain in front of her hazy eyes, protecting the last vestiges of sleep. Béatrice's round belly is draped in a large cream-coloured shawl, the folds recalling the curves of a classical statue. Her eyes sparkle with amusement. Sérénac wonders if Béatrice is always as beautiful as this, or whether it's because she's pregnant, a few days away from becoming a mother. The plenitude of pregnancy; some kind of internal joy that blossoms on the surface. The kind of thing you read about in magazines. Sérénac reflects that he must be getting older, to be having ideas like that about women. Would he have found a pregnant woman sexy a few years ago?

'Sylvio,' Béatrice says, taking a chair, 'will you fetch me a glass of fruit juice? It doesn't matter which flavour.'

Sylvio stands up and goes to the kitchen. He seems to have shrunk, like a stool that's been spun down too many times. Béatrice pulls the shawl tighter around her shoulders.

'So you're the famous Laurenç Sérénac?'

'Why "famous"?'

'Sylvio talks about you a lot. You astonish him. You shake him up. Your predecessor was more . . . more old-school.'

Sylvio's voice calls from the kitchen: 'Is pineapple all right?'

'Yes!' Then, two seconds later: 'Has the bottle been opened?'

'Yes, yesterday.'

'Then no.'

A silence.

'Fine, I'll go and see what we have in the cellar . . .'

So a pregnant woman can be sexy, but annoying too. The shawl has slipped from her right shoulder. A young person's thought, Laurenç thinks to himself, would be to wonder whether Béatrice's figure is usually so voluptuous. She turns towards Sérénac.

'He's adorable, don't you think? He's the very best kind of man. You know, Laurenç, I spotted him a long time ago, and I thought, "He's the one for me" . . .'

'He can't have resisted you for long, you're gorgeous . . .'

'Thank you.'

The shawl slips, then is pulled back up again.

'I'm touched by the compliment, particularly from someone like you.'

'Someone like me?'

'Yes. You're a man who knows how to look at a woman.'

She says that with a playful gleam in her eye. The shawl slips again, of course, and Laurenç averts his gaze to admire the manual labour of Sylvio and his father. Beams, bricks and glass.

'I like Sylvio too,' Sérénac replies. 'And not just because of his brownies and his collection of barbecues.'

She smiles. 'He's fond of you too. But I don't know if I find that reassuring.'

'Why not? Do you think I might be a bad influence on him?'

Béatrice pulls her shawl around her shoulders again and leans over to look at the photographs on the plastic table.

'Apparently you fancy one of the suspects.'

'He told you that?'

'It's his only flaw. Like all shy people, he's a bit too free and easy with the pillow talk.'

'Mango?' comes Sylvio's voice from the depths of the cellar.

'Yes, if that's all there is. But nice and cold.'

She smiles at Sérénac.

'Don't judge me, Laurenç. I can make the most of it for another few days, can't I?'

The inspector nods, sphinx-like. Super-sexy but incredibly irritating, this pregnant woman.

'He's one of a kind,' Laurenç says. 'And you found him.'

'I agree, Inspector!'

'A bit unimaginative, no?'

'Certainly not!'

Sylvio comes back carrying a big cocktail glass, decorated with a straw, a little palm tree and a slice of orange. Béatrice kisses him tenderly on the lips.

'As for me,' Sérénac says, 'I'm soaked through, so that's probably why I'm not thirsty . . .'

'Sorry, boss. What would you like?'

'What have you got?'

'Is beer all right?'

'Yes, perfect. Very cold, please. I'd like a straw and a palm tree as well.'

Béatrice holds her shawl with one hand and the straw with the other.

'Sylvio, tell him to go to hell . . .'

Bénavides' face breaks into a broad grin.

'Bitter or lager?'

'Bitter.'

Sylvio disappears into the house again. Béatrice points towards the photographs.

'So that's the teacher?'

'Yes.'

'I understand you, Inspector. She's, how can I put it, very elegant. Delicious. She looks as if she's just stepped out of a romantic painting. Almost as if she's posing.'

Laurenç is surprised. The very same thought had struck him, when he met the teacher. Béatrice parts the curtain of hair and examines the pictures, frowning slightly.

'Inspector, do you want me to reveal something to you?'

'Does it have anything to do with the case?'

'Yes. There's something quite obvious in the photographs. In any case, something that a woman would easily guess.'

19

Through the round skylight, Stéphanie Dupain has been studying the wet shadows of the last figures walking through Giverny. After a few minutes she steps back slightly. Her black dress slides down her body. Jacques is lying down on the bed, bare-chested. He looks up from the list of houses for sale in the district of Les Andelys. Their bedroom has a sloping roof, with a small bulb hanging from an oak beam that weakly illuminates the room with its woody light.

Stéphanie leans towards the skylight again, her skin a mahogany hue. She watches night falling on the street, the Place de la Mairie, the lime trees, the school playground.

Everyone can see you, Jacques thinks, looking up from his list. But he says nothing. Stéphanie presses her skin against the tiles. She is naked now, apart from a bra, a pair of black knickers and her grey stockings.

She whispers wearily: 'Why does it always rain at funerals?'

Jacques puts down his magazine.

'I don't know. It often rains in Giverny, Stéphanie. Sometimes during funerals. Maybe that means you remember them more . . . Or you think you remember . . .'

He looks at Stéphanie for a long time.

'Are you coming to bed?'

She doesn't answer. She turns on her heels and looks at her profile in the reflection on the skylight.

'I'm fatter. Don't you think?'

Jacques smiles.

'You've got to be joking. You are . . .'

He tries to find the best word to describe what he feels: that long hair raining down her long, honeyed back; those shadows that hug her every curve.

'A true Madonna . . .'

Stéphanie smiles. She brings her hands behind her back and unhooks her bra.

'No, Jacques . . . A Madonna is beautiful because she has children.'

She hangs her undergarment on a hanger suspended from a nail in the beam, then turns round and sits down on the edge of the bed, without even looking at Jacques. While her fingers slowly roll one stocking down her thigh, Jacques slips a hand from under the blankets and places it on her flat stomach. The more his wife leans over, pushing the stocking down her thigh, leg, ankle, the more her breasts press against his arm.

'Who do you want to please, Stéphanie?'

'Nobody. Who would you like me to please?'

'Me . . . Stéphanie. Me.'

Stéphanie doesn't reply. She slides under the blankets.

Jacques hesitates then finally decides to speak. 'I didn't like the way that policeman kept looking at you during Morval's funeral. I really didn't . . .'

'Don't start . . . Please.'

She turns her back to him. Jacques hears her breathing gently.

'Tomorrow morning, Philippe and Titou have invited me to go hunting, on the Plateau de Madrie. Do you mind?'

'No. Of course not.'

'Are you sure? You don't want me to stay?'

Breathing. Just his wife's back and her breathing.

It's unbearable.

He places the list of houses at the foot of the bed, then asks:

'Do you want to read?'

Stéphanie looks over at the bedside table. There's only one book lying on it. *Aurélien.* By Louis Aragon.

'No, not tonight. You can turn out the light.'

Night descends on the room.

The black panties slip to the ground.

Stéphanie turns towards her husband.

'Make me a child, Jacques. I beg you.'

20

Inspector Sérénac stares insistently at Béatrice, trying to guess what lies beneath her ironic smile. The veranda has begun to feel like an interrogation room. Sylvio Bénavides' wife shivers slightly under her shawl.

'So, Béatrice, what do you deduce from these racy shots?'

'Well, it's about your teacher. What's her name again?'

'Stéphanie. Stéphanie Dupain.'

'Yes, Stéphanie. The pretty girl who has captured your heart, according to Sylvio . . .'

Sérénac frowns.

'Anyway, I would bet my life that she's never had anything to do with that guy Jérôme Morval.'

She studies the five photographs on the plastic table one by one.

'Trust me, she's the only one of the five who has never had a physical relationship with him.'

'What makes you say that?' asks Sérénac.

The answer comes quite simply: 'He's not her type.'

'Oh . . . And what is her type?'

'You are!'

She's very direct, this pregnant woman.

Sylvio comes back with a Guinness and a large glass bearing the trademark of the beer. He sets them down in front of his colleague.

'May I stay with you while you work?' Béatrice asks.

Sylvio darts a nervous glance at them, while Laurenç blows the froth off his beer.

'I suppose what difference will it make, given that he tells you everything anyway . . .'

Bénavides avoids making any comment. His boss slides the first photograph on the table towards them.

'Right, I'll go first,' says Sérénac.

The photo shows Jérôme Morval pressed against the knees of a girl behind a cluttered desk, kissing her full on the mouth.

'The photograph was taken at Jérôme Morval's surgery. The girl is called Fabienne Goncalves. She was one of his secretaries. Young, a bit wild. White blouse, lace panties . . .'

Sylvio puts a shy arm around Béatrice's shoulder. She seems to be enjoying herself enormously.

'According to a friend of the secretary, their relationship started five years ago. Fabienne was single at the time. She isn't anymore . . .'

'That's a bit short for a crime of passion, isn't it?' Sylvio observes.

He turns the photograph over.

'And the code written on the back? 23-02 . . .'

'No idea. Not the slightest clue. It doesn't correspond to anything, not to her date of birth, or a day when they might have met. The only thing that's certain is that the second numbers don't refer to months—'

'If I can interrupt you, Chief, I've reached the same dead end. I've identified the girls, but found out nothing, absolutely nothing about the codes, 03-01, 21-02, 15-03. Perhaps that's just the way the private detective who took the pictures organised his filing.'

'Perhaps . . . But even if it is, there must be some kind of order . . . and until we have located the private detective in question, and while Patricia Morval continues to claim that she didn't send these pictures, we're going to flounder. Well, we'll see. Your turn, now.'

Sylvio keeps his arm around Béatrice, trapping the shawl firmly between his hand and his wife's shoulder. He has to twist round to pick up the next picture. The photograph was clearly taken in a nightclub. Jérôme Morval is putting his hand on the breast of a blonde who is spilling out of her sequined dress. She is tanned, caked in make-up all the way down to her toenails. Sérénac whistles between his teeth. Béatrice's eyes sparkle while Sylvio merely coughs.

'Aline . . . Malétras,' Sylvio mumbles. 'Thirty-two. Public relations, in the arts. Divorced. An independent girl. A regular on the Paris art scene. Apparently this was Morval's longest liaison.'

'Public relations, is that what they call it?' Laurenç says with a hint of irony. 'From the look of the photograph, our Aline is a bombshell in high heels . . . Have you been in direct contact with her?'

Béatrice straightens like a she-wolf sniffing danger. Sylvio's attentive fingers grip the shawl.

'No,' he replies. 'According to my information she's been in the United States for the last nine months. Old Lyme, I don't know if you've ever heard of it. Apparently it's the American Giverny, the retreat in Connecticut the American Impressionists used to go to, not far from Boston. I tried to phone her, but no success so far. But you know me, Chief, I'll keep trying.'

'Hmm, yes . . . I hope you're not saying that the lovely Aline is in exile just because Béatrice is here.'

Béatrice rests a hand on Sylvio's knee.

Sexy and irritating, these pregnant women. But affectionate, too.

'Behave yourself, boss. Do you know who Aline Malétras is working for in Boston?'

'Give me a clue?'

'The Robinson Foundation!'

'Hang on . . . That bloody foundation again! Sylvio, you've got to find me this girl,' he says, glancing at Béatrice, who looks annoyed. 'Consider that an order . . . Right, my turn . . .'

The next photograph passes from hand to hand. A woman wearing a short blue overall and skirt is kneeling in front of the ophthalmologist, whose trousers are around his ankles. Sylvio turns towards Béatrice, as if to suggest she should go on up to bed. In the end he doesn't say anything.

'I'm sorry,' says Sérénac, 'but this is where I get stuck. Without being able to see this girl's face, I haven't a hope of identifying her. I'm certain, from the paintings on the wall, that the scene is being played out in the drawing room of the Morvals' house, on Rue Claude Monet. And given the girl's outfit, the blue overall with a light check, it's possible that she's a cleaning woman, but Patricia Morval has been silent on this issue. Apparently she spends most of her time firing them, one after the other. In addition, according to Maury, who examined the paper, the photograph dates back at least ten years . . .'

'How did Morval die?' Béatrice asks all of a sudden.

'Stabbed, then his head was smashed in, then drowned,' Sérénac replies mechanically.

'I'd have cut off his balls as well.'

Sexy, irritating . . . and affectionate . . . like a snake rolling itself around your neck . . .

Sylvio smiles stupidly. 'Don't you want to go to bed, my love?'

My Love doesn't reply. Laurenç is enjoying himself hugely.

'So this relationship took place at least ten years ago,' Sylvio suggests. 'And if the girl had fallen pregnant, her child would be . . .'

'Ten years old! I can count too. I see what you're getting at,

Sylvio, but first of all we need to find the girl before we tackle the question of whether she's a mother as well. Now, your turn, the Irishwoman . . .'

'That one could take a while, Chief; do you not want another go?'

Sérénac looks up, surprised.

'If you prefer . . . Mine's going to be a short one.'

The photograph circulates. Stéphanie Dupain and Jérôme Morval are walking along a path, probably the one above Giverny. They are standing side by side, quite close, hand in hand.

'As you can see, it's rather a chaste extra-marital relationship,' Sérénac observes. 'Isn't that right, Béatrice?'

Sylvio is surprised. Béatrice gently nods.

'Yes,' Bénavides adds. 'Except that the picture appeared with the four others. And if you lump them all together . . .'

'Exactly! Hasn't anyone ever told you that you should be wary of lumping things together, Sylvio? It's the ABC of our job. Particularly when they were supplied to us by an anonymous benefactor. Besides, we already know everything about the girl in the photograph, Stéphanie Dupain, the village schoolteacher. I'm going to see her tomorrow, to ask for the list of all the children in Giverny, which will give Sylvio great pleasure, and also to find out what her husband was up to on the morning of Morval's murder.'

Laurenç waits for an encouraging comment from Béatrice, but she is leaning her head against Sylvio's shoulder, and her eyelids are starting to droop.

'So,' says Sérénac, 'your Irishwoman?'

'Alysson Murer,' Sylvio murmurs. 'But she isn't Irish, she's English, from Durham in the North of England, near Newcastle. And secondly, the beach in the photograph isn't Ireland, it's on the Isle of Sark.'

'Isn't Sark in Ireland?'

'No, it's further down. It's a small Channel Island near Jersey, the prettiest one apparently . . .'

'And what about your Alysson?'

Béatrice's eyes are closed. Her breath gently stirs the blond curls on the back of Sylvio's neck.

'It's a long story,' Bénavides whispers. 'And, with all due respect to the Bishop of Évreux, it isn't going to do much for the post-humous honour of Jérôme Morval.'

DAY SIX

18 May 2010

(Moulin des Chennevières)

Insanity

21

As you will already have worked out, my bedroom and bathroom are right at the top, in the keep of the Moulin des Chennevières, that small, square, half-timbered tower. Two tiny rooms that no one but a mad old woman would want to live in.

I slowly braid my hair. I have made my decision. I need to go and see Patricia Morval this morning. I gloomily study the dark stain on the parquet floor. Most of the clothes that I wore to the funeral are still wet. Last night I was too tired, I wasn't paying attention, and I hung them up to dry here in this room. They dripped all night and this morning I found a great puddle, and even though I've sponged it there's still a mark on the damp wood. I'm aware that it's only water, that the wood will dry, but I'm obsessed by the stain. It's just beneath my black *Water Lilies*, too.

You must be saying to yourself that I really am a sick old woman. Aren't you? And you aren't wrong. I walk over to the window. My keep has at least one advantage: there is no better observation post in the whole of Giverny. From my eyrie I can see the brook, the meadow stretching as far as Nettles Island, Monet's gardens, the

Chemin du Roy right up to the roundabout . . .

It's my lookout. I spend hours there, sometimes.

I disgust myself.

Who would have thought that I would become this person: a hag spending her life behind a grey pane of glass, spying on the neighbours, strangers, tourists?

The village concierge.

A hedgehog, without the elegance.

That's how it is.

Sometimes I weary of the ceaseless flow of cars, coaches, bicycles, pedestrians on the Chemin du Roy. The last few metres on the Way of the Cross trod by the pilgrims of Impressionism.

Sometimes not. There are good surprises, like the one just now.

That motorbike that slowed down to turn off towards the village, just before the mill. Impossible to miss.

Inspector Laurenç Sérénac himself!

I watch. No one can see me, no one can suspect me. And if they did see what I was up to, what difference would it make? For what could be more natural than a gossipy old woman, studying every detail, every morning, day after day, like a bug-eyed goldfish that forgets everything with each turn of the bowl?

Who would be wary of a witness like that?

Meanwhile, the policeman's motorbike has turned into Rue du Colombier. So this is the return of Inspector Sérénac, on his way to the great disaster.

22

Laurenç Sérénac parks his motorbike in the Place de la Mairie, under a lime tree. This time he has left nothing to chance, he has planned his arrival in front of the school just a few minutes after getting-out time. He has already encountered several children on Rue Claude Monet, who admired his Tiger Triumph T100. For the children, it's practically a collectors' piece.

Stéphanie's back is turned to him. She is filing away some

children's drawings in a large cardboard folder. He has decided to speak before she turns round, which he reckons is the best way to avoid talking gibberish – before she settles on him the infinite landscape of her gaze.

'Hello, Stéphanie. I've come back for the list of children.'

The teacher turns and holds out a gentle hand, accompanied by a sincere smile. The smile of a prisoner called to the visitors' room, Sérénac thinks, without knowing why that image should come to mind.

'Hello, Inspector. I've prepared everything for you. It's all there, in the envelope on the desk.'

'Thank you. My deputy really believes in this line of enquiry, because of that birthday card found in Jérôme Morval's pocket . . .'

'And you don't?'

'I don't know. You're probably better placed to judge than me. To tell you the truth, I think my deputy is working on the hypothesis that Jérôme Morval might have had an illegitimate child about ten years ago. That kind of thing . . .'

'You really think so?'

'Doesn't it strike you as credible? Mightn't one of your little pupils fit that profile?'

Stéphanie slides her fingers towards the white envelope, and presses it against the inspector's chest.

'Your job might be to go rummaging around in the private life of my little cubs, but it certainly isn't mine!'

Sérénac doesn't push the point. Instead he studies the classroom, pretending he's searching for a response. In fact the inspector knows exactly what he is going to say next. He has been turning the phrase round and round in his head all the way from Vernon to Giverny, like an old piece of chewing gum. His eyes settle on the pastel colours of the poster for the 'International Young Painters Challenge'. He notices that the Robinson Foundation is also mentioned on another poster hanging in the classroom, which extols the delights of the National Gallery of Cardiff, against the background of a landscape of moors painted by Sisley. After his calculated silence, Sérénac starts again:

'Stéphanie, do you know the village well?'

'I was born here!'

'I'm looking for a guide . . . How can I put it? I need to get a feel for Giverny, to understand it . . . I think that's the only way I'm going to be able to get anywhere with this investigation.'

'"Observe and imagine", like the painters did?'

'Exactly.'

They smile at one another.

'OK, I'm all yours. I'll just slip my coat on and then I'll be with you.'

Stéphanie Dupain has put on a woollen jacket over her straw-coloured dress. They walk along the Rue Claude Monet, chatting as they go, down the Rue des Grands Jardins, turn down the Rue du Milieu, then cross the stream again on the other side of the Chemin du Roy, just in front of the Moulin des Chennevières. Stéphanie has walked the children of her class along the streets of Giverny hundreds of times. She knows all the anecdotes about the place, and shares them with the inspector. She explains to him that every street corner in the village, almost every house, every tree even, is preserved and admired somewhere else, at the other end of the planet, in some prestigious museum, framed and varnished.

'Here,' Stéphanie points out with a slightly strange smile, 'it's the stones and flowers that travel, not the inhabitants!'

They cross the Chemin du Roy. The river that flows under the bridge and escapes through a brick arch, towards the Moulin des Chennevières, brings a kind of freshness to the air. Stéphanie stops, a few metres before they reach the mill.

'This bizarre house has always attracted me. Really. I don't know why . . .'

'Can I make a suggestion?' Sérénac asks.

'Go on . . .'

'You remember the book you lent me? *Aurélien*, by Aragon. I spent much of the night in its company. Aurélien and Bérénice . . . Their impossible love . . . In the chapters set in Giverny, Bérénice lives in a mill. Aragon doesn't specify which one, but if you follow his descriptions to the letter, it could only be this one.'

'Do you think so? That this is the place where Aragon's gloomy Bérénice sits around moping, torn between her two loves, reason and the absolute . . . ?'

'Hey . . . Don't give away the ending!'

They walk towards the big wooden gate. It is open. A light breeze blows along the valley. Stéphanie shivers slightly. Laurenç resists the desire to take her in his arms.

'I'm sorry to disappoint Aragon, Stéphanie, but for the dormant cop within me, this mill is, more importantly, the closest house to the spot where Jérôme Morval was murdered.'

'That's your business . . . I'm just a tour guide . . . If you must know, the mill has a long history. Without it, Monet's garden would never have existed, and nor would the *Water Lilies*. The brook that goes through the gardens is really a mill-race dug by the monks in the Middle Ages to feed the mill. Upstream, the brook passed through a field, which Monet bought centuries later in order to build his pond . . .'

And then?'

'For a long time the mill belonged to John Stanton, an American painter who was apparently better at wielding a tennis racket than a paintbrush. But since time immemorial, and no one really knows why, the children of the village have always called the Moulin des Chennevières the Witch's Mill.'

'Scary . . .'

'Look, Laurenç . . . Follow my finger.'

Stéphanie takes his hand. He lets her do it, savouring the moment.

'Look at the huge cherry tree in the middle of the courtyard. It's a hundred years old! For generations, the children of Giverny's favourite game was to creep into the courtyard and steal cherries . . .'

'And what do the police do about that?'

'Wait, look again. Do you see, among the leaves, the reflections glittering in the sunlight? Those are strips of silver paper. Ordinary silver paper cut into ribbons. It's completely stupid. They're designed to keep off the birds, which are far more dangerous to the cherries than the local kids. For the small boys of the village, it's a much more chivalrous game than trying to steal the fruit . . .'

Stéphanie's lilac eyes sparkle like an adolescent's, like the most luminous of Monet's *Water Lilies*. All melancholy seems to have fled. She continues, without allowing the inspector time to interject.

'So, the knight has to run in and steal some of those silver ribbons, then offer them to the princess of his heart, to tie up her hair.'

She laughs, bringing Laurenç's hand to her loose chignon . . .

'The incriminating evidence, Inspector . . .'

Laurenç Sérénac's fingers lose themselves in her long chestnut hair. He tries not to emphasise the gesture. Stéphanie must surely have noticed how troubled he is.

What's she trying to do? How much is she improvising? How much is premeditated?

The silver paper discreetly fastened into the teacher's hair crinkles under his fingers. He snatches back his hand as if it were threatening to catch fire. He smiles and stammers, feeling that he must look like a complete idiot.

'You're amazing, Stéphanie . . . Really. Wearing silver ribbons in your hair. I suppose it would be indiscreet to ask which knight errant gave them to you?'

She smooths her hair quite unselfconsciously.

'I shall just tell you this, to reassure you – it certainly wasn't Jérôme Morval. It wasn't his kind of thing at all, that childish romanticism. But don't imagine mysteries where there are none, Inspector. In a classroom, there are always plenty of little boys who like to give presents to their teacher. Shall we continue?'

They walk a little way along the stream and stop just in front of the wash house, at the precise spot where, a few days before, Jérôme Morval's body was found in the water.

They think about it, inevitably, and silence slips its way in between them. Stéphanie tries a diversion:

'It was Claude Monet who gave this wash house to the village. Like some other people in the commune, he tried to use gifts to win acceptance from the locals . . .'

Sérénac doesn't reply. He steps away from her, and for a moment enjoys the movement of the aquatic plants as they dance on the bed of the stream. His voice is suddenly harsh:

'I have to tell you, Stéphanie, your husband is fast becoming the chief suspect in this investigation.'

'I'm sorry?'

The sweet young fantasy has flown away like a startled bird.

'I just thought I should keep you in the picture. Those rumours about you and Morval . . . His jealousy . . .'

'That's ridiculous! What are you playing at, Inspector? I've already told you that there was nothing between me and—'

'I know, but . . .'

He stirs the mud on the riverbank with his shoes. Yesterday's rain has erased any trace of footprints.

'Does your husband own a pair of boots, Stéphanie?'

'Do you often ask such idiotic questions?'

'It's the kind of question a policeman asks. I'm sorry . . . but you haven't given me an answer.'

'Of course Jacques has boots. Everyone does. He might even be wearing them right now. He's gone hunting with some friends.'

'But it isn't the hunting season.'

The teacher's reply is crisp and precise:

'The owner of the hill above the Astragale pathway, Patrick Delaunay, has been given permission to destroy wild rabbits outside the hunting reserves and the normal hunting periods. The limestone meadows are overrun with rabbits. Your men can check; there's a file at the Department of Agriculture, along with a list of the plots concerned, the damage caused by the creatures, and the names of the huntsmen who have agreed to assist Delaunay. All his friends in Giverny, in fact, including my husband. Everything's been negotiated, Inspector. This way, they can blast away all year round, perfectly legally.'

Sérénac frowns, as if memorising every detail.

'Fine, thanks. We will check. You're going to receive a visit from my deputy, or from another police officer. Don't worry, they're much less indiscreet than I am, Stéphanie. So, what was your husband doing on the morning of the murder?'

Stéphanie steps towards the bank, rubbing a willow leaf between her fingers.

'Did you suggest coming here just to ask me about the crime scene, Inspector? To put me in the mood, so to speak?'

Sérénac stammers: 'Please . . . don't think that—'

'Jacques had gone hunting that morning,' Stéphanie cuts in. 'Early. But it's often like that at this time of year, weather permitting . . . My husband has no alibi. But no motive either . . . The fact that Jérôme Morval discreetly tried to court me isn't a reason . . . We sometimes went walking around here, just as you and I are doing right now. We talked about painting – he was interesting, cultured. But my relationship with Jérôme Morval stops there. It certainly doesn't constitute a motive for the crime.'

Stéphanie Dupain's eyes follow the water of the brook, then settle on Laurenç Sérénac.

Fathomless.

'Look, Inspector. I could slip on this wet ground and fall into your arms. Someone might see us . . . Observe us. Imagine. Take a photograph. That's what people do here. And yet we would both agree that nothing had happened.'

Sérénac can't help glancing around. He can see only a few passers-by, quite a long way off in the meadow. Apart from the Moulin des Chennevières, he can't spot a single inhabitable building.

'Forgive me, Stéphanie. It's only a lead . . . Perhaps I was exaggerating when I used the term "chief suspect".'

He hesitates for a moment before going on.

'In fact, according to my deputy, Inspector Bénavides – and I think he's right – there are three possible motives for the murder of Jérôme Morval: jealousy, because of his many mistresses; illegal art dealing, linked to his passion for paintings; or some kind of secret to do with a child . . .'

Stéphanie thinks for a moment. Her voice assumes a disturbingly ironic tone:

'Well, if I'm following you correctly, then I should be your main suspect. Because the three motives lead to me, don't they? I used to talk to Morval, I'm organising a painting competition . . . And who knows the village children better than I do?'

She bites her chalky pink lips and holds out two clenched fists, as if waiting to be handcuffed.

Sérénac's laugh sounds strained.

'There's no evidence against you! Quite the opposite, in fact. According to what you told me, you weren't Morval's lover, you don't paint . . . And you don't have any children.'

The inspector's careless words suddenly freeze in his throat. A dark veil slides over Stéphanie's eyes, as if Sérénac's words have caused her intense distress.

A violin string breaking.

Her acting skills don't go this far, Sérénac thinks. He reflects on what he has just said.

You weren't Morval's lover.

You don't paint.

You don't have any children.

Everything about Stéphanie's attitude proves that he's mistaken . . . that one of those statements is incorrect.

At least one.

But which one? And might this have something to do with his investigation, with the murder? Once again Laurenç Sérénac feels as if he is stepping into a marsh, getting bogged down in unconnected details.

Slowly, without saying another word, they head back towards the school along the Rue du Colombier. They part, troubled by an awkwardness that neither of them can express.

'Stéphanie, as the phrase goes, I'm going to ask you to remain at the disposal of the police.'

He smiles.

She replies, a forced warmth in her voice: 'Of course, Inspector. It's not hard to find me. I'm either at school or at home, just along from the playground.'

She glances towards the round skylight below the mansard roof.

'My world isn't very large, as you can see . . . Oh, but yes. In three days' time, I'll be taking the children of the village to visit Monet's gardens. In the morning.'

She runs off towards her classroom. The light mauve of her eyes lingers for a long moment in Sérénac's thoughts, distorting the reality of what he has heard, reassembling it into a strange picture, painted with chaotic brushstrokes.

Stéphanie Dupain.

What is her part in this case?

Suspect? Victim?

He is very disconcerted by her. The only reasonable thing to do would be to drop the case, call the investigating magistrate, and pass everything on to Sylvio, or any other policeman.

But one certainty, just one, holds him back.

The intuition that he can't explain, that haunting feeling, that Stéphanie Dupain is asking for his help.

23

From my keep, I didn't miss a thing. The two walkers by my cherry tree, the silver ribbons in her hair, the mud on his shoes, right by the crime scene.

In front of my house!

I would be wrong to deny myself, don't you think? And doesn't their story strike you as boringly obvious? A romance between the handsome police inspector who's come out of nowhere, and the teacher awaiting her saviour? They're young, they're attractive. Their fate lies before them, in their hands.

Everything is in place.

They just need to meet a few more times . . . The flesh will do the rest.

I come down from my tower, cursing under my breath. I take several long seconds to go down each step. It will take me several more minutes to lock those three locks. I even have trouble closing the oak door; it's as heavy and old as I am. You would think that the hinges rust overnight. To each his own rheumatism, if I can put it like that.

I think again about the policeman and the teacher. Yes, those two dream of breaking the picture. Of bursting out from the frame. An escape on a gleaming chrome motorbike. What girl wouldn't dream of escaping like that?

Unless someone puts a spanner in the works, of course.

Unless someone writes a different ending.

'Come on, Neptune!'

I walk. I walk. As so often, I cut across the car park of the American Art Museum. I pass in front of the building. As usual, I grumble to myself about the hideous, pavilion-style, seventies architecture. I know, of course, that a big garden was planned to hide the museum. A maze of privet and white cedar was planted years ago – they call it an Impressionist garden. But many people aren't even happy about the hedges. Now that the French have bought it back from the Americans, maybe they'll knock the whole thing down. I can tell you this: if they wanted my advice, I'd be in favour.

Anyway, I'll be dead before it happens. For now, they've settled on putting four old-style haystacks in the field behind the museum; the only thing that's missing is a pitchfork. I think the whole thing looks a bit odd, but people seem to like them, and you often see delighted tourists posing in front of them.

When I was younger, I often used to walk up behind the museum, past the Cambour Gallery. The view of the terraced, landscaped roofs of the museum isn't something many tourists know about, but it is quite surprising. Even if the best view is still the one from the hill above the water tower. Now that my legs are giving out, all I have is memories . . .

I continue walking. My rickety walking-stick scratches the pavement. A group of five people overtake me, old people – well, not as old as me. They are speaking English.

It's always like this during the week, Giverny is as deserted as any other village. Apart from the coaches run by the tour operators . . . Three quarters of these visitors speak English and they do a return journey along Rue Claude Monet, going as far as the church and coming back by the same route. On the way there they look at the galleries, and on the way back they buy. At the weekend it's different. Parisians disembark, and people from Normandy.

Even though the group in front is drawing away from me, I still advance, at my own rhythm. I would like to be able to speed up a little when I pass in front of the Kandy Gallery. Amadou Kandy runs the oldest art gallery in Giverny.

Thirty years I've been bumping into him. For thirty years, he's been boring me rigid . . .

Damn!

His shop looks like a kind of Ali Baba's cave. He comes out of his doorway as soon as he sees me.

'So, my lovely. Still haunting the streets?'

'Hello, Amadou. Forgive me, I'm in a hurry . . .'

He bursts into his booming Senegalese-giant laughter. To my knowledge he is the only African in the village. Sometimes I spend a bit more time with him. He tells me about his business, his dream of one day having a Monet to sell. The jackpot. A *Water Lilies*, it doesn't matter which one. In black, why not . . . Sometimes he too roams around the Moulin des Chennevières. Amadou Kandy did a lot of business with Jérôme Morval. I have to be cautious. I've also learned that he had dealings with the police not too long ago.

I continue on my way. The Rue Claude Monet seems to get longer every day. The tourists part in front of me to let me through. Sometimes some idiot might even try to take my photograph, as if I were part of the landscape.

Number 71. I've arrived.

I study the name on the letter box. *Jérôme and Patricia Morval*, as if the couple were still living under the same roof. I understand Patricia. It's not easy to scratch out the name of a dead person.

I ring the bell. Several times. She comes out.

She looks surprised.

And with good reason! We haven't exchanged more than two

words for several months, a hello in the street at most. I come closer, almost whispering in her ear.

'I need to talk to you, Patricia . . . there are some things I have to tell you. Some things that I've learned and others that I've understood . . .'

When she lets me inside, I notice that she's looking pale. The two huge *Water Lilies* in the long corridor make my head spin. Patricia even more so, clearly. I have a sense that she's about to pass out.

She's always been a little sickly, has Patricia.

'Is . . . is it about Jérôme's murder?' she stammers.

'Yes, among other things.'

I hesitate. After all, even if I have nothing left to lose, it isn't easy to throw such confessions in her face. I wait until she's sitting down on a leather armchair in the drawing room.

'Yes, Patricia, it is about Jérôme's murder. I know the name of his killer.'

24

Sylvio Bénavides has been wondering for some time what on earth those crocodiles are doing in the water-lily pond. He thinks it must be some kind of free interpretation by the painter, someone by the name of Kobamo, but he's pondering whether there's a hidden message behind it all. To pass the time, he counts the number of crocodiles. Kobamo has hidden them all over the place, under the lilies. Eyes, nostrils, tails.

Behind him, the door of the art gallery opens and Laurenç Sérénac comes inside. Inspector Bénavides smiles with relief at Amadou Kandy.

'I told you he wouldn't be long.'

Amadou Kandy slowly raises his hands. The Senegalese gallery owner must be approximately the size of two Japanese tourists. He wears an ample boubou decorated with an unlikely patchwork of African prints and pastel tones.

'I wasn't worried, Inspector, I'm just aware that my time is much less precious than yours.'

The Kandy Gallery is like a vast bric-a-brac shop. Canvases of all sizes are piled up in every corner of the room, making the place look like a museum that's about to move house, and doubtless lulling art connoisseurs into a sense that they can get themselves a good bargain from its chaotic owner.

But Amadou Kandy knows exactly what he's doing.

The policemen make themselves comfortable as best they can. Sylvio Bénavides sits on a step between two cardboard boxes, and Laurenç Sérénac's buttocks are perched on the edge of an enormous wooden bin full of lithographs.

'Monsieur Kandy, you knew Jérôme Morval well . . .' Sérénac begins.

Amadou Kandy is still standing up.

'Yes, Jérôme was an art lover, and well informed. We talked, I advised him. He was a man of good taste . . . I have lost a friend.'

'And a good client as well.'

Sérénac draws first. It's almost as if the pain in his behind is making him aggressive. Kandy retains his pastoral smile.

'If you like . . . It's your job to think like that, Inspector.'

'Fine, then you will forgive me for cutting straight to the chase. Did Jérôme Morval ask you to find him a *Water Lilies*?'

'And you are very good at your job,' says Kandy with a little laugh. 'Yes, among other things, Jérôme asked me to keep an eye on the market for works by Claude Monet.'

'*Water Lilies* in particular?'

Yes . . . It was a hopeless task, of course, and Jérôme knew that, but he liked insane challenges.'

'Why you?' Bénavides asks.

Amadou Kandy turns his head.

'What do you mean, why me?'

'Yes, why did Morval ask you and not some other art dealer?'

'Why not me, Inspector? Do you think I'm not enough of an expert?'

Kandy forces a white-toothed smile, his eyes wide. 'If he had been looking into primitive art, I might agree with you, but asking a Senegalese to do research into the Impressionists . . . Don't worry, Inspector, Jérôme also asked me to find a particularly magnificent gazelle horn . . .'

Sérénac laughs out loud, stretching his back.

'You're a clever chap, Monsieur Kandy, our colleagues told us that. But right now we're in a hurry so . . .'

'You didn't seem to be in a hurry earlier.'

'Earlier?'

'About an hour or two ago. You passed in front of the gallery, but I was careful not to disturb you, as you seemed to be concentrating very hard on what your guide was telling you.'

Bénavides is concerned. Sérénac takes the blow.

'You really are a clever man, Kandy.'

'Giverny is a small village,' the gallery owner says, turning towards the door. 'Just two streets.'

'So I've heard.'

'Having said that, Inspector, to be quite honest, it wasn't you that I noticed, but your guide, our pretty schoolteacher. I saw the two of you and I said to myself, "You lucky fellow". You know, I would've liked to have had children just for the pleasure of taking them to school and seeing Stéphanie Dupain every morning . . .'

'Like your friend Morval.'

'Except that Jérôme didn't have any children,' the gallery owner replies. 'You're a clever man too, Inspector.'

He turns towards Sylvio.

'You, on the other hand, you just like to root about. You must make an effective double act. Like the monkey and the anteater – is that how I should describe you?'

Sérénac shifts uncomfortably on his buttocks.

'Do you often invent such folktales?'

'All the time, it adds a bit of local colour, and my clients love it. I invent animal nicknames for Monsieur and Madame. It's my little commercial tic. You can't imagine how effective it is.'

Sérénac is greatly amused. Bénavides seems horrified. His feet tap nervously against the first step of the stairs.

'Do you know Alysson Murer?' he says abruptly.

'No.'

'Your friend Morval knew her.'

'Really?'

'Do you like stories, Monsieur Kandy?'

'I love them, my grandfather used to tell them to the whole tribe in the evenings. Instead of television. First we would grill some crickets . . .'

'Don't push it, Kandy.'

Bénavides grips the banister, stretches his cramped limbs a little and holds out a photograph to the gallery owner. Alysson Murer on the beach at Sark, lying side by side with Jérôme Morval.

'As you can see,' Sylvio remarks, 'she was an intimate friend of your friend, Jérôme Morval.'

Amadou Kandy appraises the picture like a connoisseur. Sérénac picks up the baton from his deputy:

'From the photograph, you might think that Miss Murer is quite pretty, but in fact our Alysson has a rather . . . unattractive face. Not hideous, but let's just say that she has no particular charm. And as we are clever policemen,' says Laurenç, glancing at Sylvio, 'clever people who like to go digging around, it occurred to us that something wasn't quite right about this Alysson, when you consider Jérôme Morval's other female conquests. Isn't it strange, Monsieur Kandy, that Jérôme Morval would have flirted with this rather ordinary-looking girl who worked in the accounts department of an insurance company in Newcastle?'

Amadou Kandy returns the photograph to the policeman.

'Perhaps you just have to put some perspective on your aesthetic judgement. After all, the girl is English . . .'

Once again, Sérénac can't help laughing. Bénavides fills the gap.

'I'd like to continue with my story, Monsieur Kandy, if you'd be so kind. Alysson's only living relative is her grandmother, Kate Murer, who has always lived in a fisherman's cottage on the Isle of Sark, an unremarkable little house that is falling to pieces. Kate Murer's home is filled with worthless old objects – knick-knacks, baubles, a series of old paintings that no one wanted, cracked crockery, and a reproduction of one of Monet's *Water Lilies*, a little canvas, sixty by sixty. Kate felt very attached to that picture, not because of its value, as you can imagine, but because it was the only thing she had left of her family. I'm talking to you about Kate because Jérôme Morval went to the island of Sark several times with the young Alysson Murer. And on this particular occasion he also formed a friendship with her grandmother. When you're a nosy policeman, Mr Kandy, an anteater, you inevitably find yourself asking a question: what the devil was Jérôme Morval doing visiting an old Englishwoman on that godforsaken island?'

25

Patricia Morval watches the stooped black figure as it moves away. The cane squeaks on the tarmac of the Rue Claude Monet with every step the old woman takes as she descends the hill towards the Moulin des Chennevières. When she is more or less level with the Immo-Prestige estate agents, Neptune joins her. Patricia Morval wonders how long their surreal conversation lasted.

Half an hour, perhaps?

Hardly more than that.

My God!

Just half an hour, yet it was enough to shake all her certainties. Patricia Morval struggles to assess the consequences of everything she has just heard. Does she have to believe this mad old woman? And more importantly, what should she do now?

She walks down the corridor, taking care not to let her eyes lose themselves in the long panels of the *Water Lilies*. She will have to tell the police. Yes, that's what she should do . . .

She hesitates.

What would be the point? Whom can she confide in?

She stares at the drooping flowers sticking out of the Japanese vase; she remembers every detail of Inspector Sérénac's visit, his inquisitor's gaze, his way of evaluating every painting hung on the wall, his discomfort at the sight of the *Water Lilies* in the corridor.

My God . . . She asks herself the question again. Who could she confide in?

Patricia sits down in the drawing room, and thinks for a long time about the conversation she has just had. There is only one question to ask, in fact: is it still possible to repair what might have been? Perhaps to reverse the course of things?

Patricia walks to a little room that is almost entirely occupied by a desk and a computer. The computer is switched on. The screensaver shows a sequence of photographs of sunlit Giverny landscapes. Patricia has only been interested in the internet for a few months. She would never have imagined she could be so excited about a keyboard and a screen. And yet it was love at first sight. She spends hours on it now. Thanks to the internet, Patricia has even rediscovered Giverny, her own village. Without the internet, would she ever have imagined that there were thousands of photographs of her village just one click away, each more enchanting than the last? Without the internet, could she have imagined the thousands of comments from visitors from all over the world, each more enthusiastic than the last? Several months ago, Patricia was stunned by the beauty of a site, Givernews. Since then, not a week has gone by when she didn't visit that blog, with its incredible daily poetry.

But not today.

Right now, Patricia is looking for something else on her canvas. Her cursor settles on the yellow star that indicates her bookmarked websites. She runs through the menu and stops on Copainsdavant. linternaute.com – a site where old friends can rediscover each other.

A few seconds later, Patricia types 'Giverny' into the search engine. The photograph she is looking for is waiting there. Impossible to miss, it's the only school photograph on the whole site that dates back before the war.

From 1936–7, to be precise.

For a moment Patricia wonders what surfers who happen upon this website must think of it.

What is this prehistoric school photograph doing there?

Who could be looking for friends who shared a school desk seventy-five years ago?

For a long time Patricia studies the docile faces of the pupils in the old photograph. My God, she is still struggling to believe the revelations that the mad old woman made to her. Is it possible? Mightn't she have invented it all? Could Jérôme's killer really be the one she named, the last individual she would ever have suspected?

Her whole body trembles at the sight of those grey faces. Cold tears flow from her eyes. After hesitating for a long time, she stands up again.

She knows what she's going to do; she has made up her mind. She crosses the drawing room again and mechanically moves the little bronze of Diana the Huntress a few centimetres along the cherry-wood sideboard.

After all, what risk is there now?

She opens one of the drawers and takes out an old black diary. She sits down again in the leather armchair and dials the number on her cordless telephone.

'Hello. Chief Inspector Laurentin, this is Patricia Morval.'

There is a long silence at the other end.

'The wife of Jérôme Morval. The Morval case, the ophthalmologist who was murdered in Giverny. That's what I want to talk about, you see . . .'

This time an appalled voice replies: 'Yes . . . of course, I remember. I'm retired, but I haven't got Alzheimer's yet.'

'I know, I know. That's why I called you. I've often read about you in the local newspapers. A lot of praise. I need you, Chief Inspector, to conduct . . . how shall I put it . . . a counter-investigation. An investigation that runs parallel to the official inquiry.'

Another long silence falls between them.

A lot of praise . . .

At the other end of the line Chief Inspector Laurentin can't help thinking again about the most important investigations of his career. His years in Canada and his involvement in the Musée des Beaux-Arts case in Montreal, September 1972 – one of the biggest thefts of artwork in history, with eighteen masterpieces whisked away: Delacroix, Rubens, Rembrandt, Corot . . . His return to the station in Vernon in 1974, and his biggest case, eleven years later, three years before he retired, in November 1985: the theft of nine Monets from the Musée Marmottan, including the famous *Impression, Soleil Levant*. It was he, Laurentin, along with the art division, or the OCBC, the Central Office against the Illegal Trade in Cultural Objects, who finally found the paintings in 1991, at Porto-Vecchio, in the home of a Corsican bandit. The case had been of national importance, with large headlines in the newspapers at the time . . . That was an eternity ago.

Laurentin breaks the silence at last.

'I have retired, Madame Morval. There is nothing exceptional about the pension of a retired chief inspector from a financial point of view, but I can't complain. Why not approach a private detective?'

'I have thought of that, Chief Inspector, of course I have. But no detective has your experience in the field of illegal art trading. I need someone with considerable competence.'

The voice of Chief Inspector Laurentin sounds increasingly astonished.

'What do you expect of me?'

'Is your curiosity starting to get the better of you, Chief Inspector? I confess that I had hoped as much. Let me paint the picture for you, and then you can evaluate it. Do you not think that the judgement of a young and inexperienced investigator who has fallen madly in love with the main suspect, would be particularly impaired? Do you think he will be able to reach a successful conclusion in his investigation? Can he be objective? Clear sighted? Do you think we can trust him to get to the truth?'

'He isn't alone. He has a deputy, a team . . .'

'Under his influence, and with no initiative of their own . . .'

Chief Inspector Laurentin coughs at the end of the line.

'Excuse me. I'm just a former policeman, almost eighty years old. I haven't set foot in a police station for ten years. I still don't understand what you expect of me . . .'

'Then I will try to pique your curiosity further, Chief Inspector. Because you still read the newspapers, I advise you to turn to the obituary section. The local pages. I'm sure you'll be interested.'

Chief Inspector Laurentin's voice is very dry.

'I will do so, Madame Morval. As I'm sure you know, a leopard can't change his spots and your strange riddle will make a change from my sudoku. It's not every day that an old bachelor like me gets such a request. But I still don't see what you're getting at.'

'Do you want me to be even more precise? That's it, isn't it? OK, let's say that a very young inspector might be a little too interested in painting, in art in general, in *Water Lilies*, and not interested enough in old people.'

There is a long silence before the chief inspector replies.

'I suppose I should be flattered, but my past as a policeman is far behind me now. I'm a bit out of touch, really. If what you want from me is a counter-investigation, I don't think you're talking to the right person. Contact the art division. I know younger colleagues who—'

'Chief Inspector,' Patricia breaks in, 'I want you to carry out your own investigation. As an amateur. With no prior assumptions. It's as simple as that. I ask no more of you. You'll see . . . Here, I'll give you a clue that I hope will whet your appetite. Go on to the internet, and click on a website, Copains d'avant. If you have children or grandchildren, they're bound to know it. Type in *Giverny 1936–7*. It's an interesting starting point for this investigation, I think . . . Look at it from another angle. Well, you'll see.'

'What do you want, Madame Morval? Is it revenge you're after?'

'No, Chief Inspector. Oh, no. For the first time in my life, it's the reverse . . .'

Patricia Morval hangs up, almost relieved.

Through the window she sees the sun, in the distance, setting gently behind the slopes of the Seine, capturing the bend of the river in a fleeting but everyday Impressionist trick of the eye.

26

In Amadou Kandy's gallery, Inspector Bénavides is rather surprised by the apparent lack of reaction on the part of the Senegalese giant.

The more Sylvio looks around the gallery, the less he finds that it resembles any other. In general, the walls of such places are immaculate, white, with a clean and discreet kind of beauty. In the Kandy Gallery, by contrast, there are blisters in the crumbling plaster, bare lightbulbs hang from the ceiling, and the bricks seem to be held together more by dust than by mortar. Amadou Kandy has clearly gone to a lot of trouble to turn his shop into a kind of cave. Sylvio insists:

'To sum up, Monsieur Kandy . . . We have a mistress without charm, a grandmother without money, and a rainy Anglo-Saxon island. Aren't you surprised by your friend Morval?'

'I always liked his eccentric side . . .'

'And Sark?'

'What about Sark?'

'You are keen on Sark too, Kandy.'

Bénavides leaves a deliberate silence before going on:

'You have been to the Isle of Sark no fewer than six times over the last few years, and you happen to have been there a few months before Jérôme Morval met Alysson Murer.'

Sérénac observes his deputy, and says to himself that if Sylvio knew how to do an impression of an anteater, he would certainly do one now. For the first time, Amadou looks shaken, and wrinkles suddenly appear on his brow. Bénavides pushes onwards:

'Monsieur Kandy, would it be indiscreet to ask what you were doing on the Isle of Sark?'

Amadou Kandy watches the passers-by walking along the Rue Claude Monet, then turns round. He has recovered his unctuous smile.

'Inspector, you know as well as I do that Sark is the last tax haven in Europe. Don't repeat this to anyone, but I go there to launder my money. Diamonds, ivory, spices, they bring in the money, you have no idea. Not to mention the trade in magic gazelle-horns . . . Sark is the British equivalent of the French Overseas Territories.'

Sylvio shrugs and goes on:

'In fact, Kandy, Alysson and her grandmother Kate have distant French roots. We have every reason to think that one of their ancestors was Eugène Murer. I suppose that you have heard of Eugène Murer?'

'If you are asking the question, I suppose you have heard that I am the expert appointed by the Regional Office of Cultural Affairs to catalogue the Murer collection.'

The art dealer leans towards some paintings that are resting against the wall and delicately extracts a landscape of an African village, both naïve in style and colourful. He stands up with a smile of delight and continues with his speech:

'Among all the Impressionist painters, there's none that has a more endearing career than Eugène Murer, don't you think? As a young man he was passionate about literature and painting . . . He became a painter and collector for the love of it but sadly for him, poor thing, because every man must earn a living, he also became a pastry chef in Paris and Rouen . . . During his lifetime, Eugène Murer was wealthier than most of his artist friends, Van Gogh, Renoir, Monet; he would help them out, support them, even feed them, good man that he was . . . He painted, too, but who today remembers Eugène Murer?'

Amadou Kandy places the African painting in front of the two policemen.

'One more detail. Eugène Murer went off to paint in Africa for two years, between 1893 and 1895, far from the influence of anyone, and he came back with suitcases full of paintings. If you have a bit of taste, you will note that Murer was an excellent colourist, and that his mixture of Impressionism and a naïve style that echoes primitive art cannot help but surprise . . .'

Laurenç Sérénac has removed his aching buttocks from the wooden bin and appraises the painting with fascination. Sylvio Bénavides refuses to be distracted.

'Well, thank you, Monsieur Kandy. So, now we know all about the Murers' ancestor, Eugène, artist, pastry chef and collector. Perhaps we could come back to his descendants, Alysson and Kate. Two years ago Kate Murer was threatened with expulsion by the Seigneur of Sark. Yes, I was surprised too, but Sark still has a Seigneur who sets out the law – what do you expect? Life is tough in tax havens. Anyway, Kate was told to renovate her dilapidated house, which was causing complaints from both neighbours and tourists, or get out. This was where Jérôme Morval came on to the scene. He was seeing her granddaughter regularly and had spent a number of weekends, which we may suppose were romantic in nature, at her grandmother's house. Our friend Morval suggested helping Kate Murer out. Fifty thousand pounds. An interest-free loan, just like that, simply out of friendship. Amazing, isn't it?

'Jérôme was a nice guy,' observes Amadou Kandy.

'Wasn't he just! Kate Murer called her granddaughter, Alysson, and told her that her good friend Jérôme Morval was the most charming of men. Not only had he lent her fifty thousand pounds, but in order to avoid embarrassing her, he had suggested that in exchange for the loan, he would relieve her of her stock of old paintings, including that cumbersome reproduction of Monet's *Water Lilies*.'

'What did I tell you?' Amadou Kandy says mischievously. 'Tact, generosity, that was typical Jérôme.'

At last Sérénac takes his eyes away from the warm colours of Murer's African village and continues where his deputy left off.

'A saint among men, we agree. Except that while our Alysson may have possessed a somewhat crude face, the girl was no fool. Morval's proposal got her thinking, so she called in an expert. Another expert, I mean, not you, Kandy.'

The gallery owner takes the blow with a smile.

I don't suppose you can guess what came next?' Sérénac goes on.

'I'm burning to know, gentlemen; you are both almost as adept at telling stories as my marabout grandfather.'

Sérénac delivers his punchline:

'Kate Murer's *Water Lilies* was a real Monet, not a reproduction. And it was worth a hundred times, a thousand times what Morval had offered . . .'

The walls of the gallery are shaken by Kandy's thunderous laughter.

'Good old Jérôme!'

'Do you know the end of the story?' Bénavides says, close to exploding. 'Alysson Murer, of course, broke off all relations with her lovely French gentleman . . . Kate, the grandmother, lost both a son-in-law and a friend. She refused to sell the painting and was thrown out of her fisherman's cottage . . . She was found two days later, having hurled herself off the top of the cliff, by the bridge of La Coupée, the isthmus that connects the two parts of the island. Do you know all that is left of her?'

Kandy, leaning on the painting by Murer, doesn't reply.

'A bench!' cries Sylvio. 'A bench with the date of her birth and the date of her death, positioned directly opposite the cliff she threw herself off. It's a tradition in Sark, no cemetery, no graves, just a wooden bench engraved with the name of the late inhabitant and placed somewhere in the landscape, facing the sea . . . Before she died, Kate had specified in her will that she was donating the paint-ing to the National Gallery in Cardiff.'

Kandy gets up again, without losing his smile.

'Then there's a moral to the tale, Inspector. Sark gains a bench, the museum in Cardiff a *Water Lilies* and Jérôme Morval a reason to part with the ugliest of his mistresses . . .'

'Monsieur Kandy,' Bénavides insists, his face blank. 'You are the expert who has been officially designated by DRAC in Normandy to work on the Murer collection . . .'

'So?'

'Given that we know Morval gave you the task of finding him a *Water Lilies*, that you were familiar with the Murer collection, and that you went to Sark on several occasions . . .'

'I might have whispered to my great friend that Kate Murer's *Water Lilies* was perhaps not a reproduction . . . Is that what you're insinuating?'

'Possibly.'

'Even if we assume that were the case, would there be anything illegal in it?'

'No, you're right.'

'So what exactly do you want to know?'

Sylvio Bénavides has hoisted himself up onto the third step, which puts him level with Amadou Kandy.

'The identity of Morval's murderer. The motive could be revenge.'

'Alysson Murer?'

'No, she has a firm alibi for the morning of the crime; she was behind her desk in Newcastle . . .'

'And so . . . ?'

'And so,' Bénavides presses on, 'there's nothing to say that Morval didn't continue looking for another *Water Lilies*, another sucker, with your help, Kandy.'

Amadou Kandy doesn't take his eyes off Sylvio. Staring contest, first to blink . . .

'If I had found one, Inspector, if I had found a *Water Lilies*, then I wouldn't be here in this wretched gallery. I'd have bought one of the Cape Verde islands near Dakar, declared independence, and built my own personal tax haven.' Amadou Kandy gives a toothy grin. 'And would you be asking me to give away a professional secret?'

'With a view to exposing your friend's murderer.'

'Let's be serious, Inspectors. Where on earth would I have been able to find another *Water Lilies* by Monet?'

Neither of the policemen answers. Both Bénavides and Sérénac get up and take a couple of steps towards the door.

'Just one more thing,' Sérénac says suddenly. 'Kate Murer didn't exactly leave the painting to the museum in Cardiff. In fact, it was the Theodore Robinson Foundation that received legal ownership, and it then loaned the work to the Welsh National Gallery.'

'So?'

Among the many posters hanging in the windows of the art gallery, Laurenç Sérénac has spotted the one for the 'International Young Painters Challenge', the same one that is pinned up in Stéphanie Dupain's classroom.

'So,' replies Sérénac. 'I think the Robinson Foundation is turning up a few too many times in this case.'

'Well that's normal, isn't it?' replies the gallery owner. 'It's an institution, that foundation. Particularly here, in Giverny . . .'

Kandy stands in front of the poster, momentarily lost in thought.

'Theodore Robinson, the Americans, their passion for Impressionism, their dollars . . . Who could imagine what Giverny would be like without all that?' he says, spreading his arms. 'You know what, Inspector?'

'What?'

'Basically I'm like Eugène Murer, here, in my shop. I'm just a grocer. But if I could go back in time, you know what I'd like to be?'

'A pastry chef?' Laurenç suggests.

Amadou Kandy explodes with laughter.

'I like you, the clever one,' he manages to articulate between hiccups. 'You too, by the way, Mr Anteater. No, Inspectors, not a pastry chef. I'm going to confess to you that I would, in fact, love to be ten years old. Still at school with a pretty teacher telling me I was a genius, and that I should put myself forward, like hundreds of other children in the world, for this competition organised by the Robinson Foundation to find a budding new artist.'

27

The sun will soon go down behind the slope. Fanette is in a hurry – she has to finish her painting. Her brush has never moved so quickly, painting in white and ochre patches, reproducing the mill and its wonky tower, the large cherry-red and silver tree in the middle of the courtyard, the waterwheel dipping into the running water. She is concentrating, but today it's the reverse, it's James who won't stop talking to her.

'Do you have friends, Fanette?'

What about you, James, do I ask if you have any?

'Of course. What do you think?'

'You're often alone . . .'

'You were the one who told me to be selfish. When I'm not paint-ing, I'm with my friends.'

James walks slowly into the field and folds his easels one by one. He always follows the same ritual when the sun starts to set.

'But since you ask, I'll tell you. They get on my nerves. Especially Vincent, the one you saw the other day. He was spying on us. He sticks to me like a pot of glue . . .'

'Of varnish!'

'What?'

'A pot of varnish. It's more useful than a pot of glue, for a girl who paints.'

Sometimes James thinks he's hilarious.

'There's also Camille, but he shows off a lot. He thinks he was born gifted, you know the type. The last one my age is Mary, but she cries all the time. The cry-baby. I don't like her.'

'You must never say that, Fanette.'

What did I say? I haven't said anything . . .

'Mustn't say what?'

'I've already told you, Fanette. Nature has been extremely kind to you, it's spoiled you, and don't pretend you don't understand. You're as cute as a button, intelligent, and full of mischief. An incredible gift for painting has been placed on your shoulders, as if a fairy had sprinkled gold dust over you. So you have to be careful, Fanette, because other people will always be jealous of you. They will be jealous, because their lives will be much less happy than yours.'

'That's rubbish! You're talking rubbish. Anyway, the only friend of mine who's worth bothering with is Paul. You haven't met him yet. I'll bring him with me, one evening. He's already agreed. We're going to travel the world together. He's going to take me to Japan, Australia, Africa so that I can paint.'

'I'm not sure there's a man who'll put up with that.'

Sometimes James annoys me too.

'Yes, there is. Paul!'

Fanette pulls a face at him as he turns around to put away his paint box.

There are times when James just doesn't get it. Besides, I don't understand what he's doing, it looks as if he's stuck in front of his tubes of paint.

'Are you stuck?'

'No, no. I'm fine.'

There's a funny expression on his face. Sometimes James is just strange.

'You know, James, for the Robinson Foundation I'd like to paint something other than the mill and the witch's house. That thing you said about reinventing the painting of Père Trognon doesn't really do it for me . . .'

'Really? Theodore Robinson did a—'

'I have my own idea,' Fanette cuts in. 'I'm going to paint some water lilies. But not in an old-man sort of way, like Monet. I'm going to paint a young person's *Water Lilies*.'

James looks at her as if she's just come out with the worst imaginable blasphemy.

He's gone all red. I think he's going to explode.

It's OK, you don't have to look like Père Trognon!

Fanette bursts out laughing.

'Monet . . . and his "old-man" *Water Lilies* . . .' James wheezes.

He coughs into his beard and then starts talking to her in a teacherly voice.

'I'm going to try to explain to you, Fanette. You know, Monet travelled a lot. All over Europe. He was inspired by all the paintings in the world – you've got to understand, they're all very different, people don't see things in the same way. Monet understood that, and he studied Japanese painting in particular. So after that, he didn't need to travel anymore, or go somewhere else. A lily pond was enough, for thirty years of his life, a perfectly ordinary pond, which was still big enough to revolutionise painting throughout the entire world . . . And even to revolutionise more than painting, Fanette. It was man's vision of nature that Monet revolutionised. A universal way of looking. Do you understand? Here, in Giverny! Less than a hundred metres away from this field! So, when you claim that Monet had an old man's way of seeing things . . .'

Blah blah blah . . .

'Well,' Fanette's bright voice explodes, 'I'm going to do the opposite. I was born here, so I'm going to start with the *Water Lilies* pond and finish with the rest of the world! You'll see, my *Water Lilies* will be unique; even Monet wouldn't have dared to paint them the way I will. Like a rainbow!'

Suddenly James bends down and gives Fanette a hug.

He's being odd again, he's got that strange, worried expression on his face. It doesn't look like him.

'I'm sure you're right, Fanette. You're the artist, after all, you're the one who knows.'

He's holding me too tightly, he's hurting me . . .

'Don't listen to anyone but yourself,' James goes on. 'Including me. You're going to win this Robinson Foundation prize, Fanette. You've got to win it! Do you hear me? So, off you go now, it's late, your mother will be waiting for you. And don't forget your painting.'

Fanette heads off across the wheat field. James calls one last piece of advice after her.

'To kill that gift within you would be the worst of crimes!'

Sometimes James says some very strange things.

James watches the slim figure running across the field, as he bends once more towards his paint box. He waits for Fanette to disappear behind the bridge, then opens it, shaking. He didn't want to let it show in front of Fanette, but he's drenched in sweat, gripped by a kind of panic. His old fingers are trembling in spite of himself. The rusty hinges squeak slightly.

James reads the letters engraved in the soft wood inside the box of paints.

SHE'S MINE,
HERE, NOW AND FOR EVER

The carved words are followed by two simple lines that cross one another. A cross. James has understood that it's a threat. A death threat. His thin, elderly body is shaken by uncontrollable tremors. The presence of the police, searching everywhere in the village because of that corpse and the murderer who hasn't been found, isn't reassuring at all. The whole atmosphere of the place oppresses him.

He reads the words, again and again. Who could have written that?

The writing looks clumsy, hasty. The vandal must have taken advantage of him falling asleep to carve this morbid threat in his paint box. It wouldn't have been difficult. He often falls asleep in the field, by his canvases, when Fanette isn't around to wake him up. But what could it mean? Who could have written those words? And does he have to take them seriously?

James studies the curtain of poplars that closes off the sweep of the meadow. The letters seem to be inscribed on his brain, as if engraved on the tender flesh of his forehead: *She's mine, here, now and for ever.* Another question troubles him now, an obsessive question that worries him even more than the desire to know who supplied the threat. His hands are shaking. He wouldn't be able to hold a brush, a knife, anything at all.

She's mine, here, now and for ever.

The seven words go round and round in his mind like some infernal merry-go-round.

Who is the threat addressed to?

He studies his surroundings as if a monster were about to emerge from the ears of wheat.

Who is in danger here?

Fanette, or him?

28

At last I pass through the gate to the mill. I feel as if my knees are about to buckle. My right arm too, from resting on the damned cane. Neptune trots by my side. For once he waits for me.

Good dog.

I take out my keys.

I think briefly of Patricia Morval. I wonder how she is taking my revelations about her husband's murder. Has she been able to resist the temptation to call the police? Even if it's too late, far too late to save anyone . . . The trap has already closed. No policeman can do anything now.

As for me, what would I do in her place?

I look up. I spot young Fanette in the distance, running through the field and passing the iron bridge. Her American is still in the middle of the wheat. He's bound to have told her scary stories about my mill, about the pair of ogres, the nasty owners who didn't like

Monet and wanted to cut down the poplars, tidy up the haystacks, allow the water-lily pond to dry up and build a starch factory in the meadow . . . The usual nonsense. The idiot! At his age, frightening children with such stories . . .

He's there every day, that American painter, that James whose surname no one knows. He stands there each day in the same place, facing the mill. He could have been standing there for ever, you might say. As if he too were part of the scenery. As if an artist God had painted him in turn. Had painted all of us. Until he felt like erasing everything. A dab of the brush and pffft, we're gone!

James will watch Fanette leaving, as he does every day, then he'll go to sleep in the field until tomorrow.

Goodnight, James.

29

Fanette goes home again. She runs. What she loves is when the lights in the streets of Giverny seem to come on as she passes.

It's magic!

But it's still too early for that today. The sun has barely started to hide itself. Fanette lives in a little house that is beginning to fall apart on the Rue du Château d'Eau. She doesn't care, she doesn't complain, she is well aware that her mother does what she can. She cleans the houses of all the well-to-do people in the village, from dawn till dusk.

Just living here, in the middle of the village, a hundred metres from Monet's garden, even in a rotten house – what more could she have hoped for?

Her mother welcomes her from behind the kitchen work surface, a simple wooden plank set on piles of bricks. She smiles wearily.

'It's late, Fanette. You know very well that I don't like you hanging around outside in the evening. Particularly at the moment, with that crime that happened a few days ago, and the murderer hasn't been found . . .'

My mother always has that sad, tired look on her face. She

119

always wears that ugly blue overall and she's always peeling vegetables, cooking soups that last a whole week, saying that I don't help her enough, that at my age I should . . . If I show her my painting, then perhaps . . .

'I've finished it, Mum.'

Fanette lifts her painting of the Moulin des Chennevières level with the work surface.

'Later. My hands are dirty. Put it over there.'

As usual . . .

'I'm going to paint another one, anyway. A *Water Lilies*. James told me that—'

'Who's this James?'

'The American painter, Mum, I've told you before.'

'No . . .'

The carrot peelings rain down into a stoneware bowl.

'I did!'

I did I did I did I did. I swear! You're doing this on purpose, Mum.

'I don't want you hanging about with strangers, Fanette! Do you hear me? Just because I'm bringing you up on my own doesn't mean you have to spend all your time outside. And don't sit there like a lump, pick up a knife. If I have to do the cooking all by myself I'll be here for an hour!'

'Our teacher told us about a competition, Mum. A painting competition.'

It's our teacher! She can't say anything. And anyway, she isn't saying anything, she's just looking at her turnip.

Fanette stands up very straight and goes on:

'James told me that . . . well, everyone says I can win it. That I have a good chance, if I work hard.'

'What would you win?'

'Lessons at an art school, in New York . . .'

'What?'

The turnip has been stabbed right through the heart. It isn't going to recover . . .

'Tell me again, Fanette, what is this competition?'

'Or maybe Tokyo. St Petersburg. Canberra.'

I'm sure she doesn't even know where that is, but it frightens her anyway . . .

'You also win dollars . . . Lots of them!'

Mum sighs. She decapitates a second turnip.

'If your teacher keeps on filling your head with such ideas, I'm going to have a word with her.'

I don't care, I'll enter the competition anyway . . .

'And I'd also like to have a word with this James of yours.'

Fanette's mother energetically slides vegetables from the work bench to the sink. The carrots and turnips plunge into the water, splashing her blue overall. She bends down to lift a bag of potatoes on to the plank.

She isn't even asking me to help her. That's not a good sign. She's babbling words that I don't understand. I'll have to ask her to repeat them.

'Are you going to leave me, Fanette? Is that it?'

And so it begins . . .

I'm exploding! I'm exploding inside my head, but no one can see it. No one but me. Mum, I want to do the washing up. I want to lay the table. I want to wipe it down with a sponge. I want to do the dusting. I want to go and get the broom, use it, put it away. I want to do all the things that a little girl should do, I want to do everything, without complaining, without crying. On condition that I'm allowed to paint. I just want to be allowed to paint.

Is that too much to ask?

Mum is still eyeing me suspiciously. She's never happy when I don't do anything and she always looks at me strangely when I do too much. I think it's New York that she can't get her head around, and the other cities too, especially when I added Japan, Russia, Australia, all at the same time!

'Three weeks of art school, Mum? Three weeks isn't a long time. It's nothing.'

She looks at me as if I am insane.

Since we finished eating she hasn't said a word. She's ruminating. It's a bad sign when she ruminates. I've never seen her ruminate and then say something I liked.

Fanette's mother gets up just as her daughter is putting away the tea towels, hanging flat on the rail rather than hurled in a pile as usual. She sends the temperature plunging:

'I've made my decision, Fanette. I don't want to hear anything more about painting competitions, American painters or anything else. It's all over and done with. I will go and talk to your teacher.'

I don't say anything. I don't even cry. I just let the rage boil up inside me. I know why Mum is saying this. She's said it a thousand times.

The old refrain. On a loop, recited by heart.

The song of lamentation.

'Little daughter of mine, I don't want you to waste your life as I did. When I was your age I too believed all those stories. I too had dreams. I too was pretty and men made promises to me.

'But look! Look at me today!

'Look at the holes in the roof, the mildewed walls, the damp, the stench; remember the cold whistling through the windows this winter; look at my hands, my poor hands, the most elegant thing I possessed, fairy hands, how many times did I hear that, Fanette, when I was your age, that I had fairy hands. Fairy hands that now spend their time washing other people's toilets.

'Don't be taken in as I was, Fanette. I won't let them do it. Don't trust anyone other than me, Fanette. Not your James, not your teacher, nor anyone else.'

OK, Mum. I will listen to you. I want to trust you.

But in that case, Mum, you'll have to tell me everything. Everything. Even the things we never talk about. The things we're not allowed to say!

I'll scratch your back, you scratch mine.

Fanette takes a sponge and spends a long time cleaning the grey tile, the one on which her mother writes her list of vegetables.

She waits a while for it to dry, then picks up the white chalk. She knows her mother is watching over her shoulder. She writes, in delicate round handwriting. The handwriting of a teacher.

Who is my father?

122

Then, just underneath:

Who?

She hears her mother crying behind her.

Why did he leave?

Why did we not follow him?

There is still some room at the bottom of the tile. The white chalk squeaks.

Who?

Who?

Who?

Who?

Fanette turns over her painting, her 'witch's mill'. She sets it on a chair, then without saying a word she goes to her room. She hears her mother weeping down below. As she always does.

Weeping isn't an answer, Mum.

Fanette knows that tomorrow the whole thing will have blown over, that they won't mention any of this again, and that her mother will have wiped the slate clean.

It's late now.

Probably nearly midnight. Mum must have been asleep for a while – she starts cleaning other people's houses very early in the morning. Often she has already left and come back by the time I get up.

My bedroom window looks out on to the Rue du Château d'Eau. The street is on a steep slope; even from the first floor you're barely more than a metre from the ground. I could jump, if I wanted to. Often in the evening, from my window, I talk to Vincent. Vincent hangs about in the streets every evening. His parents don't care. Paul is never allowed out in the evenings.

Fanette weeps.

Vincent looks at me without much of a clue about what to do. I'd rather Paul were here. Paul understands me. Paul knows how to talk to me. Vincent just listens, that's all. It's all he knows how to do.

I talk to him about my father. I only know that my mother fell pregnant when she was very young. Sometimes I think I'm the daughter of a painter, an American painter, that the only thing he left me with was his talent; that Mum posed naked for him outside, surrounded by nature, and she was beautiful, Mum was very, very beautiful – there are photographs of her downstairs in an album. And of me too, as a baby. But none of my father.

Vincent listens. He takes the hand that Fanette dangles down the wall and grips it tightly.

I go on talking. I tell him I think my father and mother were madly in love with each other, completely head over heels, and that they were both beautiful. Then my father left to go somewhere else and my mother couldn't stop him. Perhaps Mum didn't know that she was pregnant? Perhaps Mum didn't even know my father's name. Perhaps she simply loved him too much to hold him back; my father was someone good, someone faithful, perhaps he would have stayed and brought me up if he had known I existed, but Mum loved him too much to put him in a cage by telling him.

It's complicated in my head, but that's the only way it could be, Vincent, don't you think? Otherwise, where would I have got this mad desire to paint? This desire to fly away? Who else would have given me these things, these dreams that fill my head?

Vincent grips Fanette's hand. He grips it too hard. The horrible bracelet he always wears around his wrist digs into the little girl's flesh, as if to imprint there the first name engraved on the bracelet.

On other evenings, I sometimes study the clouds hiding the moon and tell myself that my father must be one of those rich bastards my mum cleans for. That I bump into him on the Rue Claude Monet, and I don't know he's my father, but he knows. He's just a big fat pig who slept with my mother, who forced her to do disgusting things. Perhaps he even slips Mum some cash from time to time. Sometimes, when I see men in the street giving me sidelong glances it drives me mad, it makes me want to vomit. It's horrible. But I don't tell Vincent any of that.

Tonight, the clouds are leaving the moon in peace.

'My father was someone who was just passing through,' says Fanette.

'Don't worry, Fanette,' says Vincent. 'I'm here.'

'Someone passing through. I'm like him. I have to leave, I have to fly away.'

Vincent grips her hand even more tightly than before.

'I'm here, Fanette. I'm here . . .'

Not far away, in the Rue du Château d'Eau, Neptune is chasing moths.

DAY EIGHT

20 May 2010

(Vernon Police Station)

Acrimony

30

Inspector Laurenç Sérénac is helpless with laughter. From time to time, through the window, he glances discreetly at the largest office in Vernon police station, Room 101, the one used most often for interrogations. Jacques Dupain is sitting with his back to him, tapping impatiently on the arm of his chair. Sérénac tiptoes into the corridor and whispers conspiratorially to Sylvio Bénavides:

'We'll let him stew a while longer . . .'

He tugs his deputy by the sleeve.

'What I'm most proud of,' he says, 'is the way I've set the scene. Come and have a look, Sylvio.'

They walk down the corridor, heading for the interrogation room.

'How many are there, Sylvio?'

Bénavides can't help smiling.

'A hundred and seventy-one pairs! Maury brought in three more a quarter of an hour ago.'

In the room where Jacques Dupain is waiting, the policemen have stored all the pairs of boots collected in the village of Giverny since the previous day. They have been placed in every corner of the room, on the shelves and on the tables, on the window sills, on the chairs, piled on the ground or balancing on top of each other. They come in all colours, from fluorescent yellow to fire-station red, although the classic khaki green predominates. The boots are sorted according to wear, size and make, and each pair bears a small cardboard tag detailing the name of its owner.

Sérénac doesn't conceal his jubilation.

'You've taken a photograph, Sylvio, I hope. I love this kind of madness! There's nothing better to put a client in the right mood. It looks like a work of contemporary art. With those seventeen bar-becues in your garden, you should appreciate a collection like this.'

'Yes,' says Inspector Bénavides, not bothering to look up. 'It's amazing, from an aesthetic point of view. A first. You could produce an exhibition. On the other hand . . .'

'You're too serious, Sylvio,' Sérénac interrupts him.

'I know.'

Bénavides studies some sheets of paper and puts them in order.

'I'm sorry, I must be too much of a policeman. Are you interested in the inquiry, boss?'

'You have no sense of humour this morning.'

'To tell you the truth, I barely slept last night. Apparently I was taking up too much room in the bed, according to Béatrice. I should add that she's had to sleep on her back for the last three months. As it was, I ended up on the sofa.'

Sérénac pats him on the shoulder.

'Come on, it'll all be over in a week and you'll be a dad. And then neither of you will be able to sleep. Do you want a coffee? We can have a catch-up in the common room.'

'A tea.'

'Of course, I'm an idiot. No sugar. You still haven't decided to go for first names?'

'I'll think about it. I can assure you, Chief, I'm really working on it.'

Sérénac laughs uproariously.

'I like you, Sylvio. And what's more, you – just you – hunt

down more information than a whole station of investigators in the Tarn!'

'You don't know how right you are. I worked all night again.'

'On your sofa? While your wife was snoring away on her back?'

'Yes.'

Bénavides grins. The two policemen go up three steps and then enter a large box room, the ten square metres of which are cluttered with an assortment of furniture: two tired sofas covered in orange fabric with a long fringe, a lilac armchair, and a Formica table laid with a cafetière, mismatched cups and some rusty spoons. A feeble lightbulb hangs from the ceiling, surrounded by a scorched cylindrical red cardboard shade. Sylvio slumps into the lilac armchair while Laurenç makes the hot drinks.

'Right, Chief,' Sylvio begins, 'shall we start with the exhibition, since you seem to be so fond of it?'

Bénavides consults his notes.

'We have a hundred and seventy-one pairs of boots, ranging from size thirty-five to size forty-six. We didn't keep any that were smaller than thirty-five. From the ones brought in, we have identified fifteen fishermen and twenty-one huntsmen, with permits. Including Jacques Dupain. We also have around thirty licensed hikers. However, as you already know, Chief, none of the hundred and seventy-one pairs has a sole that matches the plaster cast Maury made of the print near Jérôme Morval's body.'

Sérénac pours boiling water into the cafetière as he replies.

'We suspected as much. The murderer wasn't going to give himself away. Conversely we could say that it makes a hundred and seventy-one Givernois innocent . . .'

'If you say so . . .'

'And that Jacques Dupain is not among those hundred and seventy-one . . . We'll leave him to sit there a while longer. With regard to the rest, where have we got to?'

Inspector Bénavides unfolds his famous three-column sheet.

'You really are a maniac, Sylvio . . .'

'I know. I'm building this inquiry the way I built my terrace or my veranda. With patience and precision.'

'And I'm sure that at home, Béatrice is as fed up with the sight of you as I am in the office . . .'

'Exactly . . . But my terrace is still a masterpiece.'

Sérénac sighs. 'So, go on with those stupid columns of yours . . .'

'They're filling up, gradually . . . mistresses, *Water Lilies*, children . . .'

'And we'll have solved the investigation when we're able to draw a big horizontal line linking the three columns. Except that, at the moment, we're paddling about so much that even a hundred and seventy-one pairs of boots may not be enough . . .'

Bénavides yawns. The lilac armchair seems to be gradually swallowing him up.

'So, go on Sylvio, I'm listening. This evening's news.'

'Column one, the ophthalmologist and his lovers. We're starting to collect statements, but we still don't have anything that would justify a crime of passion. Nothing new, either, on the meaning of those wretched numbers on the back of each photograph. But I'll keep trying. To cap it all, we have no news from Aline Malétras in Boston, and we've reached a dead end as to the identity of the stranger in the fifth photograph . . .'

'The maid on her knees in front of Morval in the sitting room?'

'You have an excellent memory, Chief. As for the others, I've tried to order the husbands who have been cheated on by their capacity for jealousy. Jacques Dupain is without contest at the top of the list, except that we have no tangible proof of adultery on his wife's part. Have you anything new on your side, Inspector? Did you meet with Stéphanie Dupain yesterday?'

'Joker!'

Sylvio Bénavides looks at him, perplexed. He interrupts the digestion of the armchair as he struggles to sit up.

'Meaning what?'

'Joker. Full stop. I'm not going to tell about those lilac eyes sending out SOS messages, or you'll report me to the magistrate. So I'm playing my joker. Wait and see. I'll take care of that section of the investigation personally, if you prefer. But I agree with your analysis. We have no proof of adultery involving Jérôme Morval

129

and Stéphanie Dupain, but Jacques Dupain still fits the profile of our number-one suspect. So, let's move on, your column number two: the *Water Lilies*?'

'Nothing new since our meeting with Amadou Kandy yesterday. You were supposed to contact your colleagues in the art division.'

'OK. OK. I'll do it. I'll talk to them again tomorrow. I'm also going to have a look around Claude Monet's gardens . . .'

'With Stéphanie Dupain's class?'

The steam from the cafetière curls up above Sérénac's untidy hair. The inspector stares at his deputy with concern.

'It's incredible, you seem to know everything about everything, Sylvio. Have you been recording our conversations and spending your nights listening to the tapes?'

Bénavides yawns noisily.

'Why? Is the school visit a secret? For my part, I'm having a meeting tomorrow with the curator of the Musée des Beaux-Arts, in Rouen.'

'And for what reason might that be?'

'Initiative and autonomy, that's what you recommended, isn't it? Let's just say that I want to get a better grasp of the story behind Monet's paintings and his *Water Lilies*.'

'You know, Sylvio, if I were suspicious by nature, then I could take that as a lack of confidence in your immediate superior.'

Sylvio Bénavides' eyes, though weary, gleam with mischief.

'Joker!'

Inspector Sérénac carefully pours some coffee into a cracked cup. He puts a teabag and hot water in another, which he holds out to his deputy.

'I'm really having trouble understanding the Norman psychology, Sylvio. You should be by your wife's bedside instead of working overtime . . .'

'Don't worry. I'm just a tad obsessive, that's all. I know I look like a lapdog, but I can be stubborn enough. I don't know anything about art, so I just need to do some catching up. Listen, this last column, number three. The child.'

Sérénac pulls a face as he sips his coffee.

'I've been through the list of children supplied by Stéphanie Dupain. Ideally I tried to find a girl or a boy who is around ten years old and whose mother worked as a cleaner, possibly at the Morval house, about ten years ago . . .'

'And who wore a blue overall and a little short skirt . . . So, how did you get on?'

'Nothing. There isn't a single child on the list who matches that profile. There are nine children in Giverny who are more or less the same age, roughly between nine and eleven. Among those parents, there are two single mothers. The first works at the bakery in Gasny, the village on the other side of the plain, and the other one drives the local buses.'

'That's not uninteresting . . .'

'No, not uninteresting, as you say. I've also found a divorced mother who teaches at a secondary school in Évreux. All the other parents are in couples, and none of the mothers is a cleaner, either now or ten years ago.'

Sérénac leans against the Formica table. He looks disappointed.

'If you want my advice, Sylvio, there are only two possible explanations for your failure. The first is that your hypothesis about an illegitimate child is completely wrong. That's the most likely scenario. The second is that this child that Morval is wishing a happy birthday on the postcard found in his pocket isn't from Giverny, nor is his mistress, the girl in the blue overall giving him a treat. She may not even be the child's mother. So . . .'

Bénavides hasn't touched his tea. He looks up shyly.

'If I may be so bold, boss . . . There could be a third explanation.'

'Ah?'

Sylvio hesitates for a moment.

'Well . . . quite simply . . . the list supplied by Stéphanie Dupain could be wrong.'

'I'm sorry?'

Sérénac has spilled half of his coffee. Sylvio sinks back into the lilac armchair but goes on talking:

'Well, there is nothing to prove that this list of children is accurate. And Stéphanie Dupain is another suspect in this case . . .'

'I don't see the connection between her hypothetical flirtation with Morval and the children in her class.'

'Nor do I. But then there are so many other factors in this case where we can't see a connection. If we had enough time, we'd compare this list of children with a list of all the families in Giverny, first names, occupations past and present, the mothers' maiden names. Everything. You can say what you like, but that phrase of Aragon's written on the card in Morval's pocket, *The crime of dreaming, I agree to its creation*, has a direct connection with the school in Giverny; it's a poem that the village children learn by heart. You told me that yourself, Chief, and you heard it from Stéphanie Dupain.'

Sérénac drains the rest of his cup in one go.

'OK, I hear what you are saying. So imagine if you are right, what would we do next?'

'I don't know. Sometimes I feel as if the Givernois are hiding something from us. Like the kind of omertà you'd find in a Corsican village.'

'What makes you think that? They're not normally your kind of thing, impressions?'

A worrying light passes behind Sylvio's eyes.

'It's just that . . . there's something else about my third column, Chief. The kids. I warn you, it's strange . . . More than strange, in fact. Startling might be the word.'

31

This morning, in Giverny, the weather is wonderful. For once I have opened the sitting-room window and have decided to do some tidying up. The sun slips into my room with suspicious timidity, as if it were entering this place for the first time. Because there's no dust in my house for the sunlight to set dancing, it simply settles on the sideboard, the table, the chairs, making the wood seem brighter.

My black *Water Lilies* lurks in the shadows. I defy anyone, even looking up through my open window on the fourth floor, to notice the painting from outside.

I take a little tour. In the sitting room everything is in its place, which is why I'm reluctant to go rummaging about, above the wardrobe, at the bottom of the drawers, or to go down to the garage and empty mouldy cardboard boxes, lift bin bags split in two or exhume cases that haven't been opened in years. In decades, even. I know what I'm looking for, though. I know exactly what I want to find, I just have no idea where I've put it, after all this time.

I know what you're going to say, you're saying to yourself that the old woman is losing her memory. You can think that if you like . . . But don't tell me you've never turned the whole house upside down just to find something, an object you knew only one thing about: that you'd never thrown it away.

There's nothing more annoying than that, is there?

I'll tell you the truth: the thing I'm so keen to find is a cardboard box – plain, the size of a shoebox, full of old photographs. It's hardly original. I read somewhere that you can now put a whole lifetime of photographs on a memory stick the size of a cigarette lighter. That's progress, I suppose.

Without much hope, I go through the chest of drawers, slide a hand under the Normandy wardrobe, behind the rows of books.

There is nothing, of course.

I have to resign myself to the fact that what I'm looking for isn't within easy reach. My box must be somewhere in the garage, under the layers of sediment that have accumulated over the years.

I'm still hesitating. Is it worth it? Do I have to go to the trouble of moving all that bric-a-brac just to get my hands on a photograph, one photograph? A photograph that I've never thrown away, I'm sure of that. It is the only one that holds the memory of a face I would so love to see one last time.

Albert Rosalba.

Without reaching a decision, I take another look at my tidy sitting room. There are just those two boots drying by the chimney breast. Well, drying . . . Two boots that I left there, I should say. Obviously the fire is not lit.

It isn't Christmas yet.

32

Even though Sylvio Bénavides put as much emphasis as he could on those last words, his boss still doesn't seem to be taking him seriously. He gets up and pours himself another cup of coffee with a distracted air, as if he were still counting the boots in his head. His deputy brings his cup of tea to his lips and grimaces. No sugar.

Sérénac turns back towards him.

'OK, I'm listening, Sylvio. Startle me . . .'

'You know me, Chief,' Bénavides explains. 'I've gone through everything that might provide a link between Giverny and the story of an illegitimate child. In the end I found this in the local police archives . . .'

He places his cup of tea on the floor and rifles through the bundle of papers at his feet, then hands his superior a report from the police station at Pacy-sur-Eure: a yellowing piece of paper with a dozen lines on it.

Sérénac swallows hard. The cracked cup trembles in his hand.

'I'll sum it up for you, boss. I don't think you'll like it much. It's a small news story. A child was found drowned in the brook leading off the Epte, in Giverny. In the very place where Jérôme Morval was murdered. Killed in exactly the same way – the same ritual, as you put it – apart from the stabbing: the child's skull was crushed with a rock, and then the head was submerged in the stream.'

'Good God . . . What age was the child?'

'Just a few months from turning eleven.'

Cold sweat runs down the inspector's forehead.

'Bloody hell . . .'

Bénavides clutches the arms of his chair.

'There's just one hitch, Inspector. This story happened a very long time ago.' He pauses, dreading Sérénac's reaction. '1937, to be precise . . .'

Sérénac collapses onto the sofa, his eyes fixed on the yellowing report.

'1937? What on earth is going on here? A kid of eleven died in

134

exactly the same place as Morval, in exactly the same way, but in 1937? What kind of madness is this?'

'I don't know, Chief, but take a look, it's all in the police report. If you think about it, it could have nothing to do with our case . . . Back then, the child could have slipped on a stone, cracked his skull and then drowned. A horrible accident. Full stop.'

'What was this child's name?'

'Albert Rosalba. His family left Giverny shortly after the tragedy. There's been no news of them since . . .'

Laurenç Sérénac reaches out for his coffee and takes another sip.

'Christ, Sylvio, your story's still worrying. I don't like this kind of coincidence, I really don't. As if the mystery weren't confusing enough already, and now we have this as well . . .'

Sylvio gathers the papers scattered at his feet.

'Can I ask you something, Chief?'

'Go ahead.'

'What worries me most is that since the very start of this case, our instincts have been contradictory. I've thought about it all night. You've always been sure that it's all about Stéphanie Dupain, that she's in danger. I, and I don't know why, am convinced that the key lies in my third column, that there's a murderer walking around, preparing to strike again, but it's the life of a child that's in danger, an eleven-year-old child . . .'

Laurenç gets up and gives his deputy a friendly clap on the shoulder.

'Perhaps that's because you're going to be a dad any minute. As for me, being a bachelor, I'm less interested in children than in their mothers, even if they are married. It's just a matter of who you identify with. That's logical, isn't it?

'Perhaps. Each to his own column, then,' Sylvio says softly. 'Let's just hope that we're not both right.'

Sérénac is amazed by this last remark. He looks carefully at his deputy but can only see a face that is drawn and two eyes that are weary of staying open. Bénavides still hasn't finished going through all his pieces of paper. Sérénac knows that before he leaves this evening, his deputy, even though he's exhausted, will take the time to photocopy everything and put it all in the red file box. Then he will put that box in the right place on the shelf in the room in the basement. M for Morval. That's what his deputy is like . . .

'There will be an explanation for everything, Sylvio,' Sérénac says. 'There will be a way of fitting all the pieces of the puzzle together. There has to be.'

'And Jacques Dupain?' Bénavides sighs. 'Don't you think we've left him stewing for long enough?'

'Bugger! I'd forgotten all about him.'

To sit on the desk in Room 101, Laurenç Sérénac has had to move about ten blue boots and stack them in an unstable pile. Jacques Dupain is still furious. His right hand is constantly rubbing his brown moustache and his unshaven cheeks, revealing his mounting annoyance.

'I still don't understand what you want from me, Inspector. You've kept me here for almost an hour. Are you going to tell me why?'

'A conversation. We just want to have a conversation with you.'

Sérénac spreads his arms in a broad gesture that takes in the exhibition of boots.

'We're casting our net very wide, Monsieur Dupain, as you can see. Almost all the inhabitants of the village have given us a pair of boots. They are cooperating. We are checking their boots don't correspond to the print taken at the crime scene, and then we leave them alone. It's as simple as that. But . . .'

Jacques Dupain's right hand clutches at his moustache while his left hand nervously grips the arm of his chair.

'How many times do I have to tell you? I can't find my damned boots! I thought I'd left them in the shed beside the school, but they're not there. Yesterday I had to borrow a friend's . . .'

Sérénac tries an ironic smile.

'Strange, isn't it, Monsieur Dupain? Why would someone go to the trouble of stealing a pair of muddy boots? Size forty-three, your size. Exactly the same size as the print measured at the crime scene.'

Sylvio Bénavides is standing at the end of the room with his back to a shelf – the section of new and nearly new boots ranging from size thirty-nine to forty-two. He watches the conversation with weary amusement. At least it's keeping him awake. He has an answer in his head to Sérénac's question, but he isn't about to prompt the suspect with it.

'I don't know,' Dupain says, getting annoyed. 'Perhaps because that person is a murderer and came up with the idea of stealing the first pair of boots he could find, so he could frame some other poor guy?'

That's the answer Bénavides expected. This guy Dupain is no idiot, he thinks.

'And he picked you,' Sérénac presses. 'As if by chance.'

'Well he had to pick somebody, so he picked me. What do you mean, "as if by chance"? I don't like what you're implying, Inspector.'

'Then just be quiet and listen. What were you doing on the morning of the murder of Jérôme Morval?'

Dupain's feet draw large circles in the space from which all the rubber boots have been expelled, like an angry little boy clearing toys from his garden.

'So you suspect me, then? At six in the morning I was still in bed with my wife, as I am every morning . . .'

'That's another strange thing, Monsieur Dupain. On Tuesday mornings, according to our witnesses, you usually get up at dawn to go hunting rabbits on the land belonging to your fiend Patrick Delaunay. Sometimes with a group. More often alone . . . Why break with that habit on the morning of the crime, particularly that Tuesday?'

A silence. Dupain's fingers go on torturing his moustache.

'Well what bloody reason do you think would make a man want to stay in bed with his wife?'

Jacques Dupain stares straight at Laurenç Sérénac's face. His eyes are like two fists. Nothing about the confrontation escapes Sylvio Bénavides. Once again he thinks Jacques Dupain is defending himself rather well.

'No one's reproaching you for that, Monsieur Dupain. Nobody. Don't worry, we'll check out your alibi. As to motive . . .'

Sérénac studiedly pushes away the boots piled up at the end of the desk and produces the photograph of Stéphanie and Jérôme Morval, hand in hand on the path up the hill.

'Jealousy might be a motive, don't you think?'

Jacques Dupain barely glances at the picture, as if he already knows what's in it.

'Don't cross the line, Inspector. Treat me as a suspect by all means, if that amuses you, why not? But don't involve Stéphanie in your little game. Not her. Are we in agreement?'

Sylvio is wondering whether to intervene. He has a sense that the situation could degenerate at any second. Sérénac continues to play with his prey. He is holding two blue boots in each hand, distractedly trying to reconstitute the pairs. He looks up.

'That's a bit meagre as a defence, Monsieur Dupain. In a legal sense, I would even call it a tautological defence: defending one-self against a possible motive of jealousy by displaying an excess of jealousy . . .'

Dupain gets to his feet. He is shorter than the inspector, by at least twenty centimetres.

'Don't mess me about, Sérénac. I understand your little game perfectly. If you come any closer . . .'

Sérénac doesn't deign to look up at him. He throws one boot aside and picks up another, then gives a smile.

'Surely you're not going to tell me, Monsieur Dupain, that you want to obstruct the smooth running of our investigation?'

Sylvio Bénavides will never know how far Jacques Dupain would have gone that day but he doesn't care. And that's why, just in time, he rests a soothing hand on Jacques' shoulder, and gestures to Sérénac to calm down.

33

Sylvio Bénavides walked Jacques Dupain out of the police station. He used the polite set phrases, the usual veiled apologies. Inspector Bénavides is good at that sort of thing. Jacques Dupain got into his Ford, still furious, and in a gesture of defiance, he drove across the car park with his foot to the floor. Bénavides closed his eyes, then came back to the office.

Sylvio Bénavides is also good at judging his superior's state of mind.

'What did you think of that, Sylvio?'

'You were hard on him, Chief. Too hard. Much too hard.'

'OK, let's blame that on my Occitan side. But apart from that, what did you think?'

'I don't know. Dupain isn't innocent, if that's what you mean. Having said that, you can understand him. He has a wife that, naturally, he wants to hold on to. You're certainly not going to disagree with me there. But that doesn't make him a murderer . . .'

'Good God, Sylvio. And that business about having his boots stolen? It doesn't stand up for a second! Neither does his alibi. His wife, Stéphanie, told me he went hunting on the morning of the crime . . .'

'It's worrying, I agree. We'll have to compare their statements. But we also have to recognise that the evidence is piling up a little too easily. First the photograph of his wife strolling with Morval that we were sent anonymously, then his hunting boots disappearing . . . You could think that someone's trying to make him look suspicious. And then as far as that boot-print is concerned, he's not the only one who needs an excuse. We haven't managed to winkle out all the inhabitants of Giverny by any means. We've been met by closed doors, empty houses, Parisians who are hardly ever here. We need time, lots more time . . .'

'Damn it . . .'

Sérénac picks up an orange boot and holds it between two fingers by the heel.

'It's him, Sylvio! Don't ask me why, but I know it's Jacques Dupain!'

Laurenç Sérénac suddenly hurls the orange boot at the ten or so sitting on the shelf opposite him.

'Strike!' Sylvio Bénavides observes placidly.

His boss doesn't say anything for a few minutes, then suddenly raises his voice again.

'We're not getting anywhere, Sylvio. *Anywhere*! I want to see the whole team in one hour.'

Laurenç Sérénac, nerves on edge, is struggling to get some energy into the team brainstorming session he has called at Vernon police station. The bright room with the tatty curtains is flooded with sunlight. Sylvio Bénavides is dozing at the end of the table. Between two little snores he hears his boss summarising, yet again, the different lines of enquiry, and setting out the impressive list of leads that they need to follow: identifying Morval's mistresses and questioning their relatives, looking into the illegal art trade and in particular keeping a close eye on Amadou Kandy, finding out more about this Theodore Robinson Foundation, and also a closer examination of the strange case of a similar drowning in 1937. They also need to question the Givernois again, particularly the neighbours, and especially those close to Morval, those who claim they have no boots at home, or who have an eleven-year-old child. Finally they need to look into the clients at his surgery.

It's a lot, Inspector Sérénac is aware of that – far too much for a team of five people, not all of whom are working on the case full time. They will have to shoulder their picks and strike at random, then trust to luck. Hope that just one of their blows hits the spot. They're used to it, though; it's always like that. The only aspect of the operation that Sérénac hasn't reminded his colleagues of is checking up on Jacques Dupain's alibi. He's keeping that one for himself.

'Any other ideas?'

Officer Ludovic Maury has listened to his superior's muscular list of orders with the weary attention of a substitute footballer in a changing room. The sun behind him is roasting the back of his neck. During the session, he studied – yet again – the photographs of the crime scene spread out in front of him: the stream, the bridge, the wash house. The body of Jérôme Morval, feet on the bank and head in the water. He wonders why ideas come at one time and not at others, and raises a finger.

'Yes, Ludo?'

'Just an idea, Laurenç. Given where we are with this case, don't you think that maybe we should drag the bed of the stream in Giverny?'

'What do you mean?' Sérénac sounds irritated, as if he were suddenly annoyed by Officer Maury's southern use of his first name.

Sylvio Bénavides wakes with a start.

'Well,' Maury goes on, 'we've looked everywhere around the crime scene, we have photographs, prints, samples. We've also looked in the brook itself, of course. But I don't think we've dragged the riverbed. Stirred up the sand, I mean, dug down below. It occurred to me when I was looking at the orientation of Morval's pockets in the photograph: they're angled down towards the stream. Some object, anything at all, could have slipped into the water and got stuck in the sand.'

Sérénac runs his hand over his forehead.

'It's not a stupid idea. And why not, after all? Sylvio, have you woken up? Put a team together for me as quickly as you can, with a sedimentologist or whatever they're called. You know, a scientist who can give you the precise date of all the crap we're going to drag up from the riverbed.'

'OK,' says Bénavides, hoisting up his eyelids like a weightlifter lifting weights. 'I'll have everything ready for the day after tomorrow. Tomorrow, I should remind you, is cultural heritage day for us both. A visit to Claude Monet's gardens for you and the Musée des Beaux-Arts in Rouen for me.'

34

Rue Blanche Hoschedé-Monet. The evening light slips through the shutters of the Dupains' bedroom with its sloping roof. Between Jacques Dupain's nervous fingers are twisted glossy pages featuring Normandy cottages for sale.

'I'm going to get a lawyer, Stéphanie. I'll accuse them of harassment. That policeman, that Sérénac guy, there's something not quite right about him, Stéphanie. It's almost as if . . .'

Jacques Dupain turns over in bed. He has no need to check. He knows he's talking to his wife's back. To the back of her neck. Her long, light-coloured hair. A quarter of her face. A hand holding a book. Sometimes, when the blankets conspire, he can spy the small of her back, her sublime curves that he likes to stroke every evening.

'It's as if he's trying to get to me,' Dupain goes on. 'As if he's made it his personal mission.'

'Don't worry,' the back replies. 'You need to calm down . . .'

Jacques Dupain tries to immerse himself once more in his housing brochure. The minutes pass slowly on the screen of the alarm clock beside him.

9.12 . . .

9.17 . . .

9.24 . . .

'What are you reading, Stéphanie?'

'Nothing much.'

The back isn't very chatty.

9.31 . . .

9.34 . . .

'I'd like to find you a house, Stéphanie. Something that isn't this cupboard above the school. The house of your dreams. That's my job, after all. One day I'll be able to give it to you. If you're patient I can . . .'

The back moves slightly. The hand reaches out towards the bedside table and puts the book down.

Aurélien.

Louis Aragon.

She turns off the bedside light.

'So that you'll never leave me,' Jacques Dupain's voice says into the darkness.

9.37.

9.41.

'You won't let him do it, will you, Stéphanie? You won't let that policeman come between us? You know I had nothing to do with Morval's murder.'

'I know, Jacques. We both know.'

The back is smooth and cold.

9.44.

I'll do it, Stéphanie . . . Your house, our house, I'll find it.'

The swishing sound of a sheet.

The back disappears. A pair of breasts and her sex invite themselves into the conversation.

'Make me a child, Jacques. A child, more than anything.'

35

James, lying on his back, enjoys the last rays of the sun: another fifteen minutes before it sets behind the hill. He knows it must be a little after ten o'clock. James doesn't wear a watch, he lives by the rhythm of the sun, as Monet did. He gets up and goes to bed with it. A little later every evening, at the moment. The bright star is currently playing hide and seek with the poplars.

This unexpected warmth is very pleasant. James closes his eyelids. He is aware that he is painting less and less, and sleeping more and more. To put it the way most of the villagers must think, he's becoming more and more of a tramp and less and less of an artist.

What joy! To be seen as a tramp in the eyes of those fine people. To become the village tramp, just as every village has its priest, its mayor, its teacher, its postman . . . He will be Giverny's tramp. There was one before, apparently, in the days of Claude Monet. He was known as the marquis, because of the felt hat with which he greeted passers-by. But above all, the marquis was known for collecting the cigarette butts outside Monet's house, which the painter had barely smoked. He stuffed his pockets with them. Now that was class . . .

Yes, to become Giverny's resident tramp, the marquis. Now there's an ambition. But in order to get there, James is aware that there is still some distance to cover. At the moment, apart from little Fanette, no one is interested in this old lunatic who sleeps in the fields with his easels.

Apart from Fanette . . .

Fanette is enough for him.

They aren't just empty words; Fanette really is incredibly gifted. Much more gifted than he is. She has a real gift, straight from heaven, as if the Lord had deliberately ensured that she was born in Giverny, as if the Lord had made certain their paths would cross.

She called him 'Père Trognon' just now. Like Robinson's painting. *Père Trognon* . . . James would like to die like that, simply savouring those two words uttered by Fanette.

Père Trognon.

Two words that seemed to sum up his quest . . . From Theodore Robinson's masterpiece to the impertinence of a budding genius.

Him.

Père Trognon.

Who could have imagined it?

The sun isn't shining anymore.

But it isn't yet ten o'clock. Suddenly it's dark, as if the sun has abruptly changed the game, as if it has moved from playing hide and seek in the poplars to blind man's bluff. As if the sun has counted to twenty behind a poplar, giving the moon a head start . . .

James opens his eyes. Stunned. Terrified.

All he can see is a rock, a vast rock, above his face, less than fifty centimetres away.

A surreal vision.

Too late, he realises that he isn't dreaming. The rock crushes his face like some ripe fruit. James feels his temples exploding, an intense pain.

Everything collapses. He turns on to his belly and crawls into the ears of wheat. He isn't very far from the stream, from a house, that mill. He could cry out. But no sound comes from his mouth. He struggles not to lose consciousness. A terrible roaring sound saturates his thoughts, his skull swells like a steam engine that's about to blow.

James goes on crawling. He feels that his attacker is there, standing above him, ready to finish him off.

What's he waiting for?

His eyes latch on to a pair of wooden feet. An easel. His hands reach out, desperately. The muscles in his arms stretch in one last attempt to drag himself upright.

The easel collapses with a deafening crash. The paint box falls right in front of him. Brushes, pencils, tubes of paint scatter in the grass. James thinks fleetingly about the message engraved inside it. *She is mine, here, now and for ever*. He couldn't understand that threat, who engraved it or why.

Has he seen something that he shouldn't have seen?

He is going to die without knowing. He has the feeling that his thoughts are abandoning him, that they are flowing away into the earth, along with his blood, his skin. Now he is dragging himself through the tubes of paint, crushing them, eviscerating them. He continues straight on.

He is aware of the shadow, right above him.

He knows that he should stop, turn around. Try to get up. Say something. But it's impossible. He is frozen by panic. The shadow wants to kill him. The shadow is going to start again. He has to get away. He can't think anything else, there's too much roaring in his head. He can only think in primal impulses. Crawl. Get away. Escape.

He knocks over a second easel. Or he thinks he does. The blood fills his eyes now. His gaze is blurred. The landscape in front of him is stained with red, with purple. The stream can't be very far away. He might still get through, someone might come.

He crawls again.

An easel, another one, in front of him. With his palette, his brushes, his knives.

The shadow comes closer.

It is in front of him now. Through a glowing red filter, James sees a hand gripping his scraping knife. Coming towards him.

It's over.

James crawls a few more centimetres, then raises himself on his elbows, using the last of his strength. His body rolls over, once, twice, several times. For a moment James hopes he will follow the direction of the slope, that he will slide down the slight incline of the meadow towards the Epte; that he will get away.

Just for a moment.

His body topples into the crushed ears of wheat. On his back. He didn't make it two metres. He can't see anything now. James spits out a mixture of blood and paint. He can't put two thoughts together.

The shadow approaches.

James tries to move once more, a muscle, just one, but can't do it. He is no longer in command of his body. His eyes, perhaps.

The shadow is above him.

James looks up at it.

All of a sudden it's as if his brain has been returned to him. The last thought of the condemned man. James immediately recognises the shadow, but he still refuses to believe his eyes. It's impossible! Why such hatred? What madness could be feeding it?

One hand pins him against the ground, the other is about to plunge the knife into his chest. James can't move. His brain has almost stopped him from feeling pain. He is terrified.

Now, he understands.

Now, James wants to live!

So as not to die. His own life is so unimportant. He wants to live to stop what is happening, stop this monstrous, ineluctable sequence of events, this terrifying plot in which he plays only a bit part, a walk-on in a subplot.

He feels the cold blade digging into his flesh.

He is too old. He isn't even suffering anymore. His life is leaving him. He feels so useless. He was unable to halt the unfolding tragedy. He was too old to protect Fanette. Who will be able to help the child now? Who will protect her from the shadow that is about to engulf her?

With one last glance James embraces the windswept wheat field. Who will find his body amid the ears of wheat? How long will it take? Hours? Days? In one last hallucination, he thinks he sees a woman approaching with a parasol, Camille Monet, amid the wild grass and the poppies.

He has no regrets now. This is why he left Connecticut. To die in Giverny.

The sun gently sets.

The last thing James feels before he dies is the shiver of Neptune's coat against his cold skin.

DAY NINE

21 May 2010

(Chemin du Roy)

Sensitivity

36

The second sunny day in a row. In Giverny. Believe me, for the season, that's practically a miracle.

I walk along the Chemin du Roy. The older I get, the more trouble I have understanding the tourists who often wait more than an hour to get into the gardens on Rue Claude Monet, queuing up one behind the other, along more than two hundred metres of pavement. The thing is, you only have to walk along the Chemin du Roy and, through the green fence along the main road, you can see the gardens and Monet's house, take unforgettable photographs, smell the scent of the flowers – all without having to wait.

The cars pass by, skimming the greenery that separates the road from the cycle path. Each time a vehicle passes in too much of a hurry it looks as if the leaves have been seized by spasms: local boys who work in Vernon, and who stopped turning their heads towards the pink house with green shutters a long time ago. For them, the Chemin du Roy is just the D5, the road to Vernon. Nothing else.

At the speed I go at, by contrast, I have time to admire the flowers. I won't lie to you; of course the gardens are magnificent.

The cathedral of roses, the Rond des Dames, the Clos Normand with its cascades of clematis, the mass of pink tulips and forget-me-nots. So many masterpieces . . .

Who could deny it?

Amadou Kandy even told me that ten years ago, in a village in the countryside in Japan, they opened an exact replica of Monet's house, the Clos Normand and the water garden. Can you believe it? I've seen photographs, it's almost impossible to distinguish the real Giverny from the imitation. You'll tell me photographs can tell any story you like but, frankly, the idea of building a second Giverny in Japan? Really, it's beyond me.

I confess, it's been years since I've visited Monet's gardens. The ones in Giverny, I mean, the real ones. There are too many people there these days. With thousands of tourists crammed together, piled up on top of each other, treading on each other's toes, it's not a place for an old woman like me. And when the tourists visit Monet's house, they are often surprised: it isn't an art gallery. There is no painting by the master in Monet's house, no painting of *Water Lilies*, no Japanese bridge or poplars. Just a house, a studio and a garden. To see real paintings by Monet, you have to go to the Orangerie, to the Marmottan, to Vernon . . . Yes, all in all, I'm happier on the other side of the fence. And besides, I have only to shut my eyes, and the startling beauty of the garden is engraved there.

For ever. Believe me.

Those raving lunatics are still racing along the Chemin du Roy. A Toyota has just gone past at more than a hundred kilometres an hour. Perhaps you don't know, but it was Claude Monet who paid for the road to be tarred a hundred years ago, because the dust from the unsurfaced road was covering his flowers! He'd have been better off paying for a detour. They haven't a clue, honestly – a garden like that cut in half by a main road and tourists walking underneath it down a tunnel.

Well now, you've probably had enough of the reasonably interesting reflections of an old Givernois on the development of her village and its surroundings. I understand. You're probably wondering what I'm playing at. That's what interests you, isn't it? What's my role in this whole affair? At what point do I stop spying on everyone in order to make my intervention? How? Why? Patience, patience. A few more days, no more than a few more days. Let me enjoy a little while longer the general indifference towards an old woman that no one notices any more than they would a signpost or a road sign, because they have always been there. I'm not going to try to make you believe I know the end of this business, no, but I do have my little idea.

And I am the one who will supply the final parenthesis to this story, trust me. You won't be disappointed!

Bear with me, please. Let me tell you a little more about Monet's gardens. Listen carefully, because every detail counts. Mornings in May are often besieged by school outings, with the gardens as noisy as a school playground. In fact, it depends on the teacher's ability to interest the children in painting, and on the children's state of excitement, which in turn depends on the number of hours they've been banged up inside their bus. Sometimes they've spent an entire night – there are some sadistic teachers. Once the kids are inside the garden the teachers can relax; a little discreet surveillance is all that's required. The place is a bit like a public park, and it's educational to boot. The children fill in a questionnaire, they draw. Apart from the risk of drowning among the water lilies, they aren't in any danger.

On the Chemin du Roy, the Lorin bakery van goes past and honks its horn at me. I give the driver a little wave. Richard Lorin is the last shopkeeper who knows me, along with Amadou Kandy. A lot of the shop signs in Giverny change every year, along with the galleries, the hotels, the summer houses. They come, and they go. Giverny is the tide, at the mercy of the floods. I see that now, from a distance. Stranded on the sand.

I wait some more . . .

I've heard the noise of a motorbike, the characteristic sound of a Tiger Triumph T100. It has parked in Ruelle Leroy, near the group entrance. It might seem strange to you that a woman of over eighty can recognise the make of a motorbike just from the noise of its engine. An old bike, too, almost an antique. Believe me, I think I could recognise the sound of a Tiger Triumph T100 among a thousand others.

My God, how could I ever forget it?

I also note that I'm not the only one who has been listening out for it. It isn't long before Stéphanie Dupain pokes her head out through the highest window of Claude Monet's house, her face half covered by the Virginia creeper. From her lofty perch she pretends to count the children. As if.

I sense that she's trembling at the sound of the engine. Looking vaguely attentive, she watches the children running among the flower beds. I think that, in fact, the children in her class will be able to do what they like for a moment . . .

37

Stéphanie Dupain runs down the stairs. Laurenç Sérénac is there, waiting in the reading room.

'Hello, Stéphanie. It's great to see you again.'

The teacher is breathless. Laurenç performs a half-turn on his heels.

'It's the first time I've been in Claude Monet's house. Thank you for giving me this opportunity, really. I'd heard about it, but it's fascinating.'

'Hello, Inspector. It's true that you're incredibly lucky. Monet's garden is only open to the children of Giverny School this morning. It's very unusual! It only happens once a year, and we have Monet's house all to ourselves.'

All to ourselves . . .

Laurenç Sérénac can't define the feeling of excitement that washes over him. Somewhere between fantasy and unease.

'And your pupils?'

'They're playing in the garden. No harm can come to them, don't worry – I only brought the older ones. And I'm keeping an eye on them; all the windows of the house look out onto the garden. The more serious ones are supposed to be painting, looking for

151

inspiration – they're supposed to be handing over their paintings for the Robinson Foundation's "International Young Painters Challenge" in a few days. The others don't care, so they'll be playing hide and seek among the bridges, around the pond . . . It was like that in Monet's day too, you know. You shouldn't believe the myth of a silent house inhabited by a hermitic old man; Claude Monet's house was filled with his children and his grandchildren.'

Stéphanie steps forward and strikes the pose of a tourist guide.

'As you see, Inspector, here we are in the little blue drawing room. It overlooks a strange pantry. Observe the egg boxes hanging from the walls . . .'

The teacher is wearing an amazing blue and red silk dress, gathered in at the waist by a wide belt, and closed by two flowery buttons at the neckline. The dress makes her look like a geisha who has just stepped out of a print. Her hair is pulled back. Her mauve eyes merge with the pastel of the walls. Sérénac doesn't know where to look. Dressed like this, Stéphanie reminds him of a painting by Claude Monet that he admired years ago, the portrait of the artist's first wife, Camille Doncieux, dressed as a geisha. He feels almost like an intruder in his jeans, his shirt and his leather jacket.

'Shall we go to the next room?' the gentle voice of his guide suggests.

Yellow.

The room is entirely yellow. The walls, the painted furniture, the chairs. Sérénac stops in his tracks, stunned.

His hostess comes over to him.

'You are now in the dining room where Claude Monet received his most important guests.'

Laurenç admires the glow of the room. His eye finally settles on a painting that hangs on the wall. A pastel by Renoir. A seated girl, in three-quarter profile, wearing an enormous white hat. He walks over to it, appreciating the way the tones between the long brown hair and the peachy skin of the young model blend into one another.

'A pretty reproduction,' he observes.

'A reproduction? Are you sure, Inspector?'

Sérénac studies the painting, surprised by her comment.

'Well . . . if I admired this painting in a Paris museum I wouldn't doubt for a second that it was an original. But here, in Monet's house? Everyone knows that—'

'And what if,' Stéphanie interrupts, 'I were to tell you that it actually is a Renoir, an original?'

The teacher smiles at the inspector's disconcerted expression. She adds, in a lower voice:

'But shh, it's a secret. You mustn't tell anyone.'

'You're making fun of me.'

'Not at all. I'll let you into another secret, Inspector. An even more surprising one. In Monet's house, if you look very carefully, in the studio, in the attic, you'll find a whole range of masterpieces. Dozens of them. Renoirs, Sisleys, Pissarros. Real ones. Monets too, of course, original *Water Lilies* . . . all within your reach!'

Laurenç Sérénac looks at Stéphanie, perplexed.

'Stéphanie, why are you telling me such fairy tales? Everyone knows that's impossible. Paintings by Renoir or Monet have such immense financial value . . . Cultural value, too. How on earth can you imagine they'd be here, crouching in the dust? It's ridiculous.'

Stéphanie adopts a delicious pout.

'Laurenç, I grant that my revelations may seem incredible. But you disappoint me if you think they're impossible, or ridiculous, because I'm only telling you the truth. Besides, lots of Givernois know about the real treasures hidden in Monet's house. Let's just say it's a kind of open secret here, something people don't talk about.'

Laurenç Sérénac waits for the teacher to burst out laughing. It doesn't happen, even though Stéphanie's eyes are sparkling with mischief.

'Stéphanie,' he says at last. 'I'm sorry, you'll have to try out your joke on someone more gullible than me.'

'You still don't believe me, do you, Laurenç? Never mind. After all, it's not important, let's not mention it again . . .'

The teacher turns round abruptly. Sérénac is worried. He thinks that perhaps he shouldn't have come; not here, not now. He should have arranged to meet Stéphanie somewhere else. But it's too late. Everything is collapsing. So even if this is neither the time nor the place, he takes the plunge:

'Stéphanie I didn't just come here for the guided tour or to discuss art. We need to talk—'

'Shh . . .'

Stéphanie puts a finger to her lips, as if to tell him that this isn't the moment. It's probably an old teacher's trick.

She points at the glass sideboards.

'Claude Monet also insisted on refinement for his guests. Blue porcelain from Creil and Montereau, Japanese prints . . .'

Laurenç Sérénac can't help it, he grabs Stéphanie by the shoulders. He immediately realises that he shouldn't have done so. The fabric of her dress is silky, smooth, fleeting, like a skin on skin. The fabric gives him ideas, and they aren't anything to do with his police work.

'I'm not joking, Stéphanie. Things didn't go very well with your husband yesterday.'

She smiles.

'I got a slight inkling of that yesterday evening.'

'He's a suspect. It's serious . . .'

'You're wrong.'

Laurenç's fingers slip down the silk, independent of him, as if he were stroking her arms. He struggles to remain lucid.

'Stop playing with me, Stéphanie. Yesterday, during the interrogation, your husband told me that on the morning of the crime he stayed in bed with you. You told me the opposite three days ago. One of you is lying.'

'Laurenç, how many times do I have to tell you? I was not Jérôme Morval's lover. Not even a close friend. My husband had no motive for killing Morval! I know the classics, Inspector. No motive, no need for an alibi.'

She laughs deliciously.

'You like a bit of theatre, Laurenç. After your mission to collect all the boots in Giverny, are you going to ask all the couples of the village if they were making love in their bed on the morning of the crime?'

'This is not a game, Stéphanie.'

Stéphanie's voice suddenly assumes the tone of an angry teacher:

'I am well aware of that, Laurenç. So stop going on at me about this crime, this sordid investigation. That's not what's important. You're ruining everything.'

She pulls away from him and runs off, almost slipping on the brick and straw tiles. She turns round, smiling again. Angel and demon.

'The kitchen!'

This time it's blue that leaps out at Laurenç Sérénac. The blue of walls, the blue of the porcelain, every shade, from sky blue to turquoise.

Now Stéphanie sounds more like a market trader.

'Housewives in particular will appreciate the huge range of kitchen equipment: the copper pots, the faience from Rouen . . .'

'Stéphanie . . .'

She stands by the fireplace. Before Sérénac has time to react, her hands grab the lapels of his leather jacket.

'Inspector, let's be clear. Let's dot the "i"s once and for all. My husband loves me. My husband is fond of me. My husband isn't capable of hurting anyone. You need to find another suspect!'

'And what about you?'

Surprised, she relaxes her grip a little.

'What do you mean? Am I capable of hurting someone, is that what you're asking me?'

Her mauve eyes open, revealing a shade that he hadn't yet explored. Sérénac stammers, disturbed:

'N . . . no. I meant: what about you? Do you love him?'

'You're becoming indiscreet, Inspector.'

She lets go of his jacket and plunges back into the dining room, the drawing room, the pantry. Laurenç follows her at a distance, no longer sure what attitude to adopt. From the pantry, a wooden staircase rises to the first floor. Stéphanie's dress glides along the wooden steps as if polishing them.

Just before she disappears upstairs, she calls down a word. Just one word:

'Finally!'

38

Sylvio Bénavides is standing in the square in front of Rouen Cathedral. He hasn't been back to Rouen for a long time, almost a year. Clutching his guide, he imagines that people will mistake him for a tourist. He doesn't care. He has a meeting with the curator of the Musée des Beaux-Arts, one Achille Guillotin, in half an hour, but he has been careful to arrive early, as if to prepare himself psychologically and immerse himself in the Impressionist ambience of old Rouen.

He turns back towards the tourist office and consults his guide: it was from the first floor of this building that Claude Monet did most of his paintings of Rouen Cathedral, a total of twenty-eight, all different, depending on the time of day or the weather. In Monet's time the tourist office was a clothes shop, and long before that it was Rouen's principal landmark dating back to the Renaissance: the House of the Exchequer. Monet also painted the cathedral from different angles, from different houses in the square, some of which were destroyed in the war, on the Rue Grand Pont or the Rue du Gros Horloge.

Inspector Bénavides smiles as he imagines Claude Monet setting off at dawn with his easels to the sleepy town-houses, or installing himself all day, for months on end, in a ladies' fashion emporium: all to paint the same building almost thirty times. People must have thought he was mad . . .

Although deep down, people admire madmen.

Sylvio goes back towards the cathedral. Yes, people admire madness. Even to admire this building is to acknowledge that he was right, whoever it was who came up with the idea of constructing such an unlikely monument, even though it would take five hundred years; that lunatic who no doubt insisted that the spire of his cathedral should be the highest in France, even if several thousand more workmen lost their lives in the process. At the time such a building site must have been like a slaughterhouse, but we forget. We always forget in the end. We forget the slaughterhouse, we forget the barbarism, and we admire the madness.

Sylvio consults his watch – he mustn't dawdle if he doesn't want to be late; he's kept that schoolboy impulse of always arriving on time. He leaves the Place de la Cathédrale and passes under the arcades of the big shops. Rue des Carmes. The museum should be somewhere on the left, if he's understood the map correctly. He turns into a narrow little street lined with half-timbered houses. He has always had trouble finding his way around the medieval centre of Rouen. To him, the city seems like a kind of labyrinth designed by someone with a tortured mind. Maybe it was the same guy who wanted his cathedral to be the tallest in the country. An additional problem: Sylvio hasn't been concentrating very hard on the route. Instead he has been obsessing over the idea that there's something off about the Morval case. As if someone were pulling the strings, some Machiavellian Tom Thumb, leaving them clues in order to lead them wherever he wished. But who could it be?

Sylvio reaches Place du 19 Avril 1944. He hesitates for a moment and then turns sharply to the right, just as a buggy pushed by an energetic mother heads towards him. The mother rolls right over his foot without slowing down, while the inspector murmurs vague apologies.

Who?

Jacques Dupain? Amadou Kandy? Stéphanie Dupain? Patricia Morval?

Giverny is a small village, as all the Givernois keep telling them: the Givernois all know each other. So what if they are all protecting a secret? That accident, for example, the drowning of that boy in 1937? Bénavides starts coming up with the most insane hypotheses. He even finds himself wondering if his boss is being completely open with him. Laurenç Sérénac sometimes has a strange way of approaching all this business relating to art. Sylvio doesn't like that coincidence very much; the fact that his boss is such a lover of art that he hangs pictures up in his office, that he investigated the illegal art trade before he was transferred to Vernon and then, as if by chance, he finds himself having to deal with the murder of a collector . . . In Giverny! Not to mention his obsession with trying to pin everything on Jacques Dupain while flirting with the man's wife. Sylvio has discussed it with Béatrice, but for some reason his wife adores Laurenç. They've only met that one evening, but still . . .

Straight ahead of him, Silvio sees a public garden running alongside an imposing grey building in a square. About ten people are waiting in front of the steps. He recognises the entrance to the Musée des Beaux-Arts and quickens his pace. His mind is still whirring. Yes, Béatrice never stops telling him how charming, how interesting, how funny Laurenç is. She even said something like, 'For a policeman he has an astonishing sensitivity, like some kind of female intuition.' Perhaps that is why, Silvio thinks to himself, he's developing some reservations about his boss. How can Béatrice admire someone like Sérénac, who is so very different from him? Someone who is interested in nothing but art and the women Morval slept with. Or wanted to sleep with.

Bénavides climbs the steps to the Musée des Beaux-Arts and, although he can't say why, a question returns and lodges in his skull like an obsessive refrain: why do people, in the end, admire madmen? Especially women.

Inspector Sylvio Bénavides has been waiting in the hall of the Musée des Beaux-Arts in Rouen for a few minutes. He feels slightly crushed by the height of the ceilings, the depth of the room, the gleam of the huge frescoes. Suddenly, as if emerging from a trapdoor in the marble, a little bald man covered in a pair of oversized overalls heads towards him and holds out a hand.

'Inspector Bénavides? Achille Guillotin. Curator of the museum. Right, let's go. I'm afraid I can't give you very much time, not least because I don't really understand what it is that you want.'

A funny thought flashes through Sylvio's mind. Guillotin reminds him of the art teacher he had at secondary school, Jean Bardon. A teacher who was twenty-five years old and looked as if he was forty. They would be about the same size, wear the same overalls, and have the same way of talking to him. For some strange reason, throughout his school years, Sylvio was always made the scapegoat by all of his teachers, particularly the ones who lacked authority. He reflects that Achille Guillotin must belong to the same caste: little bosses who are obsequious towards authority and tyrannical as soon as they meet anyone weaker than them.

Guillotin is already far away, climbing the staircase like a little grey mouse. Sylvio imagines that with every step he could tread on his long overalls and go toppling backwards.

'Come on, then. What's this about a murder?'

Bénavides trots along behind the grey mouse.

'Quite a wealthy man. An ophthalmologist from Giverny. Among other things he collected paintings. He was particularly interested in Monet, and the *Water Lilies*. That may even be the motive for the crime.'

'And?'

'I'd just like to know a bit more.'

'And there's no one in the force who deals with such matters?'

'There is, in fact. The inspector coordinating the inquiry trained with the art division, but . . .'

Guillotin looks as him if he has just uttered the worst of heresies.

'But . . . ?'

'But I'd like to do some of my own research on the subject.'

As they reach the landing, it's hard to tell whether Guillotin is sighing or whether he is just out of breath.

'OK. So what do you want to know?'

'We could start with the *Water Lilies* perhaps? I'd like to know how many of them Monet painted. Twenty? Thirty? Fifty?'

'*Fifty?*'

Achille Guillotin utters a strange cry of horror mixed with sardonic laughter, in a sound that possibly only hyenas should be capable of producing. If he had been holding a metal ruler, he would have brought it straight down on the fingers of the ignorant inspector. The severe portraits in the Renaissance room seem to turn towards Sylvio, covering him with the utmost shame. In spite of himself,

Sylvio lowers his gaze, while Achille Guillotin gives a scornful shrug. Sylvio notices that the curator is wearing strange orange socks.

'Are you serious, Inspector? Fifty *Water Lilies*? Let me tell you that specialists have identified at least one hundred and seventy-two *Water Lilies* by Claude Monet!'

Sylvio rolls startled eyes.

'We can also compute that into metres, if that means more to you. Monet painted about two hundred square metres of *Water Lilies* for the nation, at the end of the First World War, and these were put on show at the Orangerie. But if you add up all the works that Monet didn't keep, the ones he painted when he was suffering from cataracts and half-blind, experts agree that there are over one hundred and forty square metres of "additional" *Water Lilies*, exhibited around the four corners of the world, in New York, Zurich, London, Tokyo, Munich, Canberra, San Francisco, to name but a few. Not to mention around a hundred *Water Lilies* that belong to private collectors.'

Sylvio doesn't comment. It occurs to him that he must be wearing the idiotic expression of a child who has been told that behind the wave that has just lapped his feet on the beach there is the ocean. Guillotin continues striding down the corridors. Every time he enters a room the attendants, in a moment of panic, spring to attention.

The European Baroque makes way for the Grand Siècle.

'The *Water Lilies*,' Achille Guillotin continues without pausing for breath, 'is a very strange collection, unlike anything else in the world. Over the last twenty-seven years of his life, Claude Monet painted nothing other than his lily pond. Gradually he would get rid of all the scenery surrounding it, the Japanese bridge, the willow branches, the sky, in order to concentrate entirely on the leaves, the water, the light. The last canvases, painted a few months before he died, seem almost abstract. Just marks on canvas. Tachisme, the experts have called it. It was a style no one had ever seen before. And nobody, in Monet's day, would understand. Everyone thought it was an old man's whim . . . When he died, Monet's *Water Lilies* were hidden away, particularly the later ones. People thought it was a moment of madness.'

Sylvio doesn't have time to ask what Guillotin means by 'hidden away' as the curator carries on.

'Except that a generation later it was those same, late canvases that would give rise, in the United States, to what the world would call abstract art . . . That's the legacy of the father of Impressionism: the invention of modernity! Do you know Jackson Pollock?'

Sylvio doesn't dare say no. He doesn't dare say yes either. Guillotin gives a weary-teacher sigh.

'Too bad. He's an abstract artist. Pollock and the others drew their inspiration from Monet's *Water Lilies*. It was the same in France. I hope you remember what I said a moment ago. The largest *Water Lilies* were shown at the Orangerie, the Sistine Chapel of Impressionism, given by Monet to the French State in honour of the 1918 armistice. And that's not all. If you think about the place where the *Water Lilies* were exhibited, there's something else rather fabulous . . .'

'Ah?'

Sylvio can't come up with anything more intelligent to say but Guillotin doesn't care.

'The *Water Lilies* are enthroned along the triumphal axis. That is, the major axis that runs through Notre Dame, the Louvre, the Tuileries, the Place de la Concorde, the Champs-Élysées, the Arc de Triomphe, and the Arche de la Défense. The *Water Lilies* behind the walls of the Orangerie are precisely aligned along that axis, which symbolises the whole of French history, extending from east to west, following the course of the sun. And of course Monet painted the water-lily pond at different times of day, from dawn till dusk, displaying the eternal course of the sun in the process. The course of the heavenly bodies, the triumphant history of France, the revolution in modern art . . . Now you understand why even the smallest square centimetre of these lilies is worth a fortune. This was the turning point in modern art. And it took place in Normandy, a few kilometres from Vernon, in an insignificant little pond.'

In the paintings of the Grand Siècle, the fabrics worn by the saints, queens and duchesses seem to fly in the breeze, as if stirred by the curator's lyricism.

'When you say a fortune, what do you mean exactly?'

As if he hasn't heard, Guillotin crosses the room and opens a window. Bénavides doesn't move.

'Shall we continue?'

Sylvio understands that he is to follow the curator.

'I'd like to give you an idea of what a *Water Lilies* is worth, going by the latest auctions in London or New York. So, for example, you see those grand nineteenth-century buildings facing us, along the Rue Jeanne d'Arc? Well, let's say that a Monet *Water Lilies*, a normal-sized one, about a square metre, that would correspond, at the very least, to a good hundred apartments. If we assume that there are four storeys per front door, that's already a good proportion of the street.'

'One hundred apartments? Are you joking?'

'No. And I think I could say they were worth twice that, without exaggerating. You're still looking at the Rue Jeanne d'Arc? The cars waiting at the lights? I could also work it out like this. One canvas, on the basis of the most recent sales, might be worth between one and two thousand cars. New ones, I mean. Or almost the entire contents of the shops along the Rue du Gros Horloge, the Rue Jeanne d'Arc and the Rue de la République all put together. What I'm trying to get through to you is that it's incalculable. Do you see? And that's just one *Water Lilies*!'

'You're having me on.'

'The last Monet sold at auction at Christie's in London went for twenty-five million pounds. And it was an early work. Twenty-five million pounds. Try converting that into apartments or cars!'

Sylvio doesn't have the time to recover, as the curator has already climbed to a new floor and reached the Impressionist rooms.

Pissarro, Sisley, Renoir, Caillebotte. And Monet, of course. The famous Rue Saint-Denis beneath a sea of tricolore flags; Rouen Cathedral on a cloudy day.

'And . . . are there any *Water Lilies* still on the market?' Bénavides stammers.

'What do you mean, "on the market"?'

'Well. Any *Water Lilies* that have vanished,' the inspector explains shyly.

'Vanished? What do you mean, "vanished"? Can't you be any more precise than that, given you're in the police force? Are you asking if there might be a Monet hanging around somewhere, is that it? Forgotten? In an attic in Giverny, or a cellar? You're thinking to yourself that someone would probably kill for such a discovery, for such a fortune. Well, Inspector, do listen carefully to what I'm about to tell you . . .'

39

The stairs of the pantry in Claude Monet's house creak beneath the feet of Inspector Laurenç Sérénac.

He tries to banish from his mind the parasitical thoughts, the inner voice of a kind of guardian angel that keeps murmuring that he is climbing the steps, one by one, of a terrible trap; that this staircase leads to Monet's bedrooms, and that there's no reason for him to go there, following this girl, that he is no longer in control of anything. But it isn't hard to silence that sensible voice inside him. He has only to think of the moment before, of Stéphanie's laughter, of her legs swathed in that geisha dress as she bounded towards the first floor, like two playful animals, like an invitation to indiscretion.

When Laurenç reaches the first floor, Stéphanie is standing in the doorway, in the corridor between the bedroom and the bathroom. As straight as a suited guide. Belted into her red dress, more precious and fragile than a porcelain vase.

'Monet's private apartments. More classical in style, I admit. More intimate. Laurenç, you don't look very comfortable.'

She walks into the first room and sits down on the bed. The enormous eiderdown engulfs her from her thighs to her chest.

'Is it interrogation time? I'm at your mercy, Inspector.'

Laurenç Sérénac takes an anxious glance around the room, the cream fabric stretched on the wall, the faded yellow of the bedspread, the marbled black of the chimney, the gold of the candlesticks, the mahogany of the bedside table.

'Come on, Inspector, relax. You were more talkative with my husband yesterday evening, it would seem . . .'

Laurenç doesn't respond. They are silent for a moment. Sérénac hasn't approached the bed. The joyful lanterns in Stéphanie's eyes gradually grow dim. She sits up in a flurry of feathers.

'Then I will begin. Inspector. Do you know the story of Louise, the dandelion-picker of Giverny?'

Sérénac looks at her, surprised and curious.

'No, of course you don't,' Stéphanie says. 'But it's a lovely story. Louise is a bit like our very own Cinderella. Louise was the ravishingly beautiful daughter of a peasant family, or so they say. The prettiest girl in the village. Young. Fresh. Innocent. Around 1900 she posed in the fields for some artists – in particular Radinsky, a promising Czech painter who had come to join Monet and the American artists. Handsome Radinsky was also a famous pianist. He drove an incredible car for the time, a 222 Z. He fell in love with the little dandelion-picker, he married her, and he took her home. Radinsky is now his country's most famous painter. Louise the little peasant girl became the Princess of Bohemia. It was Claude Monet himself who bought their car, the 222 Z, as a present for his son Michel, who would crash it, a few months later, into a tree on the Avenue Thiers in Vernon. Apart from the pitiful end of the poor car, it's a beautiful story, don't you think?'

Laurenç resists the desire to walk over to her, to let himself be devoured in turn by the eiderdown. His forehead is burning.

'Stéphanie, why are you telling me all this?'

'Guess . . .'

She shifts slowly on the eiderdown, as if swimming in a sea of feathers.

'I'm going to let you into a secret, Inspector. A curious secret. It's been a long time since I've found myself alone in a room with a man other than my husband. It's been a long time since I laughed while running up a staircase ahead of a man. It's been a long time since I've talked about landscapes, about painting, about the poems of Louis Aragon, to a male who is older than eleven and is capable of listening to me.'

Sérénac thinks of Morval. He is careful not to interrupt Stéphanie.

'Quite simply, I've been waiting a long time, Inspector, for this moment. All my life, I would say.'

A silence.

'Waiting for someone to come.'

Stare at something, Sérénac thinks to himself quickly. The melted candles, the flaking paint on the wall, anything but Stéphanie's eyes.

She adds: 'Not necessarily a Czech painter. Just someone.'

Even her voice is mauve.

'If anyone had told me it would be a policeman . . .'

Stéphanie leaps to her feet, and grabs one of Laurenç Sérénac's dangling arms.

'Come on. I have to check on my pupils.'

She pulls him towards the window, and gestures towards about a dozen children running around in the garden.

'Look at this garden, Inspector, the roses, the flower beds, the pond. I'll let you into another secret. Giverny is a trap! A wonderful setting, certainly. Who could dream of living anywhere else? Such a pretty village. But I have to confess: the decor is frozen. Petrified. You're not allowed to redecorate any of the houses in a different way, repaint a wall, pick so much as a single flower. There are laws forbidding it. We live in a painting here. We're walled in. We think we're at the centre of the world, that we're worth the trip, as they say. But it's the landscape, the decor, that ends up dripping all over you – like a kind of varnish that glues you to the setting. A daily varnish of resignation. Of renunciation . . . Louise, the dandelion-picker of Giverny, who became Princess of Bohemia, she's a legend, Laurenç. It doesn't happen anymore.'

She suddenly calls out to three children walking across a flower-bed: 'Go round it!'

Laurenç Sérénac feverishly seeks a diversion to stem the tide of Stéphanie's melancholy, to fight back his own desire to hold her in his arms. Here. Now. He stares at the profusion of flowers in the garden. The harmony of the colours. He is overwhelmed by the incredible charm of the park.

'Is it true,' he says suddenly, 'what Aragon says in his book? That Monet couldn't bear the sight of a wilting flower, so the gardeners changed them overnight, with a new colour every morning, as if the whole garden had been repainted?'

His ruse seems to have worked. Stéphanie smiles.

'No, not at all, that's an exaggeration on Aragon's part. So you've read *Aurélien*, then?'

'Of course . . . Read it and understood it, I think. The great novel on the impossibility of being a couple. There is no such thing as a happy love. Is that the message?'

'That's what Aragon thought when he wrote it. At that point in his life he must have thought there was no such thing as happy love. And yet he went on to experience the most beautiful, the longest, the most eternal love story that a poet has ever known. You know that. *Le Fou d'Elsa*!'

Laurenç turns round. Stéphanie's lips are still parted. He battles with the desire to bring his fingers to her quivering mouth, to stroke her delicate, porcelain profile.

'You are a strange girl, Stéphanie . . .'

'And you, Inspector, have a gift for inspiring confidences. I can tell you that in terms of questioning, you're a great deal more subtle than my husband had me believe. No, Inspector, I'm going to disappoint you. There's nothing strange about me; quite the contrary, I'm distressingly ordinary.'

The teacher hesitates and then her words rush out in one go, as if she were throwing herself out of the window.

'Ordinary, I tell you. I would love to bring up a child, my own child, but I think that my husband can't give me one. Is that why I don't love him anymore? I don't think so. I think that, as far back as I can remember, I have never loved him. He was just there. No worse than anyone else. Available. Loving. I fell on my feet. So you see, Inspector, I'm an ordinary woman. Trapped, like so many others. The fact that I'm pretty, I believe, that I was born in Giverny, and that I adore the children in my class doesn't change that . . .'

Laurenç's hand rests on Stéphanie's. They wrap their fingers around the green cast-iron balustrade.

'Why admit that to me? Why me?'

Stéphanie stares at him and laughs.

Isn't she aware that even her eyes are unique?

'Don't be under any illusion, Inspector. And don't get any ideas . . . If I've told you all this, it isn't because of your roguish smile, or the fact that your shirt is open by a button or two too many, or because your hazel eyes give away even the tiniest of your emotions. And above all, don't believe for one moment that I find you charming, Inspector . . . It's just . . .'

The hand pulls away and drifts towards the horizon. Stéphanie lets the suspense hover in the air.

'Just as Louise, the dandelion-picker, succumbed to the charm of the 222 Z, it's your Tiger Triumph that I've fallen in love with!'

She laughs.

'And perhaps also the way you always stop to stroke Neptune.'

She comes closer.

'One last thing, Inspector, but it's important. The fact that I no longer love my husband doesn't make him a murderer. Quite the contrary.'

Sérénac doesn't reply. He notices only that now, fifty metres in front of them, the passengers in the cars driving along the Chemin du Roy are systematically turning their heads towards Monet's house and spotting them, like lovers on a balcony.

Are they mad?

Is he mad?

'I think I should go and look after the children,' she whispers.

Standing on his own, Sérénac hears the teacher's footsteps fading away. His heart thumps furiously beneath his open shirt, and his thoughts explode against his skull.

Who is Stéphanie?

A femme fatale? Or a lost girl?

40

In the Impressionist hall of the Musée des Beaux-Arts in Rouen, Inspector Sylvio Bénavides opens owlish eyes. Achille Guillotin has moved again. The curator has taken out a handkerchief, and is rubbing an invisible speck of dust beside a painting by Sisley. *Flood at Port-Marly*, says the caption beneath the painting. Just as Sylvio is wondering whether Guillotin has forgotten his question, the curator turns round. He dabs a corner of his handkerchief against his forehead.

'Paintings by Monet that have disappeared, not been found, but which might come to light again, is that what you're asking me about, Inspector? OK, let's go. I can play a guessing game with you if you like . . . We know that Claude Monet's studios in Giverny contained dozens of paintings, including sketches, early works, large panels of unfinished *Water Lilies* . . . Not to mention gifts from his friends, Cézanne, Renoir, Pissarro, Boudin, Manet, more than thirty canvases . . . Do you see? That fortune, that colossal fortune, more precious than the collection of any museum in the world, was all looked after by no one other than an eighty-year-old man and his gardener, protected only by a door that barely closed, windows that were merely pushed shut, walls that were cracking. Anyone could have helped themselves. Any Givernois with an ounce of wit could have made more money by engaging in a spot of petty theft than by robbing twenty banks.'

The handkerchief wipes his face again and ends up in a ball in his palm.

'A fortune like that, just within reach, I can't imagine a similar temptation . . .'

Sylvio is beginning to understand. Around him he observes the ten or so canvases hanging on the walls. The Rouen Museum, which is supposed to house the finest provincial collection of Impressionist work, has only a quarter of the paintings that Monet's studios contained. He presses on.

'Might there still be paintings by great artists hidden somewhere in Monet's studios in Giverny?'

Achille Guillotin hesitates for a moment before replying.

'Well, Claude Monet died in 1926. Michel Monet, his son and heir, doubtless went to great lengths to look for any paintings by his father that hadn't been given to museums, and to make sure they were safe. So, to answer your question, I think it's very unlikely that we're going to find any new paintings in the pink house in Giverny today. But in the end, you never know.'

'And beyond the question of theft,' the inspector says with a little more confidence, 'might Monet have actually distributed some of his paintings, given them away?'

'The local press records the gift of a painting to a tombola stall that was raising money for the hospital in Vernon. Someone must have won that painting, at fifty centimes a ticket . . . Otherwise, we can only guess. We know that the inhabitants of Giverny didn't make life easy for Claude Monet. He had to negotiate for every aspect of his passion, for the purchase of his property, to preserve the landscapes as he painted them, and above all to divert the water from the brook towards his lily pond. Monet paid money, a lot of money, to the village. He paid to prevent a starch factory being built right next to his garden. He paid to freeze his little bit of landscape, away from any kind of progress. There again, any clever fellow, a municipal councillor or a wily peasant, could have got hold of one of the master's paintings for five hundred francs. I'm aware that specialists don't generally believe in that kind of arrangement between artists and local people, but can we really rule it out? The possibility that one of the inhabitants of Giverny might have been capable of taking an interest in painting, or at least in its saleable value? Monet would have handed the painting over, of course. He had no choice. Take that strange mill, for example, beside Monet's gardens – the Chennevières. Every time I go to Giverny I think about it, because of that painting by Theodore Robinson, the famous *Père Trognon*. Well, the countryfolk who lived in that mill had every opportunity to blackmail Monet. The brook ran right through their property. No agreement with them, no water lilies!'

Sylvio Bénavides hasn't time to note everything down, so he tries to memorise the flow of information.

'Are you serious?'

'Do I seem like I'm joking, young man? Let me tell you, there are idiotic treasure seekers who travel the world in search of three pieces of gold. If they were just a little smarter, they would visit the attics of the houses in Giverny and the nearby villages. I know what people say. Claude Monet destroyed the paintings he wasn't satisfied with, along with his early works. He was so worried that dealers would pounce on his unfinished canvases and sketches that he burned everything he didn't like in his studio, in 1921. But in spite of all the master's precautions, it's not impossible that there's another Monet hidden somewhere. Just some old, forgotten painting. But enough to buy you an island in the Pacific!'

The curator moves on to another room, and glances darkly at an attendant who seems to be more interested in the red of her nail polish than the red robe of the cardinal questioning Joan of Arc in Delaroche's painting.

'One more thing,' the inspector says. 'You mentioned Theodore Robinson, the painter and friend of Claude Monet. What do you think of the foundation that his inheritors set up?'

Guillotin opens his eyes wide.

'What makes you ask that?'

'The foundation keeps cropping up in our investigation. A lot of people involved in the case seem to have some connection with it, albeit indirectly.'

'And what do you want to know?'

'I have no idea. Just what you think of it.'

The curator hesitates, as if trying to find the right words.

'What can I tell you, Inspector? Foundations are complicated things. That kind of association is officially as altruistic and impartial as they come. I'll try to find an analogy for you. OK, imagine an association that takes care of poor people. Well, the paradox is that if the number of poor people declines, the association's reason for existence diminishes. In other words, the better it works, the more it scuppers itself. It would be the same for a foundation that campaigns against war. Peace would mean the death of that organisation.

'Like a doctor who is so good at treating his patients he puts himself out of a job?'

'Exactly, Inspector.'

'I understand, but what does that have to do with the Robinson Foundation?'

'They have a motto, I believe. The three "pros" as they call them. Prospection, protection, promotion. The motto works as well in French as it does in English. By and large, it means that they look for paintings all over the world, they buy and sell them, but also they invest in young artists, even very young ones; they buy their work, they sell it . . .'

'And then?'

'One talent follows another, Inspector. A painting isn't a record or a book; an artist's fortune isn't based on the largest number of sales. It's quite the opposite, in fact, and that's what the whole system is based on. A painting is worth a lot because the other paintings are worth much less, or nothing at all. If there is a level playing field, if there is true competition between critics, schools, and galleries, in the end everything is fine. But if a foundation finds itself in a monopoly situation, or almost, do you see?'

'Not really . . .'

Guillotin can't conceal a twitch.

'Well, if you have a monopoly, the more new talent this foundation discovers, the more it renews art – the "pro" from "prospection" if you like – the more it scuppers the sales value of its other paintings, the "pro" of "protection" . . . Do you see?'

'More or less . . .' Bénavides scratches his head. 'I'd like to ask you a more concrete question: if a Monet painting had vanished, would the Robinson Foundation be in a position to find it?'

The answer comes quickly. 'Without a doubt. More than anyone else! And probably by any means possible.'

'Well,' Bénavides continues, having adopted a slow and somewhat ponderous demeanour, which the curator seems to appreciate, 'I have one last question. It may surprise you. Are there any undiscovered paintings by Monet? I don't know, paintings that are particularly rare, or shocking, anything that could be linked to a murder?'

Achille Guillotin smiles, as if he has been expecting this question. The apotheosis of this conversation.

'Come with me,' he whispers conspiratorially.

He takes Sylvio over towards the opposite wall, to a tortured painting in which four naked men, clearly Roman slaves, are attempting to tame a wild horse.

'Observe these bodies painted by Géricault, yes, the famous Théodore Géricault. The greatest painter born in Rouen. Observe the bodies. The movement. Painters have a strange relationship with death, Inspector. We know that in order to make his *Raft of the Medusa* realistic, Théodore Géricault went to hospitals and collected amputated arms and feet, decapitated heads. His studio stank of corpses. At the end of his life, to treat his own madness, he would paint ten portraits of the insane from the Salpêtrière, ten monomaniacs who represent all the torments of the human soul . . .'

Sylvio is worried that the curator is going to lose himself in a new digression.

'But Monet wasn't mad. He didn't paint corpses.'

Achille Guillotin's hidden side seems to be coming to light. His sparse hair stands up on the lunar landscape of his head, like atrophied satanic horns.

The eleventh monomaniac?

'Come and see, Inspector.'

Guillotin dashes down the stairs, two flights, and into the museum shop, picks up a huge book and tears the transparent plastic cover with his teeth. He turns the pages, as if possessed.

'Monet didn't paint death? Monet didn't paint corpses, only nature? Ah, look now, Inspector. Look!'

Bénavides can't help recoiling.

A spectre. Filling the entire page.

The painting is a portrait of a woman. Her eyes are closed. She seems wrapped in a shroud of ice, a swirl of frozen brushstrokes, as if imprisoned by a white spider's web that devours the model's pale face.

Death . . .

'Allow me to introduce you to Camille Monet,' Guillotin says coldly. 'His first wife. His prettiest model. The girl with the parasol amid the poppies, his radiant companion on Sundays in the country. Dead at the age of thirty-two. Monet painted this accursed portrait at his wife's death bed; for the rest of his life he would reproach himself for being unable to resist the temptation to capture on canvas the colours of her ebbing life, for treating his love in her death throes as a vulgar object of study. Like Géricault and his fascination with dismembered bodies. As if the painter had taken possession of the lover. Monet later said that, by his wife's fresh corpse, he had fallen victim to a kind of automatic painting, as if he were hypnotised. What do you think, Inspector?'

Sylvio Bénavides has never felt such emotion in viewing a painting.

'Are there any other works like this? By Monet, I mean . . .'

Achille Guillotin's round face reddens again, as if a slumbering devil has woken within him.

'What could be more fascinating than painting his wife's death, Inspector? Have you thought about that? Nothing, of course.'

The red colour rises to his temples.

'Nothing, except being able to paint his own death. During the last months of his life, Monet painted incomplete *Water Lilies*, the equivalent of the score of Mozart's *Requiem* . . . Crazed brushstrokes, a race against death, against exhaustion, against blindness. Hermetic, painful, tortured canvases, as if Monet had plunged inside his own brain. *Water Lilies* have been discovered where the paint was hurled urgently onto the canvas in every colour, fiery red, monochrome blue, corpse green . . . Dreams and nightmares merged together. Only one colour was missing . . .'

Sylvio would like to reply but nothing comes out. He feels that the investigation is veering off course.

'The colour that Monet had banished from his canvases for ever.

The one he refused to use. The absence of colour, but also the union of them all.'

A silence. Sylvio gives up trying to reply, and instead scribbles nervously on his notepad.

'Black, Inspector. Black! It is said that during the last days before his death, in early December 1926, when Claude Monet understood that he was about to pass away, he painted it.'

'Wh . . . what?' Bénavides stutters.

Guillotin isn't listening anymore.

'Do you understand what I'm saying to you, Inspector? Monet observed his own death in the reflection of the water lilies and immortalised it on canvas. The *Water Lilies. In black!*'

Sylvio's pen dangles from his hand. He is incapable of taking any notes whatsoever.

'What do you think, Inspector?' the curator asks, his elation fading. The *Water Lilies* in black. Like the dahlia.'

'Is it definitely true, this story about the black *Water Lilies*?'

'No. Certainly not. Of course, no one has ever found that canvas, the famous *Black Water Lilies* . . . As you may imagine, it's a legend, just a legend.'

Sylvio doesn't know what to say anymore. He asks the first question that comes to mind.

'And children . . . Did Monet ever paint children?'

41

I watch Stéphanie at the window of Monet's pink house. She looks like the mistress of a colonial home, overseeing a swarm of servants.

Laurenç has come back down.

They are completely mad. I'm sure you agree with me this time, that you're thinking the same. The idiots, making a spectacle of themselves like that! On the balcony of Monet's house, overlooking the garden, facing the Chemin du Roy, in full view of everyone. They're asking for it!

*

I listen to the sound of the Tiger Triumph setting off. Stéphanie hears it too, but she doesn't have the courage to turn her head. She remains thoughtful, watching the children playing in the garden. It's true that she's ravishing, the little schoolteacher. It's also true that she knows how to use it, with her geisha dress clinging to her wasp waist and her dewy eyes. Trust me, she has all it takes to turn the head of any boy who comes too close to her, whether he's a policeman or a doctor, married or not. Pretty as a picture.

Enjoy it, my pretty. It won't last.

Some boys are running about in the middle of the flowers. The teacher tells them off gently. Her mind is elsewhere.

You're lost, aren't you, my dear?

This is the moment when your whole life is going to change, you've understood that, and through the most unlikely of saviours. A policeman. Charming. Funny. Cultured. Prepared to do anything – even free you from your chains. From your husband.

This is the moment. So what's holding you back?

Nothing?

Ah, if it were only up to you . . . If only death wasn't prowling around you; as if you attracted it, my darling. As if, in the end, you were only reaping what you had sowed.

Children's laughter pierces my evil thoughts. Boys running after girls.

Typical.

Make the most of it, little ones. Enjoy it. Trample the lawns and the flowers. Pluck the roses. Throw stones and sticks into the pond. Tear holes in the waterlilies. Desecrate the temple of romanticism. But don't have any delusions. It's only a garden, after all. Just because a bunch of credulous fools come from the other end of the world to pray here, it's still nothing but a pool of stagnant water.

I know, I'm wicked. Forgive me. Those two idiots have annoyed me this morning, Stéphanie Dupain and her policeman. You have to understand me too. I want to play the mute witness, the invisible black mouse, but it isn't always so easy to remain detached. You don't understand me anymore? You're still wondering what part I play in this whole story? Let me reassure you, I don't have any sophisticated aerials to pick up the conversation of those two fools through the walls of the Monet house, all the details of their loving display. Oh, no. It's much simpler than that. Dramatically simple.

I turn towards the right bank of the Chemin du Roy, towards the water garden. Along the road, a few planks have been removed from the fence, probably by some indelicate tourist in too much of a hurry to take a picture of the waterlilies, and alarmed by the queue at the entrance. The space thus revealed gives an incredible view of the pond. I observe Fanette, standing slightly apart from the other children in her class, among the willows and poplars. She has set up her easel on the Japanese bridge, propped up against the wisteria. She goes on painting, calm and concentrating, in spite of the hubbub all around her.

I cross the Chemin du Roy and come closer to get a better view. I'm practically touching the fence.

I shouldn't have done that. One little brat has spotted me.

'Miss, miss, can you take a picture of me with my friends?'

He presses a brand new camera into my hand. I don't understand it all; he explains how to work it, but I'm not listening. As I take his photograph, I squint towards the lily pond and Fanette, painting.

42

'Come on, Fanette,' Vincent insists. 'Come and play!'

'No! Can't you see that I'm painting?'

Fanette tries to fix her attention on a water lily. A lonely one, floating apart from the flock; the flower is almost heart-shaped, with a little pink flower that has only just emerged. The brush glides across the canvas. Fanette struggles to concentrate.

Someone's snivelling behind me. The willow has found someone who weeps more than it does. Mary! If only she'd shut up, with her thin little voice.

'You're cheating. I've had enough. I'm going home.'

There's more than crying behind me, there's also Vincent, still there, doing nothing, peering over my shoulder.

'You could just go and play with Mary,' Fanette says.

'She's no fun, she cries all the time.'

'And I suppose I'm no fun, painting all the time?'

He won't move. Vincent won't move. He can stay there for hours. He'd have been a great painter, if he'd put his mind to it. Observing is his thing. But I don't think he has any imagination.

The children go on running around Fanette, shouting, laughing, crying. The little girl forces herself to stay in her bubble. Selfish, as James said.

Camille rushes over and stops on the Japanese bridge. Out of breath.

It never stops. He's all I need!

He covers his fat belly by tucking his shirt in again.

'I'm knackered. I'm taking a break.'

He watches Fanette, busy painting.

'Listen, Vincent, Fanette, this one's good, I have a riddle about the water lilies. You know they double their surface area every day. So, if we say, for example, that the water lilies take a hundred days to cover a whole pond, how many days will the same water lilies take to cover half the pond?'

'Well, fifty,' Vincent replies immediately. 'That's a stupid riddle . . .'

'And what about you, Fanette, what do you think?

I don't care, Camille, if you had any idea how much I don't care.

'I don't know. Fifty. The same as Vincent.'

Camille crows with triumph.

If he ever becomes a teacher, I'm sure he'll be the most boring teacher in the world.

'I knew you'd fall into the trap! The answer isn't fifty, it's ninety-nine . . .'

'Why?' asks Vincent.

'Don't even try,' Camille says contemptuously. 'Fanette, do you get it?'

Christ!

'I'm painting . . .'

Camille hops from one leg to the other on the Japanese bridge. Large sweat stains drench the underarms of his shirt.

'OK, OK, I can see you're painting. Just one last guessing game, one more and then I'll leave you in peace. Do you know the Latin word for water lilies?'

Boring! Boring! Boring!

'No idea?'

Neither Vincent nor Fanette replies. That doesn't bother Camille at all – quite the contrary. He tears off a wisteria leaf and throws it into the pond.

'Well, it's *nymphaea*. But before that it came from the Greek, *numphaia*. The French name is *nénuphar*. And do you know the English name?'

Will this never end?

Camille doesn't even wait for an answer. He tries to hang from the nearest wisteria branch, but a cracking noise dissuades him.

'*Water lily!*' he announces.

He's so pleased with himself. He gets on my nerves, he really does, even if you have to admit that water lily is a much prettier word than nénuphar . . . I prefer nymphéa, the word that Monet used.

Camille leans towards Fanette's canvas. He smells of sweat.

'What are you doing, Fanette? Are you copying Monet's *Water Lilies*?'

'No.'

'You are! I can see you are.'

Camille always brings science back into it; the problem is that he knows everything but doesn't understand anything.

'No, you idiot, no! Just because I'm painting the same thing as Monet doesn't mean I'm doing the same thing.'

Camille shrugs.

'Monet painted loads of them. You're bound to paint one that looks the same. Even if you do a tondo. You know what a tondo is?'

He's going to get my brush in his face. That's the only way he'll understand how boring he is. And he always does both the questions and the answers.

'A tondo is a round canvas, like the one exhibited in—'

'Are you coming, boys?' Mary calls out suddenly. She seems to have dried her tears.

Camille sighs. Vincent laughs.

'I think I'm going to push her in the pond. You could paint that, couldn't you, Fanette? That would be original! *Mary in the Water Lilies.*'

He laughs, gently pushing Camille down the bridge.

'Right, we'll let you get on with your work, Fanette,' says Vincent. 'Come on, Camille.'

Sometimes Vincent understands me. Sometimes he doesn't and sometimes he does. Almost immediately.

Fanette is on her own at last. She carefully studies the reflection of the willows in the pond, or the parts of the pond that aren't filled with lily leaves. She remembers what James has been teaching her recently: vanishing points.

If I remember correctly, the originality of Claude Monet's Water Lilies *lies in the fact that the composition of the paintings is based on two opposing vanishing lines. There's the line of the leaves and the lily flowers, which broadly corresponds to the surface of the water. James called that the horizontal line. But there's also the line that governs the reflections in the water: the wisteria flowers on the banks, the willow branches, the sunlight, the shadows of clouds. Broadly, according to James, the vertical lines are reversed, as if in a mirror. That, James explained to me, is the secret of the* Water Lilies. *Fine, all right, it's hardly breathtaking as secrets go. And you don't have to call yourself James or Claude Monet to find that out. You just have to look at the pond. It's as plain as the nose on your face, those two vanishing lines. Well, I say vanishing. Where are they vanishing to? The pond with the leaves stuck on top of it is entirely motionless. There is no movement, as far as I'm concerned.*

It's rubbish. Now that I'm alone, I almost want to join the others, to run around the pond with them. But no, I've got to be selfish, James said. Think about my talent, about the Robinson competition. I'll join them in a minute.

Fanette bends over her palette and carefully mixes her paints.

Suddenly everything stops. Black! There's nothing but black.

Fanette is about to scream when she recognises Paul by his smell of freshly cut grass.

'Hey there!'

'Paul! Where were you?'

'We've had six games of tig in the garden, but we're done now. I won!' He leans towards the picture. 'Wow, Fanette, your painting is fantastic!'

'I hope so. It's for the Robinson Foundation competition. I think I'm going to be the only one to give something to our teacher.'

'You're amazing! You're definitely going to win. It's so strong, your way of painting.'

'Yeah, if only. Well I do have my idea. It was James who gave it to me.'

'Your famous American painter?'

'Yes, I'm going to see him after school. He's probably still having a snooze in the wheat field. I'm going to show him my canvas. With his advice I might just have a chance. It's true that he gets tired quickly, he sleeps more than he paints. But—'

'It's funny. Your painting doesn't look at all like Monet's *Water Lilies*.'

Fanette kisses Paul on the cheek.

I absolutely LOVE Paul!

'You're brilliant. That's exactly what I wanted. I'll quickly tell you my idea. When you look at a *Water Lilies* by Monet you feel as if you're plunging right into the picture, getting inside it, travelling through it somehow . . . I don't know, like you're sinking into a well or some sand. That's what Monet wanted, sleeping water, the impression of seeing a lifetime pass. I want to do the opposite with my *Water Lilies*. I want people to have a sense of floating on the water, you see, of being able to jump on it, bounce off it, fly away. Living water. I want to paint my *Water Lilies* the way Monet would have painted them if he had been eleven years old. *Water Lilies* in all the colours of a rainbow!'

Paul gazes at her with infinite tenderness.

'I don't understand everything you're saying to me, Fanette.'

'It doesn't matter, Paul. It's not serious, all that. Did you know that Monet painted some big *Water Lilies* that he didn't like?'

'No.'

'He gave them to the children in the pink house! When they were our age. They used the canvases he had rejected to build some canoes. If any of those were found, in the mud at the bottom of the Epte or the Seine, there would be more *Water Lilies*! Can you believe that?'

'I believe you, Fanette.'

Paul pauses.

'But it is serious, you know. I realise that you come from a different planet than the rest of us, and that one day you're going to leave, go far away. You'll become famous, and . . . well, everything! But the great thing is that for my whole life I'll be able to tell people that I knew you, here, on the Japanese bridge. And even . . .'

'And even?'

'And even that I kissed you.'

He's hopeless, Paul. When he says things like that he makes me quiver all over.

The water lilies drift slowly on the pond. Fanette shivers and closes her eyes. Paul gently places his lips on the girl's.

'And you'll even be able to say,' Fanette murmurs, 'that I promised you we'd live together, that we'd get married, and have a big house and children. And even that that's exactly what happened . . .'

The wisteria stirs.

Vincent bursts from the twisted vines like a savage beast of prey in the jungle. He stares at Paul and Fanette with a strange, worryingly empty expression, as if he has been spying on them for some time.

He scares me. Vincent is scaring me more and more.

'What are you doing?' asks Vincent blankly.

43

Still surfing the Au Bon Coin website for a wooden five-step ladder to recondition and put her plants on, officer Liliane Lelièvre glances at her watch, an elegant silver Longines: 6.45 p.m. Another quarter of an hour and she'll be able to close the reception desk of the Vernon police station. There isn't much going on this evening.

She doesn't immediately recognise the figure slowly climbing the steps to the station. But as soon as the old man comes in, turns his face towards hers and greets her, a firework display of memories explodes in her face.

'Hello, Liliane!'

'Chief Inspector Laurentin!'

My God! She hasn't seen him in years. Chief Inspector Laurentin retired what, almost twenty years ago? In the early 1990s, just after the case of the Monets stolen from the Musée Marmottan was solved. Laurentin was viewed as one of the biggest specialists in the illegal art-trade at the time. The Central Art and Cultural Property Unit automatically turned to him. Before that, he and Liliane had worked together for over fifteen years . . .

Chief Inspector Laurentin. A monument. He alone embodied the whole history of the police in and around Vernon.

'Heavens, Chief Inspector! What a pleasure it is to see you again.'

Liliane is perfectly sincere. Laurentin was a brilliant, subtle, attentive investigator. The kind of character you don't see anymore. They talk for a long time. But Liliane can't resist the curiosity that is gnawing away at her:

'So what brings you here, after all this time?'

Chief Inspector Laurentin puts his finger to his mouth.

'Shhh . . . I'm on a special mission. Wait for me, Liliane. I just need a few minutes and I'll be right back.'

Laurentin walks down the corridors that he knows so well. Liliane doesn't dare to press the issue. This is the man who ran the place for thirty-six years!

The former policeman reflects that the paint on the walls of the corridor is still flaking. Nothing changes. Room 33. The former chief inspector takes a key out of his pocket. Will it still open? It has been twenty years since the key was last put in the lock of that office.

Open Sesame . . .

So they haven't changed the lock of the office since . . . 1989. In the end, Laurentin reasons, it seems logical. Why change the lock of an office door inside a police station? As he opens the door, he thinks to himself that his most recent successor must be a boy wonder from CID, armed with computers and specialised technology, all those technological advances so beloved of police procedurals on television, and which he stopped understanding long ago.

He stops beside the desk and looks around the room. The walls are covered with Impressionist paintings. Pissarro. Gauguin. Renoir. Sisley. Toulouse-Lautrec. He smiles to himself. In fact, if he met his successor, he might be surprised. The man has good taste.

The desk is closer to what he expected: on it are a computer, a printer, a scanner. The chief inspector walks around the room. He hesitates, disappointed by his visit. He realises that in 2010 the desk of a policeman who does his job well is an empty desk. Everything will be on the hard drive of the computer. He isn't going to break into the personal work station of his successor, which is probably protected by a series of passwords. And besides, he knows absolutely nothing about computers. It would be ridiculous to deny it. He has never had the opportunity to follow the latest advances in the work of the art division. It's become a specialist area, for scientists. He was told that the OCBC, the art police, now makes use of a gigantic international database, TREIMA, or the 'Electronic Search and Fine-Art Images Thesaurus'. The TREIMA database includes more than 60,000 missing works, and is shared with the American FBI's Art Crime Team and the Art and Antiques Unit of the Metropolitan Police in London.

Laurentin sighs.

Different times, different methods.

He leaves the office and goes back to see Liliane at reception.

'Liliane, are the archives still downstairs? Red door?'

'Exactly as they were twenty years ago, Chief Inspector. Nothing's changed about the archives, at least!'

Once again, his old key lets him in. It's as if anyone could get in here. But then, he's not just anyone. A policeman, just a policeman. That's probably why Patricia Morval turned to him. She wasn't as crazy as all that, the widow.

Liliane was right, nothing has changed, and the files are still arranged in alphabetical order. One generation may succeed another, but there will always be certain officers with a mania for making sure the right files are on the right shelves, even in an age of hard disks and memory sticks.

M . . . for Morval.

The large red file is there. It isn't very thick.

Laurentin hesitates again. He knows he has no right to violate the secrecy of an investigation like that, without a mandate, without authorisation, without any reason other than his personal curiosity. Why should he open that file? Prickles of an excitement that he hasn't felt for years make the hairs on his arms stand up. Why did he come here if not to open this file? He is careful to close the door behind him, leaving the key in the lock, then sets the archive box down on the table. He opens it and inspects the pages slowly, being very careful to put them back in their exact place.

His eyes rest on a sequence of photographs of a corpse: Jérôme Morval, in a stream. The incriminating evidence passes through his fingers: other photographs of the crime scene, one of the print of the sole of a boot, a plaster cast; scientific analyses of fingerprints, of blood, of mud. He speeds up a little, stops on some other pictures: five photographs of couples, from the most platonic to the most obscene. The only point they have in common is the dead man, Jérôme Morval.

Chief Inspector Laurentin looks up, alert, listening for the faintest of footsteps through the red door. No, everything is calm. Next he studies some bundles of paper: a list of the children at

Giverny School; the more or less well-thumbed biographies of individuals related to the case: Jérôme and Patricia Morval, Jacques and Stéphanie Dupain, Amadou Kandy, other shopkeepers from Giverny, neighbours, art critics, collectors; lots of handwritten notes, practically all of them signed by Inspector Sylvio Bénavides.

Almost all the documents are lying face down on the table now. The prickling sensation on Laurentin's skin becomes even more intense. He has only one more document to examine – a yellowed report from the gendarmerie in Pacy-sur-Eure, concerning an accident: a child who drowned in 1937, one Albert Rosalba. Chief Inspector Laurentin's hands are trembling. He sits for a long time in the dark room, trying to understand, trying not to forget a single detail, attempting to forge an opinion, with no preconceptions. It would be easier just to take everything away with him or make photocopies.

But that is unthinkable.

It isn't serious. He realises, not without a certain pride, that he still has a good memory.

He returns to reception half an hour later. Good old Liliane, she waited for him!

'Did you find what were you looking for, Chief Inspector?'

'Yes. Thank you, Liliane.'

Chief Inspector Laurentin observes Liliane tenderly. He remembers the day when she was given the job at Vernon, thirty years ago now. He had called her into his office, Room 33. She wasn't yet twenty-five but already she possessed that kind of elegance that is rare among policewomen.

'What's the new boss like, Liliane?'

'Not bad. Not as good as you . . .'

'Liliane, can I ask a favour? I don't know anything about computers. You're probably more clued up than I am now.'

'I don't know. What do you want?'

'It's a kind of . . . counter-investigation, I would say. I suppose you know your way around the internet?'

Liliane smiles confidently.

'I don't,' the chief inspector continues. 'I retired too early. And I have no children or grandchildren to keep me up to date. I need to consult a website – wait, I wrote it down somewhere . . .'

Chief Inspector Laurentin rummages in his pockets and takes out a yellow Post-it with some words scribbled in clumsy writing.

'Here. It's a website called Copains d'avant. I'm looking for an item from Giverny, a school photograph dated 1936–7.'

44

'James! James!'

Fanette runs close by the wash house and crosses the wheat field where James paints each day. She is carrying, wrapped in a large sheet of brown paper, the painting of the water-lily pond that she has just begun on the Japanese bridge.

'James!'

Fanette can't see anyone in the field, not even an easel, not even a straw hat. There is no trace of James. Fanette wants to surprise the American painter, show him her rainbow *Water Lilies*, listen to his advice, and tell him her idea about painting vanishing lines. She peers around for a moment, then crouches down and hides her painting behind the wash house, in a little space that she has spotted under the cement.

Without anyone noticing.

She gets back up, drops of sweat pearling on her neck. She ran all the way here, to see that big layabout James. Fanette crosses the bridge again.

'James! James!'

Neptune, who was sleeping in the shade of the cherry tree by the witch's mill, hears her. He passes through the entrance and trots towards her.

'Neptune, have you seen James?'

Neptune isn't interested; he goes and sniffs the nearby ferns.

Sometimes that dog annoys me.

'James!'

Fanette tries to get her bearings in the sun. James always follows the sun, like a big lizard, less for the luminous quality it lends the countryside than for the comfort of his siesta.

Maybe that old slacker has fallen asleep in the field.

'James, wake up, it's Fanette. I have a surprise for you.'

She goes on walking. The wheat brushes against her waist.

My God!

Her legs collapse beneath her.

The wheat in front of her is red! Not just red. Green, blue, orange. The coloured ears of wheat have been flattened, as if someone has had a fight here, as if someone has knocked over a palette and disembowelled the tubes.

What could have happened?

I've got to think. I wouldn't be surprised if the people of the village weren't too keen on wandering painters, but to go from that to having a fight with James? An old artist who never hurt a soul . . .

An enormous shiver runs through Fanette's body. She stops, petrified. In front of her is a path of flattened wheat, the stalks red, like a bloody trail. As if someone has dragged himself through the field.

James.

Fanette's thoughts run wild.

James has had an accident, he's injured, he's waiting for my help, somewhere in the meadow.

The path of flattened wheat stops abruptly, in the middle of the field. Fanette stumbles on, parts the ears of wheat, cries out, stamps her feet. The field is enormous.

'Neptune. Please help me, help me look . . .'

The Alsatian hesitates, as if wondering what is expected of him. Then, all of a sudden, he starts to run across the plain. He goes in a straight line. Fanette tries to follow him but it isn't easy with the wheat lashing her arms, her thighs.

'Wait for me, Neptune!'

The dog waits obediently a hundred metres away, almost in the middle of the field. Fanette advances.

Suddenly her heart stops.

Behind the Alsatian, a patch of the field is flattened, one metre by two, just enough room for a prostrate body.

A straw coffin. That's the first image that comes into her head.

James is there. He isn't asleep.

He is dead.

A bloody gash opens up between his chest and his throat. Fanette falls to her knees and her mouth fills with bile.

James is dead. Someone has killed him!

Flies buzz around the open wound. They make a terrible noise. Fanette wants to scream, but she can't. The acid bile burns her throat and she vomits up a viscous liquid over her trousers and her shoes. She doesn't have the courage to rub them clean. She doesn't have any courage at all. Her hands twist together. A swarm of flies licks at her feet. She needs to get help. She straightens up and starts running like crazy. The wheat bites at her ankles and her knees. Her belly is cramped with pain. She coughs, spits, a thread of saliva splashes her cheek, but she goes on running. She passes the stream, the mill, the bridge, the Chemin du Roy, without slowing down. A car slams to a halt just in front of her.

Idiot!

Fanette runs down the road until she is in the village.

'Mum!'

She goes back up the Rue du Château d'Eau. She is screaming now:

'Mum!'

Fanette violently pushes open the door, which bangs against the coat rack that is nailed to the wall. She enters the house. Her mother is standing in the kitchen, at the work surface, as always. Blue overall. Hair pulled back. She drops everything, knife, vegetables, without thinking.

'My little one, my poor little one . . .'

Her mother doesn't understand. She spreads her arms wide, holds out her hands, instinctively. Fanette takes just the one, and pulls on it.

'Maman, you've got to come . . . Quickly!'

Her mother doesn't move.

'Please . . .'

'What's wrong, Fanette? Calm down, tell me.'

'Mum . . . he's . . . he's . . .'

'Calm down, Fanette. Who are you talking about?'

Fanette coughs, choking. She mustn't lose it. Her mother holds out a cloth. Fanette wipes her face and bursts into tears.

'Gently, Fanette, gently. Tell me what's going on.'

Her mother strokes her hands, rests her shoulder against her temple, like lulling a baby to sleep.

Fanette coughs again, then manages to articulate a few words.

'It's James, Mum, the painter. James is dead. Down there, in the field!'

'What are you saying?'

'Come. Come on!'

Fanette suddenly gets to her feet and starts tugging her mother's hand once more.

'Come quickly!'

Listen to me, just for once, I beg you.

Her mother falters. The little girl chants her command, louder each time.

'Come on! Come!'

Fanette seems almost hysterical. Some curtains on the Rue du Château d'Eau are being pulled back. The neighbours must think the little one is having some sort of tantrum. Her mother has no choice.

'I'm coming, Fanette, I'm coming.'

They cross the bridge over the stream. Neptune has returned and has fallen asleep under the cherry tree, in the courtyard of the mill. Fanette drags her mother by the hand.

Faster, Mum.

They step forward into the meadow.

'Over there!'

Fanette walks into the field. She remembers the way even without Neptune; she recognises the flattened wheat. She keeps on walking and reaches the exact spot where James is lying, she's sure it's here.

189

'This is the place, Mum, right here.'

The hand her mother was holding falls limply. Fanette feels dizzy. Her eyes widen in disbelief.

There is no one there.

No body lying in front of them.

I must have made a mistake, I must have got the wrong place, by a few metres . . .

'He was here, Mum . . . Or somewhere close by.'

Fanette's mother looks at her daughter strangely, but she allows herself to be guided by the hand pulling her. Fanette goes on looking, she searches the field for a long time. Then she starts to get annoyed, with her, with everything.

'He was here, I swear . . .'

Her mother doesn't say a word, she simply follows her calmly. A sly little voice slips inside Fanette's head, a tiny worm in the fruit.

She thinks I'm insane. My mother thinks I'm insane.

'He was—'

Suddenly her mother stops walking.

'That's enough, Fanette!'

'He was here, Mum. He had a deep wound between his heart and his throat . . .'

'Your American painter?'

'Yes, James.'

'Fanette, I've never seen your American painter. No one has ever seen him.'

Never seen him? What does she mean? Vincent has seen him, Paul knows him too. Everyone . . .

'We've got to call the police. He was dead, I tell you. Someone has killed him. Someone has taken his body and put it somewhere.'

Don't look at me like that, Mum. I'm not insane. Please believe me, you've got to believe me . . .

'No one's going to call the police, Fanette. There is no body, there has been no crime. There is no painter. You have too much imagination, my little Fanette. Much too much.'

What's she on about? What does she mean?

Fanette screams: 'No, you can't . . .'

Her mother bends down gently until she is level with her daughter's eyes.

'OK, Fanette. I take back what I said. I want to believe you, to trust in you again. But if your painter exists, if he's dead, if he's been murdered, then someone will notice. Someone will look for him and find him. And that someone will tell the police.'

'But . . .'

'This isn't the concern of an eleven-year-old girl, Fanette. The police have better things to do at the moment, believe me. They already have another corpse to deal with, a real corpse that everyone has seen, and no murderer. And we already have enough problems, without attracting even more attention to ourselves.'

I'm not insane!

'I'm not insane, Mum.'

'Of course not, Fanette. No one said you were. It's late now, it's time to go home.'

Fanette is crying. She has no strength left, she follows the hand that guides her.

He was here.

James was here. I can't have invented it all. James exists, of course he does.

And his easels? a voice screams in her head. His four easels? His lovely box of paints? His canvases? His painting knives?

Where have they gone?

You don't just disappear like that.

I am not insane!

The soup doesn't taste good.

Her mother has rubbed out the questions that Fanette had written on the slate, and replaced them with a shopping list. Vegetables, always. A sponge. Milk. Eggs. Matches.

The house is in darkness.

Fanette goes to her room.

*

That evening she doesn't sleep. She wonders if she should disobey her mother, and go and tell the police everything. Tomorrow.

I'm not insane . . . But if I go and see the police, all on my own, Mum will never forgive me. The first thing the police will do is come and tell her everything. Mum doesn't want to have anything to do with the police. That must be because of her cleaning. If the rich families thought that she was involved with the police they would be reluctant to take her on. I'm sure it's that.

But I can't just do nothing either! I have trouble thinking – my poor brain has turned to jelly.

I have to look. I have to understand what happened. I have to find some proof, take it to my mother, to the police, to everyone.

That's why I need someone to help me.

I'll start tomorrow, I'll lead the investigation. No, tomorrow there's school, it's going to be a long, long wait, locked up indoors all day. But as soon as school is out, I'm going to look.

With Paul. I'll tell Paul everything. Paul will understand.

I'm not insane.

45

Laurenç Sérénac picks up the phone with a hint of anxiety. It's rare for him to be called at 1.30 in the morning, especially on his personal number. The voice at the other end of the line doesn't reassure him. It is whispering incomprehensible words. He just manages to make out 'maternity' and 'United States'.

'Who is this, for God's sake?'

The voice becomes slightly more audible.

'It's Sylvio, Chief. Your deputy.'

'Sylvio? Damn it, it's one o'clock in the morning. Speak louder, for heaven's sake, I can only make out one word in three.'

The strength of the voice increases slightly.

'I'm at the maternity unit. Béatrice is asleep in her room, so I've taken the opportunity to slip out into the corridor . . . We have some news!'

'So it's the big day? You wanted your favourite boss to be the first to know? Congratulate Béatr—'

'No,' Sylvio cuts in, 'I'm phoning about the investigation. With the baby and Béatrice it's more a case of wait and see. We rushed to the maternity unit of Vernon Hospital because Béatrice thought she was having contractions. We waited for two hours at the so-called accident and emergency department, just to be told that Béatrice wasn't going to give birth for a while, that the baby was calm, relaxed, in the warm, and that everything was fine. In the end Béa was so insistent that they ended up giving her a room. Oh, Béatrice says hello, by the way.'

'Wish her the best of luck from me.' Sérénac yawns. 'Fine, Sylvio, go ahead. Tell me, what is this scoop of yours?'

Bénavides replies as if he hasn't been listening. 'How was your day at Monet's gardens?'

Laurenç Sérénac hesitates, trying to find the right word.

'Disturbing. And you, what about the Beaux-Arts in Rouen?'

'Instructive.'

'And that's why you've called me?'

'No. In terms of the Beaux-Arts, I have quite a bit of new information, but it complicates everything we already know, so we'll have to go through some things . . .'

The sound of footsteps echoes from the receiver, almost drowning out what Sylvio says next.

'Hang on, boss, they're bringing in a girl on a stretcher, and I don't think it's going to fit in the lift.'

Sérénac waits for a moment, then gets annoyed:

'Are they done? Right, your information.'

'OK. I've found Aline Malétras.'

Laurenç Sérénac stifles a curse.

'You mean the bombshell? Morval's mistress, the one who works for an art gallery in Boston?'

'Exactly. Because of the time difference I couldn't get through to her during the day. But in the end I managed to speak to her a quarter of an hour ago, between two cocktails. It must be about eight o'clock on the East Coast.'

'So did she tell you anything?'

'About Morval's murder, no. She seems to have a concrete alibi. On the morning of the murder she was just leaving a nightclub in a New York suburb, hold on . . .' He reads. 'The Krazy Baldhead, and there was a gang of witnesses. We'll have to check it out, but—'

'We'll check, Sylvio, but it's true that she doesn't seem to be the kind of girl to go home alone. And in terms of job, paintings, gallery, collections, do you see a connection with Morval?'

'Not from what she's told me. She hasn't heard from our ophthalmologist for almost ten years.'

'What do you think?'

'She was in a hurry. She cut me off. She only remembered that he was crazy about the paintings of Claude Monet, and that she found it a bit, how shall I put it, "common". I think she said something like that.'

'And she's still working for the Robinson Foundation?'

'Yes. According to her, she deals with exchanges between France and the United States. Exhibitions, welcoming artists on both sides of the Atlantic, exchanges of paintings.'

'At what level?'

'She seemed to imply that she was on first-name terms with all the fashionable painters on both continents, and that she went and picked up their paintings from their studios, but maybe she just goes to gallery openings and offers people champagne and canapes.'

'Hmm. We really need to know more about this damned Theodore Robinson Foundation.' He yawns again. 'Tell me, Sylvio, I don't want to offend you, but the lovely Aline doesn't seem to have told you very much. Was it worth calling me up in the middle of the night just for that?'

'There's one more thing, Chief.'

'Ah . . .' Sérénac pricks up his ears.

'According to Aline Malétras, she went out with Jérôme Morval about fifteen times, including the time we saw in the photograph. That was taken in the Club Zed, Rue des Anglais, in Paris, in the 5th arrondissement. That was ten years ago. Aline Malétras was twenty-two years old but she wasn't a blushing violet. Morval had money and everything was going well until—'

'Speak louder, damn it!'

'Until Aline Malétras fell pregnant.'

'What?'

'You heard what I said.'

'And did she keep it, the little Morval?'

'No. She had an abortion.'

'Do you know that, or is that what she told you?'

'It's what she told me. But I guess she wasn't the kind of woman who would dream of becoming a single mother at the age of twenty-two.'

'Was Morval aware of this?'

'Yes. He used his contacts in the medical world and paid for everything, according to her.'

'So, let's go back to the beginning, then. We haven't got any closer to a motive for murder.'

More footsteps echo in the hospital corridor. The siren of an ambulance wails in the distance. Bénavides waits for a moment before he starts talking again.

'Except that the child would now be ten or eleven years old.'

'There is no child – she had an abortion.'

'Yes, but what if . . .'

'There is no child, Sylvio.'

'Perhaps she was lying.'

'Then why tell you that she was pregnant at all?'

A long silence. Bénavides' voice is slightly louder.

'Perhaps she wasn't the only one?'

'The only one what?'

'The only one who fell pregnant by Jérôme Morval.'

Another long silence, then Bénavides goes on.

'I'm thinking, for example, about the fifth mistress, the one in Morval's sitting room, the girl in the blue overall that we haven't been able to identify. Perhaps if we could crack that puzzle, then those damn numbers on the back of the photographs . . .'

Down the line, Sérénac hears footsteps approaching, as if the chief nurse were running down the corridor to tell Inspector Bénavides that his nonsense had gone on long enough.

'Christ, you disturb me, Sylvio, with your twisted hypotheses and your stupid columns.'

He sighs.

'Let's try to get some sleep. We'll be up early tomorrow morning for a dip in the river in Giverny. Don't forget your fishing net.'

DAY TEN

22 May 2010
(Moulin des Chennevières)

Tributary

46

Back then, whoever built the mill, and particularly the keep in the middle, must already have had the idea at the back of their mind: the ability to survey the whole village from the fourth-floor window. Call it what you like, that tower just above the tree-tops – a lookout post, a watchtower or a conciergerie – one thing is certain: along with the church tower, it's the best observation point in Giverny. An unassailable view of the whole village, of the meadow practically all the way to Nettles Island, of the brook as far as Monet's garden and, as I'm sure you can imagine, it is above all the best and most discreet of ringside seats from which to view the crime scene. The crime scene relating to Jérôme Morval, I mean.

Look at them right now, for example: with their trousers rolled up in the stream, the police don't really look all that clever. Barefoot. No boots . . . They must be traumatised. Even the deputy, Sylvio Bénavides, is wading in the water. Inspector Sérénac is the only policeman who has stayed on the bank; he's talking to a curious character with glasses who is putting strange instruments in the river and pouring sand into funnels that fit inside one another.

Neptune is there too, of course; he doesn't miss a thing, as you can imagine. He moves from one fern to the next, sniffing heaven knows what. As soon as there's some activity going on, that dog is content. And I think he may now have spotted that Inspector Sérénac is indulgent to a fault, and doesn't stint with his stroking.

Now obviously I'm mocking them slightly, but it isn't at all stupid on the part of the police to dredge the river. Except that they ought to have thought of it before. You will deduce from this that these provincial officers aren't very quick; it's an easy criticism to make. But don't forget, also, that the handsome inspector in charge of this operation has had his thoughts elsewhere. In fact, I would go so far as to say that the river isn't the first thing he'd like to make a move on. But you know, when you're just an old witch who never talks to anyone, there's not much point in making jokes to yourself. So I just go on spying in silence from behind my curtain.

47

The three officers from Vernon are sieving the material dredged from the bed of the brook. Ten square centimetres at a time. They aren't very convinced. The mayor of Giverny has informed them that the river is cleaned every month by the council's environment officers. 'It's the least we can do,' he added. 'That tiny brook lays claim to the title of the first Impressionist river in France! That deserves some special treatment.'

The mayor wasn't lying. The dredging officers have found very little detritus in the mud at the bottom. Some greaseproof paper, some soda capsules, some chicken bones . . .

And to think that all that crap will be examined by the forensic police.

Sylvio Bénavides is struggling to keep his eyelids open. He says to himself that if it goes on like this, he's likely to fall asleep right here, in the water. He thinks these things happen very quickly. You doze off and, with a bit of bad luck, you hit your head on a stone, not very serious in itself, but it's enough to knock you out, enough to allow your head to slip into the water, beneath the water, and in the end you drown.

Sylvio is having dark thoughts this morning. After putting the phone down on Laurenç Sérénac yesterday, he couldn't get to sleep. The nurses wanted him to go home, but that was out of the question. Being a police officer gives you certain privileges. He spent the night watching Béatrice sleep, and dozing on two chairs, opposite some posters warning against the dangers of cigarettes and alcohol for pregnant women. He had time to think and rethink his damned three columns, which are still as compartmentalised as before.

Lovers, *Water Lilies*, children.

What is he supposed to think about those legendary black *Water Lilies*? Amadou Kandy must be aware of them, of course. Morval must have been too. And what about the accident involving that little boy, Albert Rosalba, in 1937? What about that postcard written for an eleven-year-old child, illustrated with a picture of the *Water Lilies* and a quote from Louis Aragon? And why Aragon? Because what could that quote, 'The crime of dreaming, I agree to its creation', possibly mean? And why were there numbers on the back of the photographs of Morval's mistresses? He guesses, he senses, that all of these pieces fit together, that he mustn't ignore any of them, they are all important.

He observes Sérénac. It isn't easy to determine whether his boss is concentrating on the sedimentologist's method of dating the samples, or whether he just isn't interested in the operation at all. The problem is that the jigsaw approach isn't really his boss's thing. Sérénac would be more inclined to tug on only one of the many threads in this tangled situation, and to tug very hard. Sylvio feels that this isn't the solution, that it will only confuse matters still further, and that Sérénac risks having the thread slip between his fingers.

Sylvio notices that Louvel has just scraped the mud off his third plastic bottle. The royal river of Impressionism isn't as squeaky clean once you start digging down to its depths. The sedimentologist analyses all the pieces of exhumed evidence with systematic professionalism, establishing in turn that if it didn't know Claude

Monet in his lifetime, it wasn't acquainted with Jérôme Morval's corpse either.

Sylvio thinks about Sérénac again. It isn't for want of trying to explain his thoughts to his boss. And Sérénac does agree with everything, his three columns, the mysteries, the whole confused mess of it all. But that doesn't stop him locking himself up in his intuition: as far as he's concerned everything revolves around Stéphanie Dupain. The teacher is in danger. That danger has a name: Jacques Dupain. He can't seem to get away from that idea. Objectively, if he examines the facts, Sylvio thinks that the teacher fits the profile of a suspect every bit as much as that of a potential victim. He said as much to Sérénac, but the pig-headed southerner seems to prefer following his instinct rather than the facts. What can Sylvio do about it then?

He thought about it a lot last night. Sylvio is like Béatrice; deep down, he rather likes Sérénac. Paradoxically, however different they might be, he enjoys being paired up with him. Perhaps it's a question of them complementing one another. But he has a strange sense that Sérénac won't stay in Vernon for long. Transfer express, by the look of it. In the north, intuition isn't the favoured method. Particularly when that intuition is being influenced less by what's going on in his brain than what's going on in his trous—

'I think I've got something!'

It was officer Louvel who shouted. All the police immediately gather round.

Louvel plunges both hands into the sand and brings out a flat, rectangular object. The sedimentologist holds out a plastic box so that the sand can flow into it. Gradually they begin to see what the policeman is holding in his hand.

Louvel has found a wooden paint box.

Sylvio sighs. They've drawn a blank, yet again, he thinks. Some painter must have dropped it there, after painting too close to the river. It could belong to anybody at all. It's certainly not Morval's, who collected paintings but didn't paint them.

Louvel sets his find down on the bank while the sedimentologist pours the sand that covered the paint box into his sieves and funnels.

'How long has it been there?' asks Maury, who is interested in such things.

The sedimentologist examines a dial in the smallest of the funnels.

'Less than ten days, no more than that. It fell into the brook yesterday at the latest and probably the day of Morval's murder at the earliest . . . It rained on 17 May and the alluvial deposits swept down by the shower are typical. They come from upstream, and it hasn't rained since then. I'd allow myself a margin of five days before and five days after that date.'

Sylvio steps towards the bank. He's intrigued by this discovery now. So the paint box has been silting up in the stream for ten days at the most . . . The date it was left there might correspond to the murder. Sérénac has come over too.

'Please, Sylvio,' says Sérénac. 'Be my guest. You deserve to be the first to open this treasure,' he adds, winking at his deputy. 'But we'll share out the booty in five equal parts.'

'Like pirates?'

'Exactly.'

Ludovic Maury laughs behind them. Inspector Bénavides doesn't need to be asked twice, and lifts the paint box right up in front of his nose. The wood is old, lacquered, curiously undamaged in spite of its sojourn in the water. Only the iron hinges look rusty. Sylvio deciphers what looks like a faded trademark, *WINSOR & NEWTON*, inscribed in capital letters beneath a logo showing a kind of winged dragon. In smaller letters is a subtitle: *The World's Finest Professional Art Materials*. He isn't sure, but Bénavides imagines that it's a prestigious brand, possibly English or American; he'll have to check.

'So,' Sérénac says impatiently, 'are you going to open that box? We want to know what's inside. Doubloons, jewels, a map of Eldorado . . .'

Ludovic Maury bursts out laughing again. It isn't easy to know whether he really appreciates the boss's sense of humour, or whether he's just laying it on thick. Sylvio, in no particular hurry, works at the rusted hinges, making them squeak. The box opens almost as if it were new, as if it had been used only yesterday. Sylvio expects to find brushes, tubes of paint, a palette, perhaps a sponge. Nothing special . . .

Good God!

Inspector Bénavides nearly drops the box into the stream. Good God . . . His head is spinning. And what if he has been wrong from the beginning, and Sérénac is right?'

His fingers tense on the wood.

'Bloody hell, Chief! Quickly, come and see this.'

Sérénac takes a step forward. Maury and Louvel too. Sylvio Bénavides holds the box open in front of their eyes. The policemen stare at the wooden frame with the fearful contemplation of Orthodox Christians in front of a Byzantine icon.

They all read the same message, carved into the pale wood of the box: *She's mine, here, now and for ever.*

The engraved text is followed by two carved notches. A cross. A death threat.

'Christ alive!' yells Inspector Sérénac. 'Someone threw this box into the stream less than ten days ago. Perhaps even on the day that Morval was murdered!'

He wipes the sweat away from his forehead with his sleeve.

'Sylvio, find me an expert in graphology this minute, and compare this message with the handwriting of all the cuckolds in the village. And put Jacques Dupain at the top of the list!'

Sérénac looks at his watch. It's 11.30 a.m.

'And I want that done before this evening!'

The chief gazes for a long time at the wash house in front of them. As his excitement subsides, he smiles at the four men surrounding him.

'Well played, guys! Let's finish the search of the river quickly and clear the area. I think we've found the biggest fish hiding there.'

He raises a thumb towards Maury.

'That was one hell of a bright idea you had there, Ludo. Dredging the river. We have some evidence, chaps. At last!'

Maury can't help it. He grins like a child who's been given a gold star. For his part, Sylvio Bénavides is habitually suspicious of such premature enthusiasm. For his boss, 'She's mine, here, now and for ever' can only refer to a woman, and the threat must have been written by a jealous husband, ideally Jacques Dupain. But, Sylvio thinks, the 'she' could refer to anyone, even a child of eleven, not necessarily a woman. It could even, at a pinch, be a painting.

The policemen go on methodically searching the river, with less and less conviction. They unearth only a few more objects. Gently, the sun turns, casting the shadow of the Moulin des Chennevières over the crime scene as the officers are preparing to leave. Before they go, Sylvio Bénavides looks up several times at the tower: he could have sworn he saw a curtain moving near the top, on the fourth floor. A moment later he dismisses the thought. He has other things on his mind.

48

'Does Claude Monet have heirs? Living ones, I mean?'

Chief Inspector Laurentin's question surprises Achille Guillotin. The retired chief inspector didn't beat about the bush, according to what the secretary of the Musée des Beaux-Arts in Rouen told him. Laurentin had phoned the museum and asked to speak to their top specialist on Claude Monet. Which is Achille Guillotin. The secretary had rushed to get hold of him on his mobile. He was in a committee meeting with the general council charged with overseeing operation 'Impressionist Normandy'. Another endless meeting. He was almost pleased to come out into the corridor and take the call.

'Heirs of Claude Monet . . . Well, Chief Inspector, it's hard to say.'

'What do you mean?'

'Claude Monet had two children with his first wife, Camille Doncieux: Jean and Michel. Jean would later marry Blanche, the daughter of his second wife, Alice Hoschedé. Jean died in 1914, Blanche in 1947 and the couple had no children. Michel Monet died in 1966, so he was Claude Monet's last living heir. A few years before his death, in his will, Michel Monet appointed the Musée Marmottan, that is, the Académie des Beaux-Arts in Paris, as his sole legatee. The museum is still home to the Monet collection, which includes more than a hundred and twenty paintings. It is the most important collection of—'

'So no heirs,' Laurentin cuts in. 'Claude Monet's descendants died out in a single generation.'

'Not entirely,' Guillotin specifies with obvious delight.

'I'm sorry?'

Guillotin leaves a moment of suspense, and then says:

'Michel Monet had an illegitimate daughter with his lover, Gabrielle Bonaventure, a ravishing woman who worked as a model. Michel finally made their relationship official, and married Gabrielle Bonaventure in Paris in 1931, after his father's death.'

Chief Inspector Laurentin explodes down the telephone:

'Surely in that case, the illegitimate daughter is the last heir? She would be Claude Monet's granddaughter?'

'No,' Guillotin replies calmly. 'Strangely, Michel Monet never acknowledged his illegitimate daughter, even after his marriage. So she's never touched so much as a penny of her grandfather's fabulous inheritance.'

Chief Inspector Laurentin's voice goes blank.

'And what was the name of this illegitimate daughter?'

Guillotin sighs.

'You can find her name in any book about Monet. She was called Henriette. Henriette Bonaventure. In fact I don't know why I'm using the past tense. She must still be alive; at least, I think she is.'

49

Four thirty-one p.m. On the dot.

Fanette doesn't waste a second. She bolts out of school and turns into Rue Blanche Hoschedé-Monet then runs straight to the Hôtel Baudy. She knows that's where American painters stayed in Monet's day – Robinson, Butler, Stanton Young. She knows the story; the teacher told her. That must be where an American painter would stay today. She glances at the green tables and chairs on the terrace opposite, then whirls into the hotel.

The walls are covered with pictures, both paintings and drawings. You would think you were in a museum. Fanette realises it's the first time she's been in the Hôtel Baudy. She would like to have the time to study the prestigious signatures in the poster corner, but a waiter is looking at her from behind his counter. Fanette walks over to him. It's a very tall counter of pale-coloured oak, and Fanette has to stand on tiptoe so that her head peeps over the top. The man has a long black beard, and looks a bit like the portraits of Renoir that Monet painted.

Fanette speaks quickly, she stumbles and stammers, but in the end Renoir seems to understand that the little girl is looking for an American painter, 'James' – no, she doesn't know his surname. Old, with a white beard. He had four easels.

Renoir looks apologetic.

'No, *mademoiselle*. We have no one staying here who resembles your James.'

The waiter's beard covers his mouth, and it's hard to tell whether he's amused or appalled.

'You know, *mademoiselle*, we don't see as many Americans here as we used to in Monet's day . . .'

Idiot! You're an idiot, Renoir!

Fanette re-emerges into the Rue Claude Monet. Paul is waiting for her outside – she told him everything at break time.

'So?'

'Nothing, no one!'

'What are you going to do? Try the other hotels?'

'I don't know. I don't even know his surname. And I think that James slept outside most of the time.'

'We could talk to the others. Vincent. Camille. Mary. If we all work together, we could—'

'No!'

Fanette is almost screaming. Some of the guests at the Hôtel

Baudy, sitting at the terrace on the other side of the road, turn round.

'No, Paul. Vincent, with that sly look of his – I've been staying out of his way for the past few days. And if you tell Camille, he'll only go and list the name of every American painter who's been to Giverny since prehistoric times. As if that's going to help.'

Paul laughs.

'Mary's even worse. The first thing she'll do is cry, and then she'll go and tell the police everything she knows. Do you want my mother to scratch out my eyes?'

'So what are we going to do?'

Fanette studies the park in front of Hôtel Baudy that stretches all the way to the Chemin du Roy: the round bales of hay that cast a bit of shade over the short-mown grass, the meadow stretching behind them all the way to the mouth of the Epte and the Seine, the famous Nettles Island.

These are the landscapes that made James dream. The landscapes for which he left everything. Connecticut, his wife and his children.

'I don't know, Paul. You think I'm mad, don't you?'

'No.'

'He was dead, I swear it.'

'Where did you find him, exactly?'

'In the wheat field, past the wash house, after the witch's mill.'

'Let's go.'

They walk down the Rue des Grands Jardins. The height of the stone façades of the houses seems to have been calculated to make sure the maximum amount of shade floods the alleyway. The cold almost makes Fanette shiver.

Paul ties to reassure his friend: 'You told me James always set up four easels. Plus there would be all of his palettes, his knives, his paint box. There must be some kind of trace up there.'

Fanette and Paul spend over an hour in the wheat field. All they can find are some flattened ears of wheat, as if someone had died there . . .

At least I didn't dream up the straw coffin . . .

. . . or, Paul suggests, as if someone had lain down there for a while. But how could you tell the difference? Paul and Fanette also find ears of wheat stained with paint. Some of them are coloured red – it might be blood, but they don't know. How can you tell the difference between a drop of blood and a drop of red paint? There are also some crushed tubes of paint. But again, that proves nothing; nothing at all, apart from the fact that someone painted here. But Fanette already knew that.

I'm not insane.

'Who else could have seen your painter?'

'I don't know, maybe Vincent?'

'And apart from Vincent? Could an adult have seen him?'

Fanette looks towards the mill.

'I don't know, a neighbour? Maybe the witch in the mill. From the top of her tower, she must be able to see everything.'

'Let's go!'

Give me your hand, Paul. Give me your hand.

50

I don't want to miss them. Here they come, the children! They cross the bridge over the stream and barely glance at the riverbank. This is the very place where the police have just fished out that paint box.

Now there isn't a single policeman there, no yellow tape, no bespectacled man with his funnels. Now there is only the brook, the poplars, the field of wheat. As if nothing was going on, as if nature didn't care.

And now, coming this way, those two children, who don't suspect a thing. Innocent. If only they knew what danger they were in, the poor things . . . Come closer, my pretties, don't be scared, dare to enter the witch's house. Like all those children's stories, like *Snow White*. Don't be afraid of the witch. Come closer, children . . . But do be careful all the same, it isn't my apple that's poisonous. It's the cherries.

*

Eventually I leave my window. I've seen enough.

From outside, no one can spot me, no one can know whether I'm here or not. Whether my mill is deserted or inhabited. No light gives me away. I'm not bothered by the dark, quite the contrary.

I turn towards my black *Water Lilies*. Increasingly now, I like looking at them this way, in the dark. In the gloom, the water depicted on the canvas seems almost to disappear, the few reflections on the surface on the pond dim, and all you can see are the yellow flowers of the water lilies at night, like lost stars in a far-away galaxy.

51

'There's no one here, I'm telling you,' says Fanette.

The little girl looks carefully around the courtyard of the mill. The worm-eaten blades dip into the water of the stream. On the edge of the stone well there is a rusted bucket, eaten away by moss. The shadow of the large cherry tree engulfs almost the entire space.

'Let's go and check,' Paul urges.

He knocks on the heavy wooden door, then lingers in the shadows. It's as if all the things in the courtyard, the walls and stones, have been abandoned there, to wither in the sun, for all eternity.

'You're right, this mill's pretty scary,' says Paul.

'It isn't really,' Fanette replies. 'To be honest, I think I'd love to live somewhere like this one day. It must be nice to live in a house that isn't like all the others.'

Sometimes Paul must think I'm bizarre.

Paul walks around the mill and tries to look through a window on the ground floor. He looks up towards the keep and then turns back towards Fanette, clumsily miming a twisted mouth and clawed fingers.

'I'm suuuure there's a witch living heeeeere, Faaaanette . . . she hatessss painting, she's going to—'

'Don't say that!'

He's terrified, Paul is. I can see that. He's showing off, but he's scared stiff.

Suddenly a dog howls on the other side of the mill.

'Shit, let's get out of here.'

Paul grabs Fanette by the hand but the little girl bursts out laughing.

'Idiot! That's Neptune; he always sleeps here, in the shade of the cherry tree.'

Fanette is right. A few seconds later, Neptune comes over, yelps once more then goes and rubs himself up against the little girl's legs. She bends down to the Alsatian.

'Neptune, you knew James, you saw him yesterday in the field. You found him. You smelled where he was. Where is he now?'

At least you know, Neptune, that I'm not insane!

Neptune sits down. He studies Fanette for a long time. His gaze flicks towards a passing butterfly, then, weary as a lizard on a stone wall, he drags himself back to the shade of the cherry tree. Fanette watches him. She realises with horror that Paul has climbed up into the tree.

'You're mad, Paul! What are you doing?'

No reply.

'The cherries aren't ripe,' Fanette insists. 'You're off your head!'

'No, it's not that,' Paul pants.

A moment later he's clambering back down. Two silver ribbons shine in his right hand.

Sometimes Paul is stupid. If he thinks he has to be Tarzan to make me love him . . .

'It's . . .' Paul explains, getting his breath back. 'It's to get rid of the birds that gather around the prettiest fruits!'

He lands on both feet, throwing up a light cloud of dust. He steps forward, rests one knee on the ground and holds out his arms in the attitude of a medieval knight.

'For you, my princess, some silver to make your hair shine, and to protect you always from wicked vultures when you are far away, when you're famous, on the other side of the world.'

Fanette tries to hold back her tears, but she can't. It's too much, far too much for a little girl like her: the disappearance of James, the arguments with her mother about her painting, about her father, about everything, the Robinson Foundation competition, her *Water Lilies*, and most of all that idiot Paul with his funny, romantic ideas.

You're too stupid, Paul! Too stupid!

Fanette holds the silver ribbons in one hand, and with the other she strokes Paul's cheek.

'Get up, you idiot.'

But she's the one who bends down, all the way down to his mouth, where she deposits a kiss.

Long, long, long. As if it was for ever.

Now she's crying fit to burst.

'Idiot. Three times an idiot. You'll have to put up with these silver ribbons in my hair for the rest of your life. I've already told you we are going to get married!'

Paul stands up and takes Fanette in his arms.

'Come on, let's go. This is madness. Someone died yesterday. And someone else was murdered a few days ago. We should leave it to the police. This is dangerous, we shouldn't be here.'

'And James? I have to f—'

'He's not here . . . there's no one here. Fanette, if you are sure of your story, then I think you need to talk to the police! You never know, James's death may be connected with that other murdered guy they found, you know the one I mean, the murder everyone in the village is talking about.'

Fanette's answer is final.

'No!'

No! Don't put doubts in my head, Paul. No!

'So who's going to believe you, Fanette? Nobody! James lived like a tramp. No one paid him any attention.'

They stop for a moment by the Chemin du Roy, wait until the main road is clear, and then cross. A few clouds are starting to cling to the tops of the hills overlooking the Seine. They set off for the village, in no particular hurry. Suddenly Paul stops.

'And Teacher? Why don't you talk to her? She likes painting. She launched the Robinson Foundation's whatsitsname competition.

She might have bumped into James . . . She'll understand you. She'll know what to do . . .'

'You think so?'

Several people pass the two children in the street.

'I'm certain! It's THE best idea.'

He leans towards Fanette.

'I'm going to tell you a secret, Fanette. I noticed one day that Teacher was wearing silver ribbons in her hair. To tell you the truth, I think that's how you can recognise a princess in the streets of Giverny.'

Fanette takes his hand.

I wish time would stop here. I wish that Paul and I would never move again, that the scenery would just keep moving ceaselessly around us, as if in a film.

'You've got to promise me something, Fanette.'

Their hands intertwine.

'You've got to finish your painting. You need to win the Robinson competition, whatever happens. That's the most important thing.'

'I don't kn—'

'You know what James would have said, Fanette, you know that very well. It's what James would have wanted . . .'

52

The children will turn towards the Rue du Château d'Eau, and I'll lose sight of them. Already, through the drawn curtain, their outlines are a little blurred . . . Neptune doesn't care about any of it. He's sleeping under the cherry tree.

That poor little girl must think she's going to get away. Don't make me laugh! She thinks she's painting a masterpiece, the one she has hidden under the wash house; she must think she's about to fly away over Monet's pond. Subsume the weightlessness of her only art, her genius that everyone's always going on at her about.

Rainbow *Water Lilies*! Poor little Fanette. How ludicrous!

I turn towards my black *Water Lilies*. The yellow corollas gleam among the shades of mourning set down by the brush of a desperate painter.

What vanity!

A fall in the pond, that's what awaits little Fanette. Drowned, trapped beneath the surface of the water lilies, like the thick layer of ice in a lake in winter.

Soon, very soon, now.

Everyone will have their turn.

DAY ELEVEN

23 May 2010

(Moulin des Chennevières)

Hostility

53

For once, I'm not spying at my window. You see, in spite of appearances, I don't just spend my days spying on my surroundings. Not just that.

This morning, outside, the noise of the chainsaws was infernal. I learned about this not long ago. Apparently they've decided to cut down fourteen hectares of poplars. Yes, felling poplars. Here, in Giverny! From what I understand, these particular poplars were planted in the early 1980s, tiny saplings at the time, probably to make the landscape look even more Impressionist. Except that since that time some specialists, probably different ones, have explained that these poplars didn't exist in Monet's time, that the landscape of the meadow that the painter admired from the window of his house was open, and that the more these poplars grow, the more their shade will cover the garden, the pond, the lilies. And the less recognisable the background on the horizon of Monet's paintings will become for the tourists. So apparently it's been decided, after planting the poplars, that they must all be cut down. And why not, after all? Some Givernois complain, others applaud. I can tell you, today, I don't give a damn.

I have other things on my mind. This morning, I tidied some old mementos, things from before the war, black and white photographs, the kind of relics that interest only old women like me. You've worked it out; I finally decided to empty my garage and find that crumpled old cardboard box tied up with twine. It was hidden under three layers of video cassettes, one layer of vinyl records and ten centimetres of bank statements from the Crédit Agricole. I folded the tablecloth into four and spread out the photographs.

After the chainsaws an hour ago, this time it was a siren that quickly brought me back to reality, the way the ringing of an alarm clock scatters your morning dreams.

A police siren, wailing along the Chemin du Roy.

The moment before, my tears were wetting the only photograph that has any importance in the end. A school photograph. Giverny. 1936–7. It's hardly yesterday, I grant you. I studied the portrait of around twenty pupils, all with their bottoms pressed obediently against three wooden steps. The names of the children are written on the back, but I didn't need to turn the photograph over.

On the bench, Albert Rosalba is sitting next to me. Of course.

I've looked at Albert's face for a long time. The photograph must have been taken shortly after the end of the holidays, sometime around Halloween.

Before the tragedy.

That was when the police siren pierced my ears.

I got up, as you can imagine. As if a prison warden, however distracted, wouldn't run to his lookout post the moment the alarm sounded. So I ran to my window. Well, ran is a figure of speech. I picked up my cane and hobbled towards the glass, discreetly pushing the curtain aside with my stick.

I didn't miss a thing. It was impossible to miss the police. The cavalry was out in force. Sirens and flashing lights.

I couldn't deny it, Inspector Sérénac was excelling himself!

54

Sylvio Bénavides looks up at the keep of the mill, which is flashing by on his right-hand side.

'Now,' Sylvio murmurs between two yawns. 'I stopped by the mill, Chief. You know you told me not to neglect a single witness, particularly the neighbours?'

'And?'

'It's strange. You would think the mill was deserted. Abandoned, if you prefer.'

'Are you sure? The garden looks as if it's being maintained, and so does the façade. Sometimes, when we were at the crime scene, I thought I spotted some movement there, particularly towards the top, on the highest floor of the tower . . . A curtain moving at the window, or something like that.'

'Me too, Chief. I had the same impression. But no one answered the door, and the neighbours tell me that no one has lived there for months.'

'Strange. You're not going to tell me it's that village *omertà* again, like there was over that eleven-year-old boy?'

'No . . .'

Sylvio hesitates for a moment.

'To tell you the truth, the locals all call that place the witch's mill.'

Sérénac smiles, watching the reflection of the tower disappearing in his rear-view mirror.

'It's more like a ghost's mill, isn't it? So, leave it, Sylvio. We have other urgent matters to take care of.'

Sérénac accelerates again. Monet's gardens pass by on their left in half a second. Neither passenger could ever have had such an Impressionist view of the garden.

'Now,' Laurenç continues. 'While we're on the subject of the village *omertà*, do you know what Stéphanie Dupain told me yesterday, about Monet's house and the studios?'

'No.'

'That if you looked properly, you would find, hidden away,

dozens of paintings by great artists. Renoir, Sisley, Pissarro . . . and, of course, some undiscovered *Water Lilies* by Monet.'

'Did you find them?'

'A pastel drawing by Renoir. Perhaps . . .'

'She was pulling your leg, Chief!'

'Of course. But why tell me a story like that? She even added that it was a kind of open secret in Giverny.'

Sylvio thinks once again about the conversation he had with Achille Guillotin on the subject of Monet's lost paintings. A painting that had been lost and found again by a stranger – why not? Like the famous black *Water Lilies*. But dozens of them.

'She's playing with you, Chief. She's taking you for a ride. I've been telling you that from the very beginning. And I don't think she's the only one, here in the village.'

Sérénac doesn't respond, and concentrates on the road once more. Sylvio leans his pallid face out of the open window. His nostrils try to inhale the scraps of fresh air.

'Are you all right, Sylvio?' says Sérénac, concerned.

'I'm OK. I must have had a dozen coffees last night to stay awake. This morning the doctors decided to keep Béatrice in till the bitter end.'

'I thought you only drank tea, no sugar?'

'I thought so too . . .'

'So what are you doing here, when your wife's in the maternity ward?'

'They're going to call me if anything happens. The gyno is dropping by. The baby is still nice and warm in its cocoon, lucky thing, and they say this could go on for days.'

'And you've spent all night on the case?'

'Got it in one. Well, I have to keep busy, don't I? Béatrice snored like a dormouse in her room for the rest of the night.'

Sérénac takes a hairpin bend towards the heights of Giverny, along the Rue Blanche Hoschedé-Monet. Sylvio glances in the rear-view mirror. Two police cars are following behind them. Maury and Louvel are just about keeping up. Sylvio manages to restrain a burp.

'Don't worry,' Sérénac goes on. 'The Morval case will be solved in the next thirty minutes. You'll be able to set up a camp bed at the hospital. Day and night. The graphology experts are clear: that message carved into the paint box, 'She's mine, here, now and for ever' matches Jacques Dupain's handwriting. You have to admit that I was right, Sylvio.'

Sylvio takes big, deep breaths of the air outside. The Rue Blanche Hoschedé-Monet snakes along the hill and Sérénac is still driving like a lunatic. Bénavides wonders if he's going to be able to survive the whole climb. He holds his breath and brings his head back inside the car.

'Only two experts out of three, Chief . . . And their conclusions are more than nuanced. According to them, there are certainly similarities between the words carved in the wood and Dupain's handwriting, but there are also a considerable number of divergent features. I get a sense that the experts haven't a clue.'

Sérénac's fingers tap nervously on the wheel.

'Listen, Sylvio, I can read the reports as well as you can. There is a similarity with Dupain's handwriting, that's the expert opinion, isn't it? As to the divergences, I just think that carving in wood with a blade isn't exactly the same thing as signing a cheque. It all links up, Sylvio; don't make life more complicated than it need be. Dupain is insanely jealous. Numero uno, he threatens Morval with the message in the postcard, the quote from Aragon, the extract from the poem "Nymphée": "The crime of dreaming, I agree to its creation"; numero two-o, he repeats his threats in the message on the paint box; numero three-o, he bumps off his rival . . .'

The Rue Blanche Hoschedé-Monet is now reduced to a two-metre-wide ribbon of asphalt that twists and turns before it reaches the Vexin plain. Sylvio hesitates to contradict Sérénac again, to point out that faced with inconsistencies in the expert testimony from the graphologists, Pellissier, the specialist from the Palais de Justice in Rouen, mentioned the possibility of a clumsy attempt at imitation.

A brief swing round to the left.

Sérénac, who was driving in the middle of the road, has a near miss with a tractor that is coming down the hill in the opposite direction. Just in time, the startled farmer abruptly steers into the ditch. He watches in disbelief as two more blue cars come speeding past him.

'Dear God!' Sylvio yells, peering into the mirror.

He takes a deep breath, then turns back towards Laurenç Sérénac.

'But how is the paint box involved in this whole story? According to the analysis, the paint box is at least eighty years old. A collector's piece! A Winsor & Newton, the best-known trademark in the world, a brand that has been supplying painters for more than a hundred and fifty years . . . Who could this damned box have belonged to?'

Sérénac goes on anticipating the hairpin bends. Indifferent sheep in the meadows barely turn their heads as the wailing cars hurtle past.

'Morval was a collector,' says Sérénac. 'He liked beautiful things.'

'No one ever saw him with this paint box. Patricia Morval, his widow, is absolutely positive on the matter. Not forgetting the fact that the link with the crime has not been established. That paint box could have been thrown into the river by anybody at all, several days after Morval's murder.'

'They've found blood on the box.'

'It's too soon, boss! We haven't had the analyses back yet. There's no certainty that it's Morval's blood. Forgive me, but I think you're going too fast . . .'

As if by way of reply, Inspector Sérénac turns off the siren, and pulls on the handbrake as they reach a small car park.

'Listen, Sylvio, I have a motive, I have a threat aimed at the victim written in the hand of Dupain, who has no alibi, but who serves us up a grotesque story about stolen boots. So I'm going in! When your jigsaw fits together differently, with your damned three columns, let me know. The other thing to support the charge against Dupain, is – even if I know you don't agree – my personal conviction.'

Sérénac gets out of the car without waiting for a reply. When Sylvio steps out of the vehicle in turn, he feels the ground spinning around him. He tells himself that he's not coping with all the coffee, or with all the excesses in general, and that he'd be better off going to throw up behind the pines at the end of the car park.

Except that it wouldn't be very discreet. Three gendarmerie trucks are parked at each end of the car park, and a dozen police officers are getting out and stretching.

The boss has pulled out all the stops on this one. About fifteen men at the very least, a good proportion of the Vernon station, plus the gendarmeries of Pacy-sur-Eure and Écos. He's put on a big spread, Sylvio thinks, chewing the chlorophyll-flavoured gum that Louvel has just given him, and he's demonstrating a liking for theatre that is perhaps a little disproportionate.

All this for just one man.

Who might well be armed.

But who might not even be guilty.

The brown rabbit bolts in desperate zigzags across the limestone meadow, as if someone has taught it that the long steel tubes carried by the three shadows in front of it are capable of taking its life in a flash of white light.

'That one's yours, Jacques.'

Jacques Dupain doesn't even raise his gun. Titou looks at him with astonishment, then shoulders his rifle. Too late. The beast has disappeared between two gorse bushes.

There is nothing in front of them now but the bare grass grazed by the recently introduced flocks of sheep. They carry on towards Giverny along the Astragale path.

'Damn it, Jacques, you're not on form,' murmurs Patrick. 'I think you might even miss a sheep.'

Titou, the third huntsman, nods in agreement. Titou is rather a good gunman. If he hadn't left that rabbit for Jacques, it wouldn't have got further than two metres . . . Quick on the draw, as his friends often tell him. Because otherwise it's a matter of finesse.

'Is it because of the investigation into Morval's murder?' he says, turning towards Jacques Dupain. 'Are you scared that the police-man's going to throw you in jail just to steal Stéphanie from you?'

Titou explodes with laughter. Jacques Dupain stares at him with controlled irritation. Patrick sighs but Titou won't let the matter drop:

'I have to say, you're having a run of bad luck with Stéphanie. First there's Morval, and now here comes this cop chasing after her.'

The gravel trickles down the Astragale path as they walk along. Behind them, on the hillside, two black and white ears appear.

When he gets going, Titou can't stop.

'You know, if you weren't my friend, I'd happily give Sté—'

Patrick voice breaks in: 'Shut up, Titou!'

Titou lets the end of his sentence disappear into his moustache. They continue down the path, sliding rather than walking. Titou seems to be ruminating over something, then he bursts out laughing once more.

'By the way, Jacques, I hope my boots aren't hurting your feet.'

Patrick stares at Titou in disbelief. Jacques Dupain doesn't show the slightest reaction.

'I'm just pulling your leg, guys. You know that, right, Jacques? I'm just pulling your leg. I know you didn't kill Morval!'

'Damn it, Titou, stop—'

This time it's the end of Patrick's sentence that is lost in his throat.

In front of them, the car park where they left their van has been turned into Fort Alamo. There are six cars with rotating lights and almost twenty policemen. Urban police officers and rural gendarmes stand in front of them in a semi-circle, hands on their hips, fingers on the white leather holsters of their revolvers.

Inspector Sérénac stands a few metres in front of the huntsmen. Patrick instinctively steps aside. His hand closes around the cold barrel of Jacques Dupain's rifle.

'Gently does it, Jacques. Gently does it.'

Inspector Sérénac steps forward.

'Jacques Dupain. You are under arrest for the murder of Jérôme Morval. Please come quietly.'

Titou bites his lip, throws his rifle on the ground and raises two trembling hands, as he has seen people do in films.

'Gently now, Jacques,' Patrick says again. 'Don't do anything stupid.'

Patrick knows his friend very well. They've been going out, walking, hunting together for years. He doesn't like that marble face, he doesn't like it at all, that absence of expression, almost as if his friend had stopped breathing.

Sérénac steps forward again. Alone. Unarmed.

'No!' yells Sylvio Bénavides.

He passes through the semi-circle of policemen and goes and stands next to Sérénac. It may be a symbolic gesture, but Bénavides has a sense that he's breaking a kind of symmetry; as if he hoped to disrupt the relentless mechanism of a duel in a western by crossing the street at the wrong time. Jacques Dupain rests his hand on Patrick's wrist. Without a word, Patrick has understood. He has no choice but to let go of the steel barrel.

He hopes he won't regret it.

He is alarmed to see Jacques's hand clenching the trigger and the barrel gently rising.

Under normal conditions, Jacques's aim is even better than Titou's.

'Stop, Laurenç,' Sylvio murmurs, his face pale.

'Jacques, don't be a fool,' Patrick whispers.

Sérénac steps forward, one more pace. The inspector slowly raises his hand and stares the suspect straight in the eye. Sylvio Bénavides is horrified to see a defiant smile appearing at the corner of his superior's lips.

'Jacques Dupain, you . . .'

The barrel of Jacques Dupain's gun is now aimed at Sérénac. An imposing silence has invaded the Astragale path.

Titou, Patrick, officers Louvel and Maury, Inspector Sylvio Bénavides, the fifteen policemen, even the least clever among them, even the least skilled at guessing what might be hiding inside a brain . . . they all read the same thing in Jacques Dupain's cold eyes.

Pure hatred.

55

The girl behind the desk at the Évreux public archives always begins her sentences with four words: 'Have you checked if . . .' She studiously does an impression of an overworked employee behind the double screen of her computer but then finally looks up, through her gold-rimmed glasses, at the old man asking her for copies of the late lamented *Républicain de Vernon*, the local weekly newspaper which became *Le Démocrate* after the Second World War. He wants all the issues between January and September 1937.

'Have you checked if they have archives in Vernon, at the offices of *Le Démocrate*?'

Chief Inspector Laurentin stays cool. He's been haunting the local archives for two hours, trying humbly to play the part of the charming old man who is kind towards women much younger than himself. It usually works. Not this time.

The girl behind her desk couldn't care less about his sweet murmurings. It would have to be said that around the wooden tables of the archive's consulting room, the ten people present are all men aged over sixty – budding septuagenarian historians or genealogical archaeologists digging for their roots – and they have all adopted the same strategy as Chief Inspector Laurentin: gallantry has become a tad outmoded. Laurentin sighs. It was all much simpler when he could simply hold his tricolore card under the nose of a disaffected civil servant. Of course, the girl has no idea that she's dealing with a police chief inspector.

'I've already checked,' Chief Inspector Laurentin explains with a forced smile. 'At the offices of *Le Démocrate,* they don't have any archives before 1960 . . .'

The girl recites her usual litany: 'Have you checked in the Vernon local archives? Have you checked the magazine department of the National Archives in Versailles? Have you checked if . . .'

Is this girl paid by the competition?

Chief Inspector Laurentin takes refuge in the patient resignation of the pensioner who has all the time in the world.

'Yes, I've checked! Yes! Yes!'

His research into Henriette Bonaventure, the mysterious potential last heir of Claude Monet, has yielded absolutely nothing so far. It isn't so important. There's another trail that he wants to pursue, unconnected. To do that he just has to persist until the girl behind the desk understands that she's going to waste more time putting this stubborn old man off than by granting him his wishes.

Finally, his tenacity pays off. Just over thirty minutes later, Chief Inspector Laurentin is holding the weekly newspaper in front of him. *Le Républicain de Vernon.*

A yellowed old copy dated Saturday, 5 June 1937. He lingers for a moment on the front page, which details a mixture of national events and local news items. The chief inspector scans a moving editorial on Europe in flames: Mussolini celebrates his entente with Hitler, the possessions of the Jews are being confiscated in Germany, Franco's supporters are crushing the Republicans in Catalonia . . . Below the dramatic editorial a blurred photograph explodes with the platinum-blond hair and dark lips of Jean Harlow, the American idol who died a few days earlier, at the age of twenty-six. The lower part of the first page is devoted to more regional concerns: the forthcoming opening, less than one hundred kilometres from Vernon, of Le Bourget airport; the death of a Spanish agricultural worker who was found with his throat slit in a Freycinet barge moored in Port-Villez, almost directly opposite Giverny . . .

At last Chief Inspector Laurentin opens the second page and finds the article he is looking for: 'Fatal accident in Giverny'.

In ten lines, over two columns, the anonymous journalist set out the tragic circumstances of the death by drowning of an eleven-year-old boy, Albert Rosalba. The incident happened in a place known as the meadow, near the wash house given to the village by Claude Monet and the Moulin des Chennevières, in the mill-race channelled out of the Epte. The boy was alone. The gendarmerie concluded that it was an accident: the little boy was thought to have slipped, his head hitting a stone on the bank. Unconscious, Albert Rosalba, who was an excellent swimmer, drowned in twenty centimetres of water. The article went on to evoke the pain of the Rosalba family and little Albert's classmates. It even slipped in a few lines on the controversy that was brewing. Claude Monet had been dead for over ten years now: shouldn't that artificial stretch of river be shut off and the insalubrious lily pond, which was now basically neglected, be allowed to dry up?

A blurred photograph accompanies the cutting. Albert Rosalba poses, his black jacket buttoned up to the neck, his hair cut short, smiling behind his school desk. A moving photograph of a good little boy.

That's him, thinks Chief Inspector Laurentin.

He takes a school photograph from the bag at his feet. The date and place are written on a black slate hanging from a tree in the school playground: 'Giverny School: 1936–7'.

It was Liliane Lelièvre who helped him unearth that image from the Copains d'avant website, as Patricia Morval had suggested on the phone. Liliane told him that the site was a place where you could stroll back through the classes you had attended, from primary school onwards; where you could find the faces of people you come into contact with during your life, and not just behind your school desk: the people with whom you'd shared a workplace, a regiment, a summer camp, a sports club, a school of music – or a school of painting . . .

It's quite surreal, thinks Chief Inspector Laurentin. It's as if there's no need to remember anything for yourself. As if your whole life has been archived, classified, revealed, and even made available to share . . . Or almost. Most of the photographs on the site date back ten years or so; twenty or thirty at the most. Strangely, that school photograph from 1936–7 is by far the oldest.

Bizarre . . .

As if Patricia Morval had put it online deliberately so that he would find it. Chief Inspector Laurentin concentrates on the photographs again.

That's definitely him . . .

The photograph from the *Républicain de Vernon* is a perfect match for the little boy in the school photograph, sitting in the middle of the second row.

Albert Rosalba.

No child's name is attached to the school photograph from the Copains d'avant website. The names must have been written on the back, on the original. Never mind. Laurentin closes the issue of *Le Républicain de Vernon* dated 5 June 1937 and opens the next few issues. He takes time to read the local pages, to examine the details. In the issue dated 12 June 1937, mention is made of Albert Rosalba's funeral at Sainte-Radegonde's church in Giverny. And of the grief of his family.

Three lines.

Laurentin continues, opening and closing the newspapers that are piling up, beneath the anxious eyes of the girl behind the desk.

15 August 1937 . . .

At last Chief Inspector Laurentin finds what he is looking for. It's an insignificant little article, a few lines, no photograph, but the headline is quite explicit:

THE ROSALBA FAMILY LEAVES GIVERNY: THEY HAVE NEVER BELIEVED IN THE THEORY OF AN ACCIDENT.

Hugues and Louise Rosalba, who have worked for over fifteen years in the foundries of Vernon, have decided to leave the village of Giverny. Let us recall that they were touched two months ago by a tragic incident: their only son, Albert, drowned after an unexplained fall in the brook which runs along the Chemin du Roy. The drowning provoked a brief controversy in the municipal council concerning the drying up of that arm of the Epte and of Monet's gardens. Explaining their departure, the Rosalbas spoke of their inability to go on living in the setting where their child had met his end. But there is one more awkward detail: Louise Rosalba claims that what is driving her to leave the village most of all is the troubling silence of the residents. According to Mme Rosalba, her son Albert never walked about alone in the village. She confirmed to me what she had said several times to the gendarmes: that, according to her, 'Albert never played alone beside the stream. There must be witnesses. There must be people who know.' According to Louise Rosalba, 'This accident affects everyone. No one wants a scandal in Giverny. No one wants to confront the truth.'

A moving conviction on the part of a distressed mother. We give the Rosalbas our very best wishes for rebuilding their lives far from these disturbing memories.

Chief Inspector Laurentin reads the article through several times, closes the newspaper, and then studies all the other copies of *Le Républicain de Vernon* for 1937, but there are no other articles devoted to the Rosalba case. He pauses. For a moment he wonders what he is doing here. Has his life become so empty that he is willing to spend his days pursuing the first fantasy that comes along? He looks around the room at the dozen or so other readers, all concentrating on their piles of yellowed documents. To each his own quest . . . The chief inspector's pen glides over his notepad. *2010–1937=73.*

Little Albert was eleven years old in 1937, which means that he was born in 1925 or 1926. The Rosalbas would now be over a hundred years old. A light appears in front of Laurentin's eyes.

Could they possibly still be alive?

The girl watches him coming towards her. She wears the expression of an official meeting a client who has turned up at closing time. Except that it's only 11 a.m., and the archives are open all day. Chief Inspector Laurentin tries out the kind of suave charm you might associate with the actors from Hollywood's golden age. A mixture of Tony Curtis and Henry Fonda.

'Excuse me, do you have an online directory? I'm looking for an address; it's quite urgent.'

The girl takes an eternity to look up, before saying: 'Have you checked if—'

The chief inspector erupts, holding his identity card under her nose.

'Chief Inspector Laurentin! From Vernon police station! Retired, I grant you, but that doesn't mean I can't go on doing my job. So, young lady, if you could kindly get a move on . . .'

The girl sighs. No panic, no apparent anger. As if she's used to the eccentricities of the pensioners who scour the archives and who, every now and again, God knows why, become hysterical. She does, however, visibly speed up the rhythm of her fingers on the keyboard.

'What name are you looking for?

'Hugues and Louise Rosalba.'

The girl's fingers dart across the keys. *Allegro.*

'Have you found an address?' Laurentin asks.

'For Hugues Rosalba it's not worth it. I always check before contacting Interpol. It's a habit. Hugues Rosalba died in 1981, in Vascoeuil.'

Laurentin thinks for a moment. There's nothing he can add. The girl at the counter is organised.

'And what about his wife, Louise?'

She taps again.

'No mention of a death . . . But no known address either.'

Dead end.

Laurentin studies the white room, trying to come up with an idea. At random he decides to try some Sean-Connery-style spaniel eyes. The girl gives an exasperated sigh in response.

'Generally,' she says wearily, 'to find people of a certain age, rather than using the directory you're better off looking among the residents of old people's homes. There are plenty of those in the Eure region, but if your Louise lived in Vascoeuil, we could start with the closest ones . . .'

Sean Connery gets his smile back and the girl, who could maybe now just about pass for Ursula Andress, begins tapping away on the keyboard like a mad thing. Minutes go by.

'I've looked up retirement homes on Google Maps,' the girl says at last. 'The closest one to Vascoeuil is Les Jardins, at Lyons-la-Forêt. We should be able to find out some information on the residents. What was the name again?'

'Louise Rosalba.'

The keys rattle.

'They must have a website. Oh, here it is.'

Laurentin cranes his neck to get a view of the computer screen. Several more minutes pass, then the girl looks up triumphantly.

'Got it! I've found the complete list of residents. It wasn't so complicated after all. The woman you're after, Louise Rosalba, went into the home in Lyons-la-Forêt about fifteen years ago, and she's still there . . . aged one hundred and two! I should warn you, Chief Inspector, that I can't guarantee the after-sales service . . .'

Laurentin feels his heart speeding up dangerously. Rest, rest, his cardiologist keeps telling him . . . My God! Is it possible? That there's still a witness?

One last witness?

And she's alive!

56

The three police vans return down the Rue Blanche Hoschedé-Monet, sirens wailing. They don't even bother skirting the village, they take the shortest route, Rue Blanche Hoschedé-Monet, Rue Claude Monet . . . Chemin du Roy.

Giverny streams past.

The town hall.

The school.

When they hear the sirens, all the children in the class turn their heads. They all want to do one thing: run to the window. Stéphanie Dupain restrains them with a calm gesture. Not a single child has noticed her distress. To keep her balance, the teacher rests her hand on the desk.

'Children, please calm down, right now. Let's get back to our lesson.'

She clears her throat, the police sirens still echoing in her head.

'So children, we were talking about the competition for promising artists organised by the Robinson Foundation. I should remind you that you have only two days to hand in your paintings. I hope a few of you will give it a go this year.'

Stéphanie is unable to dismiss the image of her husband smiling at her that morning while they lay in bed, kissing her then resting a hand on her shoulder. 'Have a good day, my love.'

She continues with the spiel she's been repeating for quite some time.

'I know that no child from here has ever won the competition, but I'm also sure that when the international jury sees that a candidate is from Giverny itself, then it will give you a huge advantage!'

Stéphanie sees Jacques slipping on his cartridge belt, Jacques unhooking his hunting rifle from the wall . . .

'Children, Giverny is a name that stirs the imagination of painters all over the world.'

Two other blue police cars pass through the village. Stéphanie starts involuntarily, panicked. Powerless. The cars didn't slow down either.

Laurenç?

Stéphanie tries again to concentrate. She looks at her class, studies each of the faces in front of her one by one. She knows that some of her pupils are particularly gifted.

'I have noticed that some of you are very talented.'

Fanette lowers her eyes. She doesn't like it when the teacher looks at them like that. It's embarrassing.

I think that may have been meant for me . . .

'I'm thinking particularly of you, Fanette. I'm counting on you!'

What did I say?

The little girl blushes to her ears. A moment later, the teacher turns back to face the board. At the back of the class, Paul winks at Fanette. He stretches across the desk in front of Vincent, who is sitting next to him.

'Fanette, Miss is right! You're going to win that competition. You and nobody else.'

Mary is sitting in front of them, sharing a desk with Camille. She turns round.

'Shhh . . .'

All heads suddenly freeze.

There's a knock at the door.

Stéphanie opens it. She finds herself looking into Patricia Morval's distraught face.

'Stéphanie . . . I need to talk to you. It's . . . it's important.'

'Wait here for me, children.'

Once again, Stéphanie tries to ensure that none of her gestures betrays her terrible fear to the children.

'I've only got a moment.'

Stéphanie goes outside. She shuts the door behind her and walks into the square in front of the town hall, beneath the lime trees. Patricia Morval doesn't even try to hide her agitation. She is wearing a crumpled jacket that clashes with her bottle-green skirt. Stéphanie notices that her chignon, which is normally impeccable, has been hastily done. It's almost as if Patricia had hurried out into the street in her dressing gown . . .

'Titou and Patrick told me,' Patricia begins breathlessly. 'They've arrested Jacques, at the bottom of the Astragale path, when they came back from hunting.'

Stéphanie rests her hand against the trunk of the nearest lime tree. She doesn't understand.

'What? What are you saying?'

'Inspector Sérénac . . . He's arrested Jacques. He's accusing him of Jérôme's murder!'

'Laurenç?'

Patricia Morval gives Stéphanie a strange look.

'Yes, Laurenç Sérénac. That policeman.'

'My God. And Jacques didn't—'

'No, don't worry, your husband didn't do a thing. But from what I've been told, it was a good thing that Patrick was there. And Sérénac's deputy, too, Inspector Bénavides. They only just averted a bloodbath. You realise, Stéphanie, that that lunatic Sérénac thinks that Jacques killed my Jérôme.'

Stéphanie feels her legs crumbling beneath her, and her body slumps against the pale trunk of the tree. She needs to breathe. She needs to think calmly. She has to get back to her classroom; the children are waiting for her. She has to run to the police station. She has to . . .

Patricia Morval's hands tug at the collar of her creased jacket.

'It was an accident, Stéphanie. Right from the start, I've always tried to believe that it was an accident. But what if I am mistaken, Stéphanie? What if I am mistaken, and someone really did kill

Jérôme? Tell me, Stéphanie: it couldn't have been Jacques, could it? Tell me it couldn't have been Jacques . . .

Stéphanie turns her water-lily eyes on Patricia Morval. Eyes like that can't lie.

'Of course not, Patricia. Of course not.'

57

I'm spying on the two women. Well, spying is a big word. I'm just sitting opposite them on the other side of the street, a few metres away from the Art Gallery Academy, and not too close to the school. Not completely invisible, but discreet; close enough not to miss anything of the scene. I'm quite good at this, as you may, I think, have realised. It's not too difficult anyway – Patricia and Stéphanie are speaking in loud voices. Neptune is lying at my feet. He's waiting for school to finish, as he does every day. He has whims, my dog has. And because I like to spoil him, I give in to him, I come here almost every day to wait with him.

As we sit there, another class is released, but this one is much less likely to make Neptune wag his tail: the students leaving the Art Gallery Academy. About fifteen artists in all, and about as promising as a bench of senators. They are pulling their paint caddies and wearing their red badges, in case they get lost. School's out for the pensioners! The international brigade: Canadians, Americans, Japanese.

I try to concentrate on the conversation between Stéphanie Dupain and Patricia Morval. They're about to reach the denouement, the last act of the Greek tragedy. The sublime sacrifice.

You no longer have any choice, my poor Stéphanie.

You will have to . . .

I don't believe it!

A painter plonks himself right in front of me: a typical American octogenarian, with a 'Yale' baseball cap wedged on his head, wearing socks with leather sandals.

What does he want from me?

'Excuse me kindly, miss . . .'

He pronounces each word with a Texan accent, putting a three-second pause between each syllable.

'I assume you're from around here, miss? You must surely know an original spot where I can paint . . .'

'Up there, fifty metres away, there's an information board. It has a map with all the paths, all the views.'

I'm barely polite, but the American is still smiling.

'Thank you very much, miss. And you have a good day now.'

He wanders off. I rage inwardly at this unwarranted invasion. The Texan has made me lose the thread of the scene. Patricia Morval is now standing by herself in the Place de la Mairie, and Stéphanie has already gone back to her classroom. Overwhelmed, inevitably. Plainly torn apart by the supreme dilemma.

Her devoted husband collared by her handsome police inspector.

My poor darling, if only you knew . . . If only you knew that you are stepping onto a plank that's been made especially slippery just for you.

Once again, I hesitate. I don't want to hide the fact that I too am plagued by a dilemma. Should I say nothing, or catch the bus to the Vernon police station and tell all? If I don't do it now, then I will probably never have the courage. I'm aware of that. The police haven't a clue . . . They haven't questioned the right witnesses, they haven't dug up the right corpses. Left to their own devices, they will never find out the truth. They won't even suspect it. Be under no illusion; no policeman, however brilliant, could put a stop to this accursed chain of events.

The Americans scatter around the village like sales reps for a cheap housing complex. Yale cap, without rancour, even gives me a little wave. Patricia Morval stands thoughtfully for a while in the Place de la Mairie, then heads back towards her house.

Inevitably, she passes in front of me.

She has the closed expression of a woman resigned never again to know a love like the one that has just been taken from her. She must be thinking once more of our conversation, the one we had a few days ago. The things I told her . . . the name of her husband's murderer. What has she done with that? Did she at least believe me? One thing is certain, she hasn't told the police. I would already know.

I force myself to say something to her; I don't talk much these days, as you will have noticed, even when Americans try to pick me up.

'Are you well, Patricia?'

'Yes, I'm fine . . . I'm fine.'

The widow Morval isn't very chatty either.

58

'Where is my husband?'

'He's in Évreux prison,' Sylvio Bénavides replies. 'Don't worry, Madame Dupain. It's just an initial charge. The investigating magistrate will have to go through all the facts again.'

Stéphanie stares at the two men in front of her, Inspectors Sylvio Bénavides and Laurenç Sérénac.

'You can't do that!'

Sérénac looks up at the walls of the office and allows his gaze to linger on the paintings hanging there: his eyes lose themselves in the meandering play of light on the bare back of the red-haired woman painted by Toulouse-Lautrec. He will let Sylvio reply. His deputy will do it so much better since he is also trying to convince himself.

'Madame Dupain. We have to face facts. The accumulation of evidence points towards your husband. First of all that pair of boots that disappeared . . .'

'They were stolen!'

'The paint box found at the scene of the crime,' Bénavides goes on, unperturbed. 'Threats carved inside it, written in your husband's hand, as most of the experts have confirmed.'

This last statement has rattled Stéphanie Dupain. Apparently she hadn't heard about the paint box, and she now seems to be probing the darkest corners of her memory. She turns her head and studies the posters fixed to the walls, lingering on the reproduction of Cézanne's *Harlequin* with his crescent-moon hat, as if seeking strength there.

'I must have gone out walking with Jérôme Morval twice, maybe three times. We just chatted. The most daring thing he did was take my hand. I clarified the situation with him, and never saw him again on my own. Patricia Morval is a childhood friend, and she will be able to confirm that. Inspectors, it's ridiculous, there is no motive . . .'

'Your husband has no alibi!' It's Laurenç Sérénac who speaks this time, cutting short Sylvio's explanations.

Stéphanie wavers for a moment. Since the start of the conversation, Laurenç has made sure that their eyes do not meet. She coughs, clenching the sides of her skirt with both hands, and then says, in a neutral voice: 'My husband couldn't have murdered Jérôme Morval. That morning he was in bed with me.'

Inspectors Bénavides and Sérénac freeze in position. Bénavides sits with one hand in the air, the one holding his pen. Sérénac has one elbow on the desk, his open palm supporting the weight of an unshaven chin and a head that suddenly feels too heavy. Room 33 is suddenly as quiet as a museum. Stéphanie decides to press home her advantage.

'If you want more details, Inspectors, Jacques and I were making love that morning. At my instigation. I want a child. We were together on the morning of Jérôme Morval's murder. It is impossible that my husband is guilty.'

Sérénac has risen to his feet. His reply is sharp:

'Stéphanie, a few days ago you told me something totally different. You said that your husband had gone hunting that morning, as he did every Tuesday.'

'I've been thinking since then. I was upset at the time. I got the day wrong.'

Sylvio Bénavides decides to come to his boss's aid.

'Your change of mind doesn't alter a thing, Madame Dupain. A woman's testimony in support of her husband isn't worth—'

Stéphanie Dupain raises her voice.

'Nonsense! Any lawyer . . .'

Sérénac now seems strangely calm.

'Sylvio, leave us.'

Bénavides tries to conceal his disappointment, but he knows he has no choice. He picks up a bundle of papers, places it under his arm and leaves Room 33, closing the door behind him.

'You . . . you're spoiling everything!' Stéphanie Dupain immediately explodes.

Laurenç Sérénac keeps his cool. He is sitting on the office chair, rolling it gently back and forth with his feet outstretched.

'Why are you doing this?'

'Doing what?'

'Giving a false statement.'

Stéphanie doesn't reply. Her eyes drift from the Cézanne to the naked back of the red-haired woman.

'I hate Toulouse-Lautrec. I hate that kind of hypocritical voyeurism.'

She looks down. For the first time in the office she meets Laurenç Sérénac's gaze.

'And why are *you* doing that?'

'What do you mean?'

'Concentrating on a single line of enquiry. Hunting down my husband because you're convinced he's a murderer. He isn't guilty, I know he isn't. Just let him go!'

'On what evidence?'

'Jacques had no motive. It's ridiculous. How many times do I have to tell you, I never slept with Morval. No motive, and he has an alibi. Me.'

'I don't believe you, Stéphanie.'

Time stands still in Room 33.

'So what are we going to do?'

Stéphanie paces nervously back and forth. Laurenç watches her, his head tilted, his chin resting on his open hand, feigning a composure he does not feel. Stéphanie takes a deep breath, as if she were lost in the spiral of the red chignon on the model painted by Toulouse-Lautrec, then suddenly turns round.

'Inspector, what choice does a desperate woman have? How far would she go to save her husband? How long would it take for her to understand the message? You are familiar, Inspector, with those American thrillers, the kind of policeman who's capable of accusing some poor fool just in order to steal his wife.'

'That's not it, Stéphanie.'

Stéphanie Dupain walks towards the desk. Gently, she pulls out the two silver ribbons, letting down her long chestnut hair. She sits down on the desk while he remains seated in his chair, looking up at her.

'This is what you're waiting for, isn't it Inspector? You see, I'm not such a fool. If I give myself to you then it will all be OK, is that it?'

'Stop it, Stéphanie.'

'What's wrong, Inspector? You're scared to take that last step? Don't ask yourself too many questions. You've caught her, the femme fatale, in your net. You're holding her, her husband is behind bars, she's trapped. She's all yours.'

Stéphanie gently raises her legs so that her skirt slides back over her bare skin. One button of her white blouse disappears between her fingers and an explosion of freckles is revealed as she exposes the edge of her bra.

'Stéph . . .'

'Unless she is the one, this femme fatale, who's been pulling the strings since the beginning. After all, why not?'

Stéphanie's eyes narrow to almond-shaped slits. To his surprise, they remind Laurenç Sérénac of a mysterious indigo sunrise. He really must pull himself together.

'There could be two of them,' the teacher continues. 'Husband and wife, accomplices. *Les diaboliques*. The infernal pair. And you would be their toy, Inspector.'

Stéphanie has put both feet on the desk, and her beige cotton skirt is now just a crumple around her waist. A second button of her blouse springs open. The areolas of the teacher's breasts are visible through the fine lace of her underwear. Drops of sweat run down the hollow of her cleavage.

Is it fear? Or arousal?

'Stop it, Stéphanie. Stop playing this ludicrous game. I will take your statement.'

Laurenç gets up and grabs a sheet of paper. Slowly Stéphanie Dupain buttons up her blouse and straightens her skirt, then crosses her legs.

'I warn you, Inspector, I'm not going to change my mind. I'm not going to change a line of what I have already said. That morning, the morning of Jérôme Morval's murder, Jacques was in bed with me.'

The inspector writes it down.

'I've taken a note of that, Stéphanie. Even if I don't believe you.'

'Do you want more details, Inspector? Do you want to test the credibility of my statement? Did we make love? In what position? Did I come?'

'The investigating magistrate is bound to ask those questions.'

'Then write it all down. Write it down, Laurenç. No, I didn't come. We did it very quickly. I was on top of him. I want a child and apparently that is the best position for getting pregnant.'

The inspector keeps his eyes lowered and writes in silence.

'Do you need any other details, Inspector? I'm sorry, I don't have a photograph, but I can describe—'

Laurenç Sérénac jumps to his feet.

'You're lying, Stéphanie.'

The inspector walks around the desk, opens the top drawer and takes out a hard-backed book. *Aurélien.*

'I'm sure you're lying.'

He opens the book at a page with the corner turned down.

'Remember, you were the one who told me to read this book, because of that strange phrase found in Jérôme Morval's pocket: "The crime of dreaming" and so on. Shall I refresh your memory, Stéphanie? Chapter sixty-four. Aurélien bumps into Bérénice in Monet's gardens, she runs off down a sunken lane in Giverny, as if trying to escape her fate. Aurélien pursues her, finds her out of breath, lying against an embankment . . . Forgive me, I can't remember the whole text by heart, but I'll read you the scene.'

Almost for the first time, Laurenç Sérénac holds Stéphanie's lilac gaze.

'"Aurélien walked towards her, he saw her heaving breasts, her head thrown back, with her blond hair falling to one side, her fluttering eyelashes, the dark circles that made her eyes even more troubling, and those trembling lips, and her gritted teeth were feline, so white . . ."'

The inspector walks forward until he is standing directly in front of Stéphanie. She can't move back, trapped as she is on the desk. Laurenç keeps advancing, until the teacher's knee is touching the denim of his jeans. The inspector's pelvis is precisely level with the base of her belly. She need only uncross her legs . . .

Sérénac is still reading.

'"Aurélien stopped. He was in front of her, very close, he loomed over her. He had never seen her like that . . ."'

He sets the book aside for a moment.

'You're the one who's spoiling everything, Stéphanie.'

He places a hand on her bare knee. Her flesh quivers, there is nothing she can do to stop it. Nor can she prevent the trembling of her legs, which are twisted around each other like wisteria around a stake.

'You're a strange man, Inspector. A policeman. An art lover. A poetry lover . . .'

Sérénac doesn't reply. He picks up the book and turns a few more pages.

'Still in that famous chapter sixty-four, a few lines on, do you remember? "I'll take you to a place where no one knows you, not even the motorcyclists . . . Where you will be free to choose . . . Where we will make our own decisions about our lives . . ."'

The book falls with his arm, down to her waist, as if it weighs a ton. He leaves his other hand on the smooth skin of her knee, as if soothing the troubled heart of a young child.

They stay like that, in silence.

Sérénac is the first to break the spell. He steps back. His fingers close around the sheet of paper on which he has recorded the teacher's statement.

'I'm sorry, Stéphanie. You were the one who asked me to read this novel.'

Stéphanie Dupain runs a hand over her eyes; tearful, emotional, and weary.

'Don't confuse everything. I've read Aragon too. I know I'm free to choose. Don't worry, I'll make my own decisions about my life, Laurenç. I've already told you that I don't love my husband. I'll give you another scoop: I think I'm going to leave him. It's been growing inside me, like a river, as if the ripples of these past few days could only herald a cascade. But none of that changes the fact that he's innocent. A wife doesn't leave a man who's in jail. A wife only leaves a free man, do you see that, Laurenç? I'm not withdrawing a word of my statement. I was making love with my husband that morning. My husband did not kill Jérôme Morval.'

Without a word, Laurenç Sérénac holds out the piece of paper and a pen. The teacher signs it without rereading it, then leaves the office. Sérénac reads the last few lines of chapter sixty-four of *Aurélien*.

He watched her leave. Her back was bent, in imitation of one who does not walk quickly . . . He was frozen by that incredible confession. She was lying, plainly! No. She wasn't lying.

How much time passes before Sylvio Bénavides knocks at the door? Several minutes? An hour?

'Come in, Sylvio.'

'So?'

'She's sticking to her version of events. She's covering for her husband.'

Sylvio Bénavides bites his lip.

'Perhaps it's for the best, in the end.'

He slips a pile of papers onto the desk.

'This has just come in. Pellissier, the graphologist from Rouen, has changed his statement. After further examination, he has concluded that the message carved into the paint box found in the stream can't have been written by Dupain . . .'

An excruciating moment of suspense, then:

'Hold on tight, Chief. In his view, the message was carved by a child! A child of around ten. He's quite positive about that.'

'Christ,' Sérénac murmurs. 'What is this nonsense?'

His brain seems to be refusing to think. But Bénavides hasn't finished.

'It's not just that, Chief, we've also had the first analyses of the blood found on the paint box. According to the results, the blood doesn't belong to either Jérôme Morval or Jacques Dupain.'

Sérénac gets up, staggering slightly.

'It's another murder, is that what you're trying to tell me?'

'We don't know, boss. To tell the truth, we don't understand anything.'

Laurenç Sérénac paces in a circle around the room.

'OK. I've got the message, Sylvio. I have no other choice than to release Jacques Dupain. The investigating magistrate will complain, of course, even though we've only held him for less than five hours.'

'He'd rather have that than a judicial error.'

'No, Sylvio. No. I can see what you're thinking: that I've been taken for a ride, all that drama at the end of the Astragale path just to nab one guy, and in the end all the evidence slips through our fingers a few hours later. We'll have to let him go. But it doesn't alter my opinion at all. Not one bit. Jacques Dupain is guilty!'

Sylvio Bénavides doesn't reply. He has worked out that in the minefield of his superior's gut feelings, it is impossible to have a reasoned discussion. However that does not prevent Bénavides thinking about all the contradictory elements building up in the columns on the folded sheet of paper that never leaves his pocket. There can't be a simple answer to all these clues; it's impossible. The further the investigation progresses, the more Sylvio has a sense that someone is playing with them, pulling the strings, enjoying themselves by sending the police down blind alleyways in order to execute his perfectly orchestrated plan.

'Come in.'

Laurenç Sérénac looks up, surprised that someone should be knocking at his door so late in the day. He thought he was alone, or nearly alone, in the station. The door to his office isn't closed. Sylvio is standing in the doorway with a strange look in his eyes. It isn't just tiredness, there's something else.

'You're still here, Sylvio?'

He consults the clock on his desk.

'It's after six o'clock! For heaven's sake, you should be at the maternity ward, holding Béatrice's hand. And getting some sleep, too.'

'I've found it, Chief!'

'What?'

Sérénac almost has a sense that even the painted figures on the walls have turned round.

'I've found it, Chief. God alive, I've found it.'

59

The sun has just hidden itself behind the last row of poplars. For any painter, the descending twilight would mean that it's time to fold up that easel, put it under your arm and return home. As Paul walks along the bridge, he watches Fanette frantically painting, as if her whole life depended on those last few minutes of light.

'I knew I'd find you here.'

Fanette waves a greeting, but goes on painting.

'Can I have a look?'

'Go ahead, I'm in a hurry. Between all the schoolwork, my mother being constantly on my back and night coming too early, I'm never going to finish my painting. I have to hand it in the day after tomorrow.'

Paul tries to be as discreet as possible, as if even the air he breathes might disturb the balance of the composition. But there are so many questions he would like to ask Fanette.

Without turning towards the boy, Fanette anticipates his questions.

'I know, Paul, there are no water lilies in the stream itself. But I don't care about reality. I painted the *Water Lilies* the other day, in Monet's gardens. As for the rest, it was completely impossible – I couldn't do a thing with that flat water. I needed to put my water lilies on a river, on running water, something that danced. A real vanishing line, do you see? Something that moves.'

Paul is fascinated.

'How do you do it, Fanette? How do you give the impression that your painting is alive, that the water is flowing, and even that the wind is stirring the leaves? Just like that, using nothing but some paint on a canvas.'

I like it when Paul pays me compliments.

'I just can't help it. As Monet said, it's not me, it's just my eye. I'm only reproducing what my eye sees.'

'You're incr—'

'Shut up, you fool. At my age Claude Monet was already a well-known painter in Le Havre, because of the caricatures he drew of passers-by. And then I'm not . . . Hey, do you see that tree over there? Do you know what Monet once asked a farmer to do?'

'No.'

'He'd started painting a tree in winter, an old oak. But when he came back three months later his tree was covered with leaves. So he paid the owner of the tree, a farmer, to take off all the leaves, one by one.'

'You're making this up.'

'No! It took two men a whole day to strip his model. And Monet wrote to his wife to say how proud he was to be able to paint a winter landscape in the middle of May!'

Paul stares at the leaves dancing in the wind.

'I'd do it for you, Fanette. Change the colour of the trees, if you asked me.'

I know, Paul, I know.

Fanette goes on painting for several more minutes. Paul stands in silence behind her as the light continues to fade. In the end the little girl gives up.

'It's no use. I'll finish it tomorrow, I hope.'

Paul walks towards the bank and studies the stream flowing at his feet.

'Still no news of James?'

Fanette's voice seems to crack. Paul has a sense that painting has allowed her to forget, and that now reality is catching up with her. He tells himself that he is stupid, that he shouldn't have asked the question.

'No, Fanette murmurs. 'No news. It's as if James never existed. I think I'm going mad, Paul. Even Vincent says he doesn't remember him. But he did see him – he spied on us every evening. I didn't dream it!'

'Vincent's weird.'

Paul tries to find the most reassuring smile he has in stock.

'If one of you is going off their head, it certainly isn't you! Have you tried to talk to the teacher about James?'

Fanette leans towards her painting to check if it's dry.

'No, not yet. It isn't easy. I'll try tomorrow.'

'And why don't you ask some of the other painters in the village?'

'I don't know. I almost don't dare. James was always on his own. I got the feeling that apart from me he didn't like many people.'

You know, Paul, I'm a little ashamed. Very ashamed, even. Sometimes I tell myself that I should forget James, that I should pretend he never existed.

Fanette firmly grips her canvas, which is almost bigger than she is, and sets it down on a wide sheet of brown paper that she uses to protect it. Her eyes turn towards the Moulin des Chennevières. The tower stands out against a sky that is beginning to turn orange. The vision is as beautiful as it is frightening. For a moment Fanette regrets having put her materials away.

'Paul, do you know what I sometimes think?'

'No?'

'I think I invented James. That he didn't really exist. That he's like a kind of figure in a painting. Paul, I think that perhaps James is Père Trognon from Theodore Robinson's painting. He got off his horse to meet me, to talk to me about Monet, to make me want to paint, to tell me I was talented, then he went back to the place he'd

243

come from, back into the painting, on his horse, into the stream, at the foot of the mill . . .'

Do you think I'm nuts?

Paul bends down to help Fanette carry her canvas.

'You mustn't get ideas like that in your head, Fanette. You really mustn't do that. Where are we taking your masterpiece?'

'Let me show you my secret hiding place. I'm not going to take it home. My mother already thinks I'm a lunatic because of James, and she doesn't want to hear another word about painting, let alone this competition. It just turns into a huge row every time!'

Fanette climbs over the bridge and jumps down behind the wash house.

'You just have to be careful not to slip on the steps or you'll fall into the water . . . Pass me the painting.'

The canvas passes from hand to hand.

'Look, there's my hidey-hole, there, under the wash house. There's a gap that's just big enough, as if someone had invented the place just to hide a painting!'

Fanette studies her surroundings with a conspiratorial air: the meadow stretching in front of her, the silhouette of the mill against the fading sky.

'You're the only one who knows, Paul. The only one apart from me.'

Paul smiles, he loves this complicity, Fanette's trust in him. Suddenly the two children give a start. Someone is walking, running nearby. In one bound, Fanette is back on the bridge. A blurred shadow comes forward.

For a moment I thought it was James.

'You idiot, you scared us!'

Neptune comes and rubs himself against her legs. The Alsatian purrs like a big cat.

'Let me correct that, Paul. Only two other people know about my hiding place. Neptune and you!'

60

Sérénac looks in astonishment at his deputy. Sylvio's eyes gleam with exhaustion like a dog that has traversed a whole country to find its master.

'What have you discovered, for heaven's sake?'

Sylvio slumps into an office chair and holds a sheet of paper under his boss's nose.

'Look, it's the numbers on the back of the photographs of Morval's mistresses.'

Sérénac lowers his head and reads.

23-02. Fabienne Goncalves at Morval's ophthalmology surgery.
15-03. Aline Malétras at Club Zed, Rue des Anglais.
21-02. Alysson Murer on the beach at Sark.
17-03. The unknown woman in the blue overall in Morval's sitting room.
03-01. Stéphanie Dupain on the Astragale path above Giverny.

'It came to me all of a sudden when I was putting my notes in order. You remember what Stéphanie Dupain said to us just now, about Morval?'

'She said a lot of things.'

Sérénac bites his tongue. His deputy holds out a sheet of paper, on which he has no doubt copied out Stéphanie's statement, word for word.

'Let me read exactly what she said: "I must have gone out walking with Jérôme Morval twice, maybe three times. We just chatted. The most daring thing he did was take my hand. I clarified the situation with him, and never saw him again on my own."'

'So?'

'OK, Chief, so do you remember what I told you two evenings ago, when I called you from the hospital? About Aline Malétras, the girl from Boston?'

'That she was pregnant.'

'And before that?'

'That she had gone out with Morval, she was twenty-two and they had arguments, Morval was ten years older and had money . . .'

The eyes Sylvio Bénavides turns on Sérénac are those of a sleep-walker who has woken up with a start.

'Yes, exactly, but she also said she went out with Morval about fifteen times!'

Sérénac stares at the lines growing blurred on his desk.

15-03. Aline Malétras at Club Zed, Rue des Anglais.
03-01. Stéphanie Dupain on the Astragale path above Giverny.

'Now you've understood. Stéphanie Dupain, three; Aline Malétras, fifteen. It was the stupidest code you can think of; the number of times the adulterous couple met, marked on the back of each photograph. The private detective, or whoever he was, must have chosen the most representative picture of each relationship from the ones he had at his disposal.'

Laurenç Sérénac stares at his deputy with admiration.

'And I suppose you've come to see me because you've already checked out the other girls.'

'Exactly,' Bénavides replies. 'You're getting to know me. I've just had Fabienne Goncalves on the phone; she can't tell me how many times she went out with her boss, but after pulling some teeth she finally gave me a ballpark figure of between twenty and thirty times.'

Sérénac whistles.

'And Alysson Murer?'

'Our good little English girl records everything in a diary, and she keeps all her little diaries from previous years in a drawer. She counted with me on the telephone because she had never asked herself the question.'

'And the final score?'

'Twenty-one.'

'Brilliant! I love meticulous people who write everything down.'

Sérénac gives his deputy a wink.

'So we're dealing with a private detective who's also particularly meticulous,' Sylvio continues. 'Given that he kept such a detailed record of each meeting.'

'More or less. Apart from Alysson Murer, there's nothing to say it's the precise figure. I suppose it's what you would ask a private detective investigating a husband's infidelities to come up with: a ballpark figure of the number of forays outside the marital bed. In sum, Sylvio, the good news is that we're not going to waste any more time on that code. The bad news is that it doesn't tell us anything at all.'

'Except that we still have the second numbers: 01. 02. 03.'

Sérénac frowns.

'Do you have any idea about that?'

Bénavides assumes a modest expression.

'When you pull one thread, the rest follows. We know that the last number is not a date. It's about the nature of the relationship between Morval and his mistresses. Information that the photographer gives to his client. Apart from the number of meetings between the lovers, what other detail might be useful?'

'Christ!' Sérénac exclaims. 'Of course! The nature of that relationship. Was Morval sleeping with the girls! Sylvio, you're a—'

Sylvio Bénavides interrupts his boss so he can have the privilege of finishing his presentation:

'Aline Malétas fell pregnant by Morval. The photograph was inscribed 15-03. So we can safely assume that 03 means that the girl in question was sleeping with Jérôme Morval.'

A big smile appears on Laurenç Sérénac's face.

'And what did Fabienne Goncalves and Alysson Murer reply just now? Because obviously you asked them. They both have the number 02.'

Sylvio Bénavides blushes slightly.

'I did what I could, boss, asking girls stuff like that isn't really my thing. So, our little English girl, Alysson Murer, swore to me on the head of the Queen of England that she had never slept with the handsome ophthalmologist. The poor thing must have dreamed of a wedding in Notre Dame or Canterbury Cathedral . . . As to

Fabienne Goncalves, she nearly hung up on me, particularly because I could hear her children shouting in the background, but just to be left in peace, she ended up telling me that she too had always refused to sleep with him. Just a few kisses and cuddles with her boss, according to her,' Sylvio says, waving the sheet of paper back and forth in front of his nose like a fan. 'So, the second figure in the code is in some way the Richter scale of Morval's sexual relations. 03, the maximum, he sleeps with them; 02, he flirts. 01, we assume that nothing happened at all. Some gallant words may have been spoken, but however much the private detective spied with his zoom, nothing! No adultery.'

'So what we have here is someone who was given the job of spying on Morval and recording his extra-marital adventures. Frequency of meetings, the nature of each relationship, photographs by way of evidence. It also seems that these numbers on the back of the photographs are not really a code designed to trap us, but just some kind of abbreviation used by a professional. But I'll ask the question again: where does it get us?'

The sheet of paper twists between Sylvio's fingers.

'I've thought about everything, Chief. For me that code – as long as we trust it, of course – gives us two important pieces of information. The first is that Stéphanie Dupain isn't lying to us, and she wasn't Jérôme Morval's mistress. And whoever ordered these photographs already knew that.'

'Patricia Morval?'

'Perhaps. Or Jacques Dupain?'

'I know, Sylvio, I've got it, I'm starting to remember the refrain. No motive. And if Jacques Dupain has no motive, he doesn't need an alibi.'

'Except that he does have an alibi.'

'Oh, bugger off.' Sérénac sighs. 'I called the investigating magistrate two hours ago to have him freed from Évreux prison. Jacques Dupain will sleep in his own house in Giverny this evening.'

Before Sérénac can venture into the terrain of his instincts, Sylvio Bénavides hurries on:

'The code also gives us a second piece of information, Chief.

According to the code, of the five girls in the photographs, only two have actually slept with Morval: Aline Malétras and the unidentified girl, the one in the blue overall in the sitting room. 17-03.'

'So, we agree,' Sérénac confirms. 'Seventeen meetings, and Morval was knocking off that girl on her knees. Where are you going with this?'

'If we assume that Jérôme Morval had a child about ten years ago, well, that girl is the only one of his mistresses who could be the mother.'

61

The terrace of the restaurant l'Esquisse Normande, nestling amid valerians, campanulas and peonies, has a pretty view of the village of Giverny. When night falls, the lamps positioned harmoniously among the flowering plants, further reinforce the image of an Impressionist oasis.

Jacques hasn't touched his starter: a carpaccio of fresh foie gras with fleur de sel. Stéphanie has ordered the same thing and is nibbling at it parsimoniously, adapting her appetite to her husband's. Jacques arrived home about an hour ago, it must have been just after nine, with a gendarme on either side.

Jacques didn't say anything, not one word. He simply signed their bit of paper without looking at it, took Stéphanie's hand and held it tightly. He hasn't let go of it since, or hardly. Just to eat. Alone on the tablecloth, orphaned, it fiddles with the crumbs.

'It'll all be fine,' Stéphanie had reassured him.

She had booked a table at l'Esquisse Normande; she didn't leave the choice up to her husband. Was it a good idea? she wonders. Are there still good or bad ideas? No, nothing but the sense that this is how things need to be done right now. The sense that it would be better to do it at l'Esquisse Normande than at home. That the context would help her. They needed a kind of protocol. The hope was that on the terrace, in public, Jacques wouldn't cause a scandal, that he wouldn't collapse, that he would remain dignified, that he would understand.

'Have you finished, sir?'

The waiter takes away the carpaccio. Jacques hasn't said a word. Stéphanie makes conversation for both of them. She talks about the children at school, about her class, about the Theodore Robinson competition, the paintings that have to be handed in in two days. Jacques listens to her with that mild expression, as he always does. Stéphanie feels she is understood. She has always felt that he knew her by heart. By heart, is the appropriate phrase. He has always liked it when she talks about the children at school, as if it were an escape that he could bear. Jailers probably like it when prisoners talk to them about birds in the sky.

The waiter sets down two thinly sliced duck breasts with pepper sauce. Jacques breaks into a smile and tries his food. He asks some evasive questions about school. He is interested in the pupils, in their characters, their tastes. Apart from the ridiculous arrest, Stéphanie is forced to acknowledge that life is simple with Jacques. So calm. So reassuring.

But that doesn't change anything.

Her decision has been made.

Even if Jacques understands her better than anyone, even if Jacques protects her, even if Jacques is incapable of hurting her, even if Jacques loves her beyond all measure, even if Stéphanie hasn't doubted that love for so much as a second . . .

Her decision has been made.

She has to go.

Jacques serves his wife some wine and then pours himself half a glass. A Burgundy, Stéphanie thinks. She read the name on the label, a Meursault. She doesn't know much about wine; Jacques has never drunk much either. He is almost the only one among his hunter friends to be so abstemious. Now he's eating. Strangely, that reassures Stéphanie a little. She's worried about her husband the way one worries about the health of a relative. Out of affection. Jacques cheers up a little and talks about a house he's spotted in the area. It's a good deal, he reckons. She knows that Jacques works hard, too hard even, he's keeping his agency at arm's length, he hasn't had much luck lately, he hasn't carried out any major transactions, but his luck should turn; luck has to turn one day, and Jacques is persistent. He deserves it. But she doesn't care about any of that. Moving house. Living with a richer man.

Jacques's hand clambers along the embroidered white cotton, looking for Stéphanie's fingers again.

The teacher hesitates. It would be so much easier to make him understand without actually saying anything, through a simple accumulation of anodyne gestures, a hand untaken, a caress ungiven, an eye averted. But Jacques wouldn't understand. Or rather he would, he would understand, but it wouldn't change anything. He would love her anyway. Maybe even more so.

Stéphanie's fingers flee, lose themselves in her hair, touch a silver ribbon. The teacher's whole body shivers. She feels ridiculous.

Why?

Why does she feel that unbearable need to leave everything behind?

Stéphanie drains her glass of wine and smiles to herself. Jacques goes on talking about the house on the banks of the Eure, the second-hand shops they would have to visit in order to furnish it . . . She listens distractedly. Why escape . . . ? The answer to her question is so banal. As old as the world. The sickness of girls who dream that they're different: that thirst for love felt by Aragon's Bérénice. The unbearable boredom of the woman who has no criticism of the man she lives next to . . . No excuse, no alibi. Just boredom; the certainty that real life is going on elsewhere. That somewhere they will find the perfect bond. That yes, these whims are not just details, but their very essence . . . That nothing matters but being able to share the same emotion about a painting by Monet or some lines by Aragon.

The waiter whisks away their plates with professional discretion.

'No,' says Jacques, 'we don't want to order more wine. Just dessert.'

Stéphanie's hand finally settles on the table, where it is immediately snatched up by Jacques. Girls, she thinks, always resign themselves, they always stay, and they live on happily, in all likelihood, or not; they find they are increasingly unable to tell the difference. In the end it's easier like that. Giving in.

And yet . . . And yet . . . The feeling in Stéphanie is rising, so dogged, so insistent: what she is feeling is unique. New. Different.

Two bowls of ice-cream and sorbet, decorated with mint leaves, land in front of them. Jacques, once again, has gone quiet. Stéphanie has decided she will speak to him after dessert. On reflection it wasn't such a great idea to come for dinner at l'Esquisse Normande. The grim wait seems to stretch for an eternity, as if filmed in slow motion. Jacques must be thinking about something else, about his arrest, about jail, about Inspector Sérénac. Pondering his shame. There is plenty to think about.

Does he suspect? Yes, probably. Jacques knows her very well.

Stéphanie devours her apple and rhubarb sorbet. She needs strength. Lots of strength. Is she such a monster that she can't wait for another evening?

Jacques has just got out of prison; he's been tested, humiliated, more than ever before.

Why tell him this evening?

Falling into the crack, slipping rather shamefully onto the battlefield, among the corpses; taking advantage of the fact that the house is burning to save her skin. Is she the most sadistic of wives?

She needs strength.

Her thoughts turn towards Laurenç, of course. The perfect bond she had longed for so devotedly. Is it an illusion, that almost instant certainty that you were fated to meet the person standing before you, that you will be happy with them and no one else, that their arms alone can protect you, that their voice alone can make you quiver, that their laughter will make you forget everything, that only they will be able to make you come like that?

Is that certainty another of life's traps?

No.

She knows it isn't.

She takes the plunge, into the void.

Into the unknown.

The endless fall, as in Carroll's *Alice*. Close your eyes and think about Wonderland.

'Jacques, I'm going to leave you.'

DAY TWELVE
24 May 2010
(Vernon Museum)

Insanity

62

The riches of Vernon Museum are largely underestimated, probably because of the suffocating shadow of the museum in Giverny. The opening of the Museum of Impressionisms, in 2009, did nothing to change that. As for me, given the option of the chaos of the museums on Rue Claude Monet, I prefer by far the calm of the sumptuous Norman building on the quays of the Seine at Vernon. You will tell me it's just my age. I'm catching my breath now; I've struggled across the cobbled courtyard and reached the entrance, bent over my cane.

I look up. Claude Monet's famous tondo hangs in the entrance hall. It has been put on display to coincide with Operation 'Impressionist Normandy': a *Water Lilies*, round, almost a metre in diameter. In its slightly old-fashioned gold circle it looks like your grandmother's mirror. Apparently it's one of only three Monet tondos on show in the world. It was given to Vernon Museum by Claude Monet himself, in 1925, a year before he died.

Very classy, don't you think?

It's the pride and joy of Vernon, which is the only museum in the

Eure département to own canvases by Monet, and not just any old paintings either. Even if the gold frame of the tondo is a bit kitsch, I challenge anyone not to be attracted by its milk-pale, chalky shades, like a porthole looking out onto a pastel Eden. When I think of the tourists in the next village, falling into ecstasies as they strut about like sheep in front of reproductions . . .

Well, I'm not going to complain; if a similar transhumance were to take place here too, in Vernon, I would be the first to groan. I walk a few steps across the terracotta tiles of the hall. Pascal Poussin passes in front of me in a gust of wind; I've just recognised the director of the museum – he's said to be one of France's greatest specialists on Monet and the *Water Lilies*, along with the eternal Achille Guillotin, the fellow at Rouen Museum. I read somewhere that he's one of the pillars of the 'Impressionist Normandy' operation. A big shot, you might say.

Poussin greets me without slowing down; he may vaguely remember my face. If he concentrated, he would make the connection between this old woman and the one who once came to talk to him about the *Water Lilies*.

But that was a long time ago.

'I don't want to be disturbed!' Pascal Poussin calls to his secretary in the hall. 'I have a meeting with some police officers from the local station. I won't be very long.'

The director stops and inspects the entrance hall of his museum. On the ground, painted ladybirds indicate the direction to take between rooms. At the bottom of the stairs, shapeless sculptures are piled up for want of room elsewhere. Pascal Poussin frowns, then closes the door to his office behind him. Through the glass of the front door I can see Inspector Sérénac's Tiger Triumph T100. The bike is parked on the cobbles of the inner courtyard. The world of the *Water Lilies* is clearly quite a small one, small as a pond.

I sigh. I'm going to do what everyone else does: I'm going to follow the ladybirds on the ground. The local archaeology to which the whole ground floor is devoted bores me to tears. I look at the stairs leading up to the other floors where the collections of landscape painters and contemporary artists are housed. The monumental staircase is another pride and joy of the museum, and you have to admit that it's got the works: marble sculptures of rearing horses and tumescent bowmen are planted all over the place, one every four steps, below huge paintings of forgotten arch-dukes, historic constables and princes that no one would want in their home. I'm worried. They're so proud of their staircase that I'm not even sure if the lift works, in this museum devoted to oblivion.

63

While Pascal Poussin carefully examines the Winsor & Newton paint box from every angle, Sérénac and Bénavides keep an eye on his every gesture. Having juddered to a halt in the investigation once more, they are mobilising every possible expert. Pascal Poussin has been presented to them as the other great specialist on Impressionist painting, particularly in Normandy. The director of the museum had told them that he was snowed under, but had also agreed to grant the police a few minutes. The character in front of them is a perfect match for the profile that Bénavides had imagined on the phone: tall, thin, grey suit and pastel-blue tie; the kind of travelling salesman who ends up either running the Louvre . . . or doing nothing at all.

'It's a lovely object, gentlemen. It's been well preserved, but it's about a hundred years old. It isn't worth a fortune by any means, but collectors might be interested in it. It matches the model that many American artists would have used at the turn of the century, but since then Winsor & Newton has become the global standard. Any slightly snobbish or nostalgic painter would dream of keeping his brushes inside one of these.'

Bénavides and Sérénac are sitting on two vintage red velvet arm-chairs, which are less comfortable than their appearance might suggest. The lacquered wooden feet threaten to break at the slightest wrong movement.

'Monsieur Poussin,' Laurenç Sérénac asks, 'do you think there might still be some Monets on the market? *Water Lilies* in particular . . .'

The director of the museum has set the box down.

'What do you mean exactly, Inspector?'

'Well, for example, could someone from the area around Vernon possess a painting given to them by Monet? And why not one of the two hundred and seventy-two *Water Lilies?*'

'When he moved to Giverny, Claude Monet was a well-known artist and each of his works was already part of the national heritage. Monet very rarely gave away his paintings, as they were worth a small fortune.' Teeth flashing, Poussin explains: 'Very unusually, he agreed to break with that principle for Vernon Museum. Hence the exceptional value of our tondo.'

Sérénac seems to be satisfied with the answer. Sylvio Bénavides, recalling the excited comments of the curator at the Musée des Beaux-Arts in Rouen, is less convinced:

'Forgive me, but didn't Monet constantly have to negotiate with his neighbours, the people of Giverny, in order to build his pond and preserve the landscape as he wanted to paint it? Is it just possible that he might have bought the agreement of his neighbours with the promise of a painting?'

Poussin doesn't bother to conceal his outrage and makes a show of consulting his watch.

'Listen, Inspector. The Impressionist era wasn't prehistoric! At the start of the century there were newspapers, notarised files, the accounts of municipal councils. All of these documents have been examined by dozens of art historians. No exchange of this kind, absolutely none, has ever come to light. But people will always go on making up stories!'

The director starts to get to his feet. Bénavides is fascinated by this attempt to bring their conversation to a speedy conclusion. He waits in vain for Laurenç Sérénac to come to his aid.

'And what about theft?' asks Sylvio.

Pascal Poussin sighs.

'I don't know where you're going with this. Claude Monet was organised and lucid until the end of his life. His paintings were listed, classified, and recorded. When he died, his son Michel never suggested that there was so much as a single canvas missing.'

The museum director's fingers dance a nervous jig on the paint box.

'Inspector, if you haven't been able to solve a crime that took place just one week ago, I doubt you would be able to find the missing link in a hypothetical theft that might have taken place before 1926 . . .'

Right hook. Bénavides takes the blow. Sérénac climbs into the ring.

'Monsieur Poussin, I presume you've heard of the Theodore Robinson Foundation?'

For a moment the director seems to be wrong-footed by this arrival of reinforcements. He adjusts the knot of his tie.

'Of course. It is one of the top three or four art foundations in the world.'

'And what do you think of it?'

'What do you mean, what do I think?'

'Have you ever had any dealings with them?'

'Obviously! What a question. The Robinson Foundation is un-avoidable as far as anything to do with Impressionism is concerned. The three "pros", as their slogan has it: prospection, protection, promotion.'

Bénavides nods and Poussin continues:

'A good third of the paintings ever shown in the world have to go through them. A foundation like that doesn't care about somewhere like our museum in Vernon, as you can imagine, but for operations on a large scale . . . A fortnight ago I was in Tokyo for the interna-tional exhibition "Mountains and sacred paths", and who was the main sponsor?'

'The Robinson Foundation!' Sérénac says like a contestant on a quiz show. 'It's a bit of an octopus, this foundation, don't you think? It seems to have many tentacles.'

'What do you mean?'

Bénavides joins in. 'Well, to someone who doesn't know much

about the art world it could look as if this foundation, which shifts millions of dollars, is a little more interested in juicy business deals than the noble and disinterested defence of art . . .'

Bénavides straightens up, smiling with false naivety. He is pleased to note that his double act with Sérénac is getting better, like tennis partners that are becoming more experienced. Pascal Poussin is starting to lose his nerve. Again he glances at his watch before replying.

'Well, to someone such as myself who does know a bit about art, the Theodore Robinson Foundation is an old and respectable institution, which has not only been remarkably good at adapting to the international market, but has also always been faithful to its initial aim: to find and support the best new talent from a very young age.'

'You're talking about the Young Artists competition?' Sérénac cuts in.

'Among other things. You can't imagine the number of new artists the foundation managed to find who are now internationally recognised.'

'So, everything comes full circle,' Sérénac concludes, 'in short, the Robinson Foundation looks after its investments, old and new.'

'Exactly, Inspector. And is there anything wrong with that?'

Sérénac and Bénavides both shake their heads in a perfectly synchronised movement. Poussin looks at his watch yet again and finally stands up.

'So,' he says, holding out the paint box. 'As I told you, Inspectors, I can't tell you very much that you don't already know.'

The moment has come. Sylvio Bénavides decides to fire his last arrow.

'One final question, Monsieur Poussin. Can you tell us anything about the rumoured black *Water Lilies*? The last painting that Monet is said to have painted a few days before he passed away, reflecting the colours of his own death?'

Pascal Poussin looks Sylvio up and down, as if listening to a child who has just claimed that he's bumped into some elves in the garden.

'Inspector, art isn't a matter of fairy tales and legends. Art has become a business. There isn't the slightest foundation for this story about a funereal self-portrait, there isn't the least bit of evidence for it except in the overheated imaginations of the type of lunatic who also believes that a ghost haunts the corridors of the Louvre and that the true Mona Lisa is hidden inside the Hollow Needle of Étretat.'

Uppercut! Bénavides is knocked out. Sérénac pauses for a moment behind the ropes, then leaps back into the ring:

'I suppose, Monsieur Poussin, that the presence of several dozen masterpieces in Monet's house and studios, stashed away in dusty attics and cupboards, is also a village myth.'

Pascal Poussin's eyes gleam strangely, as if Sérénac has just revealed a dangerous secret.

'Who told you that?'

'You haven't answered my question, Monsieur Poussin.'

'No, it's true. Monet's house and his studios are private spaces. Even though I've often visited those spaces in my capacity as an expert, you will easily understand that an answer to your question is a matter of professional confidentiality. On the other hand, permit me to ask you again. Who told you this?'

Sérénac smiles widely.

'Monsieur Poussin, you will easily understand that an answer to that question is also a matter of professional confidentiality!'

For a few seconds, a heavy silence falls on the room. Then, finally, the two inspectors get up, and the antique chairs creak with relief. The director of the museum walks them to the door and then closes it behind them.

'Not a very chatty fellow, that director,' Bénavides observes in the hall as they look up at the tondo of *Water Lilies*.

'And he seemed to be in a hurry, I would add. Tell me, Sylvio, you seem to have made some progress in terms of your knowledge of art. Do I take it your interests are no longer limited to barbecues?'

Bénavides chooses to take the remark as a compliment.

'I'm gathering information, Chief. I'm trying to pull together evidence from the very best sources. But it hasn't helped me to see things any more clearly. Quite the opposite.'

They go outside into the cobbled courtyard of the museum. In front of them, some barges are travelling up the Seine. On the right bank is the Old Mill, a strange old house that has been balanced for centuries above the river on two abandoned piers, and always seems to be on the point of collapsing into the grey water.

'Do you still have your sheet of paper with the three columns?' Sérénac asks.

Sylvio blushes and extracts it from his pocket.

'Well, Chief, yesterday I tried something else, another way of putting the clues together. It's just a sketch, but . . .'

'Show me!' says Sérénac.

The inspector barely gives his deputy time to unfold the page before snatching it from his hands. He lowers his eyes and sees a scribbled triangle with different names written on it. He runs a hand through his hair, perplexed.

'OK, so what is this weird pyramid, Sylvio?'

'I . . . I don't really know,' Bénavides stammers, 'maybe it's just another way of thinking about the case. Since the beginning, we've always been confronted with three different sets of clues that go off in different directions: the *Water Lilies*, Morval's lovers and the children. Perhaps it's a different way of formalising things. Why not imagine that the closer you get to the centre of the triangle the greater the evidence of guilt . . .'

Sérénac leans against the plinth of the statue that dominates the entrance to the museum. A bronze horse.

'Formalising everything . . . It's a bit crazy. Do you really think you can solve this investigation with some kind of Cartesian method?'

He rests a damp hand on the bronze rump.

'So, if I follow you correctly, in the middle you would put the Theodore Robinson Foundation and that girl from Boston, Aline Malétas . . . Hmm . . . The only problem is that the director of the museum seems to be seriously trying to put us off the idea of a connection to the *Water Lilies,* or some other canvas by Monet painted *ante mortem.*'

'I know. And I find his idea of professional confidentiality a little strange.'

'Me too. But I have even more trouble believing the surreal story about dozens of forgotten Impressionist paintings being hidden in the attic of Monet's house since his death.'

'I know what you mean. In any case, the Dupains aren't automatically connected with the children or the illegal art trade, particularly the husband. I'm putting them in a blind corner, along with Amadou Kandy.'

Sérénac goes on looking at the sketch with interest. Sylvio Bénavides exhales discreetly with relief. In an earlier version of his triangle he had written the name of Laurenç Sérénac halfway between the point marked 'lovers' and the point marked '*Water Lilies*'. Suddenly Sérénac looks up and stares at him strangely. Sylvio rests a finger on his drawing.

'Which leaves the girl in the blue overall, the one we haven't identified. In my triangle I've put her somewhere between the lovers and the children . . .'

'This story about a kid is turning into an obsession of yours. At least you're consistent, I suppose . . .'

'What more do you want, Chief? A birthday card intended for an eleven-year-old with a strange quote by Aragon, and now a child's handwriting on the paint box. An eleven-year-old killed in the same manner as Morval, but in 1938. An unidentified mistress who may have had a child with him, a child that would be about ten years old now, but unacknowledged by Morval . . .'

'Hmm. At any rate, no eleven-year-old could have picked up the twenty-kilo rock that shattered Morval's skull. And what are you going to do with this ragbag of clues?'

'I don't know. I can't shake off the idea that one of Giverny's children is in danger. I'm aware that it's ludicrous, and we're not about to wrap all the children of the village up in cotton wool. But still . . .'

Laurenç Sérénac claps him affectionately on the back.

'We've talked about this before; it's your dad-or-dad-to-be syndrome. And by the way, is there still no news on the maternity front?'

'A dead calm. The baby's due any time now. I try to drop by as often as I can, with a pile of magazines that Béatrice inevitably throws in my face. "It's all fine, we just have to wait, she's not dilated at all yet, it's too soon for a Caesarean, it's the baby who will decide, what else do you want me to say?" – that's what the midwives keep telling us all day long.'

'Are you going there now?'

'Well, yes.'

'I'm sure you are, Sylvio. Any other man would be burning up his last nights as a singleton with alcohol, dope or poker, but not you! Say hello to Béatrice from me, she's a terrific girl, you deserve her!' He rests his hand on his shoulder. 'I assure you, you're the last good man on this planet! I'm on my way back to hell.'

Laurenç Sérénac looks at his watch. 4.25 p.m.

He puts on his helmet and climbs onto his Triumph.

'Each to his own vanishing line . . .'

Sylvio Bénavides watches his superior driving away. As the Triumph disappears around the corner of the houses on the Seine quays, he wonders whether, in the end, he was right to delete Laurenç Sérénac's name from the list of suspects.

64

On the first floor of the Vernon Museum, the window of Room 6 looks like another painting. The right bank of the Seine, which can be seen through the window, admirably prolongs the framed landscapes of Pourville, the sunset over Veules-les-Roses, Château Gaillard, the Place du Petit-Andelys, the Seine at Rolleboise.

When Inspector Sérénac's Tiger Triumph passes across the painting, I grant you, it's a bit of an explosion in this Impressionist setting. I see his motorcycle crossing from one side of the Vernon Bridge to the other, turning right, travelling along the Seine towards

Giverny, just where the last bend of the river disappears from view.

Of course that stupid inspector is flying towards his sweetheart. Unwise. Unaware.

I move into the next room, the one with the wood panelling, the room reserved for drawings. I confess, it's my favourite! Over time, I've almost ended up preferring Steinlen's drawings to the paintings of the great masters. I love his caricatures, his portraits of workers or beggars painted in the gutter, those scenes depicting the ordinary lives of nameless people captured in pastel in just a few moments. I take my time, I linger over each sketch, I taste each line like a sweet melting under the tongue. Because it's the last time, my last visit, my goodbye to Steinlen, every detail must be savoured.

After my gaze has rested on each drawing exhibited, according to the ritual of a mad old woman, which is what I have been for over fifty years, I always stop in front of *The Kiss*. I'm not talking about the sequined embrace by Klimt, of course, that poster for some heady perfume or other. No. I'm talking about Steinlen's *Kiss*.

It's a simple charcoal sketch: a man, seen from behind, wearing tight clothes, his muscles protruding, pressing against a woman in a state of abandon. She is standing on tiptoe, her face resting against the man's shoulder, her shy arm not daring to wrap itself around his waist.

He wants her. She is reeling, unable to resist him.

The lovers are indifferent to the deep shadows that threaten in the background.

It's Steinlen's finest drawing. Believe me. It's the real masterpiece of Vernon Museum.

65

In Rue Claude Monet, school is out and the Tiger Triumph is creating a sensation among the pupils. Children slow down as they see the motorcycle and turn their heads, impressed. They are all aged between five and twelve. That's what Laurenç Sérénac would say. He can't help thinking of Sylvio Bénavides' hypothesis, the idea that a child is in danger. The faces pass before him. About ten, maybe twenty. Laughing. Carefree. Which one should he question? Which of the boys, which of the girls? To ask them what? To uncover a well-kept family secret? To try to find a resemblance, something in common with Jérôme Morval? Where to begin?

Inspector Sérénac parks his Tiger Triumph T100 under the shadiest lime tree. Neptune is sleeping at the foot of the tree, as if guarding it. He gets up lazily to demand some stroking, which the inspector does not withhold.

When Laurenç Sérénac walks into the classroom, Stéphanie has her back to him. She is busy putting away some sheets of paper in wooden boxes. Sérénac doesn't say anything. He hesitates. His breathing quickens. Has she heard him? Is she pretending to be indifferent? He walks forward a little more and rests his hands on the teacher's hips.

Stéphanie shivers. She says nothing. She doesn't turn around. She doesn't need to, she has recognised him.

The sound of the engine?

Or his scent?

She rests her hands flat on the wooden desk in front of her. The inspector's hands grip the teacher's thin waist. His body comes closer still, until he can hear the young woman's breathing. He can't take his eyes off the fine drops of sweat pearling between her ear and her neck.

His hands rise, one slides along her curved back, while the other ventures on to Stéphanie's belly as her breathing quickens. His hands rise still further, almost meeting as they come to rest on the young woman's breasts. Fingers tease the plunging shapes for several moments, as if trying to memorise the swell of them, before holding them firmly.

Laurenç presses his face against the teacher's damp profile. A dewy ear, the moist nape of her neck. Now they are one. The inspector's jeans press against Stéphanie's linen dress. Tense desire. She can't breathe.

They stay like that for a long time. Only the hands are alive; without even bothering to slip between fabric and skin, they knead the breasts.

Stéphanie tilts her head back, just a little, just enough for Laurenç to slide forward to her mouth. She murmurs, breathing more than speaking.

'I'm free, Laurenç. I'm free. Take me away.'

The inspector's hands slowly come back down, open and spread, so as not to miss a single millimetre of skin. They reach her waist but don't stop there, continuing in their descent.

For a moment, just a moment, Laurenç's body pulls away from Stéphanie's. Just long enough for his two greedy hands to grip the hem of her dress and pull it up to her waist, before his pelvis crushes the teacher's loins again, trapping the crumpled fabric and leaving Laurenç's hands free to stoke her bare thighs, to part them gently.

'Take me away, Laurenç,' Stéphanie's voice murmurs again. 'I'm free. Take me away.'

'Well?' Paul asks Fanette. 'What did she say to you?'

Fanette closes the classroom door behind her. Her face is pale. Paul suspects that this doesn't bode well.

'Hang on, that didn't take long. What did Miss say to you? Did she believe you about James? She didn't argue with you, at least?'

No answer.

Paul has never seen such distress on Fanette's face. Suddenly, without even saying a word, Fanette runs away. Neptune gets up abruptly from under his lime tree and gallops along beside her.

Paul wonders whether he should do the same. He calls out to Fanette before she disappears.

'Did you talk to her?'

'Nooooo . . .'

The only word uttered by the girl, in a torrent of tears that would be enough to flood the slope of Rue Blanche Hoschedé-Monet.

66

The local bus drops Chief Inspector Laurentin in the main square of Lyons-la-Forêt. During the journey, the vehicle's windscreen allowed him a panoramic view of the spellbinding beech grove that surrounds the town, then the row of half-timbered Norman houses that lends it a nostalgic air of the last century, as if the village has been preserved in that state solely as a setting for adaptations of Maupassant's short stories or the novels of Flaubert.

Chief Inspector Laurentin's eye settles for a moment on the square's fountain, which is just beside the imposing market halls. The pretty stone fountain doesn't look its age, and with good reason: it was only built some twenty years ago, for Chabrol's film about Emma Bovary.

Fakery! A trick.

But the chief inspector can't help making the connection between the tragic fate of Emma Bovary, that feeling of ordinary boredom, that impression of another possible life that you have been refused, and all the information he has been collecting on Stéphanie Dupain over the past few days. Leaving the central square of the village, Chief Inspector Laurentin muses to himself that such a comparison is ludicrous, he's too old to be muddling up romantic storylines. Chief Inspector Laurentin strides along. The nursing home, Les Jardins, is situated slightly above Lyons, up a steep slope, on the edge of a forest.

The pastel-blue linoleum of the foyer shines as if it's cleaned every hour. Most of the pensioners spend the late afternoon, and probably the rest of their time, in a large room to the left of it. A huge plasma screen seems to be permanently switched on in front of around thirty motionless residents. Sleeping. Lost in thought. The most active limply chew the biscuits they were served as a snack an hour ago, as they await their evening meal. In praise of slow.

A stout nurse crosses the room towards him with the supple step of a manager in a shop full of china.

'May I help you?'

'Chief Inspector Laurentin. I called this morning. I would like to meet Louise Rosalba.'

The nurse smiles. A little gold badge indicates her first name: Sophie.

'Yes, I remember. Louise Rosalba has been informed. She's waiting for you. Louise has had a lot of trouble expressing herself over the past few years, but don't worry, she still has all her wits about her, and understands perfectly what she's being asked. Room 117. Be gentle with her, Chief Inspector. Louise is a hundred and two, and she hasn't had any visitors in a long while.'

Laurentin pushes open the door of Room 117. Louise Rosalba is sitting in profile, observing the car park just beneath her window. An Audi 80 parks, and a couple gets out. The woman is carrying a bouquet of flowers and two young children kick up a rumpus as she closes the door. The chief inspector has a sense that the flow of visits to the other residents gives a rhythm to the daily life of this hundred-year-old woman.

'Louise Rosalba?'

The old woman turns her wrinkled face towards him. Laurentin smiles.

'I'm Chief Inspector Laurentin. Sophie, the nurse, told you I was coming this morning? I'm sorry, but I've come to ask you about your memories. Some very old memories that probably aren't particularly pleasant. I want to talk to you about the death of your son, Albert. In 1937 . . .'

Lacy hands tremble amid the folds of the blanket on her knees. Her bright eyes well up. Louise opens her mouth but no sound emerges.

There is no crucifix on the walls, no photographs of children, grandchildren, great grandchildren in christening gowns or first-communion dresses; no wedding pictures. The bare walls are simply decorated with a pretty reproduction of a painting by Monet, *Woman with a Parasol*: an elegant mother walking with her child in a field that blazes with the red of a sea of poppies, some-where near Argenteuil.

'I have some specific questions to ask you,' Chief Inspector Laurentin goes on. 'You don't need to move. I'll try to help you remember.'

He leans forward and takes from his bag a black and white school photograph: Giverny School: 1936–7.

He sets the picture down on Louise's knees. She seems to be fas-cinated by it.

'Is that Albert?' the policeman asks, pointing to the boy in the second row. 'Is that him?'

Louise nods. A few tears drip on to the photograph, as if it had started raining on the school playground, but the children, docile and well-behaved, didn't dare to bat an eyelash but sat patiently in front of the photographer's lens.

'You never believed it was an accident, is that right?'

'N . . . no,' Louise manages to say.

She gulps for a moment.

'He wasn't . . . alone. Not alone. By the . . . the riv . . . by the river.'

Laurentin tries to control his agitation. He thinks again of the nurse's advice. Be gentle with Louise.

'Do you know who was with your son?'

Louise nods gently. The policeman's voice becomes more hesi-tant. An extreme tension fills the air of the tiny room, as if opening up those ancient memories was releasing an inflammable gas that could ignite at the slightest faux pas.

'It was . . . was it this person, the one who was with Albert by the stream, who killed your son?'

Louise concentrates on the policeman's words and nods. A slow and unequivocal motion of her neck.

'Why didn't you say anything? Why didn't you accuse them at the time?'

A shower is now falling on the playground of Giverny School. The paper begins to curl. The children of the class, still impeccably behaved, don't move a muscle.

'No . . . no one . . . be . . . believed me . . . not even . . . my husband.'

It takes a huge effort for the old woman to utter those few words. The slack skin that hangs beneath her neck trembles. Chief Inspector Laurentin understands that he will have to tread carefully, to ask the questions and suggest the answers, so that Louise has only to confirm or deny the hypotheses that he proposes with a gesture or a single syllable.

'Then you moved? It wasn't possible to stay. And your husband passed away.'

Louise slowly nods again. The policeman leans towards her, takes a handkerchief from his pocket and delicately wipes the class photograph.

'And then?' he goes on in a voice that struggles to conceal his emotion. 'This person, this person who was with your son by the riverside. This person committed another crime, is that it? Perhaps several? This person struck again? This person will strike again?'

Louise Rosalba is suddenly breathing more easily, as if the chief inspector has just lifted a weight that had been bearing down on her chest for an eternity.

She nods her head again.

My God . . .

Chief Inspector Laurentin's arms turn to gooseflesh. Such abrupt cardiac accelerations aren't recommended for him either, but for the moment he doesn't care about the advice of his cardiologist; all that matters are these stunning revelations, hidden away in the memory of this woman for almost seventy-five years. He brings the photograph closer to Louise's fingers.

'This person we're talking about, they're sitting on the school benches too, aren't they? Can you show them to me?'

Louise's fingers quiver even more. Laurentin gently places his palm on Louise's wrist, being careful not to apply too much pressure, to avoid turning it in one direction or another. The woman's wrinkled fingers move above the school photograph and then, slowly, her index finger settles on a face.

The chief inspector feels his heart racing.

My God, my God.

An enormous wave of heat engulfs him and he clutches Louise's hand. His heart is about to burst; he needs to calm down.

'Thank you. Thank you.'

He breathes gently and the excitement subsides a little. Chief Inspector Laurentin is filled by a strange feeling: the contradiction between the size of this revelation, this testimony, this accusation, and its implacable logic. Now he knows who murdered little Albert Rosalba. Consequently he also knows who murdered Jérôme Morval. Who, and why.

His heart gradually returns to its normal rate, but he can't ignore that ridiculous satisfaction, that pointless pride in having proof at last that he wasn't mistaken, that he hadn't been duped.

That he was right, before anyone else.

His gaze drifts out through the window, beyond the car park, towards the edge of the dark beech forest.

What should he do now?

Go back to Giverny?

Go back to Giverny and find Stéphanie Dupain? Before it's too late?

At this one last thought, his heart starts beating fit to burst once more. His cardiologist would be furious.

67

10.53. I'm looking at the moon.

Seen from the window of the keep of the Moulin des Chennevières, it looks enormous, almost within reach.

Don't worry, I haven't gone mad. It isn't an optical illusion. They talked about it on Radio France Bleu Haute Normandie, and even on local television, explaining that tonight's full moon will be the biggest of the year. At its perigee, as they put it, which is to say that tonight, if I have understood it correctly, the moon will be at its nearest point to the earth. Apparently the moon doesn't orbit the earth in a circle, but in an ellipse, so there is a day when the full moon is furthest away from the earth and a day when it is closest. Once every year. The perigee.

The nocturnal brightness bathes the roofs of Giverny in a strange light. With a little motivation an artist might take out his easel and continue painting through the night, without artificial light. How many of us are looking at the same moonlight at the same time? Having listened to the radio, watched the television, and obeyed. An unmissable spectacle, they said. Thousands, tens of thousands, I'm sure.

I'm feeling very nostalgic today. After my pilgrimage to Vernon Museum, here I am spending the night by my window. I'm not going to last long, at this rate.

And in any case, I don't intend to. Believe me, it's a real privilege to know the date of the end and to be able to savour the last few hours, the last night, the last moon.

Tomorrow it will all be over.

It's been decided. I just have to choose the method.

Poison? A knife? A gun? Drowning? Suffocation?

There is no shortage of options.

Or of courage. Or determination. Or motivation.

I study the sleeping village once more. The street lights and the last windows in the village where lights still burn remind me of the yellow flowers on my black *Water Lilies*, like so many frail lighthouses lost in an ocean of darkness.

The police failed; they won't have worked anything out. Too bad for them.

Tomorrow evening everything will end with one last corpse, like a parenthesis closed once and for all.

Full stop.

It's the first time Fanette has seen such a big moon. It looks like a planet or a kind of flying saucer that is going to land just over there, among the trees, on the hill. Her teacher was right when she told her to stay up late. She explained it to them, the ellipse, the perigee, she even drew complicated diagrams on the board, with arrows and numbers.

Fanette doesn't have a watch, but she thinks it must be at least eleven o'clock. Vincent went home about an hour ago, more or less.

I thought he was going to spend the night below my window, listening to me, refusing to let go of my hand.

In the end he left.

Phew!

Fanette wanted to be alone, alone with that giant moon, like a big sister. A big sister who lives far away, and who is going to invite her to her house.

This evening Fanette finished her painting. Usually it isn't like her to be conceited, she doesn't really believe it, deep down, when everyone tells her that her drawing is brilliant, but this time . . . Yes, she can tell the moon, this time she's proud of the colours she put down on the canvas, proud of that movement of the stream running through her painting, those vanishing lines going off in all directions. She's had it all in her head for ages, but she never thought she could turn it into a painting. She has hidden the painting under the wash house. Tomorrow she will ask Paul to go and get it, then give it to their teacher.

I can trust Paul. Only Paul. None of the others, not pretentious Camille, sneaky Mary, or Vincent . . . Vincent . . . The little dog who follows me everywhere.

And certainly not Mum. Mum has been keeping an eye on me lately, she takes me to school in the morning and drops me off at the gate before going up to the villa where the Parisians live. It's the same at midday. As if she were spying on me! Sometimes I think it's weird. Perhaps Mum is worried that I will tell everyone my story.

About James. Gone. Dead.

Killed, in the field.

As if she is worried that her daughter will be taken for a lunatic.

James . . .

Fanette stretches out her hand. She feels that if she leant out of the window a little further, she might be able to touch the craters of the moon, run her fingers over the crevices.

James . . .

Did I make him up?

Didn't I just find some brushes left behind in the field by a painter, some drops of paint on the river bank, and my imagination did the rest? Mum's always telling me that I live in an imaginary world, that I invent things, I distort reality. To make it what I want it to be.

Now, the more I think about it, the more it seems to me that James never existed. I invented him because I needed him, I needed someone to tell me that I was good at painting, that I had to go on, that I was a genius, that I had to think about myself and work, work, work on my paintings.

That I had to be selfish.

Mum never tells me that. James told me all the things that a dad should have told me, everything I would have wanted my dad to tell me . . .

A dad who's an artist. A dad who's a painter. A dad who is proud of me. A dad who, one day, on the other side of the world, will read my name in the corner of a painting displayed in the most amazing gallery, and who will say to himself: I recognise her, she's my daughter. My little daughter. The most gifted of them all.

Fanette studies the façades of the dark houses.

No! No! No! My dad isn't someone from the village that my mum cleans for. Fat, ugly, old, sweaty and smelly. It's impossible.

And anyway, I don't care.

I have no dad. I invented James in his place. Thanks to him, I painted my picture, my Water Lilies. *Tomorrow they will leave to take part in the competition. My message in a bottle.*

Tomorrow.

Fanette smiles.

That huge moon might be another good omen.

Tomorrow, it's my birthday!

Under the moon, the playground of Giverny School assumes a silvery hue. It's an enormous moon. Stéphanie tried to explain the phenomenon to the children in her class by using a few simple diagrams. She recommended that they stay up later than usual, in order to witness the spectacle for themselves: she wrote everything on the board, a moon that was fourteen per cent bigger and thirty per cent brighter than usual.

The moon is the same circular shape as the skylight of their attic room, as if part of the window has become detached and floated off into the sky. The Rue Blanche Hoschedé-Monet is deserted. The leaves of the lime trees in the Place de la Mairie dance gently in the wind. A silver rain seems to have fallen on the village.

Jacques is lying in bed beside her. Without even needing to turn round, Stéphanie knows that he isn't asleep. She guesses that he's watching her, that he won't say anything, that he respects her silence. Intimacy between her and Jacques has become harder and harder for her to bear. Jacques hasn't changed any of his habits. They go on sleeping together, naked, close, even though Jacques hasn't tried to touch her, hasn't tried to win her back. Physically, at least.

Yesterday, they talked for hours.

Calmly.

Jacques has said he understands, that he'll try to change.

Change what?

Stéphanie doesn't blame him for anything. Or perhaps only for not being someone else.

Jacques says he will become someone else.

But you can't become someone else. These discussions are leading nowhere. Stéphanie knows that very well. Her decision is made. She's leaving him. She's going.

Jacques is a balanced man. He is bound to think that waiting patiently is the best way to make Stéphanie begin to doubt her decision. Let the storm clouds pass. Wait there, umbrella in hand, just in case . . . Ready to hold out that big umbrella as soon as Stéphanie comes back.

He is mistaken.

Stéphanie stares out at the playground of the school where she has taught for years, the hopscotch lines drawn on the tarmac, the climbing frame . . . The shouts of the children at break time ring in her head.

Stéphanie has arranged to meet Laurenç tomorrow afternoon. Not in the village, of course, not in front of the school, not by the stream, but further away, somewhere more discreet. She was the one who had the idea: Nettles Island, the famous field at the confluence of the Epte and the Seine that Claude Monet bought, where he set up his canvases, where he moored his boat. It's a pretty, isolated place, just over a kilometre from Giverny. The more she thinks about it, the more sure she is that Nettles Island, l'Île aux Orties, is the right place. Laurenç will appreciate it. Laurenç has an amazing instinct for all things artistic. In Monet's house, did he not guess straight away that the Renoir painting, *Young Woman in a White Hat*, was not a reproduction? Even if his reason didn't allow him to admit it, Laurenç sensed that it was a genuine masterpiece. Like dozens of other forgotten paintings in Monet's house. Renoir, Pissarro, Sisley, Boudin . . . even some *Water Lilies* too. My God, if they had the time, if they were free, Stéphanie would love to show them to Laurenç. Share such an emotional experience with him.

Jacques has turned out the light and turned onto his side as if he is sleeping. The moonlight lends the room the appearance of a fairy grotto. Stéphanie's eyes rest on the bedside table, on the book that lies there.

It hasn't moved.

Aurélien.

Louis Aragon.

Inevitably, this phrase comes back to haunt her. *The crime of dreaming, I agree to its creation.* The message discovered on the birthday card found in Jérôme Morval's pocket.

To make dreaming a crime . . .

As if the phrase had been written for her.

All those who don't know the lines that follow, all those who don't know the rest of the long poem by Aragon, 'Nymphée', are mistaken. No, of course Aragon wasn't condemning dreams.

What a misunderstanding.

It's the opposite; the poet was obviously expressing the opposite ideal.

She whispers the lines that she teaches the village children every year.

The crime of dreaming, I agree to its creation.

If I dream, it's about what I'm told I mustn't do
So yes, I'll plead guilty, I'm pleased to be wrong;
In reason's eyes dreaming is criminal too.

Stéphanie silently repeats the four lines of the verse as fervently as if it were an indecent secular prayer.

If I dream, it's about what I'm told I mustn't do . . .

Yes, dreams are outside of the law.

Yes, Stéphanie enjoys being a cruel woman.

No, she has no remorse.

Yes, in the eyes of reason her dream is criminal.

Her dream of Laurenç Sérénac taking her in his arms, of the two of them making love on Nettles Island and of him taking her away, far away . . .

Tomorrow.

DAY THIRTEEN
25 May 2010
(Chemin de l'île aux Orties)

Denouement

68

I am walking slowly along the track that begins just behind the Moulin des Chennevières and continues in a straight line across the meadow: a path that is full of ruts, dug year after year by tractor wheels.

Inspector Sérénac can't have enjoyed himself very much on his Tiger Triumph just now. I won't go into the details, but I'm not sure that his antique is very well suited to motocross. I saw him passing by a few minutes ago, turning off behind the mill and then plunging into the fields, surrounded by a cloud of dust.

There are a number of paths that lead out of Giverny and into the meadow, but they all meet at the same dead end: Nettles Island. After that, if you go straight on, there is nothing but the Epte and the Seine. This path is a direct route, and it even stops a few metres before the rivers meet, on the banks of the Epte, by a row of poplars that Monet knew well; they are protected by the pharaohs of Impressionism, every bit as much as the pyramids of Egypt.

If you want to reach the Seine, you have to continue on foot.

Neptune gallops ahead of me. He knows the path by heart, he's stopped waiting for me now. He has worked out that it is taking me longer and longer to struggle along that little kilometre that separates the Moulin des Chennevières from Nettles Island. Those ruts are a nightmare. Even with my cane, I nearly fall over every three metres or so.

Luckily this is the last time that I will ever go to that wretched 'island'. It's not suitable for my age, this kind of stroll along country lanes. And to crown it all, the heat this afternoon is suffocating. It's the finest day so far in May and there isn't a hint of shade from my mill to the Epte, except perhaps halfway, against the metal walls of the water tank. At least my scarf protects me from the sun. Out in the open, amid the sun-bleached plain, I feel like I'm an Arab woman walking in the desert.

My God, you can't imagine, it's going to take me an eternity to reach the confluence of the Epte and the Seine, that damned Nettles Island.

And to think that Neptune must already be there!

69

4.17 p.m. Laurenç Sérénac's Tiger Triumph T100 leans against the trunk of a poplar. The inspector has reached Nettles Island a little early; he knows that Stéphanie's class doesn't finish until 4.30. After that, she has a good kilometre to walk in order to join him.

Laurenç strolls along under the trees. The landscape here is odd: the Epte, surrounded by these straight trees lined up like a regiment standing to attention, looks more like a canal than a natural river. The confluence of the Epte and the Seine reinforces that impression still further: the huge river flows gently onwards, blithely ignoring the pathetic contribution made by this small stretch of water. While the banks of the Epte seem frozen in an immutable eternity, towards the Seine there are signs of bustling life: the town, factories, barges, the railway line, shops. As if the Seine were a noisy motorway crossing the countryside, and the Epte a forgotten B-road leading nowhere.

A sound behind him.

Stéphanie, already?

He turns round, smiles.

It's Neptune! The Alsatian recognises the inspector and comes and rubs himself against him.

'Neptune! Lovely of you to come and keep me company. But you know, old chap, this is a romantic assignation, a discreet tryst, so you're going to have to make yourself scarce.'

A branch cracks behind him. A rustle of leaves.

Neptune isn't alone!

Laurenç Sérénac spots the danger instantly, without even thinking. A policeman's instinct.

He looks up.

The barrel of a gun is levelled at him.

For a moment he thinks that everything's going to end like this, without any further explanation. That's he's going to die, shot down like some common game-bird; that a cartridge is going to blow up his heart and that his corpse will float down the Epte, then into the Seine, and wash up further downstream.

But the fingers don't pull the trigger.

A reprieve? Sérénac dives into the breach with apparent self-assurance.

'What are you doing here?'

Jacques Dupain pointedly lowers the gun.

'I think I'm the one who should be asking you that question, don't you think?'

Laurenç Sérénac's anger gives him fresh confidence.

'How did you know?'

Neptune has sat down a few metres away, in a ray of sunlight passing through the poplar trees, and seems uninterested in their conversation. Jacques Dupain's rifle is now pointed at the ground. His face twists with contempt.

'You're really very stupid, Sérénac. As soon as I saw you turning up in the village, like some kind of godsend with your leather jacket and your motorbike, I knew. You're so predictable, Sérénac.'

'No one could have known. No one apart from Stéphanie. She

couldn't have told you anything. Did you follow me, is that it?'

Dupain turns back to face the meadow. The village of Giverny can be seen in the distance, amid a heat haze that distorts the horizon. Dupain laughs.

'You wouldn't understand. There are some things that are beyond you. I was born here, Sérénac. Like Stéphanie. In this village. On the same day, or nearly. Only a street away. No one knows Stéphanie better than I do. As soon as you started turning her head, I noticed. The slightest detail, a book missing from a library, Stéphanie glancing at the sky, a silence . . . I have learned to interpret all the signs. A crease on a blouse, a crumpled skirt, an undergarment that she doesn't usually wear, a tiny nuance in the way she puts on her make-up, a slight change in her facial expression. When Stéphanie arranged to meet you, I knew it, Sérénac. I knew when she had arranged it for, and where.'

Laurenç Sérénac adopts a weary, irritated expression and turns towards the Epte. Dupain's long monologue has reassured him; he is dealing with a jealous husband. It was only to be expected, after all, and it's the price he must pay. The price of Stéphanie's freedom. The price of their love.

'Right,' he says. 'What's next on the agenda? Do we wait for Stéphanie to arrive and have a three-way conversation?'

A new grimace of disdain twists Jacques Dupain's features.

'I don't think so, no. You were right to turn up early, Sérénac. This is what you are going to do. You are going to write a short letter, a word of farewell; you'll know how to come up with something nice and elegant, you're clever enough to do that. Otherwise I can prompt you. You will leave the letter at the foot of a tree, in plain sight, then you will get on your motorbike and you will disappear.'

'Are you joking?'

'Inspector, you've got what you wanted. Stéphanie gave herself to you yesterday, in the classroom in Giverny. You have attained your goal. Hats off. Many people have dreamed of doing just that, but you're the first to actually achieve it. So this is where we are. You will disappear from our lives. I won't cause a scandal, I won't go and see a lawyer and tell him that the inspector in charge of the Morval case is sleeping with the wife of a suspect, a suspect that he even had the forethought to put in jail the previous day. In plain terms, I won't destroy your career. We are quits. I'm a good sport, don't you think, for someone the people of Giverny see as a husband driven mad by jealousy?'

Sérénac bursts out laughing. The wind stirs the leaves of the poplars, the walnut and the chestnut trees.

'I don't think you've understood a single thing, Dupain. This isn't about me or my career. And it's not about you and your pride either. It's about Stéphanie. She's free. Do you understand that? You and I have nothing to talk about. We're not going to make any decisions on her behalf. Do you get that? She's free . . . free to make her own decisions.'

Dupain grips the rifle with both hands.

'I didn't come here to make polite conversation, Sérénac. You're wasting precious time. The words of farewell that you choose may be important to Stéphanie; she'll have to live with them afterwards . . .'

Laurenç feels profound irritation welling up inside him. He doesn't like the situation. The man disgusts him. Behind him, the fields of nettles stretch all the way to the confluence. The place is deserted. No one will come here apart from Stéphanie. He has to get this over with.

'Listen, Dupain, don't force me to be cruel.'

'You're wasting more time . . .'

'You're a mediocrity, Dupain,' Laurenç Sérénac cuts in. 'Open your eyes! You don't deserve Stéphanie. She deserves so much more than a life lived beside you day after day. She will leave, Dupain, one day or another. With me or with someone else.'

Jacques Dupain merely shrugs. Laurenç Sérénac's salvo seems to slide off him like drops of water on a slate roof.

'Inspector, is that how you managed to get to Stéphanie, with grotesque clichés like that?'

Sérénac takes a step forward. He's taller than Jacques Dupain by at least twenty centimetres. Suddenly he raises his voice.

'Let's stop this little game, Dupain. Right now. Let me be clear, I'm not going to write your stupid note. I don't care about your mean little attempt at blackmail, what you're threatening to say to your lawyer about my career.'

Jacques Dupain hesitates for the first time, and he stares at Sérénac with renewed attention. The inspector looks away and sees in the distance the bell-tower of the Church of Sainte-Radegonde with the roofs of Giverny all around it, like the idealised village in a model train set.

'Mea culpa, Inspector,' Dupain replies. 'So, are you saying I underestimated you? That, in your own way, you are sincere?'

His face tenses into wrinkled fissures.

'Well, you leave me no choice. I'm going to have to resort to more convincing measures.'

Slowly, Dupain aims the barrel of the rifle at the inspector's forehead. Laurenç Sérénac remains motionless, staring him down. Sweat drips from his hair.

'So here we are, Dupain,' the inspector hisses. 'The mask has fallen and the true face is revealed. The face of Morval's murderer . . .'

The barrel of the rifle comes level with his eyes. It is impossible not to squint into the dark opening of the metal tube.

'Stick to the subject, Inspector!' Dupain raises his voice. 'Don't muddle everything up. We're here to sort something out between the three of us; you, me and Stéphanie. Morval has nothing to do with that.'

In his excitement, Dupain has shifted the rifle slightly in the direction of the policeman's ear. Sérénac knows he has to negotiate, gain some time, find the weak spot.

'What are you going to do, then? Kill me, is that it? Kill me here, beneath the poplar trees? It won't be hard to trace the gun. A hunting rifle. And your wife's lover shot at point-blank range. A rendezvous at Nettles Island. Everyone saw me passing through the village on my Triumph Tiger. If you end up in jail, even if you've got rid of me, it won't be the best way of keeping Stéphanie beside you.'

The rifle comes closer still, and the barrel is lowered until it's level with his mouth. Sérénac isn't sure if he should try anything. On the one hand, it would be easier to intervene now, to grab the gun and get it over with. He's stronger, faster than Dupain. It's the right moment. But the inspector hesitates.

'You're a smart one,' Dupain replies with a rictus grin. 'And you're right about that, Sérénac. But only about that. It wouldn't be very clever on my part to kill you here in cold blood. It would be like leaving a signature. But time is marching on, so let's speed things up a little. You will write that letter.'

The rifle comes down to the inspector's neck. With infinite slowness Sérénac brings his hand up along his waist and then suddenly extends it.

His fingers close on a void.

Jacques Dupain has sprung back a metre, but the rifle is still levelled at him.

'Let's not play at being cowboys, Inspector. You're wasting your time. How many times must I tell you? Write me a nice break-up letter.'

Sérénac shrugs contemptuously.

'Don't count on it, Dupain. This farce has gone on long enough.'

'What did you just say?'

'That this farce has gone on long enough!'

'This farce?'

Dupain stares at Sérénac, his eyes popping. All cynicism, all disdain has vanished from his face.

'This farce? Is that what you said? You really haven't understood a thing, Sérénac. You refuse to look reality in the face. There's something . . . something you don't know, Sérénac. You have no idea . . .'

The cold barrel of the hunting rifle settles on the inspector's heart. For the first time, Laurenç Sérénac can't manage a reply.

'You can't even imagine, Sérénac, how attached I am to Stéphanie. How capable I am of doing anything for her. Perhaps, Sérénac, you love Stéphanie; perhaps your love is even sincere. But I don't think you realise how little weight your ridiculous affection for her carries compared to my . . .'

Sérénac swallows his disgust as Dupain continues:

'My . . . call it what you will, Sérénac: madness, obsession, absolute love . . .'

His finger curls around the trigger.

'But you will write that break-up letter for me, Inspector, and then you will disappear for ever!'

70

Stéphanie Dupain can't help glancing at the clock above the blackboard.

4.20 p.m.

Another ten minutes! In ten minutes she will be leaving the children in Giverny, and will run to join Laurenç on Nettles Island. She feels as giddy as a schoolgirl whose spotty sweetheart is waiting for her by the bus shelter at the end of the school day.

She feels slightly ridiculous too. Yes, of course. But how long has it been since she had the courage to listen to that heart that is beating wildly, to look up towards that blue sky and see in it nothing but cloudless happiness, to feel that desire to leave the children where they are, right now, to give each one of them a big kiss on both cheeks and tell them she's leaving to travel the world, and that by the time she sees them again they'll be grown-ups.

To laugh out loud at the horrified expressions on their parents' faces.

So ridiculous, yes. Deliciously so. And anyway, she isn't in the right mood to teach today, she chuckles like an idiot every time a child says something vaguely silly. She didn't even deliver a lecture when none of the children handed in a painting for the Robinson Foundation competition. Not even the most gifted pupils. Any other day, she would have delivered a long sermon on opportunities that mustn't be missed, the little shoots of talent that must be cultivated, the desires that mustn't be allowed to die, the embers that must be fanned, all the advice that she drills into them all year round and which, in fact, is really addressed to herself.

Now she has listened to her own advice.

In nine minutes' time, she is running away!

The children are supposed to be solving a maths problem. It

makes a bit of a change from Aragon and painting. Some parents claim she doesn't give their offspring enough problems to solve, maths problems, science problems.

The crime of dreaming . . .

Stéphanie's water-lily gaze drifts out through the classroom window and flies far above Monet's poplars.

'You didn't hand in your painting?' Paul murmurs, turning towards Fanette.

Fanette doesn't hear him. Their teacher is looking in the opposite direction.

I'm off!

She edges over to Paul's desk.

'What?'

'Your painting, for the competition?'

Vincent is looking at them strangely. Mary seems to be itching to raise her hand and call the teacher as soon as she turns her head.

'I couldn't get it this morning. My mother took me to school and she'd have had a fit! She's picking me up at the end of the day too.'

Fanette glances out of the corner of her eye to check that the teacher isn't looking in their direction. With the other, she watches Mary. Mary is, in fact, about to get to her feet. As if he's ahead of her, Camille leans over towards Mary's exercise book and explains the question to her.

Fat Camille is being incredibly nice to me. It's as if he already understands. And Mary really isn't very good at maths. She's not very good at anything at all. Camille is the opposite, showing off is his way of flirting. With Mary, in the long term, it might just work . . .

Fanette is still crouched beside Paul's desk.

'Paul,' she whispers, 'could you go and get my painting? You know, from the hiding place. And could you bring it to Miss, just after school?'

'You can count on me. It'll only take me five minutes to get there and back if I sprint.'

Fanette slaloms back between the desks towards her seat. Discreetly. Except that stupid Pierre has left his satchel lying on the floor again. Fanette trips over the bag and knocks it against the leg of the chair. Inside it, something weird and metallic echoes like a bell around the classroom.

What an idiot she is!

The teacher turns back towards her pupils.

'Fanette,' she says. 'What are you doing? Go back to your seat this instant!'

71

The barrel aimed by Jacques Dupain is still resting on Inspector Laurenç Sérénac's leather jacket. Right against his heart. The plain looks like a classical temple, with the rows of poplars as the pillars. Silent and sacred. Behind the trees, like a distant echo, lies the turmoil of the Seine.

Sérénac tries to think quickly, methodically. Who is this individual in front of him? Is Jacques Dupain Jérôme Morval's murderer? If he is, then he's a meticulous criminal, organised and calculating. A man like that wouldn't shoot a policeman in broad daylight. He's bluffing.

Jacques Dupain's face doesn't give him a clue. He adopts the same expression as if he were hunting a rabbit or a partridge on the Astragale hill: concentrating, frowning, his hands damp and slightly trembling. The normal stance of the hunter, except that the prey at the end of his gun is a bit bigger than usual. Sérénac forces himself to reverse his reasoning. Maybe, in the end, Jacques Dupain is just a jealous husband, deceived, humiliated? In which case he's just a poor bastard who wouldn't kill anyone in cold blood.

It's obvious. Criminal or not, Dupain is bluffing.

Sérénac forces himself to sound calm:

'You're bluffing, Dupain. Mad or not mad, you won't shoot.'

Jacques Dupain blanches again, as if his heartbeat was becoming so slow that it was no longer irrigating the arteries above his neck. One hand clenches on the steel barrel, the other on the trigger.

'Don't play this game, Sérénac, don't play the hero. Stop doing your little calculations. Have you still not worked it out? Do you want an act of carnage on your conscience, is that it? Carnage rather than giving in . . .'

Everything is starting to get confused in Sérénac's head. The inspector is aware that he has to gauge the situation and react instinctively. But he wishes he had more time at his disposal, to think, to be able to discuss all the details with Sylvio Bénavides, his famous three columns, trying to find the connection between Jérôme Morval and all the unknowns in this investigation, the *Water Lilies*, the painting, the children, the ritual, 1937 . . . With every breath he feels the icy tube of the gun pressing harder against his flesh.

'You're mad,' Sérénac murmurs. 'A dangerous madman. I'm going to find you guilty, and if it isn't me it'll be somebody else.'

Neptune shakes himself under the poplar tee, as if woken by the raised voices of the two men.

'Sérénac, will you listen to me, Christ alive! There's nothing you can do. I'm not going to let Stéphanie go. If the police arrive, if you try anything, if you try to trap me, I swear, I'll kill her and then kill myself. You claim you love Stéphanie, so prove it. Just let her go. She'll live happily, and so will you. It'll all be fine.'

'Your blackmail is ridiculous, Dupain.'

'It's not blackmail, Sérénac,' Dupain yells. 'I'm not negotiating here! I'm just telling you what will happen if you don't go. I'm capable of blowing everything sky high, and myself with it, if I have nothing to lose. Do you get that? You can call all the police in the world, you still won't be able to prevent a bloodbath.'

The barrel presses still harder against his heart. Sérénac is aware that it's now too late to make the slightest movement. Dupain is alert. The inspector's only remaining option is to use words to persuade his adversary.

'If you shoot me, then you'll lose Stéphanie anyway.'

Jacques Dupain stares at him for a long time. He steps back slowly, without taking the gun off the policeman.

'Come on. We've wasted enough time. I'm asking you one last time, Inspector, scribble a few words on a piece of paper and then get out of here. It's not that difficult. Forget everything and never come back. Only you can avoid this becoming a bloodbath.'

Jacques Dupain's lips suddenly twist and a whistle comes out. Neptune runs happily to his feet.

'Think, Sérénac. Quickly.'

Sérénac doesn't say a word. His hand settles instinctively on the silky fur of the dog, who rubs up against him.

'You know Neptune, I assume, Inspector? Everyone in Giverny knows Neptune. The happy dog who runs about after the children? Who wouldn't love this innocent dog? I love him too, I love him more than anybody, he's come hunting with me a hundred times . . .'

In a flash, the barrel of the rifle comes down level with Inspector Sérénac's knees, twenty centimetres from Neptune's muzzle. One last time, the dog studies the two adults with blind trust. A baby smiling at its parents.

The shot splits the silence beneath the poplars.

Point blank.

Neptune's muzzle explodes, shattered.

The dog collapses in a heap. Sérénac's hand closes on a ball of sticky, bloody fur. The cuff of his sleeve and the bottom of his trouser-legs are spattered with scraps of skin, guts, the remains of an eye and an ear.

He feels an intense panic rising inside him, wiping out any attempt at lucid reflection. The barrel of the rifle in Dupain's hand has risen again in a fraction of a second and is once more pressed against the inspector's torso.

It is crushing a heart that has never beaten so fast.

'Think, Sérénac. Quickly.'

72

The school is a prison on such a sunny May day.

4.29 p.m.

The children run shouting from the classroom. As if in a game of tag, they are caught mid-flight by parents clustered in the Place de la Mairie, although most of them slip through the outstretched hands and the lime trees, and race down the Rue Blanche Hoschedé-Monet.

Stéphanie passes through the door of the classroom, barely a few seconds after the last child has left. As long as no child has a question to ask her . . . As long as no parent, this evening of all evenings, holds her back.

Another few minutes and she will fall into Sérénac's arms. He must have reached Nettles Island by now. Only a few hundred metres separate them. In the corridor, she hesitates a moment before lifting her jacket off the hook. In the end she leaves without it. That morning she put on the light cotton dress that she was wearing when she met Laurenç for the first time, ten days ago.

In the Place de la Mairie, a lascivious sun greedily devours her bare arms and thighs.

As if it were shining just for me . . .

Stéphanie surprises herself with these intoxicating girlish thoughts, this bargain-basement romanticism.

The windows of the town hall reflect her silhouette. She is also surprised to find herself pretty, sexy, in that insignificant little dress that Laurenç will fling into the nettles on the island. She resists the idea of running down the Rue Blanche Hoschedé-Monet, running like the children. Instead, she takes three steps towards a window to examine her face, to let down her hair and make it less modest, to spread out the silver ribbons so that they can tease the sun. She even says to herself that she could waste a few extra seconds, go back to the classroom or back home, slip off her dress, take off her underwear and slip the dress back on over her naked body. And walk through the whole of Giverny like that. She has never even imagined that before . . . Why not? She hesitates.

The desire to see Laurenç as quickly as possible carries her on. She blinks her big mauve eyes at the vague reflection in the window. She embellished her eyelids this morning with a hint of make-up. The bare minimum. Yes, if she asks Laurenç with sparkling eyes like that, eyes that implore, laugh and undress, all at the same time . . . Yes, she will be saved.

Laurenç will take her away.

Her life will never be the same again.

Stéphanie speeds up, almost trots down the Rue Blanche Hoschedé-Monet. When she reaches the Chemin du Roy, she decides not to skirt the Moulin des Chennevières and take the path, but instead cuts straight across the wheat field in front of her, as the children do.

For the children a field of wheat, with all the alleyways between the ears, is like a huge maze. She doesn't care, she isn't worried about getting lost in the labyrinth. She'll take the shortest route. She goes straight on. Straight on for ever, now.

73

Paul carefully steps onto the bridge over the Epte. Although he doesn't know why, he's feeling uneasy. Perhaps because Fanette is being so mysterious, telling him that he alone knows the hiding place of the fabulous *Water Lilies* she's painted. Fanette likes that kind of thing – secrets, promises, weird things. Perhaps he's also uneasy because of that business about the murdered painter, that American, James.

Did Fanette really see his body in the field? Or did she make it all up? And then of course there are the police, the police questioning everyone in the village because of the murder of that other man.

It's all quite frightening. He doesn't say anything in front of Fanette, he shows off a bit in front of her, playing the brave knight, but in reality he finds it all terrifying, like that mill nearby with its waterwheel and its big tower like the tower of a haunted house.

There is a noise behind him.

Paul turns round abruptly. He doesn't see anything.

He has to be careful. Fanette has trusted him with a mission, to recover her painting from under the wash house, take it to their teacher, and tell her that it's for the Robinson Foundation competition. It's an easy mission – even walking to the wash house only takes five minutes from school. Ten minutes there and back.

Paul studies his surroundings once more, checks that there's no one on the bridge, in the courtyard of the mill, in the wheat field behind it, then leans over the steps of the wash house and slips his hand into the space.

Suddenly he's frightened.

His fingers grope about in the darkness. He panics; he can't find anything. Just a void. Ideas shoot through his brain. Someone has come. Someone has stolen the painting. Someone who wanted to take their revenge, hurt Fanette . . . Or else someone who has guessed the true value of Fanette's first painting, because one day Fanette's paintings are bound to be worth a lot, as much as a Monet.

That'll be it. His fingers brush cobwebs, close on air. It isn't possible! Where could that painting have got to? He saw Fanette sliding it in there yesterday.

Behind him something moves.

There's no doubt about it now; someone is walking along the path. Paul thinks quickly. It must be someone passing by; people are always crossing the bridge, it isn't important. Paul can't turn round, not straight away. The important thing is to find the painting. Paul twists onto his belly. He reaches his other arm into the narrow hole under the wash house. He waves his hands around, searching.

He is wrapped in a vast wave of heat. He isn't going to fail stupidly like this. He isn't going to go back to Fanette and tell her, like an idiot, that the painting wasn't there. Paul realises that he can't hear footsteps on the path anymore.

It's too hot. Paul is too hot.

His arms are electrified all of a sudden, as if he had touched bare wires. Right at the back bottom, in the darkness, his fingers have closed on thick paper. Paul pulls. His hands go on exploring, blindly following the flat parcel, the right angles.

No doubt about it. It's the painting!

Paul's heart bursts with joy. The painting is there, it had just been pushed in a bit too far. What an idiot he is! He scared himself. Who could have stolen the painting? He kneels down and pulls on the package again. At last the cardboard emerges into the daylight.

Paul recognises it. The same format, about forty centimetres by sixty, the same brown paper covering it. He's going to open it to check, he's going to open it and see it once more, so that the cascading colours explode in his face . . .

'What are you doing?'

The voice freezes his blood.

Someone is standing behind him. Someone is speaking to him. A voice that Paul knows very well, too well, perhaps.

A voice so cold it's as if he's bumped into a corpse.

74

The shadow of the water tank gives me a bit of shade. It's a kind of large reservoir. Sometimes I curse myself, I curse my poor legs. Crossing the meadow from the mill to the Epte is as difficult for me now as crossing the Arctic Circle. A real expedition. Yet it's barely a kilometre. How pitiful! When I think that Neptune has already been waiting for me down there, at Nettles Island, for half an hour . . .

Right, I'd better get a move on.

I rest for another few moments and then set off again.

Don't read me the riot act, I know I'm just a stubborn old woman. But I have to get to Nettles Island, one last time. For one last pilgrimage. It's there, and nowhere else, that I will choose my weapon.

Of course just as I'm about to set off again Richard appears from behind the metal wall of the water tank. I should have recognised his blue 4L parked behind the barrier. Richard Paternoster, the last farmer in Giverny, who owns three quarters of the meadow, a countryman with the face and the name of a priest, who has never forgotten to wave at me in over thirty years, even when he was choking me from up there on his tractor and sending all kinds of insecticide into our lungs, mine and Neptune's, as he drove his engines of torture, sending death chasing after me every time I crossed the meadow.

And of course here he is now, stopping to tell me about his wretched life and share the misery of the world with me. As if I would feel sorry for him, with his fifty hectares classified as a historic monument!

Yet it's impossible to avoid him. He gestures to me to come back, to stay a while longer in the shade of the water tank.

I have no choice, I walk towards him. I just have time to see in the distance the cloud of smoke on the path, like the plume from the old trains in the Wild West. The motorbike passes by the spot without slowing down. But not so fast that I can't recognise it.

A Tiger Triumph T100.

75

Stéphanie is breathless as she arrives at Nettles Island. She ran through the field in a straight line, like an impatient teenager. As if every second that kept her from her amorous rendezvous counted.

Laurenç is waiting for her, she knows.

She pushes aside the last waist-high stems and steps into the clearing.

It's as silent as a cathedral beneath the poplars of Nettles Island.

Laurenç isn't there.

He isn't hiding, he isn't playing with her. He simply isn't there. His Triumph must be parked somewhere.

She didn't want to listen when she was crossing the field, she didn't want to look, but she distinctly heard the noise of that engine that she has learned to recognise, the engine of Laurenç's Triumph. She saw the smoke rising in the distance. She wanted to believe that she was wrong. She wanted to believe that Laurenç was coming, even if the sound seemed to be moving away; that the wind, just the wind was responsible for the illusion. It was impossible to believe that the Triumph was leaving, that Laurenç was fleeing.

Why would he have left before she even arrived?

Laurenç isn't there.

Her eyes can't miss the sheet of paper nailed to the trunk of the first poplar. It's plain white paper with some words scribbled on it.

She walks over. She already knows that she won't like what she's about to read, that those words will contain something like a death notice.

She steps forward as if sleepwalking.

The writing is jerky, nervous.

Four lines.

There is no happy love . . .
Except those loves that our memory cultivates.
For ever, for always

Laurenç

Stéphanie feels her legs giving way beneath her. Her hands claw desperately at the bark of the poplar. She falls. The vertical trunks spin around her like giants dancing in a satanic circle.

There is no happy love . . .

Only Laurenç could have written those words, she's aware of it. A memory. A pretty memory is all that the inspector was looking for.

Her light cotton dress clings to the damp earth. Her arms and her legs are filthy. Stéphanie weeps, refuses to acknowledge the truth.

What a fool!

A memory.

For ever, for always.

She will have to settle for the memory. All her life. Go back to Giverny, to the classroom, to her house. To resume the ordinary round of things, like before. To close the door of her own cage.

What an idiot!

What was she thinking?

She is trembling now, trembling with cold in the shade of the trees. Her dress is wet. Why is it wet? Her thoughts are muddled. She doesn't understand – the grass of the meadow is bone dry; it seems to have been grilled under the sun. It doesn't matter. She feels so dirty. She runs her hand over her eyes and clumsily tries to wipe away her tears.

Good God!

Stéphanie's pupils are fixed on her palms, appalled: they are red. Blood red!

Stéphanie feels that she's about to faint, she no longer understands. She raises her arms: they too are covered with blood. She lowers her eyes. Her dress is marked with large stains that drench the light cotton.

She is bathing in a pool of blood.

Red blood. Bright. Fresh.

Suddenly, the leaves of the trees rustle behind her.

Someone is coming.

76

'What are you hiding? What are you hiding in that package?'

Paul turns round and gives a huge sigh of relief. It's Vincent. He should have expected it, the boy's still spying on him. But anyway, it's only Vincent. Even if his friend's voice sounds strange and there's a weird glint in his eye.

'Nothing.'

'What do you mean, nothing?'

Fanette is right. Vincent is a pain.

'Right then, since you want to know. Have a look.'

Paul leans towards the wrapped parcel and opens the brown paper. Vincent has come over to him.

Wait until you see this, you nosy parker!

Paul pulls aside the wrapping. The colours of the *Water Lilies* painted by Fanette shimmer in the light of the sun. On the canvas, the lily flowers vibrate with the movement of the water, floating like unmoored tropical islands.

Vincent doesn't say a word. He doesn't seem to be able to take his eyes off the painting.

'Come on, let's go,' Paul says energetically. 'Help me wrap it up again. I have to take it to Teacher. It's for the Young Artists competition, but you've probably guessed that already.'

He stares at Vincent, his eyes filled with pride.

'So, what do you think? Our Fanette is a genius, isn't she! The most talented of everyone. She's going to be spoiled for choice. Tokyo, New York, Madrid – all the painting schools in the world are going to be fighting over her.'

Vincent gets up. He's staggering as if he is drunk.

Paul is worried.

'Are you all right, Vincent?'

'You . . . you're not going to do that,' the boy stammers.

'What?'

Paul starts folding the brown paper over the painting again.

'Give that painting to Miss. Send Fanette to the other end of the world . . . so that they will take Fanette away from us . . .'

'What are you saying? Come on, help me.'

Vincent steps forward. His shadow falls over Paul, who is still crouching down. Suddenly Vincent's voice assumes a strident tone that Paul has never heard from his lips before.

'Throw the painting in the river!'

Paul looks up and wonders for a moment whether Vincent is being serious or not, then bursts out laughing.

'Don't talk nonsense. Go on, help me.'

Vincent doesn't reply. He freezes for a few moments and then suddenly steps forward, raises his right foot and pushes the painting from where it lies on the steps.

The painting slides. The stream is only a few centimetres away.

Paul's hand blocks the package. He holds it solidly with one hand and rises furiously to his feet.

'You're insane! It could have landed in the water.'

Paul knows that Vincent isn't up to a fight. Paul is stronger. If Vincent goes on like that he'll make him understand.

'Move it. Get out of the way. I'm going to take the painting to Miss. After that you and I can settle our scores.'

Vincent retreats under the weeping willow whose branches dip into the stream. He rummages in his trouser pocket.

'I'm not going to let you do it, Paul. I'm not going to let you take Fanette away from us.'

'You're crazy! Clear off!'

Paul steps forward. Vincent leaps at him.

He is holding a knife.

'What the—'

Paul is stunned.

'You're going to give me that painting, Paul. I'm just going to damage it a little. Just enough . . .'

Paul isn't listening to Vincent's ravings. He is concentrating on the knife that Vincent is brandishing. A broad, flat knife. The same kind that Fanette uses when she is painting. The same one that painters use to clean their palettes.

Where could Vincent have found that tool?

Who could he have stolen it from?

'Give me the painting, Paul,' Vincent insists. 'I'm not joking.'

Paul instinctively looks for help, a passer-by, a neighbour, anyone. His eyes turn towards the window of the keep of the Moulin des Chennevières. Inside no one is moving. Not a cat. Not a dog. Not even Neptune.

The river seems to be spinning around him.

A name whirls around inside his skull, unreal, surreal.

James.

Paul stares again at the knife that Vincent is holding. A dirty knife. A painter would clean his knife.

Not Vincent.

The knife-blade is red.

Blood red.

77

Stéphanie's bare legs slip in the mixture of soil and blood, trying to find purchase.

Someone is coming.

Her hands reach out to the trunk of the poplar in front of her, gripping it like the body of a man at whose feet she lies. She struggles to her feet. She feels as if she is covered with excrement, with human remains, as if she's been thrown into a mass grave; as if she's climbing over corpses to get out of it.

Someone is coming.

Stéphanie clings to the poplar, rubs herself against it, twisting to wipe herself against the bark, as if to marry herself to its strength.

Someone's coming.

Someone is following the banks of the Epte. She clearly hears the sound of footsteps, brushing through the ferns along the confluence of the Seine, coming closer. Against the light, she sees a body standing by the row of poplars.

Laurenç?

For a moment Stéphanie thinks it is her lover. There is no pool of blood now. No filth. She is going to tear off that dirty dress and throw herself into Laurenç's arms.

He has come back. He's going to take her away.

Her heart has never beaten so fast.

'I . . . I found him like this.'

Jacques. It's Jacques's voice.

Frozen.

Stéphanie's hands scratch the wood. Her fingernails break against the trunk, one by one, each with its own fresh shard of pain.

The shadow steps forward into the sunlight.

Jacques.

Her husband.

Stéphanie no longer has the strength to think, to wonder what he's doing here, at Nettles Island, to try to put some order into the sequence of events. She merely goes through them, moving like a sleepwalker, bumping into the obstacles hurtling towards her.

Stéphanie can't take her eyes off the dark form that Jacques is holding in his arms. A dog. A dead dog whose muzzle has been torn half off and whose blood is dripping down Jacques's thighs.

Neptune.

'I found him like this,' Jacques Dupain murmurs again in a blank voice. 'It must have been a hunting accident. Someone killed him. A stray bullet. Or some bastard. He . . . he didn't suffer, Stéphanie. He died straight away.'

Stéphanie gently slides along the tree trunk. The bark lacerates her arms, her legs. She can no longer feel the pain. There is no pain at all.

Jacques smiles at her. Jacques is strong. Jacques is calm.

He sets Neptune's body down delicately on a bed of grass.

'That's enough, Stéphanie.'

Stéphanie feels all her resistance ebbing away. It's lucky that Jacques is there. Where would she be without him? What would she do without him? He's always been there. Never complaining, never judging her, never asking anything of her. Just there. Like the poplar that she's clinging to, Jacques is a tree that's been planted beside her, that doesn't react when she goes away, that knows she'll always come back to seek refuge in its shade.

Jacques holds out his hand to her. Stéphanie takes it.

She trusts him. Just him. He is the only man who has never betrayed her. She bursts into tears against his shoulder.

'Come on, Stéphanie. Come away. I'm parked nearby. We'll put Neptune in the boot. Come on, Stéphanie, we're going home.'

78

Inspector Laurenç Sérénac rests his Triumph against the white wall of the police station. It has taken him only a few minutes to travel the five kilometres that separate Giverny from Vernon. He bursts inside. Maury is on reception talking to three girls, one of whom, almost hysterical, is endlessly repeating that her handbag has disappeared from the pavement café in the Place de la Gare. Her two friends are nodding.

'Have you seen Sylvio?'

Maury looks up.

'Downstairs. In the archives.'

Sérénac doesn't slow his pace. He races down the stairs and pushes open the red door. Sylvio Bénavides is hunched over a pad, scribbling notes. He has spread out the contents of the file on the table: the photographs of Jérôme Morval's mistresses and the crime scene, the lists of children from Giverny School, the autopsy, the graphology reports, the photocopies of *Water Lilies*, his handwritten notes . . .

'Chief! Good timing. I think I've made some progress.'

Sérénac doesn't give his deputy the time to say anything more.

'Forget it, Sylvio. We're dropping the case.'

Bénavides looks at him with astonishment and goes on:

'But I've got some news. First of all, I've found the fifth mistress, the girl in the blue overall. I've made dozens of phone calls. Her name is Jeanne Thibaut. Basically she slept with Morval to keep her job, she told me. Since then she's moved to the Parisian suburbs. She lives with a postman. She has two kids, aged three and five. So you see, nothing suspicious. We've reached another dead end.'

Sérénac looks bleakly at his deputy.

'A dead end. So we agree, it's—'

'Except,' Bénavides jumps in enthusiastically, 'I've also been to the regional archives – I spent a huge amount of time there – and in the end I managed to unearth some copies of the *Républicain de Vernon* dating back to 1937. There are articles about the death of that boy, Albert Rosalba. There is even an interview with the mother of the drowned child, Louise Rosalba, and she didn't think it was an accident. She—'

Sérénac raises his voice.

'You don't understand, Sylvio. We're dropping the case! Our investigation is going nowhere; all that nonsense about *Water Lilies* hidden in the attics of Giverny, and an accident involving a little boy that took place before the war! Jealous husbands . . . We're a laughing stock!'

Bénavides lifts his pen from his note pad.

'Excuse me, but you're right, Chief, I don't understand. What do you mean, exactly, when you say we're dropping it?'

With the back of his hand, Sérénac sends a pile of papers on the table flying and sits down in their place.

'Let me put it another way, Sylvio. You were right. All along. Mixing personal feelings with a criminal investigation is folly of the worst kind. I've realised that a little late, but at least I've realised it.'

'You're talking about Stéphanie Dupain?'

'If you say so.'

Sylvio Bénavides darts him a smile and patiently gathers up the scattered pages.

'So Jacques Dupain is no longer public enemy number one?'

'We'd have to say no.'

'But . . . the—'

Sérénac brings his fist down on the table.

'Listen, Sylvio. I'm going to call the investigating magistrate and tell him I'm struggling with this case, that I'm hopelessly incompetent, and that if he wants to, he can hand the investigation over to someone else.'

'But . . .'

Sylvio Bénavides takes in the exhibits on the table and casts an eye over his notes.

'I hear you, Chief. It may even be for the best, but . . .'

His eyes come to rest on Laurenç.

'Good God, what's happened to you?'

'What?'

'Your sleeves, your jacket! Have you been carrying a corpse about or something?'

Laurenç sighs.

'I'll explain later. You had a "but"?'

'The thing is, the more I try to put all the pieces of the puzzle in order, the more I keep coming back to this child who's in danger, this eleven-year-old. If we drop the case now we risk—'

Sylvio Bénavides doesn't manage to finish his sentence. Officer Maury, who has come down the stairs four by four, bursts into the archive room.

'Sylvio! We've just had a call from the maternity ward! It's happening. I think they said her waters have broken, but the midwife didn't say anything more, just that you need to get there double quick . . .'

Bénavides leaps from his chair. Laurenç Sérénac gives him a friendly pat on the shoulder.

'Hurry up, Sylvio. Forget everything else.'

'Right . . . OK.'

'Run, you idiot!'

Sylvio slips his arms clumsily into the sleeves of his jacket. Sérénac urges him on:

'What are you waiting for? Off you go!'

'Before I leave, can I call you by your first name . . . Laurenç?'

'It was high time, you fool.'

The two men smile at each other. Inspector Bénavides casts one last glance at the sheets of paper on the table, particularly the photograph of Stéphanie Dupain, then says as he leaves: 'In the end, I really do think you're right to drop this investigation.'

Laurenç Sérénac listens to his deputy running up the stairs. The heavy footsteps fade, a door slams, then nothing. Sérénac slowly places all the pieces of the dossier together in the red filing box. The photographs, the reports, the notes. He runs his eyes along the alphabetic classification on the shelf, then puts the red box in its place.

M . . . for Morval.

He takes a step back. Now the Morval case is just another file among several hundred others that have never been solved. In spite of himself, he can't help thinking about Sylvio's last remark.

A child whose life is in danger.

One child dying. Another being born.

Sylvio will forget.

In a corner of the room Laurenç Sérénac notices, almost with amusement, some boots that the owners never came to collect, probably because they were too old or too worn. Above them, on a table, the plaster print of the boot is still on display. Quite clearly, this investigation didn't make sense from the start, he thinks to himself with a certain degree of irony. His next thoughts fly towards Stéphanie, and towards Neptune's body.

Yes, he made the right decision. There were enough bodies already.

Otherwise, Stéphanie's water-lily gaze, her porcelain skin, her chalky lips and those silver ribbons in her hair . . .

He will forget too.

At least that's what he hopes.

79

'Give me that painting,' Vincent says again.

The painter's knife that the boy is holding gives him a new confidence, as if he were a few years older, with the age and experience of a teenage street fighter. Paul presses Fanette's painting even more firmly against his waist.

Furious.

'Where did you get that knife, Vincent?'

'I found it! Who cares. Give me the painting. You know I'm right. If you really care about Fanette . . .'

Vincent's pupils dilate and the corners of his eyes appear red – like the eyes of a crazy person. Paul has never seen him like that before.

'You haven't answered my question. Where did you find that knife? And why is there blood on it?'

Vincent's arm is shaking slightly now.

'Mind your own business!'

To Paul, it's as if his friend is metamorphosing in front of his eyes, turning into a hysterical lunatic who could be capable of anything. He rests his hand on the corner of the wash house.

'It's . . . surely it wasn't you?'

'Hurry up, Paul. Just get rid of that painting. We're on the same side. If you really care about Fanette . . .'

He waves the painter's knife around chaotically in the air. Paul takes a step back.

'Christ . . . Were you the one who killed that American painter, James? He was stabbed through the heart, Fanette told me. Could it really have been you?'

'Shut up! What do you care about some American painter? Fanette's the one who matters, isn't she? Choose your side, I'm telling you! Either you chuck that painting in the water or . . . I'm giving you one last chance!'

Vincent's arm stiffens as if he has a sword in his hand and is about to launch an assault.

'One last chance, I told you . . .'

Paul smiles faintly and bends down to put the package on the tarmac along the edge of the wash house.

'OK, Vincent. Just calm down a bit.'

Then all of a sudden Paul straightens up and springs towards him. Vincent is taken by surprise and doesn't move. Paul's hand closes on his wrist and squeezes it hard, twisting the boy's forearm until Vincent is forced to kneel. He manages to croak some insults, but that only makes Paul tighten his grip.

Vincent has no choice. His red eyes are wet with tears. Pain. Humiliation. His hand opens and the knife falls to the ground. Paul swiftly kicks it away into the grass under the willow. He twists Vincent's arm up behind his back, then lifts his wrist. The boy yelps.

'Shit! My shoulder, you're going to pull my arm out . . .'

Paul continues to twist Vincent's arm up. He is stronger. He always has been.

'You're sick. You're a loony. They're going to put you away in the loony bin. I'm going to tell your parents, the police, everyone. I always thought you weren't quite right, but I didn't think you were so far gone . . .'

Vincent screams out loud. Paul has sometimes had fights in the playground, at break time, but he's never gone as far as this. How long will he go on crushing this boy's wrist? How high can he twist that arm before Vincent's shoulder is torn out of the socket? He thinks he can hear cartilage breaking.

Vincent isn't shouting any longer. Now he's crying, and his body no longer resists, as if all of his muscles have started to relax. At last Paul opens his hand and pushes the boy away. Vincent rolls off like a ball of rags.

Inert. Defeated.

'I'm watching you,' Paul says threateningly.

He glances round to check that the painter's knife is still too far away for the boy to be able to pick it up. Vincent is lying prostrate in the foetal position. Keeping his eye on him, Paul leans down by the edge of the wash house to pick up the painting. His hand touches the brown paper.

Maybe he turns away for half a second to check that he's holding the painting securely.

Barely that.

It is too much.

Vincent leaps to his feet and runs straight at him, elbows in front of him. Paul moves to the side, towards the wash house. Once again he is too quick for Vincent; Vincent's elbows glance off his torso, almost without touching him.

He's sick!

But suddenly Paul can't think about anything else, because the soil beneath his feet is slipping and he is losing his balance on the soft riverbank. His hand reaches out to find something, anything to hold on to – the roof of the wash house, one of the supporting pillars, a branch . . .

Too late.

He falls backwards. And although he curls up instinctively, his back strikes the brick corner of the wash house as he goes down. The pain is brutal and intense. Paul is still tumbling but not for long. His temple strikes the edge of one of the wooden beams. His eyes open towards the sky. A huge flash, like lightning.

He is still sliding, he can see everything, he's conscious, it's just his body that has stopped responding, is refusing to obey.

Cold water touches his hair. Paul works out that he's rolling into the stream. His eyes see only the cloudless sky above him, and some willow branches, like scratches on a blue screen.

The cold water swallows his ear, his neck, the back of his head.

He goes under.

Vincent's face appears against the blue screen.

Paul holds out his hand, at least that's what he thinks he does, it's what he'd like to do, but he doesn't know if his hand has moved at all – he can't feel it, he doesn't see it in the blue painting. Vincent smiles at him. Paul wonders what this smile means. Was it all one big joke? A laugh? Will Vincent pull him out and clap him on the shoulder?

Or is Vincent really mad . . .

Vincent leans over him.

Paul knows the answer, now. It isn't a smile that is distorting Vincent's mouth, it's a sadistic grin. Paul sees a hand, then two, emerging into the blue screen. They disappear, but he feels them settling on his shoulders.

Pushing down.

Paul wants to struggle, kick out, turn over, send this maniac flying. He's stronger than him. A lot stronger.

Yet he finds he can't make the slightest movement. He's paralysed.

The two hands push him again.

Icy water consumes his mouth, his nostrils, his eyes.

The last image that Paul is aware of is pink shapes floating above him, by the surface, just beneath the flowing water.

They remind him of Fanette's painting.

It's his last thought.

80

I struggle on along the path that leads to Nettles Island. Richard Paternoster, the farmer, has finally let me go, although not before dishing out a litany of advice. 'At your age, my dear woman, isn't a stroll all the way to the Epte a bit too much? Especially with the sun beating down on you like that . . . What are you going to do there, anyway? Are you sure you don't want me to drive you? You must be careful – even on the track you get people driving along too quickly. Tourists who have got themselves lost, or Monet fans looking for the famous Nettles Island. Did you see the speed of that motorbike a moment ago, as it crossed the meadow? And now, there, look at that car . . .'

A cloud of ochre earth has risen from the track.

The blue Ford has passed in front of the farm.

The Ford that belongs to the Dupains. In the halo of dust I just had time to glimpse the passengers.

Jacques Dupain, at the wheel, his eyes betraying no emotion.

Stéphanie Dupain, beside him, in tears.

Are you weeping, my darling?

Weep, weep, my lovely. Trust me, this is only the beginning.

This damned track seems interminable. I continue at my own rhythm, attempting to anticipate the ruts with my cane; there are only a few hundred metres to go before I reach Nettles Island. I would love to be able to speed up. I can't wait to see Neptune; I haven't seen him since I left the mill. I know that idiot dog likes to run around all day with the village children and passers-by, or chase the rabbits in the meadow.

But here . . .

A stupid anxiety rises up in my throat.

'Neptune?'

At last I reach Nettles Island.

This place, wedged between two rivers, has always felt very remote. Not an island, let's not exaggerate, but a peninsula perhaps. The wind stirs the leaves of the poplars as if it were blowing in from some great expanse of water; as if this ridiculous little stream, the Epte, a ditch less than two metres wide, were some vast, impassable ocean. As if this banal field of nettles actually stretched to the edge of the world and only Monet had understood.

'Neptune!'

I often spend quite a while here, looking from the other side of the water. I like this place. I will miss it.

'Neptune!'

I shout louder now. The dog still hasn't appeared. My anxiety is starting to turn into fear. Where could that dog have got to? I whistle this time. I can still whistle. Neptune always comes when I whistle.

I wait.

Alone.

Not a sound. Not a sign. There is no trace of Neptune.

I reason with myself. I know that my fears are ridiculous. I'm imagining things, because of this place. It's been a long time since I believed in curses, in history repeating itself and that kind of nonsense. There is no such thing as fate . . . not exactly . . .

My God. There is no sign of that dog.

'Neptune!'

I shout until I make myself hoarse.

I call out, again and again.

'Neptune. Neptune.'

The poplars seem mute for all eternity.

'Neptune . . .'

Ah!

Here comes my dog, emerging out of nowhere, parting the thicket on my right; he comes and presses himself against my dress. His cheeky eyes sparkle with mischief, as if he's asking me to pardon him for having run away for so long.

'Come on, Neptune, let's go home.'

PICTURE TWO

Exhibition

DAY THIRTEEN

25 May 2010
(Meadow, Giverny)

Renunciation

81

I'm returning from Nettles Island. This time, as I head past Richard Paternoster's farm, rather than going back towards the Moulin des Chennevières, I turn right towards the three car parks that are arranged like petals. The cars and buses are starting to leave. Several times, some idiot who is reversing without looking in the mirror almost knocks me over. Each time, I take my cane and whack their bumper, or the bottom of the bodywork. They don't dare say anything to an old woman like me. They even apologise.

Forgive me; we take our enjoyment where we can.

'Come on, Neptune.'

Those fools could even run over my dog.

At last I reach the Chemin du Roy. I walk on a little way, as far as Monet's gardens. Between the roses and the water lilies, they're in full bloom. I must say, it's a beautiful spring day. There's just an hour before the garden closes. The tourists resent the journey ahead of them, and wait patiently in single file on the paths. It's Giverny at five o'clock in the evening. Everyone's heading towards the railway station.

My gaze loses itself in the crowd. Suddenly she's all I can see.

Fanette.

She has her back to me. She is sitting by the lily pond, in front of her canvas, which rests on some wisteria. I can tell she's crying.

'Why do you want to speak to her?'

Fat Camille is standing on the other side of the lily pond, on the little green bridge with the weeping willow branches cascading down over it. He looks a bit stupid. He is twisting a card in his hands.

'Why do you want to speak to Fanette?' Vincent asks again.

Camille stammers, embarrassed:

'I . . . just to console her . . . I thought . . . I have a card for her eleventh birthday.'

Vincent tears the card from Camille's hands and studies it briefly. It's a simple postcard, a reproduction of the *Water Lilies* in mauve. All it says on the back is: HAPPY BIRTHDAY. ELEVEN YEARS OLD.

'OK. I'll give it to her. Now leave her alone. Fanette needs to be left in peace.'

From the other side of the pond the two boys watch the little girl bent over her canvas, her brushes moving in a chaotic frenzy.

'How is she?' Camille asks.

'How do you think?' Vincent replies. 'Like the rest of us. Stunned . . . Paul drowning. That funeral, the rain. But we'll get over it. Accidents happen. That's how it is.'

Camille bursts into tears. Vincent doesn't even bother trying to comfort him. Already stalking off round the pond, he adds simply: 'Don't worry, I'll give her your card.'

The path around the pond turns left and disappears in a jungle of wisteria. As soon as he's out of sight, Vincent takes the birthday card from his pocket. He walks towards the Japanese bridge, using the back of his hand to push away the irises that lean too far over the path.

Fanette is there, with her back to him, sniffing. She dips her brush, the widest one, almost like a decorator's brush, into a palette on which she has mixed the darkest colours possible.

Intense brown. Charcoal grey. Deep purple.

Black.

Fanette covers the rainbow canvas with anarchic brushstrokes, reproducing the torment in her mind. As if, within a few minutes, darkness had fallen on the pond, on the running water, on all the light of her painting. She spares only a few of the water lilies, illuminating them with a bright yellow dot using a finer brush.

Stars scattered in the night.

Vincent speaks in a gentle voice.

'Camille wanted to come over, but I told him you wanted to be left in peace. He says he wishes you a happy birthday.'

The boy's hand rests on his pocket but he doesn't take out the card that he's put there. Fanette doesn't reply. She empties a new tube of ebony paint on to her palette.

'Why are you doing that, Fanette? It's . . .'

Finally Fanette turns round. Her eyes are red with tears. She's hastily wiped her cheeks, probably with the same rag that she uses for her painting. They're black.

'It's all over, Vincent. I'm done with colour. I'm done with painting.'

Vincent says nothing.

Fanette cries out, 'It's over, Vincent! Don't you understand? Paul died because of me. He slipped on the step of the wash house when he went to look for the damned painting. I was the one who sent him there, I was the one who told him to hurry. I . . . I was the one who killed him . . .'

Vincent rests his hand on the girl's shoulder.

'No, Fanette, it was an accident, you know that. Paul slipped, he drowned in the stream; no one can do anything about that.'

Fanette sniffs.

'You're very kind, Vincent.'

She sets her brush down on the palette and leans against the boy's shoulder. Her eyes fill with tears.

'Everyone told me I was the most gifted one. That I had to

be selfish. That painting would give me everything. They lied to me, Vincent, they all lied. They're all dead. James. Now Paul.'

'Not all of them, Fanette. Not me. And besides, Paul—'

'Shh.'

Vincent understands that Fanette is calling for silence. He doesn't dare say a word. Instead, he waits. Only the sound of the girl's tears breaks the frightening calm of the pond, as well as the occasional faint splash as willow leaves or wisteria petals fall into it. At last Fanette's trembling voice speaks once more.

'I'm done with this whole game, too. All those nicknames I gave you, of Impressionist painters, to make myself more interesting. The fake first names. It's all so pointless now . . .'

'If you want, Fanette.'

Vincent's arm is now around the girl's shoulders, pressing her to him. She could go to sleep there.

'I'm here,' Vincent murmurs. 'I'll always be here, Fanette . . .'

'That too. I'm not called Fanette anymore. No one must call me Fanette ever again. Not you, not anyone. The girl that everyone called Fanette, that little girl with such a talent for painting, a genius in the making, she's dead too. She died at the wash house, beside the wheat field. There is no more Fanette.'

The boy hesitates. His hand softly strokes the top of her arm.

'I understand. I'm the only one who understands you, you know. I'll always be here for you, Fanet—'

Vincent coughs.

'I'll always be here, Stéphanie.'

The bracelet on the boy's wrist slides along her arm. He can't help lowering his eyes towards the jewel. He has understood that from now on, Stéphanie will never again call him by the painter's first name that she had chosen for him: *Vincent.*

She will use his real first name.

The one he was christened with, the one from his first communion, the one engraved in silver on his bracelet.

Jacques.

*

Water runs over Stéphanie's naked body. She rubs herself frantically under the jet of boiling hot water. Her straw-coloured dress, stained with red marks, lies in a ball nearby. The water has been cascading over her for many long minutes, but still she can feel Neptune's blood on her skin. The terrible smell. The stain.

There is no happy love.

She can't help reliving those moments of madness on Nettles Island.

Her dog, Neptune, slaughtered.

Laurenç's farewell note.

There is no happy love.

Jacques is sitting in the next room, on the bed. On the bedside table, the radio is wailing a heady hit, *Le temps de l'amour* by Françoise Hardy. Jacques is talking loudly so that Stéphanie can hear him in the shower:

'No one can hurt you now, Stéphanie. No one. We're going to stay here, both of us. No one will come between us.'

There is no happy love . . .

Except those loves that our memory cultivates.

Stéphanie is crying, a few additional drops of water under the scorching jet.

Jacques continues with his monologue from the edge of the bed.

'You'll see, Stéphanie. Everything is going to change. I'm going to find you a house, a different one, a real one, one that you will love.'

Jacques knows her so well. Jacques always finds the right words.

'Cry, my darling. Cry. You're right. Tomorrow we'll go to the farm at Autheuil and get a new dog. What happened to Neptune was an accident, a stupid accident. It happens, here in the country-side. But he didn't suffer. We'll go tomorrow, Stéphanie. Tomorrow things will look better.'

The shower has stopped. Stéphanie is wrapped in a large lilac towel. She steps into the bedroom, barefoot, her hair dripping. Beautiful, so beautiful. So beautiful in Jacques's eyes.

Is it possible to love a woman so much?

Jacques gets up, presses his wife to him, soaks himself in her.

'I'm here for you, Stéphanie. You know that, I'll always be here, with you, when things get tough.'

Stéphanie's body stiffens for a moment, just a moment, before abandoning itself completely. Jacques kisses his wife's neck.

'We can start all over again, my beautiful darling. Tomorrow we'll get a new puppy. It'll help you forget. I know you. Imagine, a new puppy to christen!'

The wet towel slips to the ground. Jacques lays his wife down on the marital bed. Naked. Stéphanie lets him do it.

She has understood. She has stopped struggling. Fate has decided for her. She knows that the years to come won't count for anything, that she will grow old like that, caught in a trap, side by side with an attentive husband that she doesn't love. The memory of her attempted escape will fade away, gradually, over time.

Stéphanie simply closes her eyes, the only act of resistance she feels capable of now. On the radio the last guitar chords of *Le temps de l'amour* merge with Jacques's raucous groans.

Stéphanie wishes she could block her ears as well.

After a brief jingle, the jovial voice of the presenter delivers the weather forecast for the following day. It will be fine, unusually warm for the time of year. Happy name day to anyone called Diane. The sun will rise at 5.49, another few extra minutes of daylight. Tomorrow it will be 9 June 1963.

> *There is no happy love . . .*
> *Except those loves that our memory cultivates.*
> *For ever, for always*
>
> *Laurenç*

I shake myself. I'm going to end up being roasted by the sun if I stand motionless like this, beside the Chemin du Roy, lost in my mad, old-lady thoughts.

I have to move. I have to loop the loop. All we need are the words 'the end' in the frame of this story.

It's a pretty romance, don't you think? I hope you appreciate the happy ending.

They got married, at least, they stayed married, they had no children.

He was happy.

She thought she was. You get used to it.

She had the time . . . Almost fifty years. From 1963 until 2010, to be precise. A lifetime, quite simply.

I decide to walk on a little, along the Chemin du Roy as far as the mill. I cross the brook at the bridge and stop by the gate. Immediately I notice that my letter box is overflowing with stupid brochures advertising the nearest hypermarket. I curse under my breath. I throw the bundle of paper into the bin by the entrance to the courtyard, which I put there for that very purpose. Suddenly I swear.

In the middle of the brochures is an envelope that almost suffered the same fate. A small, stiff envelope with my name written on it. I turn it over and read the address of the sender. *Dr Berger. 13 Rue Bourbon-Penthièvre. Vernon.*

Dr Berger. That old vulture would be quite capable of sending me a bill to extort some extra fees out of me. I assess the size of the envelope. Unless he's giving me rather belated condolences. After all, he's almost the last person to have seen my husband alive. That was exactly twelve days ago now.

My clumsy fingers tear the envelope. In it I find a small, pale grey card with a black cross in the top left corner. Berger has scribbled a few barely legible words.

Dear friend,
I have learned with sadness of the death of your husband on 15 May 2010. As I told you some days before, on my last visit, this outcome was sadly inevitable. You were plainly a solid and united couple. You always had been. It's a rare and precious thing.
With my condolences.
Hervé Berger

Irritated, I twist the card around in my hands. In spite of myself, I find I am thinking back to that last consultation. Twelve days ago. An eternity. Another life. Once again, my past resurfaces.

It was 13 May 2010, the day when everything changed, the day when an old man confessed on his death bed. Just a few confessions, before he died.

It took just less than an hour. An hour to listen, then thirteen days to remember.

I resist the desire to tear up the card. Before losing themselves again in the labyrinth of my memory, my eyes settle once more on the envelope.

I read the address. My address.

Stéphanie Dupain
Moulin des Chennevières
Chemin du Roy
27620 Giverny

DAY ONE

13 May 2010

(Moulin des Chennevières)

Testament

82

I'm waiting in the drawing room of the Moulin des Chennevières. The doctor is in the next room, the bedroom, with Jacques. I called him out at about four o'clock in the morning. Jacques was twisting and turning with pain in the sheets, as if his heart had started to slow down, like an engine that is running out of petrol, coughing before it finally stops. When I switched on the bedroom light, his arms were white, streaked with light blue veins. Dr Berger arrived a few minutes after my call. He can do that; he set up his surgery in Vernon, on Rue Bourbon-Penthièvre, but he lives in one of the finest villas on the banks of the Seine, just outside Giverny.

It was a good half hour later when Dr Berger came out of the bedroom.

I'm sitting on a chair. Not doing anything, just waiting. Dr Berger isn't someone to be handled with kid gloves. He's an abrupt old bastard who built his veranda and dug his swimming pool on the back of all the old people in the area, but his frankness, at least, is a quality to be valued. That's why he's been a family doctor for many years.

'It's the end. Jacques understands. He knows he has only a few days left at the most. I called the hospital in Vernon and they have prepared a room for him; they're sending an ambulance.'

He picks up his little leather briefcase but then pauses.

'He asked to see you. I wanted to give him something to make him sleep, but he insisted that he needed to talk to you.'

I must have looked surprised. More surprised than upset.

'And will you be all right?' Berger adds. 'Can you cope? Do you want me to prescribe you something?'

'I'm fine, thank you.'

The only thing I want now is for him to leave. He glances again around the dark room, then puts one foot outside. But then he turns back again, a strange expression on his face. He almost looks sincere. Perhaps he's not keen on the idea of losing a good client.

'I'm sorry. Good luck, Stéphanie.'

Slowly I walked towards Jacques's room, without imagining for a second what awaited me: my husband's confession. The truth, after all these years.

The story was so simple, in fact.

One killer, one motive, one place, a small handful of witnesses.

The killer struck twice, in 1937 and 1963. His sole intention was to preserve his property, his treasure: the life of a woman, from birth until death.

My life.

One criminal. Jacques.

Jacques explained everything. Nothing was left out. For these last few days, my memories have jumped from one era of my life to another, like a kaleidoscope. Yet none of these details was anything but a cog in a precise piece of machinery, a fate minutely guided by a monster.

That was twelve days ago.

That morning I pushed open Jacques's bedroom door, without knowing that I would close it on the shadows of my past.

'Come here, Stéphanie, come over to the bed.'

Dr Berger has put two big pillows under Jacques's body so that he's sitting more than lying. The blood flowing to his cheeks contrasts with the pallor of his arms.

'Come here, Stéphanie. I suppose Berger will have told you. We're going to have to part. Soon. It's . . . it's . . . I have to tell you . . . I have to speak to you while I still have the strength. I asked Berger to give me something to keep my strength up before the ambulance arrives.'

I sit down on the edge of the bed. He slips a wrinkled hand along the folds of the sheet. The hairs on his arm have been shaved for ten centimetres around a beige bandage. I take his hand.

'Stéphanie, in the garage, in the cellar, there are lots of objects that haven't been touched for years. My hunting things, for example, some old jackets, a bag, some wet cartridges, my boots, too. Mouldy old things. You're going to lift them up. You're going to move everything. Then you're going to push aside the gravel on the ground with your feet. Just underneath, you'll see there's a kind of trap door, like a small ventilation space. You won't see it unless you move everything that's on top of it. You're going to lift the trap door. Inside, you will find a small aluminium chest about the size of a shoe box. You're going to bring it to me, Stéphanie.'

Jacques grips my hand tightly, then lets it go. I don't understand, but I get up all the same. I find this whole thing strange – it isn't Jacques's style, mysteries and treasure hunts. Jacques is a simple man, plain, no surprises. I even wonder if Dr Berger hasn't overdone the medication.

I come back a few minutes later. All of my husband's instructions were rigorously precise. I found the little aluminium chest. The joints are rusty. The shining metal is stained all over with dark patches.

I put the chest down on the bed.

'It's padlocked,' I say.

'I know . . . I know. Thank you. Stéphanie, I need to ask you a question. An important question. I'm not very good at speeches, you know me, but you have to tell me, Stéphanie. For all these years, have you been happy by my side?'

What kind of answer can you give to that? What answer are you going to give a man who has only a few days left to live? A man whose life you have shared for over fifty years, sixty, perhaps. What answer are you going to give other than 'Yes . . . Yes, Jacques, of course I've been happy all these years . . .'

It doesn't seem to be enough for him.

'Now, Stéphanie, we've reached the end of the road. We can tell each other everything. Do you have any regrets? Do you think, I don't know, that your life could have been better if it had been spent differently . . . somewhere else . . . with . . .'

He hesitates and gulps.

'With someone else?'

I have a strange sense that Jacques has gone over these questions thousands of times in his head; that he has just been waiting for the right moment, the right day, to ask them. Not that I haven't asked myself these questions – my God, far from it. But I'm an old woman now. I wasn't prepared for this when I got up this morning. The fog is dispersing slowly now, in my weary mind. I too have patiently locked away questions of that kind in a chest and forced myself never to open it again. I have lost the key. I need to look for it . . . It's so far away.

'I don't know,' I reply. 'I don't know, Jacques. I don't understand what you mean.'

'Yes, you do, Stéphanie. Of course you understand. Stéphanie, you have to answer me, it's important – would you have preferred a different life?'

Jacques smiles at me. The whole of his face, all the way to the tops of his arms, is now a healthy pink. Highly effective, Berger's pills. And not just on the circulation. Never in fifty years has Jacques asked me questions like this. It's unheard of. It's not like him. Is it his way of ending his life? At over eighty, asking the other one, the one who's left behind, if her whole life deserves to be thrown in the bin? Who could answer 'yes' to that, who could answer 'yes' to her dying partner, even if they thought it, particularly if they thought it? I see the trap without knowing why it's there.

'What other life, Jacques? What other life are you talking about?'

'You haven't answered me, Stéphanie. Would you have preferred . . .'

The poisonous effluvium of the trap becomes even more apparent, like a long-forgotten perfume coming back to me, an oppressively familiar scent that faded away a long time ago but has never been forgotten. I have no choice but to answer, with nurse-like tenderness:

'I have had the life I chose, Jacques, if that's what you want to hear. The one I deserved. Thanks to you, Jacques. Thanks to you.'

Jacques sighs as if St Peter himself had come down to tell him that his name was on the list. As if now he is free to leave in peace. He worries me. His hand rises and reaches out towards the bedside table, in search of something. It bumps into a glass, which falls onto the ground and breaks. A small puddle of water flows onto the parquet.

I'm getting up to clean it and pick up the shards of broken glass when his hand rises again.

'Wait, Stéphanie. It's just a broken glass, it doesn't matter. Help me, look in my wallet, there, on the bedside table.'

I step forward. The glass crunches under my slippers.

'Open it,' Jacques says. 'Beside my social security card, there's your photograph, Stéphanie, can you see it? Run your finger under the photograph.'

I haven't opened Jacques's wallet for an eternity. The photograph must have been taken at least forty years ago. Is that really me? Did those huge mauve eyes belong to me? That heart-shaped smile? That mother-of-pearl skin on a fine, sunny day in Giverny? Have I forgotten how beautiful I was? Do I have to wait to be a wrinkled octogenarian to be able to admit it at last?

My index finger probes beneath the photograph. It finds a small flat key.

'I'm reassured now, Stéphanie. I can die in peace. I can tell you now that I've had doubts, I've had such doubts. I've done what I could, Stéphanie. You can open the padlock of the chest with the key. That key that has never left me all these years. You'll understand,

I think. But I hope I can stay strong enough to be able to explain it to you myself.'

My fingers are trembling now and a terrible feeling weighs down on me. I struggle to fit the key into the lock. It takes many long moments before finally it turns. Jacques puts his hand gently on my arm again, as if telling me to wait a little.

'You deserved a guardian angel, Stéphanie. It turns out that was me, and I tried to do my job to the best of my ability. It hasn't always been easy, believe me. I've sometimes been afraid that I wouldn't be able to do it . . . But you see, in the end . . . You've reassured me. I didn't come out of it too badly. You remember, my Stéph . . .'

Jacques's eyes close for a second.

'My Fanette . . . After all these years, one last time, will you let me call you Fanette? I've never dared to, in over seventy years, since 1937. You see, I do remember everything. I've been a good guardian angel, faithful and organised.'

I don't reply. I'm finding it hard to breathe. I have only one desire, which is to open the aluminium chest, check that it's empty, that Jacques's whole monologue is nothing but delirium caused by Berger's drugs.

'We were born in the same year,' Jacques continues, 'in 1926. You, Fanette, on the fourth of June, six months before the death of Claude Monet. Me on the seventh, three days later. You on Rue du Château d'Eau, me on Rue du Colombier, a few houses away. I always knew that our fates were linked. That I was there, on the ground, to protect you. To part the branches around you, in your way . . .'

Part the branches? Good God, these poetic images are so unlike Jacques. I'm the one who's going to go mad. I can't help it any longer, I open the chest. Immediately it falls from my hands as if the aluminium were white hot. The contents spill over the bed. My past detonates in my face.

I look in horror at three painting knives, Winsor & Newton; I recognise the winged dragon on the handle, between two red stains, dried by time. My eyes move on and settle on a collection of poetry. *En français dans la tête*, by Louis Aragon. My copy has never left the shelves of my bedroom. How could I have imagined that Jacques had another? Another copy of the book that I have read so often to the children of Giverny School. On page 146, the poem 'Nymphée'. I cling to the book as if it were a bible. The pages dance. I stop, page 146. The corner of the page is turned down. My eyes go to the bottom of the page. *Something's been cut out.* Delicately, someone has cut a piece of the page, just a centimetre, only one line is missing, the first line of the twelfth verse, a line so often recited . . .

The crime of dreaming, I agree to its creation.

I don't understand, I don't understand anything. I don't want to understand. I refuse to put all these elements in order.

Jacques's voice chills me:

'You remember Albert Rosalba? Yes, of course you do. The three of us were always together when we were kids. You gave us nicknames, the names of your favourite Impressionists. He was Paul and I was Vincent.'

Jacques's hand grips the sheet. My eyes are hypnotised by the painting knives.

'It was an accident. He wanted to take your painting to the teacher, your *Water Lilies*, Fanette, the painting in the attic, the one you never wanted to throw away. Do you remember? But that isn't the important thing – Paul, or rather Albert, slipped. We did have a fight first, admittedly, but it was an accident, he slipped near the wash house, and his head bumped against a beam. I wouldn't have killed him, Fanette, I wouldn't have killed Paul, even if he had a bad influence on you, even if he didn't really love you. He slipped . . . It's all the painting's fault. You said that yourself afterwards.'

My fingers close around the handle of one of the knives. It has a wide blade, for scraping a palette. I've never touched a brush again, not once since 1937. That's one of the vanished memories that seem to be tumbling into the huge crevasse that is opening up in my head.

'And . . . and James . . . ?'

My voice is as weak as that of an eleven-year-old girl.

'That old lunatic? The American painter? Is he the one you're talking about, Fanette?'

If I say a word, it's inaudible.

'James,' Jacques goes on. 'James, yes that's it. For years I tried to remember his name, but it escaped me. I even thought of asking you.'

Jacques is shaken by a guffaw. His back slides slightly down the pillows.

'I'm joking, Fanette. I knew I needed to leave you out of all that. That you mustn't know anything about it. Guardian angels have to be discreet, don't they? Right to the end. It's the first principle . . . Don't feel sorry for James. Remember, he used to tell you that you had to be selfish, that you had to leave your family. Everyone. He drove you mad at the time, you were so easily influenced, you weren't even eleven, and he would have had his way. At first, I just threatened him. I carved a message in his paint box while he was asleep – he used to spend almost the entire day asleep, like a big caterpillar. But he didn't pay any attention. He went on torturing you. Tokyo, London, New York. I had no choice, Fanette, you would have gone away, you wouldn't listen to anyone, not even your mother. I had to save you.'

My fingers open. My memories won't stop tumbling into that monstrous crevasse. That knife. That knife on the bed. That red knife. It's James's knife.

Jacques plunged it into James's heart. He was only eleven years old.

'I hadn't predicted that Neptune would find the body of that bloody painter in the wheat field, but I managed to move the corpse before you came back with your mother. Only by a few metres, I think, it's all so long ago. You know, I thought I would never be able to do it; I would never have thought that such a skeletal old man could be so heavy. You won't believe me, but you and your mother passed very close to me. You only needed to turn your head. But you didn't. I think you didn't really want to know. You didn't see me, and nor did your mother. It was a miracle, you understand. A sign! From that day onwards I understood that nothing else could happen to me. That my mission had to be accomplished. The next night, I buried the corpse in the middle of the meadow. It was a hell of a task for a kid, take it from me. Then I burned all the rest, one bit at a time, the easels, the canvases. I only kept his paint box as proof, proof of what I was capable of doing for you. You realise, Fanette, that I was just eleven years old. He looked after you, your guardian angel, do you see now?'

Jacques tries desperately to pull himself back up the pillows, but he goes on sliding, millimetre after millimetre.

'I'm joking, Fanette. In fact it wasn't too difficult, even for a child. Your James was a powerless old man. A foreigner. An American who had missed Monet by ten years. A tramp no one cared about. In 1937 people had other things to worry about. Also, a few days before, a Spanish workman had been found murdered on a barge just outside Giverny. The local police were all working on the case, and they only caught the killer, a sailor from Conflans, a few weeks later.'

Jacques's wrinkled hand searches for mine. It closes on air.

'It does me good to talk about all this, Fanette. Then we were peaceful together. For years . . . You remember? We grew up together, we were only separated when you took that course in Évreux, then you came back to Giverny as a teacher. Our school! We got married at the church of Sainte-Radegonde in Giverny in 1953. Everything was perfect and your guardian angel had only to twiddle his thumbs.'

Jacques bursts out laughing again. The laugh that I hear echoing around our house almost every day, in front of a television programme or behind a newspaper. That loud guffaw. How could I have failed to notice that it was the laugh of a monster?

'But the devil keeps his eyes open, eh, Stéphanie? Jérôme Morval had to come back and start sniffing around you. You remember? Jérôme Morval, our classmate at primary school, the one you used to call Camille, Fat Camille. Top of the class! The pretentious one. At school you didn't like him, Fanette, but he had changed. In the end, he even managed to drag that little sneak Patricia into his bed. The one you nicknamed Mary, after Mary Cassatt. But it wasn't long before Patricia wasn't enough for Camille. Money changes a man. He bought the most beautiful house in Giverny, and he had become arrogant, charming, even, in the eyes of certain girls . . . He didn't even bother to hide his deceptions from his wife. Everyone in Giverny knew, including Patricia, who even went to the lengths of hiring a private detective to spy on him. Poor Patricia! And Morval could deliver a well-polished speech about painting, and his collection of fashionable artists. But most importantly, Stéphanie, listen to me, Jérôme Morval, the best ophthalmological surgeon in Paris, from what people said, had come back to Giverny for one thing – just one. Not for Monet or the *Water Lilies*, no. He had come back for the lovely Fanette, the girl who had never so much as glanced at him during all their years together in primary school. Now that the wheel had turned, Fat Camille wanted his revenge.'

'You . . . you . . .' The words stick in my throat.

'I know, Stéphanie, that you weren't attracted to Jérôme Morval . . . at least not at that point. But I had to get my hand in first. Jérôme Morval lived in the village, he had all the time in the world, he was sly, he knew how to attract you, with his *Water Lilies*, his knowledge of Monet, the landscapes . . .'

Once again, the monster tries to find my hand. His hand slithers like a bedbug over the sheets. I resist the idea of grabbing the painting knife and piercing it like a harmful insect.

'I bear you no ill will, Stéphanie, I know nothing happened between you and Morval. You just agreed to go for a walk with him, have a conversation. But he would have seduced you, Stéphanie; over time, he would have got there. I'm not a wicked man, Stéphanie. I didn't want to kill Jérôme Morval. I was patient, more than patient. I tried to explain to him, as clearly as possible, what I was capable of, what risks he was taking if he went on hanging around you. The first thing I did was send him that postcard, the one with the *Water Lilies*. Morval wasn't stupid. He remembered very well that it was the card he had entrusted me with years before, in 1937, in Monet's gardens, on your birthday, just after Albert's death. I glued that phrase of Aragon's to the card, from that poem you used to make the children in the class recite. "The crime of dreaming." Morval was no fool. The message was crystal clear: anyone who tried to approach you, to hurt you, was putting themselves in danger . . .'

Jacques's fingers reach for the collection of poems by Aragon that is resting on the bed. They brush the book but lack the strength to pick it up. I don't move. Jacques coughs to clear his throat and continues.

'Can you guess, Stéphanie, what Jérôme Morval's reply to me was? He laughed in my face! I could have killed him then if I'd wanted to. But in the end I quite liked him, Fat Camille, so I gave him another chance. I sent that paint box to his surgery in Paris, James's paint box, still carved with the threat: *She's mine, here, now and for ever*, followed by a cross. If Morval hadn't got the message by then . . . Anyway, he agreed to meet me that morning in front of the wash house, near the Moulin des Chennevières. I thought he was going to tell me that he was giving you up. In fact, it was quite the opposite. Right in front of me, he threw the paint box into the middle of the stream. He despised you, Stéphanie, he didn't love you, you were just another trophy for him. He would have made you suffer, Stéphanie, he would have led you to your ruin. So what could I do? I had to protect you. He didn't take me seriously, he told me that I wasn't up to it, in my hunting boots, that I wasn't capable of making you happy, that you had never loved me. Always that same refrain . . .'

His hand goes crawling again and clutches the knife.

'I had no choice, Stéphanie, I killed him right there, with James's painting knife, which I had been careful enough to bring with me. He died on the edge of the stream, in the same spot where Albert had died years earlier. The act that followed, the rock smashing his skull, the head in the water, I know it was ridiculous. I even thought you might suspect something, particularly when the police pulled James's paint box out of the water. Luckily you never saw that box. It was important for me to protect you and make sure you didn't know anything, to take all kinds of risks for you. You trusted me, and you were right. You can admit it now, my Fanette, that you never suspected just how much I loved you, that you never guessed the lengths that I would go to for you. You remember, a few days after Morval's death, you even went to the police, to tell them that we had been in bed together that morning . . . Probably, somewhere deep inside you, you knew the truth, you just didn't want to admit it.'

I observe, petrified, Jacques's wrinkled fingers stroking the handle of the knife, as if his old man's body were still shivering from the pleasure of having stabbed two men. I don't hold back; I can't do it any longer. The words explode from my throat.

'I wanted to leave you, Jacques. That was why I gave a false statement. You were in jail and I would have felt guilty.'

The fingers twist on the knife. The fingers of a murderer, a madman. A guffaw shakes him. That crazed laugh.

'Of course, Stéphanie. You felt guilty. Obviously, everything was muddled up in your head. But not in mine. No one knows you better than I do. Once Morval was dead I thought we would live in peace. No one there to separate us any more, Stéphanie, no one to take you from me. And then, to top it all – it's almost comical, when I think about it – there's Morval's corpse luring that policeman towards you, that Laurenç Sérénac, the worst danger of all! I was stuck. How could I get rid of him? How could I kill him without being accused of it, without being arrested, without being parted from you for good? So that another Sérénac, or another Morval, could come and make you suffer because I couldn't possibly protect you if I was locked up in a cell. From the very beginning that policeman suspected me; it was as if he could read my mind . . . He followed his instinct. He was a good policeman and it was a very close thing, Stéphanie. Luckily he never managed to discover the connection between me and Albert's accident, and he never heard about the disappearance of that American painter. They came very close to the truth, back then in 1963, he and his deputy, Bénavides. But they couldn't imagine the truth, of course. Who could have understood? Meanwhile that bastard Sérénac turned your head. It was him or me. I looked at the problem from all sides . . .'

Discreetly, my hand creeps along the sheet. Jacques has slid so far, he's lying down now, he can't sit up, and he can't see me anymore,

332

he's talking to the ceiling. My hand closes on the knife again. I feel a morbid pleasure at the touch of it. As if the dried blood on the handle were insinuating itself into my veins, swelling them with a murderous impulse.

Jacques's nervous laughter turns into a hacking cough and he struggles to catch his breath. It would be better for him if he were sitting up, that much is clear. But Jacques doesn't ask me to help him.

'I've nearly finished, Stéphanie,' he says eventually, his voice faltering. 'In the end, all it took were a few threats to make Sérénac run away . . . some effectively illustrated threats.'

He laughs again. Slowly, I bring the knife towards the folds of my black dress.

'Men are so weak, Stéphanie. All men. Sérénac preferred his little job as a police officer to his grand passion for you. But we're not going to complain, are we, Stéphanie? It's what we wanted, isn't it? And Sérénac was right, in the end. Who knows what might have happened if he had decided to be stubborn. That was the last shadow between us, Stéphanie, the last cloud, the last branch to brush aside. Over forty years ago now . . .'

I fold my arms over my breasts, the knife pressed to my heart. I would like to speak, I would like to scream: 'Jacques, tell me, tell me, my guardian angel, since that's what you claim to be, is it so very easy to stab someone? To plunge a knife into a man's heart?'

'What determines a life, Stéphanie? If I hadn't been there at the right moment, if I hadn't been able to get rid of all the obstacles, one after the other. If I hadn't been able to protect you. If I hadn't been born just after you, like a twin. If I hadn't understood my mission . . . I'm leaving this earth a happy man, Stéphanie. I've succeeded, I've loved you so much, and now you have the proof.'

I get up, horrified, keeping the knife invisible against my chest. Jacques looks exhausted, as if he is struggling to keep his eyes open. He tries to pull himself up and the aluminium chest falls off the bed onto the parquet floor with a deafening crash. Jacques barely blinks but the high-pitched noise keeps ringing through my head like a dizzying echo. I feel as if the whole room is spinning around me.

I try to move forward but my legs refuse to carry me. I unfold my arms. Jacques is still staring at me. He hasn't seen the knife, yet. I raise it slowly.

Outside, Neptune howls, just below our window. A moment later, there's the sound of a siren and an ambulance enters the courtyard of the mill. Tyres crunch on gravel. Two silhouettes, white and blue in the rotating light, pass by the window and knock at the door.

They took Jacques away. I signed a stack of papers without even reading them, without asking anything at all. They asked me if I wanted to go with them in the ambulance; I said no, I would take the bus, or a taxi, in a few hours' time. The orderlies didn't comment.

The aluminium chest lies open on the floor. The painting knife is on the bedside table. The book by Aragon is lost among the bed-clothes. I don't know why, but after the ambulance leaves, the first thing that occurs to me is to go upstairs and search the attic until I find that dusty old painting, my *Water Lilies*, the one I painted when I was eleven.

The one I painted twice – first in incredible rainbow colours, to win the Robinson Foundation competition, and then in black, after Paul's death.

I've taken Jacques's hunting rifle down from the wall and put the painting in its place, on the same nail, in a corner where no one but me can see it.

I go outside. I need to get some fresh air. I take Neptune with me. It is just after six in the morning and, for a few hours at least, Giverny is deserted. I'm going to walk along the brook, in front of the mill.

And remember.

DAY THIRTEEN

25 May 2010

(Chemin du Roy)

Progression

83

That was twelve days ago, on 13 May. Since then I have spent my days reliving those few hours when my life was stolen from me, watching the film again to try to grasp the unimaginable, one last time and then be done with it.

As I walked alone through this village, you must have taken me for a ghost. In fact it's quite the opposite.

I'm all too real.

It's the others who are ghosts; the ghosts of my memories. I have peopled those places where I have always lived with my ghosts, and as I passed in front of each spot I remembered: the mill, the meadow, the school, the Rue Claude Monet, the terrace of the Hôtel Baudy, the cemetery, Vernon Museum, Nettles Island . . .

I have also populated these places with the long conversations I had with Sylvio Bénavides between 1963 and 1964, after the investigation into the murder of Jérôme Morval was dropped. Inspector Sylvio Bénavides stubbornly pursued it, but he never found the slightest bit of evidence, the smallest new clue. We sympathised. At least Jacques wasn't jealous of my exchanges with this other

335

inspector. Sylvio was a faithful husband and an attentive father to little Carina, who had had so much trouble getting out of her mother's womb. Sylvio told me all the details of the enquiry that he had led with Laurenç, at the station in Vernon, in Cocherel, in the museums in Rouen and Vernon. Then, in the mid-1970s, Sylvio was transferred to La Rochelle. A little over ten years ago, in September 1999 to be precise – you can see that my memory still works perfectly – I received a letter from Béatrice Bénavides. A short, handwritten letter. She told me that Sylvio had left them, her and Carina, one morning, after having a heart attack. Sylvio had climbed onto his bicycle, as he did every morning, to ride around the island of Oléron, where the family rented a bungalow during the low season. He had left with a smile on his face. The weather was fine, a little windy. He collapsed by the ocean, while cycling along a deceptively steep path, between Brée-les-Bains and Saint-Denis-d'Oléron. Sylvio was seventy-one.

That's what getting old is: seeing other people die.

A few days ago I wrote a short letter to Béatrice, explaining everything. A kind of memorial to Sylvio. The extremely wealthy Robinson Foundation had nothing to do with any of the murders, any more than Amadou Kandy, with his dubious art dealings did, or the rumoured Monets or Morval's mistresses. Laurenç Sérénac had been right from the start: it was a crime of passion. Only one unimaginable detail had prevented the discovery of the truth: the jealous criminal had not been content to eliminate his wife's supposed lovers, he had also killed the friends of a little ten-year-old girl with whom he was already in love. I haven't yet posted that letter. I don't think I will, in the end.

It matters so little, now.

So, I must get going!

I throw Dr Berger's envelope in the bin with disgust, then look up towards the tower of the mill.

I waver.

My legs can barely carry me. That last walk to Nettles Island has exhausted me. I am in two minds about whether I should go back to the village one last time or go on home. I thought about it all for a long while just now, on the banks of the Epte. About how I should finish things, now everything is in order.

And I've made up my mind. I've decided not to use Jacques's rifle – I imagine you can understand why, especially now. Nor am I going to swallow any pills, to spend hours, days in my death throes, at Vernon Hospital, like Jacques did, but without anyone to turn off my drip. No, the most effective way to end it all will be to finish this day peacefully, to go back to the mill, climb up to my bedroom at the top of the keep, to spend some time putting my affairs in order, then open the window and jump.

I decide to go into the village one last time. After all, my legs will hold me up for one more kilometre, one last kilometre.

'Come on, Neptune!'

If someone, anyone, a passer-by or a tourist, bothered to look at me, they might think I was smiling. They wouldn't be completely wrong. Spending these ten last days in the company of Paul, in the company of Laurenç, has finally appeased my rage.

I walk along the Chemin du Roy once more. A few moments later, I find myself by the water-lily pond.

On the death of Claude Monet, in 1926, the gardens were almost allowed to fall into a state of neglect. Michel Monet, his son, lived in the pink house until his marriage, in 1931, to the model Gabrielle Bonaventure, with whom he had a daughter, Henriette. When I was ten years old, in 1937, the other children and I used to slip into the gardens through a hole in the fence on the side of the meadow. I used to paint and the boys would play hide and seek around the pond. The only other people there were a gardener who maintained the estate, Monsieur Blin, and Blanche, Claude Monet's daughter, but they tended to leave us alone as we weren't doing any harm. Monsieur Blin wouldn't have refused little Fanette anything – she was so pretty with her mauve eyes and her silver ribbons in her hair, and such a talented painter!

Blanche Monet died in 1947. The last heir, Michel Monet, con-tinued to open the gardens and the house on special occasions for foreign heads of state, artists and special anniversaries . . . and for the children of Giverny School! I managed to convince him. It wasn't difficult. How could anyone resist little Fanette, who had become the lovely Stéphanie, the teacher with the water-lily eyes, so knowledgeable when it came to anything to do with art, and who tried, year after year, to enthuse the children of the village about Impressionism, encouraging them to take part in the Robinson Foundation competition, with such energy, such sincerity, as if her own life depended on the emotion that she communicated to her pupils? Michel Monet opened the gardens for my class, once a year, in May, when the park is at its most beautiful.

I turn round. For a moment I study the crowd gathered beneath the cathedral of roses, the dozens of faces pressed to the windows of the painter's house. To think that we were alone in that house, in June 1963, Laurenç and me. In the drawing room, on the stairs, in the bedroom. It is my loveliest memory, without a doubt. My one and only attempt at escape . . .

Michel Monet died in a car accident, three years later, in Vernon. After the reading of his will in early February 1966, an incredible stream of people converged on the house in Giverny. Gendarmes, notaries, journalists, artists . . . I was there too, like the other Givernois. Inside the house and the studios, the bailiffs were startled to discover more than a hundred and twenty paintings, eighty of them by Claude Monet himself, including some undiscovered *Water Lilies*, and forty paintings by his friends, Sisley, Manet, Renoir, Boudin . . . Can you imagine? It was an incredible treasure trove, an inestimable fortune that had been almost forgotten since Claude Monet's death. Well, I say forgotten . . . Many of the villagers knew, before 1966, the value of the masterpieces stored in the pink house, abandoned there for forty years by Michel Monet. Everyone who had been allowed to step inside the house had seen them. I had too, of course. Since 1966, those hundred and twenty paintings have been housed in the Musée Marmottan, in Paris. It's the biggest collection of Monets on display anywhere in the world.

For my part, after 1966, I stopped taking the children to Monet's garden. It only opened to the public again much later, in 1980. It was quite natural, though, for such a treasure to be shared with the masses, for the overwhelming beauty of the place to be offered to any soul capable of grasping it.

Not just that of a little girl who was so dazzled by its brilliance that she burned her dreams there.

I turn to the right and walk back up towards the village by the Rue du Château d'Eau.

My childhood home no longer exists.

After my mother's death, in 1975, it became a real hovel and had to be pulled down. The neighbours, from Paris, bought the land and put up a white stone wall more than two metres high. Where my house once stood there is probably a flower bed, a swing, a pool. In truth I have no idea. You'd have to be able to look over the wall.

At last I reach the end of the Rue du Château d'Eau. That's the hardest part over. To think that I used to run along that street faster than Neptune when I was eleven years old! Now he's the one who always has to wait for me, the poor thing. I turn into Rue Claude Monet. The tourist highway. I don't even have the desire to moan about the crowds anymore. Giverny will survive me, different, eternal, when all the ghosts of other times have disappeared: Amadou Kandy, his art gallery and his deals; Patricia Morval; me . . .

I walk. I don't resist the urge to take a detour of twenty metres to pass in front of the school. The Place de la Mairie hasn't changed in all these years, not its white stones or the shade of the lime trees, except that the school was rebuilt in the early 1980s, three years before I retired. Now it's hideously modern – pink and white like a marshmallow. In Giverny, of all places. But I lost the will to fight against this monstrosity long ago. The nursery school they've opened is even worse, in a prefab just opposite. Well, in the end none of that has anything to do with me anymore. Every day now, the children run past me without a glance, and I have to scold Neptune and tell him to leave them in peace. The only people who ever ask me for directions are old American painters.

I go back down the Rue Blanche Hoschedé-Monet. The house I used to live in when I was a teacher, just above the school, is now an antique shop. My slope-roofed bedroom, with its round skylight, along with the other dusty rooms, now furnishes city dwellers with supposedly authentic rural artefacts. Cheque in hand. No one will ever look through that round skylight to see the full moon at its perigee. My God, how many years, how many nights I spent by that window . . .

In front of the antique shop a group of adults is talking Japanese, or Korean, or Javanese. I no longer understand anything about anything. I'm a dinosaur in a zoo.

I carry on along the Rue Claude Monet. Only the Hôtel Baudy hasn't changed. The Belle Époque decor, on the terrace, on the façade and inside, is meticulously maintained by successive owners. Theodore Robinson could come back to the Hôtel Baudy tomorrow; time stopped there a century ago.

71 Rue Claude Monet.

Jérôme and Patricia Morval.

I quickly pass in front of the house. Four days ago, I went inside. I needed to talk to Patricia. Along with me, she's the last surviving person from the old Giverny. I never liked Patricia much, as you will by now understand. I think that for me she will always be Mary the sniveller. Mary the sneak.

It's ridiculous, I admit it. She has suffered so much. At least as much as me. She finally gave in to Fat Camille by marrying him, and in a cruel twist, Fat Camille became Jérôme Morval, the brilliant medical student, and the more Jérôme tried to seduce other women, the more attached to him she became. Life stopped in that house, 71 Rue Claude Monet, one day in 1963. It was once the finest house in the village. Now it's a ruin. The town council is waiting impatiently for the widow Morval to die so that it can get rid of the eyesore.

Patricia had to know. She had to know the name of her husband's murderer. I owed her that. And Patricia, the little sneak, surprised me, in the end. I expected to see the police turning up at my mill the following day. She had no hesitation, back in 1963, in sending the police in Vernon anonymous photographs of her husband's supposed mistresses. Me, among others.

But curiously, this time, it didn't happen. Life changes us, I suppose. I've heard that she barely leaves her house now, especially since one of her nephews introduced her to the internet. She, who had never turned on a computer before the age of seventy! And still, I'd like to take tea with her, one last time, to share our common hatred of a monster. Before the big jump.

I speed up, although in my case the expression isn't terribly apt. Neptune trots along thirty metres ahead of me. The Rue Claude Monet rises gently, like a long path towards the sky. *Stairway to heaven*, a guitar played, two generations ago.

At last I reach the church. The giant portrait of Claude Monet looks down at me from fifteen metres up. They're renovating Sainte-Radegonde's. The work and the scaffolding is covered by a huge canvas poster: a photograph of the master, in black and white, palette in hand. I don't have the strength to drag myself all the way up to the cemetery, on the slope behind the church, but everyone I've crossed paths with in my life, everyone who has ever meant something to me, is buried here. Strangely, it rained at almost every funeral, as if it would have been indecent for the light of Giverny to shine on the day of an interment. It rained in 1937, the day when my Paul, my Albert Rosalba, was buried. I was distraught. It also rained in 1963, when Jérôme Morval was buried. The whole village was there, including the Bishop of Évreux, the choir, journalists, and even Laurenç. Several hundred people. How strange fate is. A week ago I was alone at the burial of Jacques.

I peopled the cemetery with my memories. My memories of rain.

'Come on, Neptune!'

I'm headed for the finishing line. I go back down the Rue de la Dîme, then straight on to the Chemin du Roy. It emerges right opposite the mill. I wait a long time before crossing: the flow of cars leaving Giverny by the main road is almost continuous. Neptune waits obediently beside me. A red convertible with a complicated registration number and the steering wheel on the left finally lets me pass.

I cross the bridge. In spite of myself I stop by the brook and for the last time I examine the tiles and the pink bricks of the wash house, the green metallic paint of the bridge, the walls surrounding the courtyard of the mill, and rising above them, the top floor of the keep and the top of the cherry tree. The wash house was covered in graffiti a few weeks ago, grimacing black and white faces, but no one ever bothers to clean the bricks. Perhaps out of carelessness, perhaps not. After all, if there is one place where cleaning up the rebellious manifestations of anonymous artists could give the wrong impression, it's Giverny. Don't you think?

The little stream of clear water flows on, as if mocking the activities of the people on its banks: those monks who once dug this mill-race; the inspired painter who diverted the river to create a pond, and who locked himself away for thirty years to paint water lilies; the lunatic who, at this very spot, murdered every man who came anywhere near me, all the men I might have loved.

Who would be interested in that, today? Who could I complain to? Is there such a thing as an office of lost lives?

I walk another few metres. My eyes take in the meadow, probably for the last time. The car park is almost empty now.

No, in the end, the meadow isn't just a commercial backdrop. Of course it isn't. It's a landscape, living and changing. According to the seasons, according to the time of day, according to the light. It is overwhelming, too. Did I need to be so sure of the time of my death, so certain that I am seeing it for the last time, to understand this at last? To know just how much I will miss it? Claude Monet, Theodore Robinson, James and so many others didn't end up here by chance. The fact that it is a place full of memories doesn't strip the landscape of its beauty.

Quite the contrary.

'Isn't that right, Neptune?'

My dog wags his tail as if he can hear my ravings. In fact he already knows what I'll do next. He knows it's rare for me to enter the courtyard without taking a quick tour of the little clearing just behind it. A willow, two pines. Today the clearing is protected from the tourists by a fence. You can't see it from the road. I step forward.

Neptune is ahead of me once again. He waits for me, lying in the grass, as if he were aware of the significance of this spot. When I finally arrive, I place my cane in the soft earth and stand, leaning on it. In front of me I see the five little tumuli with their five little crosses.

I remember. How could I forget? I was only twelve. I held Neptune tightly, and he died in my arms. A year after Paul drowned. Old age, my mother told me.

'He didn't suffer, Stéphanie. He just fell asleep, like an old dog.'

I was inconsolable. I didn't want to be parted from my dog.

'We'll go and get another one, Stéphanie. A little puppy. Tomorrow.'

'The same one, I want the same one.'

'Fine, Stéphanie. The same one. We'll go to the farm at Autheuil. What would you like to call your new puppy?'

'Neptune!'

I've had six dogs in my life. All Alsatians. I've called them all Neptune, out of fidelity to the whim of a lonely, unhappy little girl, who so wanted her dog to live for ever, who never wanted him to die.

My gaze shifts from right to left. Beneath every cross, on a little plaque, the same name is engraved. *Neptune.*

The only difference is the numbers beneath each name.

1922–1938
1938–1955
1955–1963
1963–1980
1980–1999

Neptune gets up, comes and rubs himself against me as if he has understood that for the first time I'm the one who's leaving, and not him. Neptune will be taken in by the farm at Autheuil. They've been raising dogs there for generations; his mother probably still lives there. He'll be fine. I'm going to leave a letter with precise instructions, about his food, the fact that children should be allowed to play with him; and that he should be buried here when his time comes.

I stroke him. He's never pressed himself so tightly against me. I want to cry, more and more. I'll have to get a move on. If I dawdle, I won't have the courage.

I leave my cane there, planted in the ground by the five tumuli. I won't be needing it anymore. I walk back to the courtyard and Neptune stays right beside me. That damned sixth sense that animals have! Usually, Neptune would have gone to lie down beneath the cherry tree. Not this time. He doesn't leave me. He's going to trip me up. For a moment I wish I hadn't left my cane behind.

'Gently now, Neptune. Gently.'

Neptune pushes against me again. There haven't been silver ribbons among the leaves of the cherry tree for a long time now. The birds are singing their hearts out. I stroke Neptune again, for a long time. I look up towards the keep of the Moulin des Chennevières.

Jacques bought the mill in 1971. He kept his word. I believed him, my God, I believed him at the time. He bought it for me, the house of my dreams, that wonky house that had attracted me so much ever since I was a child. When the Parisians started coming, his estate agency finally went into profit. He had been biding his time, waiting for the right moment. The mill had been unoccupied for a long time, but then the owners finally decided to sell. He was the first on the case. He renovated the entire place over a period of several years. The wheel, the well, the keep.

He thought it would make me happy. It was so pathetic. Like a jailer decorating the walls of a prison. When it was finished, the Moulin des Chennevières no longer resembled the ruined old house that had fascinated me, 'the witch's mill', as people called it back then. Washed stones. Varnished wood. Trimmed trees. Flower-covered balconies. Raked courtyard. Oiled gate. Built fence.

Jacques was obsessive. So obsessive.

How could I have imagined . . .

I always refused to let him cut down the cherry tree. He yielded to all my whims. Yes, yes, that's what I really believed.

Then the tide turned at the agency. We found it difficult to pay for things. At first we rented out part of the mill, then we sold it to a young couple in the village. We only held on to the keep. Some years ago they turned the rest of the Moulin des Chennevières into holiday homes. It's going well, apparently. I think they're just waiting for one thing, for me to depart, so they can build a few extra rooms. There are swings in the courtyard now, a large barbecue, parasols and garden furniture. They're even talking about turning the field behind the mill into a small zoo. They've started bringing in llamas, kangaroos, emus . . . I don't know.

Can you imagine?

Exotic animals to amuse the children. You can't miss them, when you arrive in Giverny, travelling from Vernon along the Chemin du Roy.

To think that for decades this place was just the witch's mill . . .

All that's missing is the witch.

Me.

I won't be around much longer, don't worry. The witch is going to take advantage of the full moon and disappear. She'll be found in the early morning, lying at the foot of the cherry tree. Whoever finds her will look up and decide that she probably fell from her broom.

I grip Neptune's fur in my hand one last time, tightly, oh so tightly, then I close the door of the keep behind me. I climb the stairs quickly before I hear him whine.

DAY FOURTEEN
26 May 2010
(Moulin des Chennevières)

Silver Ribbons

84

I've opened the window. It's just after midnight. I thought it would be easier to jump once night had fallen. I've tidied everything in the room, like a crazy old woman, as if the worst of Jacques's obsessive behaviour has finally rubbed off on me. On the table I have left the letter asking for Neptune to be looked after. I didn't have the courage to take down my black *Water Lilies*.

I have no illusions; some junk-shop vultures from the Eure Valley will come and help themselves. Furniture, pots and pans, knick-knacks. Perhaps some objects will make their way to the antique shop on Rue Blanche Hoschedé-Monet, to my old house above the school. But I'd be surprised if anyone troubled themselves to take an interest in my *Water Lilies*, that hideous painting daubed with black.

Who could imagine that another life full of light might be hidden underneath?

To the bin with it!

To the hole in the ground, beside her lovely husband, the old woman who leaned too far out of the window.

The wicked old woman who no longer spoke to anyone, who never smiled, who barely said hello. Who could imagine that beneath that wrinkled skin there was once a little girl with talent. Perhaps even genius . . .

No one will ever know.

Fanette and Stéphanie have been dead for so long now, murdered by an over-zealous guardian angel.

I study the courtyard of the mill through the window. The grey gravel is lit by the light from the porch. I'm not scared, I have just one regret. Little Fanette had such a love of life.

I don't think she deserved to die feeling so bitter.

85

The Citroën Picasso stops almost below my window. It's a taxi. I'm used to it; taxis often drop off tourists at the holiday homes at the end of the evening. They take the last train from Paris to Vernon station, suitcases full to bursting.

Neptune goes over, of course. Usually taxi doors open to release a horde of children, still excited by the journey and Neptune loves to welcome them.

No luck for him this time; there isn't a single child in the taxi.

Just a man, an old man.

No luggage, either.

Strange . . .

Neptune goes and stands in front of him. The old man bends down. He strokes my dog for a long time, as if he's an old friend.

My God!

Is it possible?

Everything explodes, my heart, my eyes, my head.

Is it possible?

I lean out still further. Not in order to fall, this time. Oh, no! A terrible wave of warmth fills me. I see myself at the window of another house, a pink house, Monet's house, in another life; a man was standing beside me, a very charming man. I said some strange things to him back then, some words I never thought would come out of my mouth.

Some words like a poem by Aragon . . . lines learned by heart for ever . . .

'It's just your Tiger Triumph that I've fallen in love with!'

I laughed then, and added,

'And perhaps also the way you always stop to stroke Neptune.'

I lean even further over the window sill. The voice rises up the tower. It hasn't changed, or has changed so little, in almost fifty years:

'Neptune . . . Old man, I never thought I'd find you here after all this time, alive!'

I go back into the bedroom and press myself against the wall. My heart is thumping. I try to reason, to think.

For ever, for all time.

I never saw Laurenç Sérénac again. Inspector Laurenç Sérénac was a good policeman, very good. Some months after the Morval case, at the end of 1963, I learned from Sylvio Bénavides that Laurenç had asked to be transferred to Quebec, as if he had to escape to the other end of the world. Escape from me, I thought. Escape from Jacques's murderous jealousy, I now realise. It was in Canada, over the years, that everyone got used to calling him by his nickname, Laurentin. In Quebec, that's what they call the inhabitants of the St Lawrence Valley, from Montreal to Ottawa. It must have been too tempting for his colleagues to turn Laurenç's Occitan name into a good Quebecois Laurentin. I learned that he'd gone back to his job in Vernon when I read about him in the national press. Some of Monet's paintings had been stolen from the Musée Marmottan, in 1985, and he was involved in the case. At that time, some photographs of him appeared in the newspapers. How could he not have been recognised? Laurenç Sérénac, who was Chief Inspector Laurentin to everyone else. Amadou Kandy told me that they hadn't even taken down the paintings in his office at Vernon police station, twenty years after he retired. Cézanne's *Harlequin*, Toulouse-Lautrec's *Red-Haired Woman* . . .

*

I'm trembling like a leaf. I don't dare to return to the window . . .

What is Laurenç doing here?

It's crazy.

I have to put my thoughts in some sort of order. I pace around the room.

It can't be a coincidence. I walk towards the mirror, even though my feet didn't ask for permission.

There's a knock on the door, a few floors down.

I panic like a teenager who's been caught coming out of the shower by a potential boyfriend. My God, I must look ridiculous . . . Just for a moment I think of Patricia Morval, little Mary, the sneak, Jérôme's wife, collapsing into my arms a week ago. Life changes you. For the better, sometimes. Did she call Laurenç? Who put him on the trail of the truth, the abominable truth? I have no time to try to understand.

There's another knock down below.

My God . . .

I look at this cold and wrinkled face in the mirror, my hair covered by that black scarf that never leaves me now, the face of a bad-tempered old hag.

Impossible, just impossible to imagine opening the door to him.

I hear the sound of someone pushing open the door to the tower. I didn't close it behind me. To make it easier for whoever found my body.

A voice, in the spiral staircase:

'You stay there, Neptune. I don't think you're allowed upstairs.'

My God. My God.

I tear off my black headscarf. My hair cascades down onto my shoulders. I'm almost running, now, I'm the one issuing commands to my legs. And they're keen to obey.

I open the second drawer of the side table, scatter old buttons, rolls of thread, a thimble, needles. I don't care if I prick myself.

I know they're there!

My trembling fingers find two silver ribbons. Images pass in rapid succession before my eyes. I see Paul in the cherry tree in the

349

courtyard of the mill, unhooking silver ribbons and offering them to me, calling me his princess; I see myself kissing him for the first time, promising to wear them all my life; I see Laurenç, some years later, stroking the ribbons in my hair.

My God, I need to concentrate.

I run to the mirror again. Yes, I swear, I run. Feverishly, I knot the silver ribbons into my hair in a makeshift chignon.

I laugh nervously.

A hairstyle fit for a princess, that was what Paul said, a hairstyle fit for a princess . . . How mad I must seem!

The footsteps approach.

There's another knock, this time at my bedroom door.

It's too soon. I don't turn round, not yet.

Another knock. Gentle.

'Stéphanie?'

I recognise Laurenç's voice. It's almost the same as before. A little more serious than I remember, perhaps. It seems like only yesterday, he wanted to take me away. My whole body is shivering. Is it possible? Is it still possible?

I look at my face in the flaking gold mirror.

Do I still know how to smile? It's been so long.

I try.

I pass through the mirror.

What I see in the glass isn't an old woman anymore.

It's the joyful smile of Fanette.

It's the water-lily eyes of Stéphanie.

Alive. Oh, so alive.

AFTER THE CRASH

Michel Bussi

On the night of 22 December, a plane crashes on the Franco-Swiss border.

All the passengers are killed instantly, apart from one miraculous survivor – a three-month-old baby girl. But who is she? Two families step forward to claim her, but is she Lyse-Rose or Emilie?

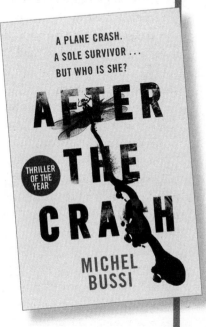

A PLANE CRASH.
A SOLE SURVIVOR . . .
BUT WHO IS SHE?

AFTER THE CRASH

THRILLER OF THE YEAR

MICHEL BUSSI

Two decades later, on the eve of her eighteenth birthday, the detective who investigated the case makes a discovery that could change everything . . .

'One of the most remarkable books I've read in a long time . . . I doubt I'll read a more brilliant crime novel this year' *Sunday Times*

DON'T LET GO

Michel Bussi

In an idyllic resort on the island of La Réunion, Liane Bellion and her husband Martial are enjoying the perfect moment: blue seas, palm trees, a warm breeze.

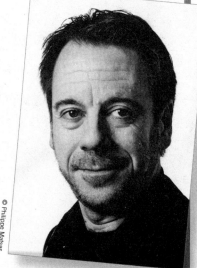

© Philippe Matsas

Then Liane disappears. Despite his protestations of innocence, the police view Martial as their prime suspect. Helicopters scan the island, racial tensions surface, and bodies are found.

Is Martial really his wife's killer? And if he isn't, why does he appear to be so guilty?

Available from W&N 27 April 2017

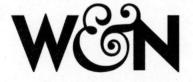

blog and newsletter

For literary discussion, author insight,
book news, exclusive content,
recipes and giveaways, visit the
Weidenfeld & Nicolson blog and
sign up for the newsletter at:

www.wnblog.co.uk

For breaking news, reviews and exclusive competitions
Follow us 🐦 @wnbooks
Find us 📘 facebook.com/WNfiction

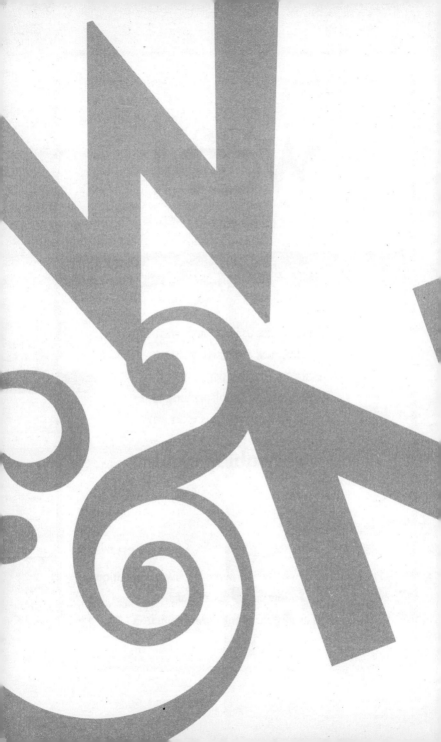